No matter when,

No matter where,

I will love you always.

Foul Rift

By:

Gregory John T Pardo

ISBN 979-8-9889825-0-0

Table of Contents

Dedication

To my beloved daughter, Hayley Grace A Pardo, and my
cherished son, Bo Everest G Pardo,

This story is dedicated to both of you as a reminder that life is
a grand journey filled with countless opportunities for
discovery and wonder. Just like the brave souls in our tale,
Captain Kidd's gold was not the only treasure waiting to be
found—it lies everywhere if you have the courage to seek it.

As you navigate through life, remember the importance of
being there for each other. Cherish the bonds that tie you as
siblings, for they are unbreakable and will always guide you
through both calm and turbulent waters.

Embrace every moment with open hearts, making countless
memories along the way. Each memory is a treasure of its
own, forever etched in the tapestry of your lives. Whether
you are exploring the world or creating new experiences
close to home, let the spirit of adventure guide you and bring
joy to your souls.

May the lessons from this story resonate in your hearts,
filling you with the determination to embrace life's
adventures fearlessly, always supporting and caring for one
another. Your love and bond as siblings will be the compass
that leads you through the myriad of experiences that await.

Hayley and Bo, as you venture forth into the vast unknown,
remember that life's greatest treasures are not always buried
gold but lie within the shared moments you create together.
Keep your hearts open to the magic of the world, for
adventure waits around every corner.

With all my love and unwavering support,
-Dad

Preface

Welcome to the world of "Foul Rift," where adventure and metaphor intertwine to create a tapestry of thrilling experiences. This tale is more than just a narrative—it is a homage to two timeless movies that have shaped the author's creative spirit: "The Goonies" and "Jaws." With a nod to these cinematic treasures, "Foul Rift" emerges as a story of camaraderie, courage, and the pursuit of something greater than oneself.

Inspired by real places, the backdrop of "Foul Rift" is grounded in authenticity. Many of the settings, ranging from the enchanting Field of Dreams Playground to Wind-Chime Woods, are either real or based off real locations.

The characters that populate this tale are not mere figments of imagination; they are inspired by real individuals who inhabit the author's world. Hayley and Bo, the heart and soul of the adventure, mirror the author's own children and their friends, whose personalities and bonds fuel the story's dynamics. Amidst the twists and turns, you may catch glimpses of the author and his friends embodied in some of the protagonists, breathing life into their experiences.

A pivotal element of "Foul Rift" revolves around Captain Kidd's "magic numbers" and his chest with its false bottom. These intriguing aspects are steeped in historical fact, adding layers of authenticity to the story's adventurous narrative. They provide a bridge between the fantastical and the real, inviting you to explore the intersections of history and fiction.

Chapter 1:

There's No Place like Drone

The sun was beginning its descent, casting a warm golden glow over the tranquil town of Foul Rift. In the outskirts of the town, a young man in his early 20's stepped out of the mechanic's garage. Covered in grease and grime, he had just finished a long day's work, his jumpsuit proudly displaying the name "Retnik" embroidered on the chest.

With a tired smile, the mechanic glanced at his faithful companion, a black Labrador retriever by his side. The mechanic fondly called out, "C'mon, Xela! Let's go for a walk!"

Without wasting a moment, the mechanic and Xela ventured into the nearby woods, seeking solace and escape from the bustle of daily life. The air was crisp and filled with the scents of nature, as they made their way along a well-trodden path that led to the river.

The sound of their footsteps echoed through the quiet woods, the rustling leaves and occasional chirping of birds accompanying their journey. The towering trees provided a comforting canopy overhead, while sunlight pierced through the gaps, casting dappled patterns on the forest floor.

As they walked, glimpses of the river came into view, its shimmering surface reflecting the fading light. The Delaware River, the lifeblood of Foul Rift, flowed calmly, its waters carrying stories of the past and secrets yet to be discovered.

The mechanic and Xela continued their leisurely stroll, the town of Foul Rift standing at a distance, its old buildings and quaint charm nestled along the riverbank. The sleepy town had its own mysteries, whispered tales of the river witch and the uncharted depths harboring untold secrets.

Unbeknownst to them, a presence lurked beneath the surface, waiting patiently. A monster was biding its time in the murky depths of the river, its hunger growing with each passing day.

As the sun lowered in the sky, casting an amber hue over the river, the mechanic and Xela ventured further along the overgrown path. The serenity of the woods surrounded them, broken only by the occasional chirping of birds and the rustling of leaves beneath their feet.

They reached a secluded spot where the path opened up to reveal an eddy in the river. The water appeared still and murky, its depths concealing a hidden world. The sides of the eddy were mushy and muddy, making it an inviting playground for Xela.

With a grin, the mechanic unclipped Xela's leash, allowing her to explore the muddy terrain. Xela dashed off, her black fur blending with the darkening landscape as she joyfully rolled around in the mud. The mechanic watched with a mix of amusement and reflection, the events of the day lingering in his mind.

As Xela frolicked near the edge of the eddy, she suddenly emerged from the muck, carrying something in her mouth. Her fur was caked in mud, and droplets of water dripped from her soaked coat. The mechanic extended his hand, and Xela obediently dropped the object—a dog collar with the name "Pippet" engraved on it.

Curiosity piqued, the mechanic examined the collar, flipping it over to check for any additional information. On the back, he discovered the initials "B. Q. H." and an address—515 North Road. The collar belonged to another dog, and the muddy circumstances raised questions in the mechanic's mind.

Lost in his thoughts, Retnik shortly diverted his attention from Xela's playfulness. Unbeknownst to him, an abnormally large carapace silently broke the surface of the water, a menacing head now facing Xela. Retnik's senses suddenly heightened, and he realized the impending danger.

"Xela! Come!" He called urgently, his heart pounding in his chest. He sprinted toward the edge of the eddy, but his feet sank deep into the treacherous mud, trapping him in place. Panic set in as he watched the terrifying sight unfolding before his eyes.

The top points of a massive shell and a menacing maw rose above the water, closing in on Xela, who had inadvertently become trapped in the sticky mud. The deafening sound of a snap echoed through the air, followed by a tumultuous splash as the mechanic and Xela were pulled beneath the surface, disappearing into the murky depths.

Silence enveloped the scene, broken only by the gentle ripples on the water's surface. The once playful eddy now held a secret, its muddy depths concealing the fate of the mechanic and his dog. The monster, having satisfied his hunger momentarily, retreated beneath the surface, leaving no trace of the horrific event that had unfolded.

Back in Foul Rift, the fading light of the setting sun cast an eerie ambiance over the town. Unbeknownst to its residents, darkness had crept into their midst, and the legend of a monster had claimed its first victims.

The next day, the town of Foul Rift basked in the glow of a late spring day, its old-world charm radiating from the quaint homes that lined its streets. Nestled along the banks of the Delaware River, the town wore its history proudly. Most of the houses, with their wraparound porches and timeless architecture, harkened back to the mid-1800s and early 1900s.

As the sun bathed the town in warm hues, the residents of Foul Rift went about their day, savoring the simplicity and whimsy of their beloved home. A few old factories stood nearby, a reminder of the town's industrial past. Stories of a bygone era lingered in the air, whispered from generation to generation.

In the heart of town stood "Rambo's," a general store that had been a staple in Foul Rift for decades. It offered a variety of grocery items and mouthwatering sandwiches, attracting both locals and visitors alike. The store was a hub of community, where people shared stories and laughter over simple pleasures.

Foul Rift not only thrived along the Delaware River but also boasted an old railroad that ran through its core. Once a bustling route for transporting goods, the railroad now meandered peacefully, reflecting the town's timeless charm.

Within Foul Rift, there were two charming bed and breakfasts, a couple of cozy coffee shops, and an inviting ice cream parlor that always tempted passersby with cold, sweet treats. Two churches, with their towering steeples, provided solace and a sense of community. The town even boasted three cemeteries, each one with its own stories etched into the weathered headstones.

Every evening at 6 pm, the church bells chimed, their melodious tones resonating through the town, a gentle reminder of the passage of time. Fishing enthusiasts cast their lines into the river while others embarked on adventures along the towpath, riding their mountain bikes or hiking amidst the picturesque scenery.

In the heart of Foul Rift, a small museum stood proudly, attached to the historic town hall. The museum celebrated the town's rich history, preserving artifacts and stories that spanned generations. Visitors would stroll through its exhibits, gaining a deeper understanding of the town's heritage.

On this particular day, as the townsfolk went about their routines, six teens found themselves scattered throughout Foul Rift. Bo, his sister Hayley, their friends Andy, Ryan and Hayley's best friend Cassidy and her sister, Charlotte were each engrossed in their own explorations, unknowingly drawing closer to their destiny.

In a dimly lit room, Bo tiptoed across the creaky wooden floor towards the old stereo. With a press of a button, the room filled with Cindy Lauper's iconic tune, "The Goonies 'R' Good Enough." A grin spread across Bo's face as he bobbed his head to the music.

Sneaking back to his bed, Bo reached under the mattress and retrieved a worn-out case. With careful hands, he unlatched it, revealing an aging, beat-up drone. The memories flooded back as he held the device, recalling countless adventures it had been on.

Stepping out onto the deck, Bo took a deep breath of the cool morning air. "Okay, Bo. Don't mess this one up. Prepare for the wings of flight," he whispered to himself, a mix of excitement and nervousness evident in his voice. Bo pressed a button, and the drone's propellers whirred to life, lifting it off the ground.

With deft movements of his controller, Bo skillfully navigated the drone through the air. The drone's camera feed displayed on his controller, giving him a bird's-eye view of the backyard. His gaze fixed on Hayley, his older sister, ankle-deep in the creek behind their home.

Hayley Grace stood inside the glistening stream, her eyes scanning the water's edge in search of her favorite amphibian companions: frogs. It was one of her cherished pastimes, catching frogs and letting them hop about in her hands. Occasionally, she would even playfully accessorize them with tiny hats and capture their adorable moments on camera for her whimsical Instagram account.

Intrigued, Bo flew the drone closer, hovering above Hayley. He chuckled softly as he watched her gentle gestures, captivated by her compassion for small creatures. The drone's camera captured every detail, and Bo felt like a curious observer of his sister's world.

Hayley crouched near the water; the melodic sounds of nature surrounded her, mingling with the distant hum of Bo's drone. She tilted her head, listening curiously, but her focus returned to the stream as a small drama unfolded before her eyes. A sly snake stealthily hunted an unsuspecting frog, quickly seizing its prey. Hayley's empathetic heart stirred.

"Uh-oh, that's not fair!" Hayley exclaimed in her signature cute voice, akin to a mother talking to a baby. She gently approached the snake; her fingers delicately prying its jaws open to release the frightened frog. "Now, now, you two. Let's play nice and be friends, okay?" She playfully booped the frog on its tiny nose, as if imparting a gentle scolding, before sending it on its way.

With the freed frog leaping happily back into the safety of the water, Hayley turned her attention to the snake, her voice filled with kindness. "Don't cause any more trouble, Mr. Snake. Behave yourself, alright?" She cradled the slithering creature carefully in her hands, its smooth scales glinting in the dappled sunlight.

Carrying the snake with her, Hayley began ascending the gentle slope that led to their backyard, her eyes sparkling with affection for her newfound reptilian friend. The sound of the drone had dissipated, replaced by a moment of serenity.

As Hayley neared the deck, she placed the snake gently on the ground, offering it one last affectionate pat. "Be good now, Mr. Snake. Find a nice spot to relax." With a tender smile, she bid the snake farewell.

As the music continued to play in the background, Bo's heart swelled with affection for his big sister. He had always admired Hayley's kindness and sense of wonder, and in that moment, it was as if the drone's lens was capturing not just a scene but also the essence of their special bond.

With a fond smile, Bo gently maneuvered the drone away from Hayley, exploring other parts of Foul Rift. The drone soared over the trees and glided over the neighborhood, giving Bo a bird's-eye view of the familiar houses and streets. He marveled at how different everything looked from up above.

Feeling a surge of curiosity, Bo guided the drone towards the nearby park. As he flew closer, he spotted a familiar figure among the greenery. It was Andy Zzobi, his close friend. Andy was dressed in his highly decorated Boy Scout uniform, engrossed in his latest endeavor - earning a merit badge for identifying local plant species.

Andy, with his phone in hand recorded himself. "Here we have a prime example of Prunus Spinosa, commonly known as the Blackthorn Shrub," Andy declared, his voice carrying an air of self-assuredness. He gestured towards the shrub, its branches adorned with sharp thorns. "This particular species is known for its impressive thorny defenses, serving as protection against browsing animals."

With a mischievous grin, Bo decided to have some fun. He used the drone's built-in microphone to say a friendly "hi" to Andy. Unaware of the drone's approach, Andy was taken aback by the unexpected voice from above and stumbled over a root, falling into a thorny shrub. Bo watched the whole scene unfold on the drone's camera with a mix of amusement and concern.

"Whoa!" Andy yelped, his voice filled with surprise and mild pain. The thorns pricked his skin, leaving scratches and tiny cuts on his arms and face. He winced, feeling a mixture of embarrassment and discomfort, as he lay tangled within the prickly branches.

With careful movements, Andy carefully disentangled himself, mindful of avoiding further scratches. Though a few lingering thorns remained stubbornly lodged in his clothes, he managed to regain his footing and stand free from the thorny bush.

Seeing Andy's less-than-graceful tumble, Bo quickly realized he may have startled his friend more than intended. "Sorry, Andy," Bo called out over the drone's speaker, feeling guilty for the unintended mishap.

Andy, now brushing off leaves and thorns from his uniform, looked up at the drone and grinned. "Bo, you really know how to surprise a guy," he chuckled, displaying his easygoing nature.

"I didn't mean to startle you, sorry about that," Bo apologized sincerely, relieved that Andy took it in good spirits.

"It's alright, Bo. Just one of those moments, I guess," Andy replied, flashing a friendly wave at the camera.

Bo smiled and continued to watch Andy as he resumed his plant identification with renewed caution. Deciding to make it up to his friend, Bo adjusted the drone's camera angle and began recording Andy's expertise. He captured every detail of Andy's passionate explanation of the Blackthorn Shrub, impressed by his friend's vast knowledge.

As Andy wrapped up his recording, Bo seized the moment to reconnect. He pressed the microphone button again, calling out, "Hey, Andy! Great job on plant identification!"

Startled once more, Andy looked up at the drone, this time with a grin. "Thanks, Bo! You caught me off guard, but it's all good!" he said, chuckling at the amusing encounter.

As Bo zoomed the drone away from Andy, he could not resist the temptation to check on his other friends. He navigated the drone around the corner and spotted Cassidy and Charlotte's house. Cassidy, engrossed in her book, sat on a swinging chair on the porch, her eyes captivated by the pages of "Kaiju Rising." Charlotte, on the other hand, was focused on perfecting her volleyball skills, determined to prepare for an upcoming competition.

Bo grinned mischievously, knowing just how to liven up their day. He decided to put his drone skills to the test and have some playful fun with the sisters. As Charlotte tossed the ball into the air, preparing for a powerful spike, Bo seized the opportunity. With a loud "Whoooooo Hoooooo," he maneuvered the drone towards the ball, attempting to intercept it in mid-air.

His daring move was a success, as the drone collided with the ball, altering its trajectory. The ball bounced off Cassidy's face, causing her to let out a surprised yelp. Charlotte turned to see what had happened and noticed the drone hovering nearby. Both sisters immediately recognized Bo's drone and realized what had transpired.

"Bo!" Cassidy called out, her laughter mixing with a touch of annoyance. "You can't do that! I was just getting to the best part of the book!"

Charlotte chimed in, her competitive spirit temporarily set aside, "And I was in the zone for my volleyball practice! Seriously, be careful with that thing!"

Through the drone's microphone, Bo sheepishly apologized, "Sorry, girls! I couldn't resist having a little fun. My bad!"

As the sisters playfully scolded Bo, he swiftly zoomed the drone away, leaving Cassidy and Charlotte to continue with their respective activities. His laughter echoed through the drone's speaker as he playfully teased, "Maybe next time, I'll bring you some ice cream to make up for it!"

The sisters could not help but smile, knowing that Bo's antics were all part of their close-knit friendship. As Bo guided his drone away from Cassidy and Charlotte's home, he decided it was time to head back. He skillfully piloted the drone through the streets, enjoying the sights from above. Suddenly, he spotted his good friend, Ryan Shawl, strolling down the sidewalk. Excited to say hello, Bo lowered the drone to almost head level with Ryan.

"Hey Ryan, what are you up to?" Bo called out through the drone's speaker, a smile in his voice.

Ryan immediately recognized the familiar drone and grinned. "Hey Bo! I'm heading to a garage sale up the street. They've got a bike that I've been eyeing. Do you want to hang out later?"

"Sure, that sounds great!" Bo replied enthusiastically. "I have to go for now, though. My drone's battery is running low."

"Alright, catch you later then!" Ryan waved, and the drone began to ascend. "If I manage to get the bike, I'll ride it over and show you!"

"Awesome, looking forward to it!" Bo said, already imagining the fun they would have with the new bike.

With that, Bo soared his drone higher into the sky, glancing back at Ryan as he continued on his way to the garage sale. He couldn't help but feel grateful for the special connections he had with his friends. It seemed that no matter where they were or what they were doing, they always found a way to stay connected and share their adventures together.

As Bo guided the drone back home, he could not help but feel a sense of contentment. He knew that the friendships he had were irreplaceable, and the memories they created together were truly priceless. With a full heart and a curious mind, Bo looked forward to the next time they would all be together, exploring their neighborhood and making new memories that they would cherish for a lifetime.

With the echoes of Cindy Lauper's song fading away, Bo stood on his deck, taking in the serenity of the day. He noticed that he had just enough battery life to swing by a neighbor's house. It was a place he had explored with his drone on previous occasions. To his surprise, the middle-aged woman who lived there, known for her playful spirit, spotted the drone and playfully motioned for it to come closer. Bo's eyes widened, unsure of what to expect, but he obliged, gradually lowering the drone until it hovered at eye level with her. The drone's built-in microphone allowed him to hear her voice as she addressed the machine.

"Well, well, what do we have here?" she said with a teasing tone. "Playing the neighborhood spy, are we? You had better watch out, young man. I've got my own eyes everywhere!"

Bo chuckled nervously, his cheeks flushing slightly. "Just having some fun, ma'am," he replied through the drone's speaker. "No harm intended, I promise."

The neighbor seemed satisfied with his response and waved the drone off, indicating that it was time to leave. Panic started to rise within Bo as he hurriedly tried to make the drone fly away. But just as he was about to retreat, an unseen figure approached from behind and grabbed hold of the drone's landing legs.

The propellers screeched to a halt, and Bo's heart sank as the neighbor's husband revealed himself. He was a burly man with a stern expression on his face. He turned the drone around, his frustration and annoyance evident in his voice.

"I'm sick and tired of this thing buzzing around our property," he declared firmly. "If you want your precious drone back, you better be brave enough to come knock on our door and get it!"

Bo's heart pounded in his chest as he realized he was caught in a tricky situation. Taking a deep breath, he knew he had no choice but to face the music.

Bo's worry intensified as he watched the man through the drone's camera carry the drone in his house. It left Bo with a sense of trepidation. Retrieving the drone would require him to confront the neighbor and her husband face-to-face, and he couldn't help but wonder what other repercussions might follow.

A moment later, Bo's big sister walked up on the deck, wet from being in the creek. "What's wrong, Bo?" she asked, her voice filled with warmth and curiosity, her eyes reflecting genuine care for her brother.

Bo hesitated for a moment, then spoke with a mixture of relief and apprehension. "I had a bit of a drone mishap, and I need your help."

Hayley's heart fluttered with a mix of excitement and concern, her playful demeanor shifting to a determined focus. She nodded, ready to face the challenge alongside her brother.

As Bo nervously explained what had happened to his drone to Hayley, she listened attentively and reassured him that everything would be fine. "Accidents happen, Bo," she said with a comforting smile. "Let's see if the others have any ideas on how we can fix this."

Hayley quickly sent out a text to Cassidy, Charlotte, Andy, and Ryan, asking them to meet at the Field of Dreams Playground. Bo felt a pang of guilt as he thought about how his drone had inadvertently caused trouble for his friends. He remembered how he disrupted Charlotte's volleyball practice, made Andy trip, and even accidentally hit Cassidy with the volleyball. He worried that they might be upset with him and hesitant to help.

Cassidy approached her sister, who was still diligently practicing spiking a volleyball. Cassidy called out to her, trying to catch her attention amidst the rhythmic thuds of Charlotte's workout. "Hey, Char! Did you see the text from Hayley?" she asked, hoping to share the news with her sister.

Charlotte remained focused on her exercise, not breaking her concentration. She continued her vigorous jumps, determination etched on her face. Cassidy raised her voice a little louder, trying to reach through to her. "Char, Hayley sent a text! She wants us to meet at the Field of Dreams. We should head there!"

Charlotte paused for a moment, her chest heaving with exertion, and finally released the ball. She glanced at Cass, sweat glistening on her forehead, and nodded in acknowledgment. "Got it," she replied curtly, her voice filled with determination.

Cassidy could sense the intensity in her sister's actions, knowing that her sister was focused on her goals. "I know you're dedicated to your training, but this might be important. Hayley wouldn't send a message like this unless it was urgent. We should go and see what's going on," Cassidy insisted, her voice tinged with concern.

Charlotte took a deep breath, her competitive spirit temporarily set aside. She recognized the urgency in her sister's words and the significance of Hayley's message. Nodding in agreement, she wiped the sweat from her brow and adjusted her volleyball gear. "You're right. Let's go to the Field of Dreams and find out what's happening," Charlotte replied, her voice resolute.

With a shared understanding, Cassidy and Charlotte headed out of the yard, leaving behind the fragrant blooms and embracing the sense of adventure that awaited them at the Field of Dreams.

At that moment, in another corner in Foul Rift, Ryan stood in front of a garage sale, his eyes fixated on the Cannondale mountain bike. He knew it was a steal at $250, but his theater skills and natural knack for negotiation urged him to aim for an even better deal. With a determined expression, he approached the owner and engaged in a friendly battle of wits.

They went back and forth, each presenting their arguments with conviction. Ryan's charisma and persuasive abilities came to the forefront as he skillfully tried to lower the price. Just as they seemed to reach an impasse, Ryan's phone buzzed, drawing his attention away from the negotiation.

Curious, Ryan glanced at his phone and saw Hayley's text message. His eyebrows furrowed slightly, momentarily distracting him from the bike negotiation. Realizing this could be his last chance, he seized the moment and incorporated it into his negotiation strategy.

Looking back at the bike owner, Ryan sighed and said, "Sorry, it's my mother texting me. She just told me she wasn't approved for summer overtime at the diner. Times have been tough for us lately." He put on a slight pout and did his best to appear saddened by the news. "I guess I shouldn't buy it now no matter what. Thank you for your time. I hope you are able to sell it to a deserving person."

His words struck a chord with the woman. She empathized with Ryan's situation and reconsidered her initial stance. Understanding the importance of helping others, she decided to extend her kindness and generosity to him.

Moved by his apparent need, the woman softened her expression and said, "You know what? You can have the bike. I don't need the money as much as I thought. Consider it a little help for your family."

Ryan's eyes widened with genuine gratitude. "Thank you so much," he exclaimed, repeatedly expressing his appreciation. He wanted to ensure the woman knew just how grateful he was for her act of kindness.

With a smile and a nod, the woman assured Ryan that he could take the bike. Ryan thanked her once again, feeling a mix of relief and excitement. With the bike now his, he hopped on and pedaled away, eager to join Hayley and the rest of his friends at the Field of Dreams Park.

As he rode towards their gathering spot, his heart filled with gratitude for the woman's compassion and the chance to join his friends. The bike's wheels spun beneath him, carrying him closer to a day filled with camaraderie and memorable moments.

At the Field of Dreams, a wooden playground that stood like a fortress of childhood dreams, children laughed and played. The structure, crafted entirely from wood and old tires, resembled a castle, its towers and bridges inviting young adventurers to scale its heights. A giant wooden globe beckoned curious minds to step inside, while a wooden train offered the perfect backdrop for imaginative journeys.

Bo, Hayley, Andy, Ryan, Cassidy and Charlotte gradually converged upon the Field of Dreams, their paths intertwining like the currents of the river. As they all gathered at the playground, Bo could feel the weight of his mistake on his shoulders. But to his surprise, Cassidy, Charlotte, Andy, and Ryan greeted him with warm smiles. They could tell something was bothering him, and they were eager to find out what had happened.

Bo shifted nervously, feeling the weight of their expectant gazes. He took a deep breath and recounted the incident with the neighbor and the drone. "So, I was flying the drone, just for fun, you know, and the neighbor spotted it. She waved it down and started jokingly scolding it. But then her husband came out, grabbed the drone, and told me to come knock on their door if I wanted it back."

Bo took a deep breath and told them the whole story, starting from causing Andy to trip in a thorn bush and ending in his drone being confiscated by the neighbor down the street.

To his relief, his friends were understanding and supportive. "We all make mistakes, Bo," Charlotte said, patting him on the back.

"Yeah, accidents happen," Andy chimed in. "We've all had our fair share of mishaps."

Cassidy smiled warmly at Bo. "Don't worry, we've got your back. Let's think of a plan together to fix this."

Ryan nodded in agreement. "Yeah, we're a team, remember? We'll figure this out together."

Bo felt a wave of gratitude wash over him. He was relieved to have such understanding and forgiving friends. With their support, he knew they could come up with a solution to repair the damage caused by his drone. As they huddled together to brainstorm ideas, Bo realized that even in the face of mistakes, true friendship meant standing by each other and finding a way to make things right.
The group exchanged glances and began a lively back-and-forth discussion. Charlotte raised an eyebrow and asked, "Why won't you just go get it, Bo? It's your drone."

Bo's cheeks flushed with embarrassment as he replied, "I don't know... I just feel awkward about it. It's better if someone else goes."

Ryan, always ready for a challenge, spoke up confidently. "Well, if no one else wants to do it, I'll go get it. I'm pretty good at convincing people and getting what I want."

The others nodded in agreement, relieved that Ryan had taken charge of the situation. With the matter seemingly settled, Cassidy interjected with a tidbit of information.

"Hey, did you guys hear about the missing person the police are looking for?"

Curiosity sparked within the group as they turned their attention to Cassidy. Bo, Hayley, Charlotte, and Andy shook their heads, indicating they were unaware of the situation.

Cassidy continued, her voice carrying a sense of intrigue. "Yeah, apparently there's this mechanic in town who went for a walk and never returned. The police are searching for him."

Some of the group shrugged indifferently, their focus still on the drone retrieval. Others showed a hint of concern but didn't dwell on the news. It seemed like just another piece of gossip in their small town.

With the conversation momentarily shifted, the group made their way out of the park together, heading towards the neighbor's house to watch Ryan negotiate for the drone. Their collective curiosity and anticipation carried them forward, their friendship and shared adventures binding them tightly as they embarked on this new escapade.

The group of five friends crouched behind the large shrub across the street from the neighbor's house, anxiously awaiting Ryan's encounter. Ryan took a deep breath, steeling himself for the task at hand, and approached the door.

As the door opened, the man who had taken the drone appeared, a stern expression on his face. Ryan mustered his best negotiating skills and explained, "Hi, sir. I'm here to pick up the drone that accidentally flew into your yard."

The man's gaze hardened as he scrutinized Ryan. "So, you're the person who's been flying the drone around my house, spying on my wife?" he questioned, his voice laced with suspicion.

"Do you like spying on my wife? Would you like me lingering around your home watching your mother?"

Ryan's nerves heightened as he quickly replied, "No, sir! I assure you, I am not spying on your wife or anyone else. It was purely for fun."

Just then, the wife approached from behind her husband, having overheard Ryan's response. Annoyed, she demanded her husband give Ryan the drone, "Oh, for heaven's sake, give the kid his drone. Stop being an idiot!"

"For heaven's sake go back in the house, I'll handle this", the husband demanded.

Ryan stammered, trying to defuse the awkward situation. "I'm…I'm sorry. I promise that I will not fly it around your house anymore."

The tension in the air grew palpable as the couple's argument escalated. The husband became agitated with his wife, criticizing her for worrying about a high school boy. The wife fiercely defended herself, their voices echoing through the open doorway.

As the wife stormed off, her footsteps echoing through the house, the husband hesitated for a moment, torn between his desire to continue arguing and his concern for his wife's anger. Finally, with a frustrated sigh, he turned and followed her, leaving the door ajar.

Ryan's eyes widened as he spotted the drone sitting on the nearby coffee table, its familiar shape a beacon of hope. Without a second thought, he seized the opportunity. Darting into the house, he navigated the unfamiliar surroundings, his heart pounding in his chest.

He could still hear the distant sound of the couple's argument, their voices intertwining in a heated symphony. Ryan's senses heightened, fueling his determination to retrieve the drone before they noticed his presence.

With agile steps, he reached the coffee table and snatched the drone, clutching it tightly in his hand. A surge of adrenaline coursed through him as he turned to make his escape, silently praying that luck would be on his side. At that moment, the husband spotted him through his periphery and yelled, "Hey, get the hell out of my house!" Ryan, in a panic, ran for the door. In the heat of the chase he called out, "so long sucka."

As he sprinted through the door, a wave of relief washed over him. The husband gave chase, consumed by his own grievances. Ryan's heart raced with anticipation as he burst out of the house, the drone held aloft like a victorious trophy.

Reuniting with his friends, Ryan couldn't help but grin with satisfaction. He had managed to retrieve the drone without capture, seizing the opportune moment amidst the couple's discord. The group shared a mixture of relief, excitement, and admiration for Ryan's daring feat.

Little did they know that this was only the beginning of their thrilling adventure, a series of events that would intertwine their lives and lead them into the heart of a mystery. But for now, in the glow of their small victory, they stood together, ready to face the unknown.

Chapter 2:
Wind-Chime Woods

The sun cast a warm glow over the quaint town of Foul Rift as the six friends gathered outside Rambo's, indulging in their savory pork roll, egg, and cheese sandwiches. The aroma of sizzling bacon mingled with the crisp morning air, creating an inviting atmosphere.

Seated at the metal tables, their laughter and chatter filled the space, temporarily oblivious to the world around them. But as they savored their breakfast, a movement caught their attention—a woman, a touch of worry etched upon her face, hanging "missing" signs on nearby telephone poles.

The group's gazes converged upon her, their sandwiches momentarily forgotten. The woman seemed determined, methodically placing each flier with care. Her eyes scanned the surroundings, as if hoping to catch a glimpse of something or someone that could offer solace or answers.

Intrigued by the woman's actions, the teens exchanged glances and wordlessly agreed to observe from a distance. As she finished attaching the last flier, the woman approached their table, her footsteps tentative but purposeful.

"Excuse me," she said softly, her voice tinged with concern. "I'm sorry to interrupt, but my brother, a mechanic at the garage up the street, has gone missing. I've been putting up these flyers in the hopes that someone might have seen or heard something."

Her words hung in the air, enveloping the group in a shroud of uncertainty. They took the flyers she offered, their eyes scanning the photograph of the missing man, his smile frozen in time.

"We haven't seen him," Cassidy replied, her voice filled with empathy. "But we'll keep an eye out and let you know if we hear or see anything."

The woman nodded, gratitude flickering in her eyes. "Thank you, thank you so much. It's been days, and we're all worried sick. He's never disappeared like this before."

As the woman turned to leave, the weight of the situation settled upon the friends. Their once carefree morning had taken an unexpected turn, the specter of the missing mechanic casting a shadow over their thoughts.

With a shared sense of responsibility, they pledged to keep a vigilant watch over the town, their minds filled with questions. What had happened to the mechanic? Was there a connection to the recent disappearance mentioned by Cassidy earlier? The mystery had begun to unravel, and their journey into the unknown had only just begun.

As the six friends sat at the metal tables outside Rambo's, finishing their breakfast, their eyes shifted toward the commotion that disrupted the tranquility of the small town. A red 2-door Jeep Wrangler, its top and doors absent, screeched to a halt in front of the store. The engine's roar subsided, only to be replaced by the boisterous voices of four seniors from their high school—Greg, Rick, Sean, and Sanj.

The boys, oblivious to the concerned glances directed their way, leaped out of the jeep, their exuberance filling the air. Their arrival seemed to herald an unwelcome storm, disturbing the peace that had enveloped Foul Rift. The friends' attention shifted entirely to the unruly quartet as they swaggered past them, their carefree demeanor suggesting a disregard for those around them.

Inside Rambo's, the foursome continued their disruptive behavior, their voices resonating against the store's walls. Their presence loomed over the six who observed them with an intensity that conveyed their displeasure. It was evident that a deep-seated animosity existed between the two groups—a tension that crackled with unspoken grievances and unsavory histories.

Hayley's eyes narrowed, her jaw clenched, as she focused on the four seniors. Bo's expression hardened, a flicker of defiance igniting in his gaze. Cassidy, though composed, radiated a quiet strength, her body poised for whatever might transpire. Charlotte, her determination unwavering, met their gaze head-on. Andy's grip on his phone tightened, ready to document any potential confrontation. And Ryan, his acting skills honed, concealed a smoldering fury behind an impassive facade.

The six friends shared an unspoken understanding, their collective disdain fueling a determination to stand against the boys. The air grew thick with silent tension between them as the seconds ticked by, each passing moment heightening the anticipation of what lay ahead.

As Greg, Rick, Sean, and Sanj exited Rambo's, their mouths filled with hastily devoured food, their attention shifted towards Hayley and Bo. Greg's eyes narrowed as he caught sight of the two siblings, their happiness a stark contrast to his own inner turmoil. The resentment that simmered within him boiled over, fueled by envy and a sense of superiority.

"Hey dorks," Greg spat out, his words dripping with disdain. The sharpness of his tone lingered in the air, drawing the attention of Sean, who listened intently, ready to follow his friend's lead.

Sean, recalling his own history with Andy and fueled by the desire to fit in with the others, took a jab at his former comrade. "How's boy scouts, Andy? Still dorking out with the rest of the little douche-canoes?" The words were laced with mockery, intended to belittle and provoke.

Greg and Rick erupted into laughter, their amusement feeding off the taunting words. The six friends on the receiving end of the insults remained silent, their faces a canvas of mixed emotions. Hayley's brow furrowed with a mix of indignation and defiance, while Bo clenched his fists, his eyes shining with an inner fire.

A charged silence hung in the air, pregnant with unspoken words and unbridled emotions. The six friends were confronted with a choice—retaliate and sink to the same level of aggression or rise above the provocation and maintain their composure.

For a brief moment, time stood still, the tension palpable. As the six friends remained silent, a tense standoff unfolding, Sanj seized the opportunity to assert his own dominance. With a mischievous grin, he reached over and snatched the last bite of Andy's sandwich from the paper plate, devouring it greedily. His mouth full, Sanj casually wiped his mouth with his hand, a smug expression on his face.

"Thanks, I was still hungry," Sanj mumbled, his words barely intelligible through the mouthful of stolen food. Ryan's face flushed with anger, his frustration boiling beneath the surface. The audacity of Sanj's actions sparked a fire within him, fueling his desire to stand up for himself and his friends.

In that pivotal moment, Ryan's calm and collected demeanor took center stage. He saw the brewing conflict and recognized the need for intervention. His voice broke the uneasy silence, carrying a measured tone as he addressed the boys.

"Guys, leave us alone," Ryan spoke with a firmness that belied his youth. "Most of us are younger than you. Why don't you pick on someone older and see how that works out!"

His words hung in the air, challenging the antagonistic behavior of the four seniors. Ryan's calm demeanor and rational appeal to fairness highlighted the imbalance of power in their actions, drawing attention to the inherent injustice of their harassment.

The six friends, though outnumbered the boys, faced a palpable imbalance of power, found solace in their unity and Ryan's voice of reason.

Ignoring the taunts and derogatory remarks hurled their way, the six friends maintained their composure. Greg, Sean, Rick, and Sanjay dismissed their comments with an air of superiority, emphasizing their intention to cross paths again within the confines of their school. Their departing insults echoed through the air, staining the atmosphere with negativity.

As the jeep sped away, leaving a trail of disdain in its wake, the six friends gathered themselves, their silence thick with unresolved emotions. It was Bo who broke the quietude, proposing a diversion to shift their focus and regain a sense of peace.

"Hey, guys," Bo's voice cut through the lingering tension, "Let's go walkthrough Wind-Chime Woods."

Hayley's eyes brightened at the suggestion, and Charlotte readily agreed. The idea held a certain allure—an opportunity to immerse themselves in the tranquility of nature, away from the verbal assaults and the weight of the encounter.

With a shared nod, the group discarded their empty plates and cups, disposing of the remnants of their interrupted breakfast. Stepping away from Rambo's, they made their way toward the trailhead, located a few blocks from Rambo's. As they ventured forth, their collective presence became a shield against the lingering negativity, their determination to find solace and peace prevailing over the insults thrown their way.

Wind-Chime Woods is a hidden gem nestled within the heart of nature, where the remnants of an old railroad trail have been transformed into a tranquil pathway. Once occupied by the rhythmic chugging of locomotives, it now welcomes visitors with a wide expanse of crushed gravel, inviting them to wander beneath the shade of towering trees.

The path meanders through a verdant canopy, providing respite from the sun's relentless rays. Towering oaks, majestic maples, and elegant birches intermingle, their branches reaching towards the sky, creating a natural ceiling of foliage. The air is alive with the vibrant melodies of countless birds, their songs intermingling with the rustle of leaves and the distant scurrying of woodland creatures."

As walkers tread upon the gravel path, their steps are accompanied by a symphony of sound. Wind chimes, an enchanting presence in Wind-Chime Woods, adorn the branches of the surrounding trees. Each chime tells its own unique story, resonating with different materials and craftsmanship. Some chimes are grand in scale, their large metallic tubes capturing the wind's embrace and producing deep, melodious tones that reverberate through the forest. Others are delicate and tiny, ringing with delicate notes as the breeze dances through their forms.

The wind chimes themselves are a testament to creativity and resourcefulness. Homemade creations hang alongside store-bought treasures, forming a tapestry of whimsy and ingenuity. Discarded pots and pans, forgotten utensils, metal pipes, and even recycled soda cans have been repurposed into enchanting musical instruments. The chimes sway and collide, forming an ever-changing symphony of delicate harmonies, interweaving with the natural soundscape of Wind-Chime Woods.

Amidst this harmonious symphony, the forest teems with life. Squirrels traverse branches, chasing one another in playful pursuit. Rabbits hop through the undergrowth, their cotton-tails bobbing with each agile movement. Deer, elegant and cautious, occasionally grace the scene with their graceful presence, their eyes alert to any sign of intrusion. And in rare moments of chance, a black bear may amble by, a majestic reminder of the wilderness that encircles Wind-Chime Woods.

But it is the ephemeral breezes that breathe life into this enchanting sanctuary. When the wind stirs, the chimes respond, their harmonies carried on the delicate currents. The resulting concert, a blend of nature's whispers and the crafted melodies of the chimes, fills the air with a sense of serenity and wonder. It is during these breezy days that Wind-Chime Woods truly comes alive, offering visitors an immersive and captivating experience—a respite from the world's clamor, where the interplay of nature and human artistry creates a symphony for the soul.

In the embrace of Wind-Chime Woods, the six friends sought refuge and a momentary respite from the troubles that plagued their minds. They weaved through the sun-dappled paths, the soft tinkling of wind chimes accompanying their steps, soothing their spirits and rekindling a sense of unity among them.

As they ventured deeper into the forest, a renewed sense of camaraderie took hold, their bonds strengthened by the shared desire to rise above the conflicts and negativity that sought to divide them. In the embrace of nature's gentle embrace, they found solace and a renewed determination to navigate the challenges ahead, both within the winding trails of Wind-Chime Forest and beyond its leafy canopy.

As the group continues walking through the Wind Chime Woods, Bo's frustration from their encounter at Rambo's lingers in his mind. The serenity of the trail inspires him to speak up about an idea he's been brewing. With a determined look on his face, he takes a deep breath and addresses his friends, "Hey, guys, I've been thinking about something. I'm sick of all the negativity and drama in high school. It's exhausting, and I believe we can change the culture." His friends turn their attention towards Bo, intrigued by his serious tone.

Bo continues, "I want to start a group, a club, whatever you want to call it. Something that promotes positivity, kindness, and integrity. I've been calling it 'The Noblemen' for now. The idea is simple and, I believe, powerful. We'll follow a set of tenets that define what it means to be a noble person." He pauses, giving them a moment to absorb his words.

"We'll challenge ourselves to be better every day. As an example, we should stop cursing, because it only spreads negativity. Instead, we'll choose our words carefully, better and stronger words, and work on uplifting others. We'll be the ones who stand up for those who can't stand up for themselves. Like heroes in comic books, we'll protect others from harm and strive to make a positive impact in their lives."

Bo looks around at his friends, sensing their interest and curiosity. "This isn't about being perfect. It's about taking a stand against the negativity we see every day. It's about being accountable and holding ourselves to a higher standard. I believe we can create a ripple effect of goodness and make our high school a better place."

He finishes with a determined expression, waiting for his friends' responses, eager to hear their thoughts and whether they are willing to embark on this journey with him.

As Bo finishes sharing his idea of starting "The Noblemen," Charlotte and Cassidy can't help but burst into laughter. Charlotte manages to stifle her laughter enough to say, "Bo, it's a nice thought, but isn't it a bit... corny?" Cassidy joins in, unable to contain her giggles. They exchange amused glances, clearly finding the concept a little amusing.

Amidst their laughter and playful criticism, Andy steps forward, defending Bo's idea. He interjects, "Hold on, guys. I actually think it's a great concept. It's like Boy Scouts, but without all the knot-tying and camping. Bo's talking about spreading kindness and positivity, helping others, and being standup people. Isn't that something we can get behind?"

Charlotte and Cassidy exchange skeptical glances but let Andy's words sink in. They consider his perspective and the sincerity in Bo's eyes. Gradually, their laughter subsides, and they begin to see the potential value in the idea.

Cassidy chimes in, a hint of seriousness in her voice, "Well, I guess it wouldn't hurt to give it a try, right? We could be like modern-day knights, standing up for what's right."

Charlotte, still wearing a playful smile, nods in agreement. "Fine, I'm in. But only if we can come up with cooler names than 'The Noblemen'."

Bo's face lights up with a mix of relief and excitement as the group starts to warm up to his idea. He's grateful for Andy's support and the willingness of Charlotte and Cassidy to give it a chance. Together, they continue walking through Wind Chime Woods, brainstorming ideas and discussing the possibilities that lie ahead for their newfound club.

As the group walks through Wind Chime Woods, Ryan listens to the conversation with a pensive expression. He nods along to Cass's suggestion about defining what it means to be a Noblemen, and then chimes in, "You know what, guys? I think it's important to establish a clear definition of what being a Nobleman entails. We should set certain values and expectations for ourselves, like Bo mentioned earlier. Do you know what the difference is between superheroes and villains? They both, typically, have tough childhoods."

Bo looks at Ryan with admiration. "What is the difference?"
Ryan, expecting Bo to ask 'why', says, "They both have had hard lives. The difference is, choice as result of having a strong mind or a weak mind. You see, when the world hurts a villain, the villain wants to hurt the world back. When the world hurts a superhero, the superhero wants to protect the others from the world."

Bo says loudly, "I like that. I never thought of it that way.

Ryan glances at Charlotte, who had suggested considering a new name. "And speaking of which, Charlotte might be onto something. 'The Noblemen' does sound a bit outdated. Maybe we can brainstorm some alternative names that still capture the essence of our mission but still sound cool."

Charlotte raises an eyebrow, a mischievous smile forming on her lips. "Finally, someone agrees with me. Alright, let's put our heads together and come up with a name that reflects our modern-day knightly virtues."

Hayley listens intently to the conversation, a proud smile spreading across her face as Bo shares his idea. She clears her throat and speaks up, her voice filled with admiration for her little brother. "I have to say, Bo, I think this idea of yours is cool. It takes courage to stand up against negativity and strive to make a positive difference."

She takes a deep breath before continuing, "One of the tenets you mentioned, Bo, about not cursing, really struck a chord with me. I think we should strive to reserve cursing for those moments when it's genuinely hard to stop, like when we get hurt and it slips out unintentionally. But let's make it a point not to use curse words in our general speech like so many kids do. You know, some kids think it makes them sound cool, but in reality, it's just a form of toxic speech. It's like when a baby throws a tantrum. People curse because they don't have a better way to express themselves. As Noblemen, we should hold ourselves to a higher standard."

Hayley looks around at her friends, her eyes filled with determination. "What do you all think about that? I really like the idea of the Noblemen promoting a culture of positive and respectful communication. Let's add that to our list of tenets.

Bo speaks up, "Ok, Tenet number one is 'No Cursing' in regular conversations. What is Tenet 2?"

Cass listens attentively to Hayley's words, nodding in agreement. She waits for a moment before speaking up, her voice filled with thoughtful consideration. "I really like the idea of not trash talking people," she says, her tone firm yet compassionate. "I've noticed how often people resort to gossiping when they simply don't like someone for superficial reasons. It's a way of bullying someone behind their back, and it serves no purpose other than spreading negativity."

She takes a deep breath, her eyes focused as she continues, "As Noblemen, we should hold ourselves to a higher standard. If we ever find ourselves speaking badly about someone, let it be because that person has done something morally wrong, something that truly warrants criticism. But let's refrain from engaging in gossip or trash-talking people for the sake of it."

Cass's gaze softens as she recollects a quote she recently stumbled upon on the Internet. "There's a quote that comes to mind," she says, a faint smile gracing her lips. "It goes, 'Small minds discuss people, average minds discuss events, great minds discuss ideas.' Let's strive to be great minds, to focus our conversations on meaningful ideas rather than tearing others down."

With a determined nod, Cass suggests, "So, let's make our second tenet not to gossip or trash talk people without a valid reason. It's about promoting kindness, understanding, and genuine conversations that uplift and inspire."

Bo: "Great! Tenet 1: 'No cursing' and Tenet 2: 'No gossiping or bad mouthing others'. I love it!"

Char listens intently to Cass's words, her eyes shining with agreement. She nods in approval and then takes a step forward, ready to contribute her own idea for the next tenet. "I've got an idea for our third tenet," she says, her voice filled with determination. "As Noblemen, we must always stand up for others when they're being picked on or bullied. We can't just stand by and watch, as if it's some kind of Saturday morning cartoon. It's our duty to be the ones who intervene, who lend a helping hand when someone is in need."

She pauses for a moment, gathering her thoughts. "Too often, I've seen kids turn a blind eye or even join in on the bullying, as if it's some twisted form of entertainment. But that's not who we are as Noblemen. We stand up for the little guy, for the underdog, and we don't let them face adversity alone."

Char's gaze shifts from person to person, her expression firm yet compassionate. "Let's make it our third tenet: Noblemen always stand up for others. We become their voice, their shield, and their support. It's about creating a safe and inclusive environment where everyone feels valued and protected."

She finishes her statement, a resolute smile spreading across her face. "What do you all think?"

As the group listens to Char's passionate words, they nod in agreement, their expressions reflecting a shared sense of purpose and determination. Bo, feeling the energy and support from his friends, steps forward and takes a deep breath.

"Alright, let's recap our tenets," Bo begins, his voice filled with enthusiasm. "As Noblemen, we've established three guiding principles, so far, that will define who we are and how we conduct ourselves."

He raises his hand, counting off each tenet on his fingers. "First, Noblemen do not curse unnecessarily. We understand that words hold power, and we choose to use them wisely, avoiding unnecessary negativity in our speech."

Bo continues, "Second, we do not engage in gossip or speak ill of others without a justifiable reason. We recognize that superficial judgments and gossip can harm and bully others, so we rise above it."

A smile spreads across Bo's face as he reaches the third tenet. "And finally, Noblemen always stand up for others. We become the champions of those who need support, the defenders against bullying and injustice."

Bo: "Let's add some more."

Ryan listens intently to his friends, nodding in agreement with their ideas. When Bo finishes listing the three tenets, Ryan raises his hand, a thoughtful expression on his face.

"I have another idea for a tenet," Ryan begins, his voice filled with sincerity. "It may not be as grand as the others, but it's something my father always emphasized to me: never shake a person's hand while sitting down. It's a simple gesture, but it signifies respect."

He continues, "Perhaps we can expand on that and make respect a core value for the Noblemen. It's about truly listening to others, hearing their thoughts and opinions, and validating their experiences. We can focus on the little acts of kindness, like opening doors for people and always being willing to lend a helping hand."

Andy's eyes light up as he recognizes the parallel with his own experiences. "In Boy Scouts, we call that 'doing a good turn daily,'" he adds. "But maybe as Noblemen, we can take it a step further and strive to 'do a good turn always.'"

The group exchanges approving glances, realizing the significance of this new tenet. It encapsulates the essence of their vision – to be respectful, compassionate, and continuously committed to making a positive impact on the lives of others.

With the addition of Ryan's tenet, the list of Noblemen's principles grows stronger, embodying a code of conduct that encompasses integrity, kindness, and empathy. They feel a renewed sense of purpose, ready to embrace this path and spread goodness in their community.

Andy listens attentively to his friends' ideas, feeling inspired by the noble tenets they have already discussed. He raises his hand, eager to contribute his own suggestion.

"I have something to add as well," Andy says, his voice filled with enthusiasm. "In Boy Scouts, we have a motto that was devised by Baden Powell, the founder of the scouting movement. The motto is 'Be Prepared.'"

He pauses for a moment, gathering his thoughts. "Being prepared means more than just physical readiness. It's about cultivating a mindset of readiness, being prepared to face challenges, adapt to different situations, and seize opportunities."

Andy continues, "As Noblemen, we can embrace the idea of being prepared in all aspects of our lives. It means being mentally and emotionally prepared to tackle obstacles, being proactive in our pursuits, and always striving for personal growth."

The group listens intently, realizing the value of Andy's suggestion. Being prepared encompasses not only practical skills but also a mindset of readiness and resilience. It reinforces the idea that as Noblemen, they are committed to self-improvement, always striving to be their best selves and to be ready to make a positive impact whenever the opportunity arises.

With Andy's contribution, the list of tenets grows stronger, reflecting the values and aspirations of the Noblemen. The group feels a sense of unity and purpose, eager to embrace these principles and carry them forward as they embark on their journey of spreading goodness in their community.

As the group absorbs Andy's suggestion, their excitement grows palpable. They can feel the power of their collective vision taking shape. Bo takes a moment to let the anticipation build, and then he enthusiastically lists all the tenets they have established:

"So, our tenets are: No cursing, always come to the aid of others, no gossiping or trash-talking, stand up for the little guy, always give respect and have good manners, and be prepared," Bo recites, the words carrying a sense of purpose.

The friends exchange proud glances, their unity strengthening with each reaffirmation of their shared values. But before they can bask in the moment, Char interjects, her voice filled with playful humor, "You know, we really need to consider a new name."

Ryan, always ready to lighten the mood, jumps in with a mischievous smile, "How about 'The Extraordinary League of Do-Gooders'?"

Hayley calls out, "The E.L.D.G.!"

Laughter erupts among the friends as they realize the absurdity of the suggestion. It breaks the tension and brings a sense of lightheartedness to the conversation. They understand that while the name might need some consideration, it is the principles and actions behind it that truly matter.

With their first 5 tenets firmly established and their spirits lifted, the group feels a renewed sense of purpose and camaraderie. As they made their way out of Wind Chime Woods, the gentle melodies of the chimes accompanied their every step, creating a serene atmosphere. Just ahead, a missing person sign fluttered on a post at the end of the trail, displaying a picture of the mechanic. The wind rustled the paper, as if trying to catch their attention. Lost in their own world of ideas and laughter, none of them noticed the sign as they passed by, moving towards their next adventure while the chimes softly faded into the distance.

Chapter 3:
The Eddy

Foul Rift, bathed in the warmth of a picturesque day, exuded an undeniable charm. With summer on the horizon, the town had come alive, vibrant and bursting with life. The landscape was adorned with lush greenery, as trees swayed gently in the breeze, their branches reaching towards the azure sky. Colorful flowers bloomed, dotting the sidewalks and gardens, adding splashes of vibrant hues to the already picturesque scene.

As people went about their daily routines, Foul Rift seemed to hum with activity. The town's streets buzzed with the cheerful chatter of neighbors and friends, exchanging greetings and catching up on the latest news. Beautiful houses stood proudly, showcasing their grandeur and architectural splendor. Elaborate millwork adorned the facades, accentuating the timeless elegance of the buildings. Expansive porches invited residents to relax and bask in the beauty of the day, while intricate windows framed scenes of everyday life with an artistic touch.

Foul Rift, like a character in its own right, exuded a sense of history and community. Its well-preserved charm whispered tales of generations past, offering a glimpse into a bygone era. The town's beauty and ambiance permeated every corner, weaving a tapestry of nostalgia and warmth that embraced all who called it home.

Detective Brien Chotdyfo, a seasoned investigator with seven years of experience in the Foul Rift Police Department, was tasked with the investigation into the disappearance of the mechanic. In a small police department consisting of a chief, a couple of detectives, and a few patrolmen, Brien took on the responsibility of delving into the mysterious case.

The mechanic's sister, his sole family member, had reached out to the police, her concern apparent in her voice. She revealed that her brother had a history of heart issues, having suffered a heart attack in the past. She feared that he may have experienced another health-related episode while in the woods, possibly leading to his demise.

The mechanic's solitary nature and limited circle of friends added a layer of complexity to the investigation. Brien recognized the significance of the case, understanding the weight of responsibility in uncovering the truth and providing closure for the worried sister. As she delved deeper into the investigation, she meticulously examined the mechanic's background, looking for any leads or clues that could shed light on his whereabouts.

Brien's determination and commitment to her role as a detective propelled her forward. With the assistance of the small police force in Foul Rift and the potential collaboration with the state police, she was determined to leave no stone unturned in her pursuit of answers. The missing mechanic's fate hung in the balance, and it was up to Brien to unravel the mystery and bring a sense of peace to the concerned sister and the tight-knit community of Foul Rift.

Having exhausted the search efforts in the surrounding woods, Detective Brien Chotdyfo couldn't shake off the nagging thought that perhaps the mechanic's fate had taken an unexpected turn—one that led to the treacherous eddy. Brien had a deep-rooted aversion to that dark and enigmatic place, a feeling stemming from her childhood experiences.

The eddy, hidden from casual observation, lurked like a shadow within the river's flow. It was an ominous entity, larger and deeper than the surrounding waters. Encircled by a series of small cliffs and concealed caves, it exudes an aura of mystery and danger. A barely discernible tributary, its entrance disguised amidst the river's natural landscape, served as the pathway to this foreboding abyss.

Brien's unease with the eddy traced back to her childhood adventures, where she had ventured too close for comfort. Its haunting presence and concealed secrets had always sent shivers down her spine. Yet, driven by her unwavering commitment to her duty as a detective, she steeled herself for a visit to this eerie location. The potential resting place of the mechanic's remains compelled her to confront her fears and delve into the depths of the eddy's murky waters.

Detective Brien Chotdyfo reached for her radio, her hand trembling ever so slightly with a mix of anticipation and unease. She clicked the button, activating the device, and spoke into the microphone with a steady voice.

"Patrolman Hendricks, this is Detective Chotdyfo. Over," she relayed, her words carrying a hint of resolve.

A brief moment passed before a crackling response came through the radio. "This is Patrolman Hendricks. Go ahead, Detective Chotdyfo. Over."

Brien took a deep breath, steadying herself before she replied, "I'm proceeding to investigate the eddy. I have a hunch I might find something there. I'll need you to maintain communication while I'm there. Copy?"

Patrolman Hendricks voice came through with a tone of reassurance, "Copy that, Detective Chotdyfo. I'll keep the lines open and be ready to assist if needed. Please stay safe out there. Over."

A sense of gratitude washed over Brien as she acknowledged the patrolman's support. "Thank you, Patrolman. I appreciate your assistance. I'll update you as soon as I have any significant findings. Over and out."

With the confirmation that her message had been received, Brien clipped the radio back to her belt and prepared to venture into the foreboding depths of the eddy. Brien Chotdyfo stepped out of her parked car, leaving behind the familiar comfort of the vehicle as she embarked on her journey through the woods. What was once a serene and picturesque landscape seemed to transform before her eyes. The sunlight that had bathed the area moments ago now cast eerie shadows, elongating the gnarled tree trunks that surrounded her path.

As she ventured deeper into the woods, the sounds of chirping birds and rustling leaves were replaced by an unsettling silence. Unfamiliar noises echoed through the dense foliage, faint whispers carried on the wind, as if the very forest itself held secrets it dared not reveal. The air grew stale and heavy, tinged with a hint of decay, making each breath an uncomfortable reminder of the unknown lurking in the shadows.

Branches twisted and reached out like skeletal fingers, their gnawed bark adding to the macabre atmosphere. The once vibrant colors of the flowers and foliage now appeared muted and somber, as if drained of their vitality. Brien couldn't help but feel a shiver run down her spine, a primal instinct warning her of the foreboding presence that lingered within the depths of the woods.

With each step, the path seemed to shift, the terrain becoming more treacherous, as if nature itself conspired to impede her progress. A sense of isolation enveloped her, a feeling of being watched by unseen eyes. Shadows danced and swayed, playing tricks on her senses, as if the very fabric of reality was distorted within this foreboding realm.

Though she pressed on, fueled by determination and duty, Brien couldn't shake the unsettling sensation that she was an intruder in this enigmatic domain. Every rustle, every snap of a twig, sent her senses into heightened alertness. She became acutely aware of the weight of her footsteps, the creaking of her worn boots, each sound magnified in the eerie stillness of the woods.

As she neared her destination, the presence of the eddy loomed in her mind like a specter. It called to her, a dark and mysterious force pulling her deeper into the heart of the woods. Brien's steps quickened, her heart pounding in her chest, a mixture of apprehension and determination propelling her forward.

Amidst the palpable unease, Brien Chotdyfo remained resolute, her commitment to finding the missing mechanic unwavering. She pressed on, navigating the unsettling atmosphere, determined to uncover the truth that lay hidden within the twisted embrace of the woods.

Brien Chotdyfo's steps grew cautious and deliberate as she approached the edge of the foreboding eddy. The unease that had accompanied her throughout the journey intensified, the sensation of being watched becoming almost suffocating. She couldn't shake the feeling that unseen eyes were fixed upon her, observing her every move with a sinister intent.

As she stood at the precipice of the murky abyss, a sense of tension coiled within her, causing her muscles to tighten involuntarily. The air seemed to pulse with an oppressive presence, as if the very essence of the eddy exuded an otherworldly malevolence.

Her gaze darted around the surroundings, peering into the shadows and across the expanse of the eddy. She strained to listen, hoping to catch any sound that might reveal the source of her unease. A distant rustle, a faint echo of footsteps, teased at the edge of her perception, taunting her senses.

With each careful step she took, her eyes scanned the surface of the eddy, searching for any sign of the missing mechanic. Her heart raced in her chest, anticipation mingling with trepidation as she desperately sought confirmation that her fears had been unfounded.

A flicker of relief coursed through her when she initially saw nothing but the swirling darkness within the eddy.

However, a glimmer of contrasting color caught her attention, drawing her gaze back to the depths. There, amidst the churning waters, was an ominous sight—a tangled mass of fabric, akin to clothing, caught in the grasp of the eddy's grip.

Her pulse quickened, and a chill ran down her spine as she realized the gravity of the discovery. The missing mechanic's fate seemed to stare back at her from within the mysterious eddy, a silent witness to the secrets concealed within its depths. The realization that she had found a potential clue sent a surge of determination coursing through her veins, overriding the lingering unease that enveloped her.

Brien's instincts urged her to proceed with caution, warning her of the perils that lay ahead. With a steady resolve, she continued to peer into the heart of the eddy, determined to unearth the truth that lurked beneath its enigmatic surface. The presence that had plagued her throughout the journey seemed to grow more tangible, its weight pressing upon her as she braced herself for the daunting task that lay before her.

Brien's attention zeroed in on the elusive garments trapped within the clutches of the eddy. Determined to retrieve them as a potential piece of evidence, she assessed her surroundings, searching for a means to bridge the distance between herself and the clothing.

Her eyes scanned the immediate area, desperately seeking a suitable tool. Spotting a dead tree branch nearby, she hastened towards it, hope swelling within her. With careful consideration, she assessed its length, but alas, it fell short of the reach required to grasp the clothing.

Undeterred, Brien's gaze returned to the eddy, her mind racing to find an alternative solution. As her eyes swept across its tumultuous surface, she noticed a specific section caked with thick mud, an anomaly amidst the swirling chaos. Intrigued, she fixed her attention on the hardened mound jutting out from the mud's grip.

Though cloaked in layers of mire and moss, the mound appeared solid, a promising foothold in her quest to bridge the gap. Without hesitation, Brien leaped from the safety of the bank, expertly maneuvering over treacherous stretches of mud, her determination serving as her guide.

Her boots sank into the mire, each step demanding her unwavering focus as she inched closer to the protruding mound. With a careful balance of agility and caution, she ascended the mound's surface, relying on its sturdy form to support her weight. Mud clung to her boots and splattered across her clothing, testament to the treacherous terrain she navigated.

Finally, she reached the end of the mound, a vantage point that brought her within arm's reach of the clothing tantalizingly trapped within the eddy's grasp. With her makeshift tree branch extended, she stretched her arm out, straining against the limits of her reach to make contact with the fabric.

Every ounce of her being was focused on this pivotal moment, the anticipation building as she attempted to ensnare the clothing. The branch wavered precariously, mud slipping from its makeshift grip, as Brien fought against the swirling currents that threatened to thwart her progress.

A surge of determination coursed through her, lending her strength as she leaned forward, inch by painstaking inch. Just as the branch's tip brushed against the fabric, a renewed sense of purpose surged within her. She would not be deterred. With a final, determined lunge, she succeeded, the garment curling around the branch, claiming them as a crucial piece of the puzzle.

Brien's heart pounds in her chest as she fights against the muck, struggling to maintain her balance on the shifting mound. With a determined grip on her stick, she pulls the garment in closer, her focus unwavering. But the treacherous terrain has other plans.

Suddenly, her foot slips on the slimy surface, and she crashes hard against the mound, the impact reverberating through her body. Gritting her teeth, she quickly pushes herself back up, ignoring the throbbing ache in her side. The urgency to retrieve the clothing compels her to try again.

Taking a deep breath, Brien steadies herself and extends the stick, carefully hooking it onto the fabric. Just as she starts to pull the garment towards her, she feels a jolt beneath her feet. The mound beneath her begins to quiver and sink, sending a surge of panic through her veins.

Time seems to slow as Brien scrambles to keep her footing. Her heart races, and a cold sweat forms on her brow as she desperately tries to regain stability. The mud oozes and churns around her, threatening to swallow her whole.

In a heart-stopping moment, the mound gives way, and Brien's body slides off its crumbling surface, plunging her into the thick, clinging mud below. She gasps as the cold, mucky substance engulfs her, making every movement a struggle against its relentless grasp.

Her heart pounding, Brien fights against the mud's suffocating grip, clawing at the slimy terrain in a desperate attempt to pull herself free. But the more she struggles, the deeper she sinks, the mud clinging to her like a sinister embrace.

Brien's heart pounds in her chest as panic grips her tightly. Covered in mud, her vision obscured, she strains to make sense of her surroundings. Through the murky haze, she catches a glimpse of a shadowy figure, but her muddied eyes deceive her, leaving her uncertain.

Suddenly, a piercing cry in an unfamiliar accent cuts through the eerie silence, jolting Brien from her disoriented state. The words, "NUHR ZEELP NUHR," echo in her ears, sending a shiver down her spine. The foreign utterance only adds to her bewilderment, heightening the sense of danger that looms in the air.

As if in response to the enigmatic call, the very ground beneath Brien begins to shift and stir. With wide eyes, she watches in disbelief as the mound she had been standing on moves beside her, rising ominously from the clinging mud. Simultaneously, another massive mound emerges from the depths, its other end facing the distant banks.

A mixture of awe and terror washes over Brien as she realizes the truth that unfolds before her. She finds herself stuck in the mud next to a gigantic alligator snapping turtle, a creature of colossal proportions unlike anything she has ever encountered. Its sheer size and strength are enough to render her efforts to escape futile.

Frantically, Brien fights against the viscous mud, struggling to free herself from its unforgiving grip. With every exertion, the thick sludge seems to tighten its hold, entwining her further in its mire. Her heart and mind races with a blend of survival instincts and confusion.

Fear courses through Brien's veins as she desperately searches for an escape route, her mind racing to find a solution. The massive turtle, its presence both awe-inspiring and terrifying, now represents a formidable obstacle between her and freedom. Every move she makes feels futile against the relentless hold of the mud.

In the midst of her struggle, Brien's thoughts whirl in a maelstrom of confusion and urgency. The strange words that reverberated through the air, the shadowy figure lurking in the periphery—everything adds to the surreal and treacherous nature of her predicament.

With each passing second, Brien fights against the mud's suffocating grip, her muscles straining against the weight and resistance. But the inescapable truth remains: she is trapped, ensnared in a deadly dance with the colossal turtle and the unforgiving elements that surround her.

As desperation seizes her, Brien musters every ounce of strength and determination, driven by the primal instinct to survive. The mud clings relentlessly, but she refuses to surrender. With renewed resolve, she continues to fight, hoping for a chance to break free from the clutches of this watery prison and find her way back to solid ground.

Brien's heart pounds in her chest as she struggles to retrieve her revolver, its once gleaming surface now encased in thick layers of mud. The snapping turtle's unwavering gaze remains fixed on her, its massive body slowly pivoting to face her directly. The weight of the moment hangs heavy in the air, every passing second feeling like an eternity.

With a final desperate tug, Brien manages to free her revolver from its muddy holster. She raises the weapon, her hands trembling slightly, but her determination unwavering. Locked in a chilling stare with the formidable creature before her, she steadies her aim, her finger caressing the trigger.

Time seems to slow as the gravity of the situation unfolds. Brien's senses heighten, her focus honed solely on the snapping turtle. Beads of sweat mingle with the mud on her brow as she waits for the opportune moment, her finger gently squeezing the trigger, preparing to unleash the deadly force of her weapon.

The air crackles with anticipation, the tension reaching its climax as the snapping turtle's colossal form looms just a few feet away. Brien knows this moment is her only chance for survival, her resolve tested to its limits.

The beast looked like a creature from the primordial era. Its immense size is awe-inspiring, its shell as colossal and round as a hulking SUV. With a head resembling a weathered boulder, it exudes an air of prehistoric power. Its gaping maw, large as an oven, reveals a menacing razor-sharp beak and jagged points protruding from its rugged exterior. Every inch of its monstrous form evokes a sense of primal ferocity, an embodiment of ancient strength and untamed wilderness.

Brien squeezes the trigger, but her gun jammed from the mud caked on it. Frustration fills her as she tries again, desperately attempting to unjam the weapon. Meanwhile, the turtle's head inches closer, its eyes fixed on Brien's face. Determined to defend herself, Brien clears the mud from her gun and takes aim at the turtle's menacing head. With a final effort, she pulls the trigger, but nothing happens. The turtle's jaws snap shut, freeing Brien's head from her body.

Detective Brien Chotdyfo was gone. Snappy took his time to take small, anticipatory bites. The tender flesh yielded effortlessly, revealing the juiciness within. With each subsequent bite, Snappy relished the combination of textures and flavors. The sound of his beak crunching through the bones added an element of satisfaction to each bite for Snappy.

The woods around the eddy fell into a heavy silence, disturbed only by the gentle rustling of leaves in the breeze. The absence of Detective Brien's presence left a void, a sense of loss that hung in the air. The once vibrant and inviting woods now seemed desolate, their beauty overshadowed by the weight of sorrow.

The surrounding trees stood as silent witnesses, their branches reaching out like mournful arms. The sun, which had bathed the woods in warmth and light, now seemed to cast a melancholic glow, casting long shadows that stretched towards the edge of the eddy.

The echoes of Brien's final struggle faded, swallowed by the stillness of the forest. It was as if the woods themselves mourned the tragic fate of the detective, their silence a somber tribute to a life extinguished too soon. The tranquility of nature now held an eerie quality, as if the very essence of the place had been forever changed.

Chapter 4:
Privateer and Pirates

As the sun begins to rise, casting a soft golden hue across the sleepy town of Foul Rift, the six friends go about their morning routines, preparing for another day at school. Bo, with a spark of excitement in his eyes, feels a surge of anticipation within him. Today is the day he has been eagerly awaiting – the day he will present his idea to the school principal about starting a club called "The Noblemen." He believes that this club can make a positive impact on their school and bring about meaningful change.

Meanwhile, the rest of the group feels a sense of excitement as well, albeit for a different reason. With only a couple of weeks left until the much-anticipated summer break, they can almost taste the freedom and adventure that awaits them. The promise of lazy days, endless laughter, and memorable adventures fills their thoughts, heightening their anticipation.

As they gather their belongings, say their goodbyes to their parents, and head out the door, the air is filled with an electric energy. Each member of the group carries their own hopes and dreams for the day ahead, their minds buzzing with possibilities. Little do they know that this ordinary morning will mark the beginning of a remarkable journey, where the bonds of friendship will be tested and the true essence of nobility will be revealed.

In different corners of the school, the six friends find themselves immersed in their respective classrooms. Cassidy sits in her Fictional Literature class, where the topic of discussion revolves around the renowned author Peter Benchley. The class delves into the complexities of Benchley's feelings of guilt, stemming from the negative portrayal of sharks in his works. A thoughtful conversation ensues, exploring the power of storytelling and its impact on public perception.

Across the hallway, Char finds herself in the midst of a lively P.E. class. The sound of pickleball paddles striking the ball fills the air as her classmates engage in a spirited match. Char joins in the action, her competitive spirit shining through as she skillfully maneuvers on the court, determined to claim victory.

Meanwhile, in study hall, Ryan observes his peers engrossed in the glow of their cell phone screens. He can't help but ponder the role of technology in their lives, wondering about the lost moments of connection and the beauty of the world outside the virtual realm.

Andy and Hayley find themselves captivated by the lessons of history in Mr. Odrap's classroom. They listen attentively as their teacher sheds light on the rich tapestry of their local history, connecting the past to the present, and instilling a sense of pride for their community and its heritage.

In the midst of numbers and equations, Bo sits in his math class, where the engaging game of "24" is in full swing.

With numbers dancing before his eyes, Bo's mind races with anticipation. He raises his hand, eagerly awaiting his turn to present his idea to the principal, determined to bring his vision of "The Noblemen" to life. He makes the request of his teacher to see the principal and she obliges.

Bo enters the front office and finds it momentarily empty, save for the diligent secretaries manning their desks. They glance up from their work, offering friendly smiles as they acknowledge his presence. The sound of ringing phones and the soft hum of office equipment fill the air, creating a bustling yet organized atmosphere.

One of the secretaries, Mrs. Shannon looks up from her computer screen and warmly greets Bo. "Good morning, Bo," she says cheerfully. "How can we help you today?"

Bo explains his intention to speak with the principal about his idea for the club. The secretaries exchange a knowing glance and assure him that they will check if the principal is available. They pick up the phone and make a brief call, ensuring that Bo's request can be accommodated.

"Mr. Fratelli is currently available," Mrs. Shannon informs Bo with a friendly nod. "You can go right in. Good luck!"

Grateful for their assistance, Bo offers a polite thank you before heading towards the principal's office. The support and encouragement from the secretaries give him an added boost of confidence as he prepares to pitch his idea to the school's leader.

Meanwhile, in the history class, Mr. Odrap stands at the front of the room, an aura of enthusiasm surrounding him.

He addresses the class with a smile, energizing the students for the day's lesson.

"Good morning, everyone! As we approach the final stretch of the school year, let's keep the learning journey exciting and delve into our local history," Mr. Odrap announces, his voice filled with anticipation.

Hayley and Andy, seated attentively in their desks, exchange curious glances. They eagerly await what Mr. Odrap has in store for them.

Just as Mr. Odrap begins discussing the rich history of Foul Rift, a student calls out, "Nothing ever happens in Foul Rift!"

Mr. Odrap's eyebrows raise, and he grins mischievously. He swiftly responds as if he was hoping a student would question him, countering the statement, "Oh, but that simply isn't true. Foul Rift, my dear boy, has witnessed remarkable tales, intriguing events, and hidden gems that shape our town's identity."

The class leans forward in their seats, captivated by Mr. Odrap's words. He proceeds to recount fascinating anecdotes of Foul Rift's past, weaving stories of triumph, mystery, and community resilience. Hayley and Andy eagerly soak in the historical narratives, their imaginations sparked by the tales of their town's rich heritage.

With each passing moment, the perception that "Nothing ever happens in Foul Rift" fades away, replaced by a newfound appreciation for the town's vibrant history.

Back at the front of the school, Bo enters Mr. Fratelli's office, a mixture of nerves and excitement coursing through his veins. The principal warmly welcomes him, gesturing for Bo to take a seat. With a determined look in his eyes, Bo begins to explain his vision.

"Mr. Fratelli, I have an idea for a club that I believe would be a great addition to our school next year," Bo starts, his voice filled with enthusiasm. "It's called The Noblemen."

As Bo speaks, he passionately describes the concept of The Noblemen, emphasizing the core tenets of the club: kindness, integrity, leadership, and service. He shares his belief that fostering these qualities among students would not only contribute to a positive school environment but also help individuals grow and thrive.

"I think The Noblemen can make a real difference in our school community. It will encourage students to be their best selves, to support one another, and to make a positive impact both inside and outside the school," Bo explains earnestly.

Throughout Bo's presentation, Mr. Fratelli attentively listens, nodding occasionally and taking notes. The principal recognizes Bo's passion and the potential of The Noblemen to promote character development and student engagement.

Mr. Fratelli listens intently to Bo's explanation, nodding along and genuinely impressed by the concept of The Noblemen. As Bo finishes speaking, a smile forms on the principal's face.

Principal: Well, Bo, I must say, your idea for the Noblemen reminds me of the International Order of Odd Fellows.

Bo: The what, sir? I've never heard of that.

Principal (in a soft and low voice): Allow me to enlighten you, Bo. The International Order of Odd Fellows is a longstanding organization that promotes friendship, philanthropy, and community service. They have lodges all over the world.

Bo: Really? I had no idea. Can you tell me more?

Principal: Have you ever visited Clinton, in Hunterdon County, Bo?

Bo: Oh, yes, we go there quite often. We usually have breakfast on Main Street by the waterfall.

Principal: Ah, excellent. Now, have you ever taken a good look at the buildings on Main Street? Specifically, have you noticed the big eye atop one of the buildings towards the center of town?

Bo: Oh, yes! I've seen it many times. I always wondered what it was about. It's quite weird to have a giant eye on a building. There's even an address written above it, saying 100F.

Principal: Laughs Bo, that's not the address at all. Those aren't numbers, they are letters. It stands for I. O. O. F, which stands for the International Order of Odd Fellows. It used to be one of their lodges many years ago. My grandfather was a member. It's quite an interesting group, and strangely enough, their organization shares similarities with what you are creating. As a matter of fact, the gentleman who runs the museum in town is a former member, at least I heard that he was.

Bo: Wow, that's amazing! I never knew about the International Order of Odd Fellows. I will have to do some research about them. I'm even more excited about the Noblemen now!

"Bo, I must say, I'm truly impressed by your idea and the principles behind 'The Noblemen'. It's clear that you've put a lot of thought into this", Mr. Fratelli expresses, his voice filled with admiration. "I believe it has the potential to make a significant impact on our school community.

Mr. Fratelli leans in with a playful gleam in his eyes. "Although, I must admit, the name 'The Noblemen' does have a certain noble ring to it," he remarks, a hint of mischief in his voice. "But what if we considered something like 'The Virtuous Vanguard' or 'The Valiant Heroes'? Just a thought!"

Mr. Fratelli chuckles lightly, the atmosphere in the room becoming more lighthearted. He appreciates Bo's creativity and the seriousness with which he has approached the club's concept.

"But in all seriousness, Bo, I genuinely like the idea and the name you've chosen. It embodies the values you're aiming for, and I can see the positive impact it could have on our students," Mr. Fratelli adds, a warm smile on his face. "I'll be sure to review the proposal thoroughly and discuss it with the administration. We'll work together to make this club a reality."

Bo's face brightens with a mixture of relief and excitement, grateful for Mr. Fratelli's support and open-mindedness. They exchange a final handshake, sealing their agreement to pursue the creation of 'The Noblemen'.

As Bo steps out of the principal's office, he can't help but feel a renewed sense of purpose. With Mr. Fratelli's encouraging words and jesting suggestion, Bo is more determined than ever to bring 'The Noblemen' to life and inspire his peers with the values it represents.

At that very moment, a sense of tension fills the air as Mrs. Shannon bursts into the principal's office, her expression filled with concern. Bo's curiosity piques, but he understands that it's best to give them their privacy. He nods respectfully as Mr. Fratelli apologizes and asks him to excuse the interruption, promising to address their discussion later. Bo exits the office with a mix of wonder and unease.

As he walks down the hallway, his thoughts are interrupted by a sight that catches him off guard. Two state police officers are standing near the entrance of the office, their presence an unexpected addition to the usual school environment. Bo's mind races with questions, wondering what could be happening and how it might be connected to the urgency in Mrs. Shannon's demeanor. He can't help but feel a sense of uneasiness settle over him as he continues on his way, his mind buzzing with possibilities and concerns.

Meanwhile, back in Mr. Odrap's class: Mr. Odrap's eyes light up with enthusiasm as he poses a question to the class, "Have any of you ever heard about the history of

Captain William Kidd, the infamous pirate, and his connection to our very own Foul Rift and the Delaware River?" The students perk up, their curiosity piqued by the mention of pirates in their local area. One eager student blurts out, "Pirates on the Delaware?" Mr. Odrap chuckles warmly and responds, "Yes, indeed! The Delaware River holds its fair share of pirate tales. Would you like to embark on a historical adventure with me?"

The classroom erupts in excited chatter as Mr. Odrap begins his vivid storytelling. With animated gestures and a flair for dramatic retelling, he paints a colorful picture of Captain Kidd's exploits and the mysteries surrounding his ill-gotten treasures. The students lean forward in their seats, hanging on every word, their imaginations ignited by visions of swashbuckling pirates, hidden maps, and daring escapades along the treacherous waters.

As Mr. Odrap delves deeper into the stories, he interweaves historical facts with legends, evoking the spirit of adventure and the allure of hidden riches. He describes how Foul Rift became a den of secrecy and a strategic haven for these seafaring outlaws, highlighting the area's rugged cliffs and treacherous currents that kept authorities at bay.

Mr. Odrap, with an air of authority, delved into the true story of Captain William Kidd, unraveling the captivating tale of his rise and fall. The class listened intently as he explains that Kidd initially began his seafaring career as a privateer, a sanctioned pirate employed by Great Britain during times of war. With a letter of marque in hand, Kidd and his crew were authorized to attack and plunder enemy ships, with the promise of keeping a generous 80% share of the spoils.

As the conflicts subsided, Kidd's ambitions lingered, and he sought to continue his pursuit of wealth through piracy. However, unbeknownst to him, he had crossed the line into unlawful activities and soon found himself a wanted man. In a desperate bid for protection, Kidd penned a letter to Lord Bellomont, the influential Governor of New York and Massachusetts in the British American Colonies, seeking his aid.

Regrettably for Kidd, his plea for sanctuary was in vain. The authorities had caught wind of his piratical deeds, and he was arrested, facing charges of piracy. In a final attempt to secure his fate, Kidd tantalizingly informed Lord Bellomont of the hidden treasures he claimed to have buried on Gardiner's Island, just off the coast of New York.

Eager to uncover the rumored riches and maintain his reputation, Lord Bellomont dispatched search parties to scour Gardiner's Island, their eyes gleaming with visions of untold wealth. Alas, despite their thorough efforts, no treasure was unearthed, leaving them with nothing but a tale of missed opportunities and dashed hopes. Bellomont ordered the execution of Kidd where he would be hanged.

Meanwhile, in study hall, Ryan finds himself overwhelmed by boredom. He sits among two senior students whom the group had encountered at Rambo's. Seeking respite, Ryan rests his head on the desk, inadvertently falling asleep. Unbeknownst to him, as he dozes off, a small amount of drool escapes his mouth and collects on the desk.

Greg and Sean, seeking amusement at Ryan's expense, notice the drool and hatch a mischievous plan. Greg grabs a bright-blue dry erase maker and outlines the drool on the desk with it. He then proceeds to write in big block letters, "Me Sweepy - Me Make Big Mess" Sean pulls his phone from his pocket and makes sure the teacher is not paying attention and then continues to take photos of Greg's handiwork. Sean begins sending the photo to various upperclassmen. Photos of Ryan napping in a pool of drool circulated through the entire school by noon.

Meanwhile, back in history class, as Mr. Odrap reaches the dramatic climax of Captain William Kidd's story, he shares a curious detail that piques the interest of Hayley and the rest of the class. With a slight grin, he reveals that when Kidd faced his ultimate fate on the gallows, the rope actually broke upon his initial hanging attempt. The second attempt, however, proved successful in bringing an end to his life.

Intrigued by the connection between Kidd's tale and Foul Rift, Hayley raises her hand and curiously asks Mr. Odrap about the significance of this historical event to their town. She questions the geographical distance between Gardiner's Island, where the supposed treasure was buried, and Foul Rift, highlighting that the two locations are over 100 miles apart.

With a knowing smile, Mr. Odrap responds, acknowledging Hayley's observation. He confirms that the distance from Foul Rift to Gardiner's Island is indeed approximately 160 miles, emphasizing the specificity of her statement. Hayley persists, pointing out that Mr. Odrap never mentioned Captain Kidd's presence in Foul Rift during his narrative.

Mr. Odrap nods in agreement, acknowledging Hayley's astute observation. He explains that while he didn't explicitly mention Foul Rift in connection to Captain Kidd, historical records indicate that in 1699, the colony authorities apprehended four men suspected of serving under the infamous pirate captain. This suggests a local link to the larger narrative of Captain Kidd's exploits, hinting at the possibility that his presence or influence may have touched the shores of Foul Rift.

The class buzzes with excitement, their imaginations ignited by the prospect of pirates lurking in their own historical backyard.

Back in Cass's fictional literature class, the discussion transitions to comparing Peter Benchley's novel and the corresponding movie adaptation. Cass actively engages in the conversation, eagerly sharing her favorite scene from the story. She vividly describes the part where two young boys ingeniously create a fake fin to startle the swimmers.

As Cass is in the middle of narrating the thrilling scene, the room is abruptly interrupted by a scratching sound emanating from the back. A boy, seemingly seeking attention, uses his fingernails to scratch down the surface of a chalkboard hidden behind a newer dry erase board. The unexpected sound captures the class's collective attention, causing Cass to pause her storytelling.

Everyone's gaze shifts towards the boy, waiting to see what he has to say. In a whisper that's both urgent and hushed, he holds his hand up to his mouth and utters, "Check your text." The students discreetly retrieve their phones, cautiously keeping them below their desks. A wave of whispers and murmurs spreads throughout the classroom as they receive and view the image that has been shared.

The picture displayed on their screens reveals Ryan, peacefully sleeping at his desk, with drool visibly beside his mouth. Words inscribed next to him convey a sense of mockery and humiliation. The class collectively feels a mix of shock and humor as they openly chuckle and giggle at the image.

Cass's initial enthusiasm fades as she realizes the negative turn the situation has taken. She, along with some compassionate classmates, immediately recognizes the need to address the incident and support Ryan.

With resolve in her eyes, Cass stands up, ready to speak up against such hurtful behavior. She looks directly at the boy who shared the image and addresses the class, urging them to consider the impact of their actions and to prioritize empathy and respect above all else.

The room falls into a reflective silence as Cass's words sink in. Slowly, one by one, students begin to put their phones away, realizing the harm caused by spreading such images.

Back in history class, Hayley's eyes widen with excitement as she grasps the implications of Mr. Odrap's words. She contemplates the possibility of the treasure being hidden in one of the towns along the Delaware River, much closer to their own Foul Rift than previously thought. Eagerly, she asks Mr. Odrap if he believes that the treasure could be buried in their very own community.

A knowing smile tugs at Mr. Odrap's lips as he leans in slightly, his eyes sparkling with intrigue. "That's exactly what I'm suggesting," he confirms. "Consider this: four of Captain Kidd's men were captured in the Philadelphia area, a mere 60 miles from Foul Rift. It's a documented fact that these men were spotted in various towns and ports along the Delaware River. Captain Kidd was a cunning and intelligent individual. It would make perfect sense for him to keep the true location of his buried treasure a well-guarded secret. I'm not merely speculating when I say this; I've heard whispers and rumors suggesting that Kidd had the treasure moved far away from the bustling ports of New York."

Hayley's mind races with possibilities as Mr. Odrap's words sink in. The tantalizing prospect of an undiscovered treasure hidden within the reaches of their own community fills her with a sense of adventure. She can't help but imagine the thrill of uncovering a piece of history and the potential impact it could have on their small town.

Back inside of the gymnasium, the freshmen have been matched up against the seniors in a heated game of pickleball. Charlotte finds herself pitted against senior player, Erin Panfile, who exudes an air of anger and disdain towards her. Despite Charlotte's lead in points, Erin's frustration grows as she struggles to accept the idea of freshmen outperforming seniors.

Erin, known for her snobbish demeanor, holds firmly to the belief that there should be a clear divide between freshmen and seniors. She sees no reason to mix or befriend underclassmen, and the thought of freshmen excelling in any aspect challenges her perception of hierarchy. It has always irritated her to witness her own classmate, Ryan, forming friendships with underclassmen, particularly Bo, a freshman.

As the pickleball game intensifies, Erin's anger becomes more apparent in her playing style. She directs her shots aggressively towards Charlotte, trying to regain control and assert her seniority. However, Char's skill and determination persist, and she continues to outperform Erin, further fueling her opponent's frustration.

Amidst the heated competition, Charlotte maintains her focus and refuses to let Erin's animosity affect her. She displays sportsmanship, responding to Erin's aggressive shots with grace and precision. The contrast between their attitudes becomes increasingly evident, with Charlotte embodying the spirit of fair play and respect for her opponents.

Throughout the game, Char's performance serves as a quiet challenge to Erin's prejudice and the notion that grade levels should determine friendships or abilities. As the pickleball game concludes, Charlotte emerges as the victor, earning the respect and admiration of her peers, both freshmen and seniors alike, except for Erin. Erin is not happy that she has been beaten by a freshman. Erin turns her back to the class and walks to the bleachers where her phone is waiting for her. Her grimace turns to a menacing smile when she opens up her text messages.

Back in history class, Andy eagerly interjects, unable to contain his curiosity. "But what kind of treasure are we talking about here?" he asks, his eyes gleaming with anticipation. "Are we talking about silk scarves, exotic spices, or something even more valuable?"

Mr. Odrap, pleased with Andy's inquisitiveness, chuckles softly before providing an answer. "Ah, Andy, you've hit upon an intriguing point," he replies. "While Captain Kidd did amass a variety of valuable plunder during his piracy days, the treasure that has captured the imagination of many is the one associated with the Quedagh Merchant Ship."

The classroom falls silent as Mr. Odrap leans in, his voice filled with excitement. "Legend has it that Kidd captured this very ship, which was laden with an astonishing fortune in gold and other precious treasures," he continues. "We're talking about riches worth millions of dollars, Andy."

Eager to learn more, Andy asks Mr. Odrap how they can find out more about the Quedagh Merchant Ship and its connection to Captain Kidd's treasure. With a knowing smile, Mr. Odrap points to a classroom computer and encourages Andy to delve into the vast ocean of information available at their fingertips.

"Google the Quedagh Merchant Ship, my young treasure hunter," Mr. Odrap suggests. "You'll find a wealth of stories, historical accounts, and even some ongoing research surrounding this elusive piece of history. Who knows what hidden clues and secrets await your discovery?"

Andy nods eagerly, already envisioning himself embarking on a virtual journey of exploration, unearthing the secrets of Captain Kidd's treasure and the captivating tales that surround it. With newfound determination, he heads towards the computer, ready to immerse himself in a world of history, adventure, and the tantalizing promise of untold riches.

Meanwhile, the rest of the class buzzes with excitement, inspired by the possibility of unraveling the mysteries that lie within their own community.

Mr. Odrap's eyes light up as he addresses the students' curiosity about learning more about Captain Kidd and his legendary treasure. "If you're eager to delve deeper into this captivating topic," he says, "I encourage you all to visit the Foul Rift Museum. It's a treasure trove of knowledge, and our very own Harvey Ambrose, a long-time resident of Foul Rift, serves as the curator."

He pauses for a moment, excitement evident in his voice, and continues, "Harvey Ambrose possesses a wealth of information about Captain Kidd, his daring exploits, and the enigmatic tales surrounding his hidden gold. He has spent countless hours researching and investigating, even sharing with me his own personal quest to find the elusive treasure."

One of the students can't contain their surprise and exclaims, "Wait, we have a museum here in Foul Rift?" Mr. Odrap's face briefly reflects a hint of disappointment before he smiles warmly and responds, "Yes, indeed! We have a museum dedicated to our town's unique history, including the intriguing stories of Captain Kidd. It's a remarkable place that offers a glimpse into our past."

He emphasizes, "The Foul Rift Museum holds valuable artifacts, documents, and accounts that shed light on the enigmatic figure of Captain Kidd and the legends that surround him. It's an opportunity for you to explore, learn, and perhaps even uncover some hidden truths this summer."

The students exchange excited glances, realizing the hidden gems that their town holds. They eagerly make plans to visit the museum, intrigued by the possibilities that lie within its walls. Mr. Odrap beams with pride, delighted by the newfound curiosity ignited within his students.

A few moments before the bell rings, the p.a. system crackles to life, catching the attention of the students throughout the school. The voice of the principal echoes through the corridors, carrying a tone of concern and urgency.

"Attention, students. This is Principal Fratelli. I have an important announcement. When the bell rings, I kindly request that all students make their way to the auditorium immediately.

The unexpected and somber tone in the principal's voice spreads a wave of curiosity and speculation amongst the students. Whispers ripple through the hallway as they wonder what could have prompted such a summoning.

As the final moments tick away, anticipation builds with their minds racing with questions and possibilities. The urgency in the principal's voice leaves little room for doubt that something significant awaits them in the auditorium.

Within minutes, the bell rings, signaling the end of the current class period. The hallways flood with students, all directed to the central gathering space. The atmosphere is tinged with a mix of apprehension, intrigue, and a shared sense of unity as everyone converges making their way to the auditorium.

The auditorium doors swing open, revealing rows of seats, bathed in the dim glow of stage lights. The principal stands at the front, a serious expression etched across his face as he waits for the student body to take their seats.

As the last stragglers find a seat, the auditorium falls into an expected silence. All eyes are on the principal, awaiting the reason behind the impromptu gathering. The hushed anticipation hangs heavy in the air, as the principal steps forward, ready to address the student-body.

Clearing his throat, the principal takes a deep breath, his voice steady, but filled with genuine concern. He begins, "Thank you all for coming here today. I understand that this unexpected meeting has raised many questions. I want you to know that the safety and wellbeing of our school-community are of the utmost importance."

Mr. Fratelli's eyes darted toward the state troopers standing off to the side, their stern gazes fixed upon the students.

"I have an important announcement to make. The state police are currently conducting an investigation in our town of Foul Rift. Unfortunately, we have two individuals who have gone missing."

A hushed murmur swept through the crowd as the students exchanged worried glances.

"The first person is a local mechanic who has not been seen for several days," the principal continued, his voice tinged with solemnity. "The second is a detective from our own Foul Rift Police Department. As of now, the investigation is underway, and we are cooperating fully with the authorities."

The principal's eyes scanned the room, his expression urging the students to listen carefully to his next words.

"The state police have advised us to take precautions. They recommend that you travel in groups and avoid venturing into the woods north of Foul Rift. Additionally, it is strongly advised that all students be in their homes by nightfall. Your safety is our utmost priority."

A palpable tension settled over the auditorium as the students absorbed the gravity of the situation. The principal's gaze softened, and he offered a reassuring note.

"I want to assure you all that the school counselor will be available for any student who needs someone to talk to. We are here to support each other during this challenging time. We will be contacting your parents and guardians through our digital phone service and email to ensure they are kept informed about the ongoing situation."

He paused, his gaze sweeping across the attentive faces before him, their eyes reflecting a mix of concern and determination.

"Remember, students, your safety is paramount. Please be vigilant and look out for one another. If you see or hear anything unusual or have any information that might aid the investigation, please report it to a trusted adult or directly to the authorities."

The principal's words resonated through the auditorium, embedding a sense of responsibility within the students. With those parting words, the principal stepped back, allowing the weight of his message to sink in. The students exchanged solemn nods and shared glances, ready to face the unknown challenges ahead while keeping a watchful eye on their peers. The auditorium fell into a moment of silence, broken only by the faint rustling of unease, as they absorbed the gravity of the situation and prepared to heed the principal's advice.

Chapter 5:
Somber Day

As the new day dawned upon Foul Rift, the atmosphere in the town mirrored the somber mood that had settled over its inhabitants. A collective sense of fear and worry permeated the air, casting a shadow over the once vibrant community. The weather itself seemed to reflect the town's disquiet, with heavy clouds shrouding the sky in a dismal gray. The absence of sunshine, usually a comforting presence during late spring, only intensified the feeling of unease.

People moved about the town with cautious steps, their expressions etched with concern. The streets, once bustling with lively conversations and laughter, now echoed with hushed whispers and solemn silence. Neighbors exchanged worried glances, sharing their fears and hoping for answers that remained elusive.

The cold temperature seemed to pierce through the layers of clothing, serving as a chilling reminder of the uncertain times that gripped Foul Rift. The usual signs of spring's warmth and blossoming life were overshadowed by a sense of foreboding, leaving a void in the hearts of the townsfolk.

Yet amidst the gloom, a quiet resilience emerged. The community banded together, seeking solace in each other's company. They offered support, lending a listening ear and a comforting presence to those most affected by the disappearances. Though fear still lingered, there was a determination to persevere, to find answers, and to reclaim the sense of security that had been shaken.

As the day unfolded, the town of Foul Rift navigated its new reality, united in their shared concern and a shared hope for the safe return of their missing friends.

Gray clouds moved across the expansive sky, casting a solemn ambiance over the town of Foul Rift. Inside his room, Bo Everest sat by the window, his gaze fixed upon the shifting shades of gray. His mind was consumed with thoughts of the recent disappearances, their mystery hanging heavy in the air.

A gentle knock on the door interrupted Bo's contemplation, and without waiting for permission, Hayley entered the room. As Hayley stepped into Bo's room, her expression weary and glum, she searched for a distraction from the weight of her thoughts.

Hayley: Come on, Bo! We're heading to the Field of Dreams to meet up with everyone.

Bo looked up from his desk, a hint of confusion on his face.

Bo: We are? What's happening?

Hayley let out an exasperated sigh, rolling her eyes.

Hayley: Seriously, Bo? Did you even check your text messages? We're going to hang out, we should try to have some fun. So, get moving! I don't want to sit around here all day.

Bo gave a small smile, realizing his oversight, and quickly got up from his chair.

Bo: You're right, Hayley. I should've checked my phone. Let's go then!

They swiftly gathered their belongings, grabbed a quick bite to eat, and made their way to the shed to retrieve their bikes.

As Hayley and Bo made their way to the Field of Dreams to meet the others, a sense of unease settled over the town. They couldn't help but notice the heightened police presence, with state troopers patrolling the streets and patrol cars scattered throughout.

They pedaled past the entrance of the woods that lie north of Foul Rift, where a larger gathering of police officers, firefighters, and concerned community members had assembled. Among them stood Mr. Odrap, their history teacher.

Hayley approached him with a heavy heart, seeking answers. "What's going on, Mr. Odrap?" she asked, her voice tinged with worry. Mr. Odrap's expression reflected the gravity of the situation as he explained, "We're forming a human chain to search the woods for evidence of the missing people." Bo jumped in, "And bodies too? You're also looking for their bodies?" Mr. Odrap, with a somber tone answered, "Yes, Bo. Unfortunately, we are also looking for remains." Bo, unable to contain his concern, interjected, "Can we help?" With a sigh, Mr. Odrap replied, "Unfortunately, you both have to be 18 to help, but your willingness means a lot."

The three sat quietly for a moment when Hayley's eyes locked onto Ryan's familiar figure. "There's Ryan," she whispered, a mix of surprise and curiosity in her voice. Bo, equally puzzled, questioned, "What's he doing here? Wasn't he supposed to meet us at the park?" Hayley shrugged her shoulders, admitting that Ryan hadn't responded to their text message. They maneuvered through the gathering crowd, navigating between police officers and firefighters who were organizing their search efforts. Finally reaching Ryan, Bo wasted no time in posing his question, "Hey, Ryan, are you helping too?" Ryan's response was affirmative, as he revealed that his parents had encouraged him to participate and, being 18 years old, he met the age requirement to join the efforts.

Ryan adds, "Hey, guys, guess what? I've got some news. I'll be taking my driving test in a few weeks!" Hayley's eyes widened with excitement as she exclaimed, "That's awesome, Ryan! Finally, we won't have to rely on bikes for getting around."

Bo, joining in on the conversation, teasingly adds, "Does that mean you'll be giving me your bike, Ryan?" Ryan laughs, "You mean the one that I scammed from that garage sale? Hmm, we'll see about that, Bo." Bo adds, "Yeah, that is not something that a 'Noblemen' does." Ryan playfully defends himself, saying, "Well, the concept of noblemen wasn't a thing back then. Cut me some slack…AND, let me remind you that it was not very 'noblemen-ish' to spy on your neighbors with a drone and then have your close friend pretend he was you to go and get it."

Bo let out a soft and quick burst of laughter, "That's true, Ryan. You got me there."

Hayley spots Cassidy and Char nearby, she eagerly goes over to join them, leaving Bo and Ryan to continue their conversation.

As Ryan and Bo continue their conversation, Ryan's tone becomes bittersweet as he brings up the upcoming chapter in his life. He says to Bo, "You know, Bo, I'll be leaving for college in August." Bo's smile fades a bit, and he nods understandingly, acknowledging the inevitable change that will come when Ryan is no longer around. Deep down, Bo feels a pang of sadness, realizing how much Ryan means to him as a friend, almost like an older brother. Bo wants to express how much he'll miss Ryan's presence, but he can't find the right words. Instead, he simply says, "Yeah, I know. We'll make the most of the time we have left." They both share a silent understanding that things will be different when they're no longer in the same high school together.

Hayley approaches Cassidy and Charlotte, curious about why they're at the scene. Cassidy explains that they were heading to Field of Dreams but decided to check out the commotion instead. Hayley quickly fills them in on Mr. Odrap's explanation and the purpose of the search.

Just as they're talking, a police officer steps up to the front and addresses the gathered crowd through a bullhorn. He announces that they are about to commence the search and offers the public the opportunity to ask any questions they may have by speaking to one of the commanding officers from the state police. Hayley, feeling the urgency, suggests that she will text Andy to inform him of the situation and invite him to join them.

Meanwhile, Ryan turns to Bo, a tinge of sadness coloring his voice, as he mentions that he needs to get into position. Bo watches Ryan's retreating figure, a wave of melancholy washing over him. He can't help but ponder the impending changes that college will bring, wondering if he'll still have a place in Ryan's life or if their friendship will fade amidst new experiences. With a heavy heart, Bo watches as Ryan walks away, heading towards his parents and preparing to fulfill his crucial role in the search effort.

Hayley, Bo, Cassidy, and Charlotte stand there, their eyes fixed on the retreating figures of Ryan, his parents, Mr. Odrap, and the assembled group of dedicated searchers. They watch as the human chain, formed by the police, firemen, and familiar community members, ventures into the dense woods just north of Foul Rift. A sense of solemnity hangs in the air, intensified by the steady patter of raindrops that begin to fall.

At first, the rain is gentle, a soft drizzle that seems to mirror the melancholy of the moment. But within moments, the rain intensifies, transforming into a downpour, each droplet landing with a resounding splash. Hayley retrieves her cell phone from her pocket, as she wakes it up from its sleep and begins typing, she can feel the raindrops splatter against her phone screen. With determined fingers, she sends a message to Andy, informing him that they will be meeting inside Rambo's, seeking solace and shelter from the inclement weather.

Under the shelter of the cantilevered edge of the second story of Rambo's General Store, Hayley, Cassidy, Charlotte, Andy, and Bo find refuge from the rain. Their limited resources are evident as Hayley and Cass sip on sugary coffee while the others share a meager sleeve of powdered donuts. Despite the modest provisions, their spirits remain hopeful as they discuss the events of the search party.

Just as Hayley begins to delve into the conversation about her and Andy's discussion in history class with Mr. Odrap, a sudden burst of music shatters the air. A vibrant red Jeep Wrangler pulls up, its speakers blaring tunes that resonate through the rainy surroundings. Behind the wheel is Greg, with Rick, Sean, and Sanj crammed in the backseat. To Hayley's surprise, Erin, a senior who had lost to Charlotte in a pickleball match during gym class, occupies the front seat.

The unexpected arrival interrupts the conversation, and the group turns their attention towards the lively scene unfolding before them. The vibrant energy emanating from the Jeep contrasts with the somber mood brought by the rain and recent events.

Cassidy's anger flares up at the sight of the Jeep, her clenched fists and furrowed brows reveal her brewing frustration. The unresolved issue surrounding the photo the group had posted of Ryan weighs heavily on her mind, intensifying her anger with each passing moment. Hayley and Charlotte, attuned to Cass's emotions, sense the building tension and exchange worried glances.

Hayley, curious yet apprehensive, wonders how her friend will respond to the boys in the Jeep. She contemplates the potential consequences of Cass's impending outburst, hoping that the situation can be diffused without escalating into further conflict. Charlotte, too, holds her breath, uncertain about the outcome but ready to support her big sister through whatever unfolds.

Amidst the rain-soaked atmosphere, the group's camaraderie hangs delicately, teetering on the edge of turbulence. The next few moments will determine whether Cass's anger will be vented or if a path towards resolution can be found. Hayley and Charlotte brace themselves, ready to navigate the shifting dynamics, hoping to maintain the unity they had forged thus far.

As the group exits the Jeep and seeks refuge under the overhang, Cassidy's anger ignites like a spark in the night. She stares at the boys, her eyes blazing with fury, and announces loudly, "What you did to Ryan was absolutely wrong! It wasn't cool at all. You only did it for attention!"

Hayley, sensing her friend's rising anger, leans in and whispers, "Stay calm, Cass. We've got your back." Bo chimes in, "Yeah, remember, you're a Noblemen. We can stand up for Ryan, but let's do it calmly." His words resonate with determination and a hint of authority.

Andy, Hayley, and Charlotte exchange determined glances, ready to support Cassidy in her stance. Andy speaks up, his voice steady, "Cass is right."

Cassidy takes a deep breath, feeling the support of her friends, and continues, her voice unwavering, "We won't tolerate what you did to Ryan. He deserves an apology, and we're going to make sure he gets it."

The air around them crackles with a mixture of tension and determination. They stand together as a united front ready to defend their principles and support Ryan. They face the boys with unwavering resolve, their eyes filled with determination.

Cass's voice trembles with anger as she responds, " What you did was mean-spirited and hurtful. We stand by…"

Erin's eyes narrow, and a malicious grin spreads across her face. She is enraged to see her friends get lectured by the sister of the freshman that beat her at pickleball. Erin does not like underclassmen by default and there is no way she is going to let her friends be yelled at by someone beneath them.

Erin rolls her eyes dismissively and interrupts, "Oh please, Cassidy. Can you be any louder? You're always making a scene, trying to be some kind of hero."

Cassidy's face flushes with anger, momentarily taken aback by Erin's comment.

Andy, maintaining his composure, adds, "Cass is not loud. She's right. What they did to Ryan was not cool."

She takes a step closer to Andy and sneers, "And you, Mr. Boy Scout, with your little badges and uniform. What a pathetic sight. Do you honestly think it makes you special? Do you think you're a big tough army guy?"

Andy's expression remains composed, though his eyes reflect a tinge of hurt. He responds calmly, "Being a part of the Boy Scouts has taught me important values like respect, responsibility, and service. It's about helping others and making a positive impact."

Hayley steps forward, her voice filled with determination, "Don't belittle Andy's commitment to the Boy Scouts. It shows his character and his willingness to contribute to the community. What have you done lately, Erin, besides tearing people down?"

Erin scoffs, rolling her eyes, "Oh please, spare me the moral high ground. Your little 'Noblemen' group is just a bunch of wannabes. What difference do you think you're making? Oh-Yes, I heard all about it. News travels fast…just like the photo of your loser friend."

Charlotte steps up, her voice steady and firm, "We may not have it all figured out yet, but at least we're trying to do something good. We support each other, watch each other's backs, and strive to make a difference. What about you, Erin? What positive contribution can you claim?"

Bo, his voice filled with conviction and intelligence, steps forward and begins his impassioned speech. His words resonate with sincerity and a sense of moral righteousness.

"Do you know where Ryan is? Right at this very moment, Ryan is out there in the pouring rain, searching for two missing individuals in the woods. He's sacrificing his comfort and safety, taking on a responsibility that we would all share if we were old enough. Instead of standing alongside him, offering support, you choose to mock and belittle him. But let me tell you, your actions reveal more about your character than his."

Bo's gaze sweeps across the group, his voice unwavering in its conviction. "You are all 18, the same age as Ryan, yet while he's out there, selflessly trying to make a difference, what are you doing? Driving around in your fancy red Jeep, thinking that makes you superior? Is that your idea of being cool? Let me tell you, it's nothing but shallow and empty."

He directs his attention specifically to Erin, his voice tinged with disdain. "You have the audacity to mock Andy for being a part of the Boy Scouts. But what about you, Erin? What do you contribute to the betterment of others? What impact do you make? You seek attention by tearing others down, but all it reveals is your own insecurities and lack of purpose."

Bo's voice grows stronger, his words filled with righteous indignation. "You know what? You guys suck! You're all shallow, devoid of empathy and compassion. While Ryan and the rest of us strive to do good, you choose to revel in negativity and feed off of others' pain. We won't stoop to your level, because we know what it means to be Noblemen".

The rain intensifies, its steady rhythm accentuating the weight of Bo's words. The group stands in awe of his eloquence, feeling empowered by his passionate defense of their principles.

Erin feels diminished by Bo's speech. She is angered, but also feels embarrassed and unsure of how to respond to Bo. This is twice within a week's span that she was humiliated by an underclassman.

Rick, the largest of all of the boys, saw that Erin was at a loss for words and stifled by the 14-year-old. He steps forward closer to Bo.

Rick: You're lucky you're smaller and younger than me. I would keep my mouth shut if I were you. One day someone your size is going to lay you out".

Sanj: Yeah, you and your little group of losers should know your place. Hayley, control your brother before he gets hurt.

Bo: (Taking a deep breath) Physical threats and insults won't change the truth, Rick. Resorting to violence only shows your own insecurities. And Sanj, name-calling won't diminish our principles.

Hayley: (Supportively) Bo's right. We won't be intimidated by your attempts to undermine us.

Cassidy: We believe in standing up for what's right, even if it means facing opposition. You're not tough, you're weak. (Cassidy remembering Ryan's words about superheroes) The weak want to hurt the world when they have been hurt by it; The strong want to protect everyone else from being hurt because they know what it feels like. That's all you are… you're weak.

Charlotte: You may think we're losers, dorks, and nerds, but at least we're not afraid to make a difference. We are glad that we're not like you.

Andy: (Calming the situation) Let's not resort to violence or name-calling. Those things will not get us anywhere.

Rick: (Growing more agitated) Yeah, well, whatever. You're still a bunch of losers and one day you're going to find that out the hard way.

Sanj: (Eying them with disdain) One day you're going to find yourself in a world of trouble and nobody is going to bail you out.

The confrontation escalates, the tension thickening in the air. Bo and his friends hold their ground, their words and determination challenging the hostility of Rick, Sanj, and their group.

Greg: (Feeling hungry and not in the mood) I don't have time for this. I am going in and getting something to eat.

Greg's abrupt interruption shattered the charged atmosphere, diverting the focus from the ongoing conflict. He pushed past the group with an air of indifference, his hunger overriding any interest in the heated exchange. Sean trailed behind him, snatching the last remaining donut from Andy's grasp, a mischievous grin on his face. He wasted no time devouring it, the powdered sugar leaving traces on his lips.

Sean: Thanks buddy.

Rick's laughter echoed through the air, a mocking soundtrack to the unfolding scene. As if synchronized, Sanj and Erin joined the procession, their contemptuous gazes lingering on the others. Sanj muttered the word "losers" under his breath, adding a final touch of disdain before disappearing into Rambo's.

The porch was left tinged with a mixture of disappointment, frustration, and lingering tension. Bo, Hayley, Cassidy, Charlotte, and Andy exchanged glances, their disappointment palpable. They understood that their voices were not heard, their attempts at reason falling on deaf ears. Now, faced with the aftermath of the encounter, they took a collective breath, regrouped and contemplated their next steps.

Bo's voice carried a hint of introspection as he spoke up, addressing his friends. "I think we need to add a new tenet for being a Nobleman," he stated, his gaze searching each of their faces. Hayley, genuinely curious, inquired, "What's that?"

Bo took a moment to gather his thoughts before continuing. "A Nobleman is calm," he emphasized. "We need to work on that. I'm not sure if our tone with Erin helped the situation." His words hung in the air, the weight of self-reflection evident in his expression.

Andy nodded in agreement, his eyes reflecting a mix of concern and weariness. "I agree," he chimed in. "Self-Control is strength. Calmness is mastery. You have to get to a point where your mood doesn't shift based on the insignificant actions of someone else. Don't allow others to control the directions of your life. Don't allow your emotions to overpower your intelligence. Our scout leader says that all of the time. It's finally making sense to me."

Cassidy: Can we get out of here? I don't want to be around when they come out.

The group exchanged silent nods, their shared understanding cementing their decision. Leaving behind the remnants of tension and unproductive confrontation, they gathered their belongings and prepared to depart from the shelter of Rambo's. As they walked away, a renewed sense of unity and a determination to embody the virtues of being noblemen took root within each of them, paving the way for a calmer and more thoughtful approach in future encounters.

Charlotte, looking up at the pouring rain, couldn't help but voice her uncertainty. "Okay...where are we going in this rain?" she asked, her words punctuated by a hint of concern. As if in response to her inquiry, the rain eased up slightly, transitioning from a downpour to a gentle drizzle. Andy, quick with a playful remark, chimed in, "Looks like Char here is a magician."

Hayley, seizing the moment, took charge with a determined expression. "I know somewhere we can go," she said, her voice carrying a sense of purpose and hope. The group turned their attention to Hayley, their curiosity sparked. In the midst of the dampness and lingering tension, her suggestion offered a glimmer of anticipation and relief. Trusting in Hayley's intuition, they eagerly awaited her response, ready to embark on a journey to find shelter and respite amidst the drizzle.

Hayley's eyes sparkled with anticipation as she revealed her plan. "Guys, let's go to the museum," she exclaimed, her voice filled with excitement. Andy, catching onto her enthusiasm, chimed in, "I'm all in. Mr. Odrap shared some cool things about our town's history, and I'm dying to explore it further…especially the part about hidden gold."

Charlotte, Cassidy, and Bo exchanged puzzled glances, unfamiliar with the museum's allure. They had heard about it vaguely but never ventured inside its doors. Uncertainty flickered across their faces as they contemplated the idea. The museum represented uncharted territory, a realm shrouded in mystery and potential discovery.

Charlotte, breaking the silence, questioned, "What's so special about the museum, Hayley? I've never been there before." Cass and Bo nodded in agreement, their curiosity piqued by the unknown. Hayley grinned, ready to share her newfound knowledge. "Well," she began, "Mr. Odrap told us about some fascinating aspects of Foul Rift's past. Do any of you know anything about Captain William Kidd? He was a privateer turned pirate and later hanged leaving his body outside in a gibbet for two years."

Charlotte's eyes widened with intrigue as Hayley mentioned Captain William Kidd and his intriguing pirate tales. The unknown history of Foul Rift began to unfold before them, capturing their imaginations like a swashbuckling adventure come to life. Cassidy and Bo leaned in, their curiosity ignited by the mention of buried treasure and a hidden connection to their own town.

Hayley, unable to contain her excitement, reveled in their captivated attention. "You won't believe it," she exclaimed, her voice brimming with enthusiasm. "Captain William Kidd, a privateer turned pirate, once roamed the Atlantic Ocean. And get this, he had millions in stolen gold, which he claimed to have buried on an island near Long Island's coast...Gardiner's Island, I think"

Bo, his curiosity piqued, interrupted, "Hold on, what's a gibbet?"

Hayley momentarily brushed off Bo's question, too engrossed in her narrative to explain. "But here's the twist," she continued. "The treasure was never found on Gardiner's Island. Instead, after Kidd's capture, his crew members were seen roaming the Delaware River's shores. They were even arrested in Philadelphia for piracy, but they had no trace of gold on them."

Cass interjected, recognizing Hayley's audacious plan. "So, you're suggesting that the treasure may have been hidden along the Delaware River by Kidd's crew and you want us to go have a "Goonie-Weekend" and try to find it," she exclaimed, a sense of thrilling possibility coloring her words.

Bo, still longing for an answer, couldn't resist asking again, "Seriously, what's a gibbet?"

Hayley pressed on, undeterred by Bo's repeated question. "Exactly! And that's where the museum comes in," she revealed, her eyes sparkling with anticipation. "Mr. Odrap mentioned that the museum's curator holds a wealth of knowledge about Captain Kidd and his ties to Foul Rift. Perhaps they can shed light on the hidden connection and provide us with clues to embark on our own treasure hunt."

Andy chimed in, joining the spirited discussion. "We can gather information, study some maps, 'play the bones' and unravel the secrets of the Delaware River. It's like being real-life treasure hunters."

Cassidy couldn't help but smile, caught up in the allure of their ambitious quest. "Okay, I'm in," she declared. "But before we set off on a treasure hunt, can someone please explain to Bo what a gibbet is?"

As laughter filled the air, the group's excitement grew, fueled by the mysteries and possibilities that awaited them at the museum. Their Goonie-esque adventure was about to begin, with Captain Kidd's pirate legacy as their guiding star and the museum as their gateway to a world of hidden treasure and thrilling discoveries.

Chapter 6:
Picking Marigolds

Hayley, Bo, Andy, Cassidy, and Charlotte finally arrived at the Foul Rift Museum, a humble structure tucked away next to the town hall. From the outside, it appeared unassuming, blending into the surrounding buildings without drawing much attention. None of them had ever felt the inclination to venture inside its doors before, as it seemed like a forgotten relic of the past.

With a determined push, Hayley swung open the door, and the group stepped into the museum, their senses immediately met with a surprising sight. The interior was remarkably clean, a stark contrast to their expectations. A pristine Berber carpet adorned the floor, seemingly untouched by footprints. The kids exchanged curious glances, their interest piqued as they took in their surroundings.

The room unfolded before them, revealing a collection of historical artifacts and exhibits. Photographs depicting Foul Rift's bygone days adorned the walls, offering glimpses into the town's rich history. A series of weathered maps hung nearby, their faded lines and markings telling tales of exploration and discovery.

A display case, carefully arranged, housed a collection of old relics, each one whispering stories of the past. From weathered tools to fragments of ancient pottery, these artifacts carried the weight of forgotten lives and long-gone eras. Framed newspapers, their yellowed pages preserved for posterity, showcased significant moments in Foul Rift's history, capturing the essence of the town's triumphs and trials.

In one corner, a small shelf displayed a modest assortment of souvenirs, perhaps once cherished mementos of visitors who had journeyed to this hidden gem of a museum. Bo, ever curious and drawn to the tangible, gravitated towards the shelf, inspecting the trinkets with fascination.

Despite the intriguing displays, there was an absence of visitors. The kids scanned the room, their gazes searching for any sign of life, but not even the curator was visible. It felt as though they had stepped into a forgotten chapter, left to unravel the secrets of Foul Rift's past on their own.

The stillness enveloped them, amplifying their sense of awe and wonder. In this quiet sanctuary of history, they stood united, ready to uncover the mysteries that lay dormant within the museum's walls. It was a moment of anticipation and possibility, a collective journey into the depths of the past, fueled by their shared determination and newfound fascination for the stories waiting to be unraveled.

As Hayley's eyes roamed the walls, her attention was immediately captured by the immense map of the Delaware River prominently displayed. Stretching across the expanse of the wall, the map detailed the meandering course of the river, revealing the various towns and landmarks that lined its shores. Foul Rift, their own hometown, was marked with a small dot, nestled amidst the intricate network of waterways. The map beckoned

Hayley to explore the river's secrets, inspiring thoughts of adventure and discovery.

Meanwhile, Andy's gaze fell upon an old photograph mounted on a wooden frame. It depicted a boy scout troop proudly posing in front of a backdrop that unmistakably represented Foul Rift. The date inscribed beneath the picture read June 7, 1985. Andy's curiosity ignited as he examined the faces of the young scouts, wondering what adventures and memories they had forged in their scouting days. The photograph served as a reminder of the town's enduring traditions and the camaraderie shared by those who came before them.

Over by the souvenirs, Charlotte joined Bo, their shared curiosity drawing them towards the display. The assortment of trinkets showcased tokens of Foul Rift's identity, capturing glimpses of its charm and character. Together, they explored the shelf, their fingers gently touching the small figurines, keychains, and postcards that represented cherished memories and symbols of local pride.

Cassidy, ever the avid reader, discovered a book rack nestled in a corner of the museum. Its shelves were lined with an intriguing assortment of books, each title offering a glimpse into the surrounding towns and their unique histories. Among the collection, Cassidy found books on gardening and farming, a testament to the region's agricultural heritage. A few volumes explored local ghost stories, igniting a flicker of excitement within her. And hidden within the rows, she stumbled upon a couple of titles dedicated to the daring exploits of pirates, fueling her imagination with tales of treasure and adventure.

In this museum, where the artifacts whispered stories of the past, each member of the group found a piece of intrigue that resonated with their interests and curiosities. The room was alive with the echoes of history, inviting them to delve deeper into the narratives woven by the towns and people that had shaped their own lives. It was a place where the past met the present, where hidden tales awaited discovery, and where the seeds of their own journey were planted amidst the rich tapestry of Foul Rift's heritage.

Hayley's eyes darted around the museum, searching for any signs of a staff member or curator. Her question hung in the air as her friends, now sharing her urgency, also began scanning the room for any indication of a presence. Their focus shifted from the intriguing artifacts to the pressing need to find someone who could provide them with information or assistance.

Just as the group's collective attention turned towards their search, a faint sound caught Bo's ears. It was the distinct creak of a door opening and closing. His gaze sharpened as he fixed his eyes on a framed-out opening in the wall, concealed behind a shelf. A corridor lay beyond, and the sound of footsteps grew nearer, accompanied by the subtle shuffling of movement. The anticipation filled the air, and the group stood motionless, their gazes fixed on the concealed opening, awaiting the emergence of the mystery person.

Time seemed to slow as the footsteps drew closer, the anticipation mounting with each passing second. They stood at attention, their eyes wide and alert, brimming with curiosity and a hint of apprehension. The room was filled with an expectant hush, broken only by the soft echoes of approaching footsteps. As the figure neared the opening, the tension reached its peak, their senses on high alert, ready to greet the individual who would finally reveal themselves from the hidden corridor.

Harvey Ambrose, the museum curator, stepped through the concealed portal, his eyes widened in surprise as he beheld the sight of the five kids standing before him, their gazes fixed upon him with a mix of curiosity and anticipation. The room seemed to come alive with their presence, and Harvey, an elderly man in his eighties, appeared fragile yet full of life.

His hair, gray and thin, adorned his head with wisps of silver, while a neatly trimmed white mustache framed his white-toothy smile. Harvey's hunched posture suggested the weight of age, and he leaned upon a cane for support as he navigated the space. His eyes, though weathered, held a twinkle of warmth and wisdom.

In his sweet, gentle voice, Harvey extended a warm greeting to the group, a kind and welcoming tone that seemed to echo the passage of time. "Ah, welcome, young ones! Welcome to the Foul Rift Museum," he said, his voice carrying the gentle lilt of a storyteller. "It seems you've sought shelter from the rain, am I correct?"

Hayley, taking a step forward, nodded with a smile. "Yes, sir," she replied. "We were caught in the rain and thought the museum would be an interesting place to wait it out. But we also heard that you know a lot about Captain Kidd the pirate."

Harvey's eyes crinkled with amusement as he chuckled softly. "Of course, my dear, of course. The museum is always open to those seeking refuge or seeking knowledge. Please, feel free to explore and indulge your curiosity. There's much to discover within these walls."

The kids exchanged excited glances, grateful for the unexpected invitation. With a renewed sense of purpose, they dispersed throughout the museum, their eyes alight with anticipation as they delved into the secrets and stories that lay hidden within its exhibits. And as they embarked on their exploration, Harvey stood in the midst of it all, a guardian of the town's history, ready to guide them on their journey through time.

Hayley: (approaching Harvey Ambrose) Excuse me, sir. I heard you know quite a bit about Captain Kidd and his treasure. Is it true that it might be hidden somewhere along the Delaware?

Harvey Ambrose: (smiling, looking at Hayley) Now, who told you that?

Hayley: My history teacher told me. He said you know quite a bit about Captain Kidd. We were hoping to learn more about him and his treasure.

Andy: (leaning in) Yeah, we're really interested in the history of our town.

Harvey Ambrose: (chuckling softly) Well, well, it seems the legends of Captain Kidd's treasure still captivate young minds. There have been stories, whispers, and theories about the treasure being hidden along the Delaware, but it's all part of the mystery, my young adventurers.

Charlotte: (excitedly) Do you think there are any clues or maps that could lead us to the treasure?

Harvey Ambrose: (stroking his chin thoughtfully) Ah, the allure of hidden maps and undiscovered riches. While I can't make any promises, the river has a way of holding secrets, you know. Some believe there may be clues waiting to be found.

Cassidy: (eagerly) Have you come across any evidence or stories about the treasure in your research?

Harvey Ambrose: (leaning closer) Ah, my dear, the treasure of Captain Kidd is a tale intertwined with many legends and myths. Over the years, countless stories have emerged, but it's up to each generation to uncover the truth hidden within the tales.

Bo: (grinning) So, you're saying there's a chance that there's still treasure out there?

Harvey Ambrose: (winking) Indeed, my young friend. The past has a way of revealing itself to those who seek its secrets. But remember, the true treasure lies not only in gold and jewels but in the knowledge gained on the journey itself.

Hayley: (filled with excitement) We're ready for the adventure, Mr. Ambrose. Can you guide us through the history of Foul Rift and share any tales that might lead us closer to finding Captain Kidd's treasure?

Harvey Ambrose: (smiling warmly) It would be my pleasure, young explorers. Let us embark on this journey through time, unraveling the enigmas of our town's past, and who knows, perhaps along the way, we may catch a glimpse of the hidden treasures that lie within our reach.

Harvey chuckled softly, relishing in their enthusiasm. "You see, young explorers, history is not merely confined within the pages of textbooks or the confines of museums. It is alive, waiting to be discovered and experienced. Captain Kidd's tale is but one thread in the rich tapestry of our town's history."

He gestured towards the exhibits surrounding them, each one offering a glimpse into the past. "Within these walls lie stories of brave pioneers, resilient settlers, and the legends that have shaped Foul Rift. If you seek knowledge and adventure, you shall find them here."

The kids exchanged excited glances, their spirits ignited by Harvey's words. They embarked on their exploration with newfound enthusiasm, ready to uncover the mysteries that lay hidden within the museum's walls and along the shores of the Delaware. And as they ventured forth, Harvey Ambrose stood there, a guardian of secrets and a conduit to the past, eager to accompany them on their journey through history.

Hayley: (eagerly) Please, Mr. Ambrose, tell us more about Captain Kidd. We're fascinated by his journey and the tales of hidden treasure.

Harvey Ambrose: (smiling, amused) Ah, it seems you have quite the appetite for adventure! Well, let me share another captivating aspect of Captain Kidd's story. You see, after Kidd's successful capture of the Quedagh Merchant, his fortunes took a sharp turn. The weight of his actions began to catch up with him.

Andy: (curious) What do you mean, Mr. Ambrose? Is it true that he was a privateer and then turned to piracy?

Harvey Ambrose: (nodding) Yes, indeed. Kidd's once-illustrious reputation as a privateer quickly transformed into that of a notorious pirate. The English government, eager to maintain control over their territories, branded him a criminal and set out to capture him. A fierce pursuit began, with Kidd sailing the treacherous seas, constantly evading capture.

Hayley: (intrigued) So, did he manage to escape with his treasure? And where did he hide it?

Harvey Ambrose: (leaning in, his eyes gleaming with intrigue) Ah, my dear, that's the million-dollar question, isn't it? The truth is, the whereabouts of Kidd's hidden treasure remains a mystery to this day. Legends and rumors abound, with countless theories and speculations, but no definitive answer has been found.

Andy: (excitedly) That's incredible! The idea of a hidden treasure waiting to be discovered is so awesome.

Hayley: (nodding) Absolutely! Imagine unraveling the secrets of the past and unearthing a long-lost fortune. It's like stepping into a real-life treasure hunt.

Harvey Ambrose: (chuckling) Indeed, young adventurers, the allure of treasure has captivated countless souls throughout history. But remember, the journey is often as valuable as the destination. It's about the discoveries you make along the way, the knowledge you gain, and the stories you uncover.

Charlotte:(in a sassy tone) It sounds great and all, but if nobody has found it by now, I doubt it will be found. He either hid it extremely well, or someone has it sitting in their vault.

Harvey Ambrose: (leaning in, his voice filled with intrigue) Ah, the plot thickens, my young adventurers. Captain Kidd, ever the shrewd strategist, realized the gravity of his situation. He decided to make a daring move in an attempt to clear his name and salvage his reputation.

Hayley: (leaning closer, captivated) What did he do, Mr. Ambrose? How did he plan to convince Lord Belemont of his innocence? (Hayley wanted to compare Odrap's story with Ambrose's)

Harvey Ambrose: (smiling knowingly) Kidd knew that evidence of his innocence was crucial, so he devised a plan. Before sailing back to Boston to face Lord Belemont, he cunningly concealed his loot in a secret location. This ensured that even if he faced scrutiny, the treasure would remain hidden and secure.

Andy: (intrigued) That's quite the calculated move.

Harvey Ambrose: (pausing, his eyes gleaming with anticipation) My dear adventurers, that is where the tale takes a twist. Despite Kidd's efforts, fate had a different plan in store for him. Upon his arrival in Boston, he was betrayed by those he once considered allies. Lord Belemont, under pressure from the English government, turned against Kidd, and he found himself arrested and thrown into prison.

Hayley: (gasping) How unfortunate! After all his efforts, he still faced an unjust fate.

Harvey Ambrose: (nodding sympathetically) Indeed, my dear. Captain Kidd's journey was a tumultuous one, fraught with unexpected turns and betrayal. But remember, every story carries its own lessons, its own truths to be discovered.

Andy: (thoughtfully) So, what happened to Kidd's hidden treasure? Did anyone ever find it or at least part of it? (Andy also was checking to see if Odrap's story aligned with Ambrose's)

Harvey Ambrose: (mystically) Ah, that remains a mystery, my young adventurers. The fate of Captain Kidd's hidden treasure, scattered among legends and whispers, has captivated treasure hunters and historians alike. The allure of discovering unimaginable wealth continues to beckon brave souls to embark on their own quests.

Andy: (interjecting) Mr. Ambrose, our teacher, mentioned that Kidd, in a desperate attempt for freedom, informed Lord Belemont that the treasure was hidden on Gardiner's Island in NY. Was there any truth to that? Did Kidd hope to use the treasure as a bargaining chip for freedom?

Harvey Ambrose: (smiling knowingly) Ah, clever young minds indeed! It seems your teacher has shared some intriguing details. Yes, it is believed that Kidd, aware of the allure the hidden treasure held, hoped to strike a deal with Lord Belemont. By revealing the supposed location of the treasure, he aimed to negotiate his release and redemption.

Hayley: (leaning in, her eyes shining with curiosity) Did Lord Belemont believe him?

Harvey Ambrose: (continuing the tale) Ah, you have delved into the depths of the story, my young historians. After Kidd's mention of the treasure, Lord Belemont, eager to prove Kidd's guilt or perhaps intrigued by the possibility, dispatched his men to scour Gardiner's Island in search of the hidden wealth. However, their efforts yielded no tangible results. The island's secrets remained firmly guarded, defying their best attempts to unearth Kidd's rumored treasure.

Hayley: (leaning closer, captivated) So, even Lord Belemont's men couldn't find it? What happened to Kidd after that?

Harvey Ambrose: (nodding) Correct, my inquisitive young scholar. Frustrated by the fruitless search and perhaps driven by anger at Kidd's failure to deliver the promised riches, Lord Belemont resolved to sever ties with the enigmatic captain. Kidd was sent back to England to face trial for piracy, his fate hanging in the balance.

Cassidy: (concerned) What happened to Kidd in England? Did he receive a fair trial?

Harvey Ambrose: (his tone turning somber) Alas, the wheels of justice turned against Kidd. He was subjected to a trial that many deemed unfair and biased. Found guilty of piracy, he met a grim fate at the gallows, where he was hanged for his alleged crimes. Thus, the tale of Captain Kidd reached its tragic climax, leaving behind a legacy shrouded in mystery, adventure, and unanswered questions.

Andy: (reflecting) It's both thrilling and disheartening to think about Kidd's journey. He sought fortune and redemption but met an unfortunate end. Yet, the mystery of his hidden treasure lives on.

Hayley: (leaning in, eyes shining with anticipation) Mr. Ambrose, please tell us about the connection between Captain Kidd and Foul Rift. Our history teacher mentioned that Kidd's treasure might be hidden along the Delaware River. Can you tell us more about that?
Harvey Ambrose: (smiling kindly) Ah, young girl, your curiosity serves you well. The tale of Captain Kidd and Foul Rift holds an air of mystery. While I cannot claim certainty, there are whispers of a fascinating connection worth exploring.

Hayley: (leaning closer, eager to hear more) Please, Mr. Ambrose, we're all ears. We want to uncover the secrets of Captain Kidd and his hidden treasure.

Harvey Ambrose: (nodding) Lord Bellomont, angered by the lack of success in recovering the treasure, sent his men to scour Gardiner's Island. However, they came back empty-handed, much to his dismay. It is believed that Kidd's treasure remained elusive, defying all attempts to locate it on that particular island.

Hayley: (intrigued) So, where does the Delaware River come into play? Our teacher mentioned four of Kidd's men seen along the Delaware. Is there a connection?

Harvey Ambrose: (smiling knowingly) Ah, the Delaware River. A waterway teeming with history and legends. It is true that four of Kidd's men were captured in Philadelphia, a bustling port city along the Delaware. These men were known to wander along the river, visiting various ports and settlements. Some speculate that they might have sought refuge or hidden the treasure within the nooks and crannies of the Delaware's shores.

Hayley: (excitedly) So, the Delaware River holds the key to uncovering Captain Kidd's secrets! Could his treasure be hidden somewhere along its banks, waiting to be discovered?

Harvey Ambrose: (leaning in, his eyes twinkling) Ah, actually my sweet girl, I hold the key. I've been waiting to share this with you. You see, before Captain Kidd was whisked away to face his trial in England, there was a remarkable moment that took place during his visit with his wife in Massachusetts. It was a clandestine meeting, guarded closely by the watchful eyes of the authorities.

Hayley: (leaning forward, intrigued) What happened during that meeting, Mr. Ambrose?

Harvey Ambrose: (nodding) As Captain Kidd embraced his wife one last time, he managed to slip her a small piece of paper, hidden from prying eyes. It was a moment of secrecy and hope, for within that folded note lay a clue, a glimpse into the whereabouts of his fabled treasure.

Cassidy: (leaning closer, excitement evident) What was written on that piece of paper? What did the clue reveal?

Harvey Ambrose: (smiling knowingly) With a slight hobble, Harvey Ambrose disappeared behind the wall from which he had emerged earlier. The kids exchanged curious glances, their anticipation mounting. Moments later, he returned, a small piece of paper delicately held in his hand. With a gentle nod, he placed it in Hayley's outstretched palm, almost recreating the exchange between Captain Kidd and his wife.

Hayley carefully unfolded the paper, her eyes scanning the mysterious numbers written upon it: 44106818. The room fell silent as the significance of the digits began to sink in.

Andy: (whispering) Could these numbers be coordinates? A secret location that holds the key to Captain Kidd's treasure?
Harvey Ambrose: (smiling, his voice filled with anticipation) Indeed, my astute young scholar. Those numbers hold the key to unlocking the next chapter of our quest. They are a clue, a breadcrumb leading you closer to the hidden riches of Captain Kidd.

Bo: (grinning with excitement) We've come this far, and now we have a solid lead! Let's see if we can decipher the meaning behind these numbers and follow the path they reveal.

Harvey Ambrose: (pausing for a moment, a gleam in his eyes) Ah, my young friend, you have stumbled upon a revelation. Indeed, those numbers have already been deciphered, and the truth behind them lies within the confines of my own experience. You see, I am the one who cracked the code, nearly three decades ago. It was a discovery that changed the course of my life and led me to this very moment.

The children's eyes widened in astonishment, hanging onto every word Mr. Ambrose uttered.

Cass: (leaning forward, her voice filled with wonder) Mr. Ambrose, you deciphered the numbers? What did they lead you to?

Harvey Ambrose: (smiling fondly) Aye, my young sleuths, they led me to a hidden trove of knowledge, to a realization that the legends surrounding Captain Kidd's treasure were more than mere folklore. But more importantly, they led me to Foul Rift. But truth be told, I have kept this secret locked away for all these years, waiting for the right time and the right people to unveil it to.

Hayley: (leaning in, her voice filled with anticipation) Please, Mr. Ambrose, tell us what you discovered. We're ready to dive into the depths of history and be part of this incredible journey.

Harvey Ambrose: (with a gentle smile) Very well, my young adventurers. The truth is this: the numbers, 44106818, were indeed coordinates. They pointed to the rugged coastline of our beloved town.

Bo: (in awe) So, the treasure is real and it's here in Foul Rift?

Harvey Ambrose: (nodding) It is as real as the salt in the sea and the wind in our sails. Captain Kidd's treasure exists, and its essence has been carefully guarded, waiting for those worthy enough to unlock its power.

Andy: (excitement bubbling) We're honored to be a part of this, Mr. Ambrose. To carry on the legacy, you began so many years ago.

Bo: (grinning wide) This is beyond anything we could have imagined! Let's embark on this journey together, guided by your wisdom and our determination. We will pick-up where you left off.

Hayley: (holding the piece of paper tightly) We promise to keep this secret and follow the path that leads us to Captain Kidd's treasure. It's a journey we won't take lightly.

Harvey Ambrose: (his voice filled with pride) I have faith in you, my young companions. With your unwavering spirit and my guidance, we shall unravel the mysteries that have haunted the shores of our town for centuries. The path to the treasure awaits us, and together, we shall claim what Captain Kidd left behind.

And so, the group forms an unbreakable bond, their minds brimming with excitement, curiosity, and a shared determination to unveil the secrets that have remained hidden for far too long. Their journey has only just begun, but they walk forward with the knowledge that they carry a legacy, a treasure of knowledge that has the power to change their lives and the history of Foul Rift forever.

Hayley: (curiosity filling her voice) Mr. Ambrose, forgive me for my skepticism, but I can't help but wonder how you were able to crack the code. These numbers appear to be just a random sequence. How did you come to realize they are coordinates?

Harvey Ambrose: (smiling knowingly) Ah, a valid question, young Hayley. The path to deciphering those seemingly random numbers was not without its challenges.

It required a keen eye, a touch of intuition, and a deep understanding of Captain Kidd's mindset.

Cassidy: (leaning forward, eager to hear the answer) So, how did you do it? What was the key that unlocked the meaning behind those numbers?

Harvey Ambrose: (his eyes glimmering with the memory) It was a combination of research, historical knowledge, and a stroke of luck. I delved into the accounts of Captain Kidd's voyages, studied his interactions with key figures, and pieced together the puzzle of his life. In doing so, I discovered that Captain Kidd had a penchant for hiding clues in plain sight, utilizing what others might perceive as randomness to veil his true intentions.

Andy: (intrigued) That's fascinating! So, the numbers held a deeper significance beyond their appearance?

Harvey Ambrose: (nodding) Indeed, my young friend. Captain Kidd, being a cunning strategist, chose to encode the coordinates of his treasure in a way that would confound those who stumbled upon them. The numbers themselves were carefully chosen to mimic a random sequence, thus diverting attention from their true purpose.

Bo: (leaning in, captivated) But how did you crack the code, Mr. Ambrose? What led you to realize they were coordinates?

Ambrose: (chuckling) Well, my young friend, allow me to share a tale that sheds light on how I cracked the code. It was many years ago when I heard a rumor about a wealthy millionaire that lives in Florida had come into possession of a chest believed to belong to Captain William Kidd himself. This chest had been passed down through generations of Kidd's family until it finally found its way to an auction.

Bo: (leaning in, captivated) A chest belonging to Captain Kidd? That's incredible! What does it have to do with the numbers?

Ambrose: (smiling nostalgically) My curiosity got the better of me. At that time, I was fervently seeking any clue or artifact that could lead me to Kidd's treasure. I managed to track down the millionaire and, after some persuasive words, convinced him to let me see the chest.

Cassidy: (intrigued) What did you find inside? Did it hold any answers?

Ambrose: (nodding) The chest was truly a sight to behold. It was a weathered wooden box, its once vibrant hues faded with time. Brass hinges held its worn lid in place, and a sturdy lock secured its contents. But what caught my attention was the engraving on the brass hardware, above the keyhole —the name 'William Kidd'.

Hayley: (leaning closer) William Kidd's initials were engraved on the chest? That's incredible!

Ambrose: (smiling) Indeed, it was a remarkable detail. It immediately sparked my imagination and fueled my determination to delve deeper into the mysteries it held. With bated breath, I carefully opened the chest, revealing a treasure trove of papers that adorned its interior.

Cassidy: (intrigued) Papers? What kind of papers?

Ambrose: (gesturing with his hands) The inside of the chest was wallpapered with sheets from the British Britannica. These were no ordinary papers, my young sleuths. They were filled with information about history, geography, and the secrets of the world that Captain Kidd had collected on his voyages. Each of them carefully glued in a collage covering the chest's walls.

Bo: (wide-eyed) So, the chest not only contained his personal belongings but also his thirst for knowledge?

Ambrose: (nodding) Exactly, my observant adventurer. The papers inside the chest were a testament to Kidd's intellectual curiosity, his hunger for understanding the world beyond the pirate's life. It was as if he sought to surround himself with knowledge and keep it close, even while pursuing his daring exploits on the high seas.

Cassidy: (impressed) Captain Kidd was a man of many facets, it seems. A pirate with a thirst for knowledge and a secret treasure to protect.

Ambrose: (smiling knowingly) Indeed. Captain Kidd's legacy is more complex than meets the eye. His chest held not only material wealth but also a wealth of knowledge and untold secrets that have captivated countless seekers throughout history.

As the group absorbs the significance of the papers inside Captain Kidd's chest, they can't help but feel a deeper connection to the enigmatic pirate. The intertwined themes of knowledge and hidden treasure evoke a sense of wonder and excitement within them, fueling their determination to solve the mysteries that lie ahead.

Hayley: (curiously) Mr. Ambrose, if the papers glued inside the chest didn't help you crack the code, then what did? How did you uncover the hidden secret?

Ambrose: (smiling) Ah, my inquisitive young mind, the papers may have provided valuable insights into Captain Kidd's knowledge, but they did not hold the key to the code itself. It was something else entirely that led me to the hidden secret. As I was examining the box with the owner still in the room, I noticed something peculiar—the bottom inside the box seemed to wiggle ever so slightly.

Cassidy: (leaning forward) A false bottom, perhaps?

Ambrose: (nodding) Precisely, young lady My instincts told me that there was more to the chest than met the eye, that a hidden compartment lay beneath the surface. However, I needed to be cautious. I wasn't certain what awaited me in that concealed space, and I certainly didn't want the man to catch wind of it just yet. I had a lingering suspicion that he might snatch whatever I found and withhold it from me, not letting me view it.

Bo: (excitedly) So, what did you do? How did you check out the secret compartment?

Ambrose: (with a hint of mischief) Patience, dear boy. Timing is everything in such delicate matters. I waited for the opportune moment, a moment when the millionaire's attention was diverted. It just so happened when he received a phone call and had to walk over to his desk on the other side of the room to take the call. That's when I discreetly lifted the false bottom of the chest.

Charlotte: (leaning closer, captivated) What did you find inside, Mr. Ambrose? Was it the key to the code?

Ambrose: (nodding) Oh, indeed it was, little miss. Nestled within that secret compartment, I discovered more than just papers from the British Britanica wallpapering the bottom. Glued to the bottom were additional fragments of the encyclopedia, but amidst them, something extraordinary caught my eye. It was a handwritten poem, carefully disguised by the aged pages.

Hayley: (intrigued) A poem? Was it a clue to deciphering the numbers?

Ambrose: (smiling) Precisely. As time was of the essence, I quickly pulled out my old camera and snapped a few shots of it. We used film back in those days. I then scanned the verses, realizing its potential significance. Knowing the uncertainty of the pictures I took, I committed the poem to memory as best as I could. Just as I finished, I heard the gentleman concluding his phone call and approaching.

Cassidy: (eagerly) What did you do next? Did you manage to replace the false bottom before he noticed?

Ambrose: (nodding) Indeed. With haste, I returned the false bottom to its original position, carefully concealing the hidden compartment once more. Though the poem's words echoed in my mind, I knew it was crucial to maintain the element of secrecy, ensuring the millionaire remained oblivious to my discoveries—for the time being, at least.

Bo: (excited) So, you have the poem memorized, Mr. Ambrose? What did it say? Did it hold the key to figuring out the meaning of the numbers?

As the group absorbs the gravity of the hidden poem and the significance it holds, their determination intensifies.

Mr. Ambrose reaches into his pocket and retrieves a folded piece of paper, a glimmer of excitement in his eyes. "I have it right here, dear boy," he says, carefully unfolding the paper. He reads the poem written on it aloud: "It's called, 'Picking Marigolds':"

<u>Picking Marigolds</u>
Skip and take,
Skip and take,
Skip and take.
Do it Slow,
Make no Mistake.
Kill one flower,
Kill one more,
Grow one flower, evermore.
Skip a petal, Skip a petal, Skip a petal, Skip.
Skip a petal, grow two more, and go be on your trip.

Mr. Ambrose: I wasn't certain if the poem was connected to the numbers either. It seemed out of place, yet held a glimmer of significance. When I returned home, I anxiously had the film developed, hoping the pictures would provide clarity. I feared that I had forgotten most of the poem, and my only hope lay in those developed images. I worried about the possibility of having to find a way back into the millionaire's home if the pictures turned out unclear or indecipherable.

Hayley: (leaning forward, curiosity evident in her eyes) So, Mr. Ambrose, how do the numbers and the poem correlate? What's the connection between them?

Mr. Ambrose: (smiling mischievously) Ah, my dear, this is where the fun begins. The numbers and the poem hold the key to unraveling Captain Kidd's hidden treasure. Allow me to shed some light on their correlation.

Hayley: (leaning closer, eager to understand) Please do, Mr. Ambrose. We are all ears.

Mr. Ambrose: Each line of the poem corresponds to a specific instruction related to the numbers. For instance, "Skip then take" signifies that we need to skip certain digits and take others in a specific sequence. And when we encounter "Kill one flower," it means we have to subtract one from a particular number.

Cassidy: (intrigued) So, the poem guides us on how to manipulate the numbers?

Mr. Ambrose: Exactly. As we follow the poem's instructions, we manipulate the numbers accordingly.

Bo: (excitement building) So, by following these instructions, you decoded the numbers to find the treasure's location?

Mr. Ambrose: Precisely! The carefully crafted correlation between the poem and the numbers is the key to revealing the hidden treasure's location.

Andy: So what is the location?

Mr. Ambrose: Let me show you. Let me grab a piece of paper and a pen.

Mr. Ambrose carefully hobbles over to a hidden corridor, retrieving a piece of paper and a pencil. With a sense of excitement in the air, he returns to the group, ready to unveil the next step of their journey.

Mr. Ambrose: (holding the paper and pencil) Let's write down the numbers in a clear and prominent manner: 4 4 1 0 6 8 1 8. Now, let's follow the guidance of the poem, "Picking Marigolds." It instructs us to "Skip then Take, Skip then take, Skip then take." So, we'll start with the first number and follow the pattern.

As Mr. Ambrose writes down the process, the group watches intently, their anticipation growing.

Mr. Ambrose: (writing) We will skip the first digit and take the second. (He writes the number 4 on the paper) Now, we skip the one and take the zero. (He adds 0 to the number) And finally, we skip the 6 and take the 8. (He writes down 8)

Hayley: (leaning closer, following along) So, if I understand correctly, the new number sequence is 4, 0, and 8. Is that right, Mr. Ambrose?

Mr. Ambrose: (nodding, pleased with Hayley's understanding) Yes, indeed. You're following along perfectly. The sequence we have now is 4, 0, and 8.

The group, fully engaged in the process, nods in agreement, their excitement building.

Mr. Ambrose: (looking at the group) Are you all staying with me?

Everyone: (nodding eagerly) Yes, Mr. Ambrose. We're right here with you, ready to uncover the secrets hidden within these numbers.

With their determination renewed, the group focuses their attention on the next step of the puzzle, eager to see where the path will lead them.

Mr. Ambrose: (enthusiastically) Onward to the next step! According to the poem, it instructs us to "kill one flower, then kill one more." The next number in our sequence is 1, so 1 minus 1 equals 0. (He writes down the number 0)

Mr. Ambrose continues: Now, let's subtract one from the last number, which gives us 7. So, our updated number is "40807."

Hayley: (eagerly) Can I give it a try?

Without waiting for an answer, Hayley takes the opportunity to delve into the puzzle.

Hayley: (confidently) The poem says, "grow one, flower evermore." Since we have gone through all the numbers, we start back at the beginning. That's why it adds the phrase "evermore."

Hayley's excitement fills the room as she continues: We add one more to 4, and we get 5. (She writes down the digit 5) Now, our number reads 408075.

Hayley proceeds to read the next part of the poem: "Skip a petal, skip a petal, skip a petal. Skip, skip a petal…"

She pauses, contemplating the instructions, and then declares: So, let's skip the four, the one, the zero, the six, and the eight. Finally, we add the last two digits to the sequence.

With anticipation, Hayley announces the resulting number: 9. Our new number is 40807509.

The group eagerly observes the growing sequence, their curiosity piqued by each step they unravel. They realize they are inching closer to uncovering the hidden secrets that lay ahead.

Hayley gazes at the perplexing numbers, her brows furrowed in confusion. She voices her frustration, "These are just as perplexing as the first set. I don't understand."

Mr. Ambrose, taking the piece of paper, smiles reassuringly. He explains, "You see, these numbers are actually coordinates, representing lines of latitude and longitude. Allow me to demonstrate." With a steady hand, he places a decimal point between the zero and eight, and another between the five and zero. He then adds the letter 'N' after the second zero, signifying the north direction, and the letter 'W' after the nine, indicating the west direction.

"Now," he proclaims, "We have 40.80N 75.09W." His voice brimming with certainty, he continues, "I am certain that one of you, if not all of you, is carrying one of those hi-tech phones. Punch those numbers into your search engine."

Excitement fills the room as the children swiftly retrieve their phones, eagerly typing the newly revealed coordinates into their search engines. Their eyes widen as information unfolds before them, unraveling the mystery that has captivated their imagination.

Cass's voice fills the room, brimming with astonishment, "OMG...FOUL RIFT!" The kids gather around, their eyes fixated on the maps displayed on their phones, each one marking the location of Foul Rift. A collective gasp escapes their lips as they realize the significance of their discovery.

Hayley's excitement is palpable as she exclaims, "So the treasure is in Foul Rift? Captain Kidd arranged everything, ensuring that his wife and son would have a chance to find the treasure in case he didn't make it out of prison alive."

Mr. Ambrose, a gleam in his eyes, responds, "Precisely! You now share the same enthusiasm I felt thirty years ago when I deciphered the letter. It was that very enthusiasm that led me to Foul Rift all those years ago. Regrettably, despite a lifetime of searching, I never managed to locate the treasure. Perhaps, my dear children, luck will favor you where it eluded me."

The room fills with a mixture of hope and determination as the kids realize the weight of the adventure that lies ahead. They understand that this journey, fueled by curiosity and the spirit of Captain Kidd, may hold the key to unraveling an age-old mystery and fulfilling the legacy of a legendary pirate.

Hayley's excitement bubbles over as she fires off a flurry of questions. "Where have you looked, Mr. Ambrose? Are you the only person who knows about these coordinates? And what about the four men who worked with Kidd? What happened to them? How is it possible that nobody has found the treasure? And how have you, with all your searching, not been able to find it? Where do you think it could be?"

Mr. Ambrose, taking a moment to compose himself, responds with a mix of nostalgia and contemplation. "Oh, my dear girl, I have searched far and wide, exploring countless nooks and crannies in pursuit of Kidd's treasure. From the coastal shores to remote river islands, my quest has taken me to various corners of the county. But alas, the elusive treasure has remained elusive."

He continues, his voice filled with a mix of intrigue and determination. "As for the knowledge of these coordinates, it has been a closely guarded secret of mine, known only to a select few. The four men who worked alongside Kidd, I believe they played a crucial role in hiding the treasure. Kidd was aware that the British Crown would be hot on his trail, searching tirelessly for his ill-gotten gains. He knew that hiding it along the Atlantic Seaboard would be far too predictable."

Mr. Ambrose leans closer, his eyes shining with a sense of adventure. "So, instead, Kidd and his men embarked on a journey northwest, venturing away from the coast. They followed a path, which in those times was nothing more than a humble horse trail, now known as Interstate 80. Their path led them towards a place that we now call Portland. It was there that they devised their plan. Kidd intended to plead innocence and, if found guilty, make a daring escape."

A touch of sadness creeps into Mr. Ambrose's voice as he continues, "The four men, faithful to Kidd's cause, awaited his arrival in Philadelphia, eager to reunite with him and the treasure. However, their hopes were shattered when they were captured and met the same tragic fate as Kidd himself—hanged by the authorities. It was a heartbreaking end to their loyalty."

He sighs, a mix of remorse and admiration evident in his expression. "Kidd's true intention was for his beloved wife and son to discover the treasure. He wanted to ensure their future, free from the clutches of the Crown. However, his wife could never decipher the significance of the numbers. The key was hidden in plain sight— at the bottom of Kidd's chest, where the poem about his wife's favorite flowers, perhaps the last letter William wrote to his beloved wife Sarah, layed concealed. Both the numbers and the chest were passed down through the generations, eventually falling into the hands of treasure seekers. But it was this old man, with a passion for solving puzzles, who finally cracked the code."

As the kids listen attentively, they grasp the magnitude of the story unfolding before them. They realize that the curator's journey to Foul Rift carries a weight of history, tragedy, and the allure of unimaginable wealth. The torch has now been passed to them, the next generation of treasure hunters, to unravel the mysteries left behind by Captain Kidd and his ill-fated crew.

With a sigh, Mr. Ambrose offers his perspective, "As for where I think it may be, Foul Rift is undoubtedly a significant piece of the puzzle. Its name alone suggests a connection. But beyond that, I can only speculate. Perhaps it lies hidden in a cave, buried at the bottom beneath layers of earth, or concealed in the depths of the river. The possibilities are endless, my dear Hayley."

The kids listen intently, their imaginations running wild with visions of buried treasure and untold riches. They understand that their journey will require courage, wit, and a touch of luck to succeed where others have failed.

As the rain subsides, the gentle rays of the sun filter into the room, illuminating the space with renewed hope. Mr. Ambrose, sensing the change in weather, smiles warmly at the group of young adventurers. He acknowledges the shift in their collective mood and begins to speak with a sense of contentment.

"You know, my days of treasure seeking are long gone," Mr. Ambrose admits, his voice tinged with nostalgia. "I find great joy in maintaining the town museum, preserving the stories and artifacts of our rich history. But I must implore you, if you do decide to embark on this quest, be cautious. The path to hidden treasures can be treacherous."

Pausing for a moment, Mr. Ambrose's gaze turns to his cane, and he taps it against his fake leg, the sound reverberating in the room. The kids glance at each other, their curiosity piqued, yet unsure how to broach the subject delicately.

With a hint of wistfulness in his eyes, Mr. Ambrose decides to share a glimpse of his own journey. "You see, there was a time when I was consumed by the allure of the treasure. I wish I had heeded the advice I now offer you. The pursuit led me down perilous paths, and in the end, I paid a personal price." He pauses, his voice filled with a mixture of acceptance and regret.

Understanding their unspoken question, Mr. Ambrose continues, his tone gentle and sincere. "I lost my leg, my dear children, in an unfortunate accident during my quest. It serves as a constant reminder of the risks one faces in the pursuit of hidden riches. But please, don't be burdened by my experience. It's simply a reminder to tread carefully and prioritize your well-being above all else."

The kids absorb his words, a mixture of empathy and respect filling their hearts. They recognize the weight of Mr. Ambrose's cautionary tale, appreciating the wisdom he imparts through his own personal sacrifice. They are grateful for his vulnerability and understand that their journey, though filled with excitement, has the potential to be filled with risks.

Mr. Ambrose glances at the kids, anticipating their eagerness to embark on their adventure now that the sun is peeking through the clouds. Do any of you have a final question before I bid you adieu and start locking up the museum?"

Bo takes a moment to gather his thoughts before speaking up. "Actually, Mr. Ambrose, I have one last question before we head out… What is a gibbet?"

Hayley rolls her eyes playfully. "Leave it to Bo… Alright, Mr. Ambrose, we should get going now."

Mr. Ambrose chuckles and nods. "Of course, my dear. Good luck on your journey, and remember, be cautious in your search. If you have any more questions along the way, feel free to return and ask. Now, go and make some history of your own!"

Chapter 7:
Hotdog Johnny's

The next day dawns, and the six friends begin their usual routine, starting with school. Excitement fills the air as the end of the school year draws near, bringing with it the promise of long-awaited freedom and adventures yet to come.

Meanwhile, the tight-knit community of Foul Rift strives to maintain a sense of normalcy despite the lingering worry caused by the disappearance of two beloved members. The town's residents grapple with various theories circulating about what might have happened, ranging from plausible explanations to outlandish speculations.

The presence of law enforcement is palpable, with a heavy concentration of state police stationed throughout the town. Rumors swirl about reporters seen questioning people, adding an extra layer of intrigue and uncertainty to the situation.

After a full day of classes, the bell finally rings, signaling the end of the school day. Ryan, Hayley, Cassidy, Andy, Charlotte, and Bo convene outside the school's entrance, ready to embark on their next adventure. Ryan takes the lead, suggesting that they join other students that are heading over to Johnny's Hot Dogs in Buttzville, where he intends to share the details of yesterday's search.

However, Bo interjects, expressing his desire to take a walk through Wind-Chime Woods. He remarks on the present wind and suggests it as an alternative plan. Ryan swiftly dismisses the idea, revealing that the police have blocked off all trails and wooded areas, aiming to prevent anyone from venturing into isolated locations until the disappearance of the two community members is solved.

Undeterred, Ryan proposes heading to Johnny's instead, assuring them that it will be fun. Bo voices his concern about the distance, but Ryan counters by promising to buy him a birch beer as an incentive. Bo eagerly agrees, and the group sets off towards their destination, ready to share their museum experience and intriguing discoveries from the previous day.

Hayley asserts that they have a lot to discuss and piques Ryan's curiosity, hinting that he will find their revelations fascinating. With anticipation in the air, they embark on their journey, eager to unravel the secrets that lie before them.

The six friends arrive at Hot Dog Johnny's in Buttzville and park their bikes on a nearby bike rack. As they approach the bustling roadside eatery, they notice that it's already teeming with fellow students from their high school, creating a lively and energetic atmosphere.

They make their way to the ordering window, where they encounter an elderly man with short white fluffy hair, adorned in a 'Hotdog Johnny' golf shirt bearing the name "Putz" embroidered on it. He addresses the group with a friendly yet concerned tone, expressing his observations about the rowdy behavior of some of their classmates.

Putz assertively requests that the six friends relay a message to their peers, urging them to be mindful of their language and conduct. He emphasizes that Hot Dog Johnny's is a family-oriented establishment, and the inappropriate language being used by some individuals is not in line with the atmosphere they strive to maintain.

Concerned about the possibility of everyone being asked to leave if the behavior continues, Putz hopes that the six friends can help ensure a pleasant and respectful environment for all customers. The group nods in understanding and assures Putz that they will relay the message and do their best to foster a more appropriate atmosphere among their peers.

As the six friends make their way towards one of the weathered picnic tables, their ears are filled with the clamor of unruly behavior emanating from a nearby group of kids. Loud cursing and unnecessary noise pierce the air, while a couple of kids disregard proper seating etiquette and occupy the table's surface instead of the designated benches. The scene becomes even more disheartening as they witness napkins, wrappers, and even fries being carelessly thrown among them trying to engage in a food fight.

As the six friends draw nearer to the source of the commotion, they realize with little surprise that the culprits responsible for this disruptive behavior are none other than Greg, Rick, Sean, Sanj, and Erin—a group known for their disregard of rules and attention-seeking mischief-making tendencies. Their presence casts a negative shadow over the otherwise enjoyable atmosphere of Hot Dog Johnny's. However, amidst this chaotic scene, Bo's attention is drawn to a different area approximately fifty feet away. There, he observes young children happily swinging on the wooden slat swings, their innocent enjoyment contrasting starkly with the rowdy antics of the older troublemakers. Bo also notices the mounting frustration on the faces of parents nearby, clearly becoming exasperated by the disruptive behavior exhibited by Greg, Rick, Sean, Sanj, and Erin, among others.

As Bo approaches the group of troublemakers, his heart beats a little faster, but he remains steadfast in his commitment to the principles of the Noblemen. His friends, seated at the picnic table, watch in a mix of awe and concern, unsure of how Bo will handle the situation. They hesitate, unsure whether to intervene or support him, their eyes locked on the unfolding scene.

Bo stands beside their table, projecting a calm and composed demeanor. His friends hold their breath, waiting to hear his words and see how the confrontation will unfold. Erin, the first to notice Bo's presence, halts her conversation with a curious expression. The rest of the group's attention soon follows, and they all fix their gazes on him, their annoyance apparent.

Erin (loud and assertive) YES, CAN WE HELP YOU?

In response to Erin's confrontational tone, Bo remains unfazed. He looks each of them directly in the eyes, a firm resolve shining through his own. With measured words, he addresses them, conscious of his surroundings and the impact of their behavior on others. "Can you guys bring it down a little? There are little kids right there swinging," Bo states calmly, his voice carrying a tone of sincerity. "At least stop cursing. Those are their parents and they don't want to listen to you guys."

The five, their attention redirected towards the swings, finally notice the presence of the innocent children for the first time. The realization dawns on them, causing a momentary pause in their otherwise defiant attitudes. However, Sanj, seeking to maintain his tough façade, decides to challenge Bo's request. He rises from the bench, standing tall and attempting to intimidate Bo with his larger stature.

Sanj, looking down at Bo, attempts to dismiss him with a taunting remark. "How about you mind your own business, little boy?" he retorts, his voice carrying an air of bravado.

Bo maintains his composure, un-swayed by Sanj's attempted intimidation. He stands tall, his gaze unwavering, and calmly responds, "I'm just asking for some consideration. We're all here trying to have fun and enjoy ourselves, and that includes the little kids. Is it too much to ask for a bit of respect?"

The atmosphere becomes tense as the confrontation hangs in the balance, the outcome uncertain. Bo's friends watch anxiously, ready to support him if needed, but also hoping for a peaceful resolution to the situation.

As Sanj moves closer to Bo and gets in his space, Ryan and Andy quickly rise from their seats in solidarity with Bo. Their actions catch the attention of Greg and Rick, who, sensing the escalating tension, also stand up. The atmosphere becomes charged with an undercurrent of hostility, leaving Hayley, Cass, and Char frozen in shock, their mouths agape. Hayley's concern for her younger brother intensifies, fearing that the situation may escalate into a physical confrontation.

Ryan, his voice steady but firm, addresses Sanj and the others. "We're just asking for a little respect and consideration here, for God's sake, there are little children right behind you," he states, his words emphasizing the importance of maintaining a peaceful environment. Andy, standing beside Ryan, adds his support with a determined expression, ready to stand up for their principles.

Sanj adjusts his stare at Ryan.

Sanj:(with a look of annoyance with Ryan) Hey Ryan, how can you tell when the white-trash student's desk is level in class.

Sanj pauses for a brief second. Ryan doesn't like where this is going.

Sanj:(with a giggling arrogance) Drool comes out both sides of his mouth.

Ryan can feel his blood boil and feels embarrassed over the picture incident which he has never been able to address. He is unsure of how to proceed.

Ryan: (seething with anger) Sanj, that's clever! Do you feel like a big man now?

Sanj: (smirking) Oh, look who's standing up for his little buddy. What's the matter, Ryan? Can't handle a little joke?

Ryan: (taking a deep breath) It's not about jokes. It's about respect. You need to consider others. You should try listening more and speaking less.

Sanj pays no mind to what Ryan says. He redirects his focus on Bo and then places one hand on Bo's chest and gives him a shove. "Go back to your drool-daddy".

Ryan: (stepping forward, fists clenched) That's enough, Sanj! He's four years younger than you. Why don't you try that with someone your own age?

Sanj: (pausing, then smirking) Fine, if it makes you happy, sorry for hurting your delicate feelings, drool boy.

Sanj places both of his hands on Ryan and pushes him backwards causing him to fall back and land on his backside.

Putz: (storming over) I've had enough of your nonsense. You five need to get your things, right now, and go. We have had several complaints from customers here. Gather your things, clean up your mess and make like a tree and get outta here.

Greg: (muttering) Whatever, old man. Let's go.

Putz: (firmly) Leave, and clean up your mess before you go. And don't come back until you learn some manners.

Greg, Rick, Sean, Sanj, and Erin grumble as they reluctantly gather their belongings and head towards Greg's red jeep. They leave their scattered trash behind, displaying their disregard for Putz.

Putz: (turning to Bo) I want to thank you for speaking up. It's swell to see someone with manners and decency.

Bo: (cheeks red) Thank you, sir. I just thought someone needed to say something.
Putz: Whew, that was quite an intense situation, wasn't it? I must say, more teenagers could certainly learn a thing or two from all of you. I'll take care of this mess. You kids enjoy the rest of your time here.

[Putz starts clearing the table and disposing of the leftover trash.]

Putz: Oh, by the way, are you kids planning on participating in the Snakehead Derby next week? I'll be there selling hotdogs. I'll have my pontoon set up on the river. If you float over to me, I'll make sure each of you gets a free hotdog and birch beer.

[The six friends exchange excited glances, their interest piqued by the offer.]

Bo: That sounds awesome. I completely forgot about the derby.

Ryan:(dusting himself off) Absolutely! Thanks for the offer. We'll be sure to catch you at the Snakehead Derby.

Putz: Excellent! I'll be looking forward to seeing you there. Enjoy the rest of your day, and remember, free hotdogs are waiting for you next week!

The six friends, still in a state of disbelief over what just transpired, thank Putz again for his intervention and offer of free dogs at the derby. As they return to their table, they talk about the incident and realize the importance of standing up for what is right, even in the face of adversity.

As the 6 of them settled down, the atmosphere began to relax. They started eating their hot dogs and sipping their birch beers, enjoying the well-deserved break. Cassidy, unable to contain her curiosity, broke the silence.

Cassidy: "Okay, Ryan, spill the beans. What happened during the search? Did you guys find anything? And what about the police? Did they uncover anything?"

Ryan took a deep breath, preparing to recount the events that had unfolded yesterday.
Ryan sat at one end of the table, leaning forward to ensure his voice carried to everyone gathered around. His eyes scanned the faces of his friends, capturing their undivided attention.

Ryan: "Alright, listen up, guys. I have to be honest with you. Our search didn't turn up any concrete evidence linked to the mechanic, John Retnik or Detective Chotdyfo. It's like they vanished into thin air. And here's the weirdest part: his dog is missing too."

Bo: (Blurting out his question without hesitation) Wait, you mean you found nothing? No trace of either of them?

Ryan glanced at Bo, his eyebrows raised.

Ryan: No, Bo, we didn't find anything linked to either of them. But, let me tell you about the strange things we did encounter.

The rest of the group leaned in, their curiosity piqued.

Ryan: As we formed a human chain, we combed through the forest. The police were there too, using poles to help in the search. But as we went deeper, something felt off. It was like an eerie silence hung in the air, and a sense of emptiness filled the woods.

Cassidy leaned forward, her eyes shining with anticipation.

Cassidy: What do you mean by 'strange things'? Did you stumble upon any clues?

Ryan nodded, a serious expression on his face.

Ryan: Well, not exactly clues, but odd occurrences. We found an abandoned campsite deep in the woods, as if someone had been staying there recently. But it was deserted, with no signs of life. It was as if whoever was there vanished without a trace.

Charlotte's voice filled with intrigue as she chimed in.

Charlotte: That's so weird. Did you find anything else?

Ryan paused for a moment, a hint of fascination in his eyes.

Ryan: "Yes, actually. We discovered a series of peculiar markings on dead trees and logs. They were just random letters. We tried to decipher them, but had no clue what they were or who did them. I took pictures of them.

Ryan reached into his pocket, retrieved his cellphone, and displayed an image to his friends. The image showcased a log with the letters carved: "R E G N A D." Intrigued, his friends leaned in closer, their curiosity piqued.

Ryan began sharing the speculations surrounding the mysterious carvings. Initially, some of the searchers believed it to be the last name of a mechanic named Retnik, but that assumption quickly proved wrong. Another theory emerged, suggesting that "R E G N A D" might be an abbreviation for something like "Regulation North American Datum." This idea proposed a connection to an environmental group responsible for mapping the surrounding area, hypothesizing that the log served as a marker of their presence. This idea was somewhat popular among the group.

Adding weight to the theory, Ryan mentioned that the state police had confirmed recent sightings in the vicinity, bolstering the notion that the enigmatic "R E G N A D" log held significance beyond its initial appearance. The friends exchanged glances, captivated by the unfolding mystery, eager to uncover the truth behind the peculiar markings and their potential connection to the environmental group's activities.

Hayley's curiosity got the better of her.

Hayley: And what did the police say about all this? Did they have any leads?

Ryan's voice took on a more serious tone as he shared the latest information with his friends. He spoke with a sense of concern and urgency, striving to relay the gravity of the situation.

"The police are perplexed. Currently, their leading hypothesis revolves around wolves. Timber wolves, specifically. Reports of their presence in the area have surfaced, but here's the catch: typically, there would be some remnants left behind, like bones or shreds of clothing, but nothing like that has been found so far."

Lowering his voice, Ryan continued, "However, there's more to this story. I overheard the police discussing dredging parts of the Delaware River and the big eddy that's back there. They may even send in scuba divers. It gets stranger. As we were walking closer to the edge of the river we found these weird tracks. It looked like someone was dragging a boat in and out of the river, except they weren't just dragging it a little way on the shore. It looked like they pulled it up to the eddy and around in the mud. I am not sure why anyone would drag a boat around in the woods."

Hayley shifted the conversation. She found what Ryan was saying to be interesting, but she wanted to start telling him about the museum and Captain Kidd's treasure possibly being in Foul Rift "Did you see Odrap? Did he say anything? Any talk about Captain Kidd?"

Ryan's voice held a hint of intrigue as he responded to Hayley's questions about Captain Kidd. He shook his head slightly, dismissing the notion.

"But I did see Odrap, though he had to leave in a hurry. He seemed pretty nervous the whole time he was there. I didn't talk to him."

A thoughtful expression crossed Ryan's face as he continued, recalling another peculiar encounter. "But here's something interesting. We saw the 'river witch', that homeless woman that you see walking around the outskirts of town sometimes. My parents told me that she spends most of the year at a shelter, but then comes back to Foul Rift in the spring and stays with family, except she has been kicked out and now she squats in one of those old abandoned factory buildings up the road, behind the bio-science plant. Apparently she has been sleeping there." Pausing for a moment, Ryan continued with a touch of uncertainty. "The police actually came across her while we were there. She was yelling at them from a distance in some strange language. My parents said it was just gibberish. The police tried to call her over, but she wouldn't listen to them. When they tried to approach her, she took off running."

Leaning in closer, Ryan added, "According to my parents, she's been around for years, harmless for the most part. The police have already questioned her and even searched the building where she stays. They don't suspect her of having anything to do with the disappearances. They were supposed to contact the shelter she stays at in the winter since she is not welcome with her family anymore. They don't want her squatting in the old buildings."

Ryan's words hung in the air, leaving a lingering sense of mystery surrounding the enigmatic river witch and her presence in the town of Foul Rift.

Bo expressed his mixed emotions, reflecting on the absence of any significant findings while acknowledging the unsettling nature of the wolf reports. Concerned for their safety, he anticipated that their parents would likely restrict their access to the woods and the river.

"Yeah, I agree with you, Bo," Ryan chimed in, his tone somber. "The thought of wolves roaming around is definitely unsettling. It's better to err on the side of caution and stay away from those areas for now."

Hayley caught Ryan's gaze, her eyes gleamed with determination. She took a deep breath before addressing the group with conviction. "Ok Ryan, my turn. We have a unique opportunity here. We met Mr. Ambrose, an old man who runs the museum in town and he told us some intriguing stories about Captain Kidd's hidden treasure."

She paused for a moment, allowing the weight of her words to sink in. "We are going to look for pirate treasure! It's here in Foul Rift!"

Hayley's words hung in the air, a spark of excitement igniting the imaginations of her friends. They exchanged glances, a mixture of enthusiasm and uncertainty dancing in their eyes. The prospect of a thrilling quest lay before them, beckoning them to explore the secrets that lay hidden within their town.

Chapter 8:
The Snakehead Derby

On a scorching Saturday morning, the Snakehead River-Derby descended upon the Foul Rift area of the Delaware River, transforming it into a hub of activity and anticipation. The atmosphere crackled with excitement as anglers, both local and from distant corners, flocked to participate in this highly anticipated event orchestrated by the Delaware River Fishermen's Association (DRFA). However, this year, there was an added element to the festivities – a heightened presence of security personnel. State police, fish and wildlife officials, and park rangers could be seen patrolling the area, ensuring the smooth operation of the derby and the safety of its participants. This visible display of authority served as a reminder that despite the festive ambiance, rules and regulations were in place to preserve the integrity of the event and protect the delicate balance of the river ecosystem.

As the sun climbed higher in the sky, the event unfolded in full swing. Vendors lined the streets of Foul Rift, offering a variety of goods and services to the enthusiastic participants. Fishing enthusiasts, equipped with their boats and fishing gear, filled the river, their crafts spread out along the water, each angler searching for that prized catch.

The riverbanks were alive with spectators, their eyes fixed on the water, waiting for the sight of a triumphant fisherman reeling in a mighty snakehead. Cheers and applause erupted each time someone successfully hooked a fish, their efforts met with admiration from the onlookers.

The DRFA had set up a central stage, where the winners would be announced and prizes awarded. The anticipation grew as the record-breaking size of the largest snakehead caught in the Delaware River—measuring a staggering seven feet—was shared among the crowd. Everyone wondered if this year's derby would produce another extraordinary catch.

Hayley, Andy, Ryan, Cassidy, Charlotte, and Bo navigated through the lively scene, weaving between anglers and spectators alike. They made their way to the boat launch dock towards the pontoon boat where Putz had set up shop, the aroma of sizzling hotdogs filling the air. The group exchanged excited glances, their mouths watering at the thought of the free hotdogs promised by Putz.

Reaching the pontoon, they found Putz beaming behind the grill, wearing a bright yellow silk screened T-shirt bearing the words "Hotdog Johnny's." He greeted them warmly, flipping burgers and hotdogs with expertise.

Putz: "Hey there, folks! Welcome to the Snakehead River-Derby! I hope you're all ready for some delicious tube-steaks. Climb-aboard and take a seat and I'll get those hotdogs sizzling for you."

The six friends settled on benches along the rail of the pontoon, their eyes fixed on the river, where the fishermen continued their quest for the elusive snakeheads. The sound of excited chatter filled the air as people swapped stories of their angling adventures.

Hayley: I can't believe the size of some of these snakeheads. They are huge.

Andy: Yeah, they look like something out of a horror movie. I wonder if anyone will manage to top the record.

Cass: I love the derby. It's always so much fun. Charlotte and I have been coming since we were babies.

Putz: (bringing the cooked hotdogs over to the teens) You know why the snakeheads are so big in this section of the Delaware, don't you?

As Putz shared his insights, the six friends listened intently, their curiosity piqued by the revelation about the snakeheads and Foul Rift. The information painted a more intricate picture of the derby and the unique conditions that made it possible.

Hayley: So, you're saying that the Foul Rift section of the Delaware is known for producing the largest snakeheads because of the presence of a nearby bio-science laboratory?

Putz nodded, a knowing expression on his face.

Putz: That's right. The laboratory's activities and the oxygen-rich waters of this section of the river contribute to the extraordinary growth of the snakeheads. It's a combination of factors that make Foul Rift the perfect breeding ground for these massive fish.

Ryan: Wait, what are they making there?

Putz: They are one of the world's largest producers of hormones and pharmaceuticals for animals. They provide products to farmers, veterinarians, zoos, park services and even pets.

Cassidy: But if the laboratory is producing growth hormones and pharmaceuticals for animals, couldn't it have an impact on other species in the river too?

Putz: It's certainly a possibility. While the exact extent of the laboratory's influence is unknown, there have been reports of unusually large catfish caught in these waters as well. It suggests that certain species that reside and thrive in this area may be affected by the conditions created by the laboratory's activities.

Andy: That's fascinating. I remember talking about this at a scout meeting. I remember our scoutmaster talking about the ecological impact the factory has. Do you know if the EPA has been actively monitoring the situation?

Putz: Indeed, the EPA has been conducting regular water tests in the area to ensure safety. Surprisingly, the results have consistently shown the water to be clean and within acceptable limits of any chemicals. Scientists believe that the abundance of oxygen in this stretch of the river plays a role in the size of the snakeheads. It's a unique combination of factors that has led to the reputation of Foul Rift as a hotspot for these impressive fish.

The friends exchanged glances, their minds buzzing with newfound knowledge about the ecological dynamics of Foul Rift and its remarkable fish population.

Putz, with a friendly smile, proposed an enticing idea to the kids. "I'm about to set sail up the river, and there are plenty of eager fishermen up there who requested a visit from me. How about I take you all for a ride? We'll cruise up the river, explore the surroundings, and then make our way back down. I'll drop you off back here," he gestured to the dock. Hayley's eyes sparkled with an idea forming in her mind. This boat ride could provide an excellent opportunity to survey the river and potentially uncover clues about Kidd's treasure's whereabouts.

As the boat glided up the river, the scene unfolded into a fishing frenzy. Fishermen lined the banks, their fishing rods casting lines into the water, hoping to hook one of the elusive snakeheads. Some were in small boats, their excitement palpable as they discussed strategies and shared stories of past catches.

A few minutes into the journey, a couple of guys in a nearby boat suddenly shouted with excitement. "Hey, we got one! It's a big one!" they cheered, as their fishing rods bent under the weight of the catch. The kids watched in awe as the fishermen expertly reeled in the struggling snakehead fish. Its distinctive snake-like appearance sent shivers down their spines.

"Wow, that's massive!" Bo exclaimed, leaning over the side of the boat to get a closer look.

Ryan nodded in agreement. "I didn't realize they could get that big. No wonder this derby is so popular."

Hayley, taking mental notes, observed the riverbanks, thinking about where a treasure might be hidden. Maybe, she thought, it was at the bottom of the Delaware.

As they continued up the river, the number of fishermen increased, and the excitement in the air was contagious. The kids could feel the sense of camaraderie among the anglers, all united by their shared passion for fishing and the thrill of the Snakehead River-Derby.

Putz skillfully navigated the boat, and they soon arrived at Mack Island. It was bustling with activity, and several other boats were already anchored there. Fishermen exchanged stories and tips, while others proudly displayed their catches, hoping to win the prize for the largest snakehead.

"Welcome to Mack Island, folks!" Putz announced cheerfully, his smile reflecting his genuine enthusiasm. "If you guys want to hop off and explore while I serve up some hotdogs, feel free to do so. I assure you, I won't leave without you."

As the six kids disembarked from the boat, their excitement palpable, Hayley's sharp eyes caught sight of an intriguing opening amidst the lush trees and bushes. She instinctively pointed towards it and asked Putz, "What's that over there?"

With a knowing expression, Putz replied, "Ah, that's a distributary, the opposite of a tributary. It's a small waterway that winds its way to an eddy hidden in the depths of the woods. I must warn you, though, it's quite swampy with treacherous cliffs and flooded caves. I don't advise going back there."

Hayley's curiosity piqued, she interrupted him eagerly, "Caves? There are caves back there?"

Putz nodded, his face filled with reminiscence. "Oh, indeed, several of them. Some are even partially submerged. Many years ago, someone had a mishap in those caves, and since then, the park rangers have been strict about prohibiting anyone from venturing in that area. They consider it quite hazardous."

Hayley's mind raced with thoughts, connecting the dots between the mention of caves and the legendary Captain Kidd's treasure. She couldn't help but wonder if these hidden caverns held the secrets they were seeking.

In that moment, the allure of adventure and the possibility of discovering the long-lost treasure intensified, igniting a spark of determination within Hayley's eyes. She realized that the forbidden nature of those caves made them a perfect hiding place for a valuable treasure like Captain Kidd's.

Excitement coursing through her veins, Hayley knew that exploring those caves held the potential to unravel the mystery that had captivated their imaginations for so long. With her newfound knowledge and the thrill of the unknown ahead, she couldn't wait to share her thoughts with the rest of the group.

The kids thanked Putz and stepped onto the island, immediately greeted by the enthusiastic crowd. Hayley, with her eyes on the river's edge, couldn't help but wonder if there was something hidden among the chaos of the

Snakehead River-Derby that might lead them closer to Kidd's treasure.

As the kids leisurely strolled around Mack Island, taking in the lively atmosphere of fishermen and the aroma of sizzling hotdogs, Hayley's excitement couldn't be contained. She eagerly brought up the topic of the distributary, their potential gateway to uncovering Captain Kidd's hidden treasure.
"What if the treasure is hidden in one of those caves or at the bottom of the eddy?" Hayley mused, her eyes glimmering with a sense of adventure. "Imagine, gold hidden underwater. It would be the perfect hiding spot."

The rest of the group listened intently, captivated by Hayley's ideas. Cassidy's voice carried a hint of caution as she added, "But what if the treasure is cursed? Isn't that a common theme in pirate stories? The books I've read always had curses attached to their treasure."

Bo chimed in, offering a practical solution. "We could easily hike to the eddy and explore it, right?"

However, before Bo's suggestion could be fully discussed, Ryan interjected with a serious tone. "The woods are currently closed off. They have barriers and police tape preventing anyone from entering. It's off-limits due to the ongoing investigation. We could get in trouble and face fines if we're caught."

Charlotte's voice quivered slightly as she voiced her concerns. "I don't know if it's a good idea to venture into the woods, especially with people going missing. What if there are wild animals like wolves? Or worse, what if some deranged person is living out there? Ryan, didn't you mention a campsite? What if it belongs to a serial killer?"

The gravity of Charlotte's words hung in the air, causing the group to exchange uneasy glances. The allure of hidden treasure was met with the reality of potential dangers lurking within the woods. The prospect of treasure hunting suddenly seemed entwined with the unsettling mysteries that surrounded Foul Rift.

With these thoughts in mind, the kids found themselves at a crossroads. Their desire for adventure and the anticipation of discovering Captain Kidd's treasure collided with the looming uncertainty and potential risks ahead. The decision they would make would require careful consideration and a collective agreement that weighed both the allure and the dangers they faced.

As the kids immersed themselves in their discussion about Kidd's treasure, their peaceful stroll along the banks of Mack Island was suddenly interrupted by a commotion. Cassidy's keen ears detected the sound first, and Bo's sharp eyes spotted the unfolding spectacle on the nearby riverbank. It was as if the air had been pierced by screams, drawing the attention of everyone around.

Curiosity piqued, the six friends hurriedly made their way through the bustling crowd of fishermen, eager to catch a glimpse of the unfolding drama. They followed the source of the commotion, their gazes directed across the wide expanse of the river. There, not far from the distributary, stood an old woman who seemed to be causing quite a scene. Her voice carried over the river, sharply cutting through the ambient noise, as she directed her loud accusations at some of the fishermen.

Intrigued and concerned, the group gathered at the riverbank, straining their eyes and ears to piece together the fragments of the unfolding drama. The old woman's passionate outburst captured the attention of both the fishermen and the onlookers, creating an air of curiosity and suspense. Whispers and murmurs circulated among the crowd, attempting to decipher the reason behind the woman's distress.

The six friends exchanged curious glances, their minds buzzing with questions. What could have caused the old woman to become so agitated? Was there something significant happening at the distributary? Their collective curiosity fueled their desire to investigate further, prompting them to linger on the riverbank, hoping to uncover the truth behind the old woman's alarming behavior.

Amidst the clamor and confusion, the haunting cries of the old woman echoed through the air, piercing the tranquility of the riverbank. Her voice resonated with an otherworldly quality as she repeated the enigmatic words, "Rej-Naid, Rej-Naid, Rej-Naid, Ret-Snom, Ret-Snom, Ret-Snom." The six friends drew closer, captivated by the strange scene unfolding before them.

As the commotion subsided for a moment, the kids managed to catch a better glimpse of the woman. Her appearance was as ragged and unkempt as the tales that surrounded her. With tattered clothes, disheveled hair, and a wild look in her eyes, she bore the marks of a figure that had long been dubbed the "river-witch" by the townsfolk. Their collective curiosity mingled with a hint of trepidation as they watched her frantic outburst.

"What is she saying?" Bo's voice broke the silence, reflecting the perplexity shared by the group. The onlookers, sensing the peculiar nature of the situation, began to record the scene on their smartphones, capturing the old woman's haunting cries for posterity.

In the midst of the unfolding chaos, the distant sound of approaching sirens signaled the arrival of the state police. Responding to a call, their boat made its way across the river with purposeful determination. The officers disembarked at the riverbank, attempting to calm the distressed woman whose tears mingled with her desperate pleas. With gentle reassurance, they guided her into their boat, setting course downstream toward Foul Rift.

As the boat carrying the old woman disappeared down the river, the six friends remained transfixed by the sequence of events. It was then that Bo's keen eyes spotted a familiar figure seated in a jon boat at the edge of Mack Island not far from where they were standing. Mr. Ambrose, the enigmatic museum curator, sat serenely with a fishing rod in hand, as if unaffected by the commotion that had just unfolded.

Hayley approached the riverbank closest to Mr. Ambrose, her friends trailing behind her. "Hi, Mr. Ambrose," she called out with a friendly smile.

"Ahoy, treasure hunters," Mr. Ambrose replied, his eyes twinkling with amusement. "How is your hunt going?"

Hayley nodded enthusiastically. "Good. Did you catch anything today?"

Mr. Ambrose chuckled softly, shaking his head. "Indeed I did, I think I managed to catch the smallest snakehead out here." Mr. Ambrose holds up a 12-inch snakehead he pulled from the bottom of his jon boat. "Perhaps the fish aren't in the mood for biting today, given all the commotion."

Andy, impressed with the idea of catching the smallest snakehead, asks if he can take a selfie with the fish. He plans on putting in his portfolio for boy scouts on his 'community events' page. He hoped to get a selfie with the smallest and largest snakehead on the river.

Mr. Ambrose: Sure thing. (Ambrose holds the fish up and high as Andy turns himself around to make sure that he, Ambrose and the fish are all in the picture. Andy checks the photo for clarity), "perfect!"

Charlotte chimed in, "Mr. Ambrose, do you know what language the old lady was speaking in? It didn't sound like English."

Mr. Ambrose paused, his gaze thoughtful. "Oh, yes, it did sound like she was speaking a different language. In a sense, she was. You see, that woman has a rare form of a rare condition called aphasia. It causes her to reverse word sounds when she speaks and writes. It's called 'backwards speech.'"

Charlotte's eyes widened in astonishment. "Backwards speech? That's fascinating."

Mr. Ambrose nodded, a slight smile playing on his lips. "Indeed, it is. Her unique condition can make it challenging to understand her at times, but she is speaking

English, albeit in a reversed manner. It's quite a remarkable linguistic phenomenon."

Hayley listened attentively to Mr. Ambrose's explanation, absorbing every detail. "So, she's actually speaking real words, but backwards? That's both fascinating and sad," she remarked with a tinge of empathy in her voice.

Mr. Ambrose nodded solemnly. "Yes, indeed. It's a condition that brings its own set of challenges. The poor old thing has had her fair share of difficulties. She does have family that she can stay with in the area, but for some reason, she's chosen not to stay with them. Instead, she resides in the old vacant buildings adjacent to the bio-science labs."

A mix of concern and compassion filled the air as the friends exchanged worried glances. Hayley's voice trembled slightly as she spoke, "That must be tough for her. Is she getting enough support? I mean, with food and everything?"

Mr. Ambrose's expression softened, reflecting the weight of the situation. "There are a few townsfolk who bring her food and try to help out as best they can. But I must admit, I fear she may struggle through this winter without proper support."

A sense of urgency washed over the group as they pondered the old woman's plight. They understood the importance of community and the need to lend a helping hand to those in need. Hayley's voice carried determination as she spoke, "We should do something to help her, to make sure she's taken care of."

The friends nodded in agreement, their hearts swelling with a newfound purpose. As they stood by the riverbank, surrounded by the excitement of the Snakehead River-Derby, their minds were already racing with ideas on how they could make a difference and provide assistance to the old woman.

Putz's arrival interrupted their conversation with Mr. Ambrose, but the group welcomed his presence. Putz nodded to Ambrose, acknowledging their interaction, and turned to the six teens. "Well, folks, it's about time for me to head back. If you want a ride, hop aboard."

Ambrose: (to the kids) Don't forget to keep me filled in about your adventure. Let me know if you make any new discoveries or uncover new information.

The teens bid farewell to Mr. Ambrose, expressing their gratitude for his insights and promising to visit the museum soon to continue their treasure hunt discussions. As they boarded the pontoon, settling in for the ride, Bo couldn't contain his curiosity. "What do you all think the woman was trying to say? She seemed really upset."

The group exchanged glances, contemplating the mysterious encounter. Hayley spoke up, her voice filled with concern. "It's hard to say, but there was definitely a sense of distress in her words. Maybe she was trying to communicate something important, it's difficult to decipher what she was saying without hearing it or writing it down."

Cassidy nodded in agreement. "It seemed like she was desperately trying to convey something."

Andy, always the practical thinker, suggested, "I am going to do some research on her condition, aphasia. The next time we come across her on our path, I am going to try to figure out what she is saying."

The group embraced the idea, especially Hayley, who realized that unraveling the woman's message might hold the key to finding Captain Kidd's hidden treasure. Hayley couldn't help but wonder, that maybe the river witch, having an intimate knowledge of the woods, has stumbled across a clue that could lead them to Kidd's treasure.

As the kids settled in on the Putz Pontoon, they turned their attention to Putz's excited call. Their gazes followed his outstretched finger, and their eyes widened in awe at the sight before them. A family of deer, several does accompanied by two delicate fawns, gracefully navigated the waters of the Delaware River.

"We're going to follow them," Putz exclaimed, a hint of wonder in his voice. With careful maneuvering, Putz guided the pontoon to a safe distance behind the swimming deer. The kids leaned against the railings, their eyes fixed on the serene scene unfolding before them.

The deer moved together in perfect harmony, their elegant bodies gliding through the water. The sun's rays glistened on their sleek fur as they swam with a gentle grace, creating ripples that mirrored the tranquility of the moment. The kids watched in awe, captivated by the rare sight of nature's beauty.

As they floated along the river, the only sounds were the soft lapping of the water against the pontoon and the distant chirping of birds in the trees. The 6 friends shared a sense of calm and reverence, grateful for this unexpected encounter with the natural world.

Time seemed to stand still as they silently observed the deer, marveling at the quiet strength and resilience of these magnificent creatures. In that serene moment, surrounded by the beauty of the river and the gentle presence of the deer, the kids felt a deep connection to nature and the mysteries it held.

The atmosphere on the pontoon shifted from tranquility to concern as the kids realized that one of the fawns had vanished beneath the water's surface. Their eyes scanned the river, desperately searching for any sign of the missing deer. Putz maneuvered the pontoon closer to the area where the fawn had disappeared, his brows furrowed with worry.

The fishermen on the riverbanks had also noticed the peculiar incident and were pointing and murmuring among themselves. The air was filled with a sense of anticipation and concern. The 6 friends huddled closer together, their eyes fixated on the spot where the fawn had last been seen.

Seconds turned into minutes, and the silence was broken only by the gentle lapping of the water against the pontoon. Every eye remained trained on the river's surface, hoping for a glimpse of the fawn emerging unharmed. But there was no sign of the young deer.

Bo's voice trembled with worry as he asked, "Where did it go? Did it get caught in something? Is it alright?" The other kids shared his concern, their hearts heavy with the unknown fate of the missing fawn. They exchanged worried glances, their minds racing with possibilities.

Putz, his voice filled with reassurance, said, "Sometimes, deer can dive underwater and stay submerged for longer periods than we expect. They have a natural ability to hold their breath. Let's stay hopeful and keep watching."

The minutes stretched on, and anticipation turned to a mixture of hope and unease. The kids continued their vigil, their gazes scanning the water's surface for any sign of movement. And then, as if responding to their collective longing, a small head emerged from the river's depths.

Relief washed over the group as they saw the fawn's head resurface, its tiny head bobbing in the gentle currents. The kids let out sighs of relief, their worry dissipating like ripples on the water.
As the deer family swam towards the riverbank, the fishermen and the kids watched in awe, their hearts filled with gratitude for the resilience and beauty of nature.

The pontoon boat continued to glide smoothly down the river, leaving the family of deer behind, and the group of friends let out a collective sigh of relief. Putz, the driver of the pontoon, increases the speed, eager to take them further downstream. Hayley, Bo, Ryan, Andy, Cassidy, and Charlotte turn their attention away from the deer and focus on the journey ahead.

Unbeknownst to them, the family of deer make it to the river's coast. The last fawn continues to bob in the water. As the other deer exit the river and disappear into the safety of the forest, the little fawn is left behind. Between two groups of fisherman, a compassionate man notices the distressed fawn and decides to lend a helping hand.

With a caring heart, the fisherman wades into the water, reaching out to assist the stranded baby deer. He gently attempts to lift it out of the water, hoping to guide it to safety. To his horror, he only manages to lift the fawn's head, which is detached from its body. Shocked and confused, the fisherman immediately releases the head, his mind filled with questions and concern.

He gazes out to the river, trying to comprehend what could have caused such a tragic sight. Thoughts of a boat's propeller crossing the fisherman's mind, but the isolated nature of the incident leaves him puzzled. He wonders if something more mysterious and sinister could be lurking beneath the river's surface.

Back on the pontoon, the group of friends continues their journey, blissfully unaware of the dark discovery made by the fisherman. The river flows peacefully around them, but unknown to them, a sense of unease lingers beneath the calm waters. The day's adventure has taken an unexpected turn, and the secrets of the river begin to unravel, hinting at something more profound and enigmatic lying ahead.

On the pontoon boat, the atmosphere is a mix of curiosity and concern as the kids discuss the mysterious occurrence of the fawn. They exchange glances, each trying to make sense of what they had witnessed.

Bo breaks the silence, "You guys think maybe a large snakehead pulled it under? I've heard those things can be aggressive."

Andy nods thoughtfully, "Could be. Or maybe it got caught in an underwater tide pool or a strong current that dragged it down."

Hayley chimes in, "Maybe it was disoriented and weak and it went under, but somehow managed to summon more strength to resurface."

Putz, who has always been attuned to nature, leans in with a gentle smile, "Nature is full of mysteries, kids. Sometimes we may never know the answers to everything that happens out here. It's just the way things are."

Bo nods in agreement, "You're right, Putz. But maybe we should report it to the police or the rangers. They should know what happened, in case it's something serious."

Putz pats Bo on the shoulder, "It's a good idea to be vigilant. If you feel it's necessary, we'll let them know once we're back on land."

The boat continues down the river, the conversation occasionally returning to the incident with the fawn. As they soak in the beauty of nature around them, they are reminded of its unpredictability and its delicate balance.

Bo's voice filled with determination as he spoke up, "Guys, I really think we should report what we saw. Something doesn't feel right about the fawn's disappearance below the water. It was like it was pulled under the water. We need to let the police know."

Ryan nodded, acknowledging Bo's concern. "You're right, Bo. It did seem as if something pulled the fawn under. Maybe you're right about it being a giant snakehead."

Cassidy added, her voice filled with worry, "Snakeheads are an invasive species, and they can have a devastating impact on native fish populations. I am not sure if one would go after a deer but I guess the larger the snakehead, the larger the appetite."

Hayley chimed in, "I agree. Let's report it."

As the kids approached a group of police officers, their attention was immediately drawn to the exhausted figure of the river witch. She sat on a stone wall with her head hung low, her presence captivating and mysterious. The police officers stood nearby, keeping a watchful eye on her but maintaining a respectful distance.

Ryan hesitated for a moment, considering whether it was appropriate to approach. Andy suggests waiting, but Ryan assured the group that they can just inform the officers and leave without intruding. With a shared nod, they gathered their courage and approached the scene.

As they drew closer, the river witch suddenly lifted her head and locked eyes with Bo, gripping his shirt sleeves tightly. Her voice broke through the air, filled with a mix of desperation and urgency as she repeated her peculiar chant, "Ret Snom - Ret Snom - AWA ATS."

Startled by the unexpected encounter, the kids glanced at each other, unsure of how to react. The police officers swiftly intervened, attempting to calm the old woman and gently pry her hands off Bo's sleeves.

Ryan stepped forward, his voice steady and empathetic, "We apologize if we've caused any disturbance. We simply wanted to report something we witnessed—an incident involving a baby deer which appeared to have been pulled down beneath the water. We thought it might be important to bring to your attention."

The river witch's eyes widened, her expression shifting from distress to a mixture of confusion and recognition. She released her grip on Bo and took a step back, still muttering softly to herself.

Approaching the group, one of the officers, a compassionate woman, addressed the kids, her tone soothing, "Thank you for letting us know. We'll certainly look into it."

Hayley, always eager to help, and secretly wanting to ask the old woman questions, offered her assistance, "Is there anything we can do to help her? Maybe we can try to understand what she's trying to say."

The officer appreciated Hayley's concern, her voice filled with gratitude, "Your willingness to help is commendable. She has her own unique way of expressing herself, and we're doing our best to understand and communicate with her. For now, it's important to give her the space she needs."

Curiosity brimming within her, Cass couldn't resist asking, "What does she mean by 'Ret Snom' and 'AWA ATS'? Do those words hold any significance?"

Pausing for a moment, the officer shifts her gaze toward the river witch, observing her in contemplation. "I think she's Dutch."

Grateful for the officers' dedication and insight, the kids express their appreciation and understanding. They take a step back, allowing the river witch and the officers to focus on their interaction.

Walking away from the scene, the group reflects on the encounter. Though they couldn't report the incident with the fawn accordingly, they recognize the importance of compassion and understanding in such complex situations. They hope that the authorities' efforts will lead to unraveling the mysteries surrounding both the river witch and the reason the fawn was pulled below the water.

As the kids continue their walk, their eyes are drawn to three fishermen who pass by them, their strides burdened by the weight of a colossal snakehead fish. The creature's massive size, measuring around 7 feet, captivates their attention. Bo's mind races with curiosity, contemplating whether a fish of that magnitude would be capable of targeting and overpowering a baby deer.

His thoughts spill out as he poses the question to his friends, "Do you think a fish like that could pull down a baby deer? I mean, it is huge!"

Andy considers the idea, his brow furrowing in contemplation. "It's hard to say. Snakeheads are known to be aggressive predators, but their usual prey consists of smaller fish, amphibians, and even small mammals. A fawn would be quite a challenge for a fish, even one as large as that."

Cassidy interjects, her eyes fixed on the snakehead being carried by the fishermen, "But who knows? Nature can be unpredictable, and we've already seen some unusual things today. Maybe a snakehead felt ambitious or it felt threatened. It's hard to imagine, though."

The group falls into a momentary silence as they walk along the base of Foul Rift, their thoughts absorbed in the mysteries of the river. The gushing sound of the rushing water provides a steady soundtrack to their contemplations.

Bo glances back towards the boat launch area, still processing the encounter with the river witch, and muses, "Perhaps there's more to this river than we could ever imagine. Maybe there's a reason why Captain Kidd chose this place to hide his treasure."

The group continues their walk, their minds buzzing with thoughts and questions. They can't help but feel that there's a connection threading through the events of the day—a web of intrigue, mystery, and unforeseen encounters waiting to be unraveled.

In the days that followed, the memory of the fawn remained etched in the hearts of the 6 friends, leaving a lasting impact on their journey and strengthening their resolve in their pursuit of Kidd's treasure. The image of the fawn disappearing beneath the river's surface served as a constant reminder of the risks and challenges they might encounter on their quest, propelling them forward with unwavering determination. It ignited a deeper sense of purpose, uniting them in their mission to unravel the enigmatic mysteries concealed within the depths of Foul Rift. Each step they took was now infused with a profound sense of responsibility, and they knew that they couldn't turn back until they had unearthed the hidden truths and reclaimed the long-lost treasure of Captain Kidd.

Chapter 9:

The River Witch

School is finally out, and the long-awaited summer vacation has arrived. The days blend into a haze of freedom and endless possibilities. The six friends find themselves gathered at Ryan's house, their laughter and excited chatter filling the air.

Hayley sits in a cozy corner, lost in her own thoughts. Her mind is consumed by the enigma of Captain Kidd's treasure. She can't help but fixate on the idea that it might be hidden within one of the caves near the eddy they discovered during their trip to Mack Island. The possibility lingers in her mind like a tantalizing secret waiting to be unveiled.

Meanwhile, the rest of the group engages in the typical activities of carefree summer days. They sprawl across the living room, their energy vibrating with a shared sense of camaraderie and anticipation. The room is alive with the sounds of their laughter, the clattering of board games, and the occasional burst of music from a nearby speaker.

Ryan's mom pops in, offering snacks and refreshing drinks, her warm smile mirroring the summer sunshine streaming through the windows. She knows how precious these moments are and cherishes the friendships that have blossomed between the six young adventurers.

Cass flips through a magazine, occasionally sharing interesting tidbits with the group. Andy is engrossed in a video game, his eyes focused and fingers dancing across the controller. Bo challenges Charlotte to a friendly game of Connect Four, their competitive spirit fueling their laughter and banter.

Amidst the carefree atmosphere, the topic of the treasure resurfaces. The friends gather around Hayley, intrigued by her persistent thoughts and theories. They offer their own ideas and suggestions, each contributing to the ever-growing tapestry of possibilities.

As the evening stretches on, the sun casting its golden hues across the sky, the friends relish in the simplicity of being together. Their summer adventures await, brimming with excitement, mystery, and the promise of cherished memories.

Ryan, excitement gleaming in his eyes, gestures for his friends to gather around as he shows them a video he discovered on social media. It was shared by a friend of a friend of one of the fishermen at the snakehead river-derby. The video depicts the River Witch, captured in her intense moment of distress. The friends huddle close, their curiosity piqued, eager to decipher the cryptic messages she attempts to convey.

As the video plays, the River Witch's words spill out in a jumbled, reversed manner, a linguistic puzzle that demands their attention. Hayley, being particularly intrigued, focuses intently, her mind racing with possibilities. The rest of the group follows suit, their eyes fixed on the screen, ears attuned to the garbled sounds.

Silence envelops the room as they listen, straining to discern the hidden meaning behind the River Witch's backwards speech. Each word becomes a piece of a complex puzzle, and they embark on a collective mission to unravel the tangled threads of her message.

Ryan, with his sharp intuition, picks up on a recurring phrase. Andy, always attentive to details, notices patterns within the reversed words and offers his insights. Cassidy, armed with her research skills, quickly scours the internet for linguistic resources to aid in the translation.

As they collaborate and exchange ideas, a sense of excitement fills the air. The friends lean in closer, their collective intelligence and determination merging to decipher the enigmatic language of the river witch. They are determined to bring clarity to her words.

As Bo frantically writes down the reversed words spoken by the River Witch, Hayley's eyes widen with realization. She interrupts his scribbling and exclaims, "Wait, Bo, I think I understand what she's saying!" The group looks at her, eager for an explanation.

Hayley takes a moment to gather her thoughts before continuing, "She's saying 'danger, danger, monster!' It's not just random words, it's a warning!" Bo stops writing and looks at Hayley in astonishment. The others lean in, captivated by her revelation.

Hayley explains, "Think about it. The river witch, in her own way of speaking, is trying to alert everyone to a potential threat." Her words hang in the air, filling the room with a sense of unease.

Cassidy: Do you think she was warning every one of the snakeheads? Something did pull that fawn under.

The group falls into a contemplative silence as they absorb the gravity of the situation. The idea of a lurking monster in their midst sends shivers down their spines, but it also fuels their determination to uncover the truth.

With newfound urgency, they realize that the treasure hunt has transformed into something much bigger. It's no longer just about uncovering Captain Kidd's treasure; it's about solving the mystery of the river and ensuring the safety of their town.

As their minds race with possibilities, they begin to discuss their next steps.

Andy: Let's go see her. She might tell us why she was yelling "danger and monster". We can also find out if she has seen any clues in the woods that would help us. She lives out there, she probably has seen something. We will bring her some food to help her. We can trade it for information.

Ryan: I agree; it could be valuable to learn from her first hand. But we have to be careful and plan how we are going to approach her.

Cassidy: I understand the idea of asking her what she meant and to see if she has come across anything out there that might help us find the treasure, but she can also be dangerous. We need to think about this.

Hayley: I think we should go, but we have to be cautious. Let's do what Andy said and bring her some food and let her know that we want to help her.

Ryan: Yeah, we will approach her calmly. If she seems agitated, we will keep our distance and still try to communicate.

Andy: It's a risky idea, but it might be worth it. We should prepare ourselves and have a plan in case things don't go as expected.

Ryan: Alright, let's gather some supplies and make sure we're prepared. We'll approach her with caution, keeping our safety in mind. Everyone, make sure your phones are fully charged. Let's bring her a couple of jugs of clean water and maybe some canned food. We can also bring her a sandwich that she can eat while we are there.

The evening sky transformed into a canvas of warm hues as the sun set behind the horizon, bidding farewell to the day. The town of Foul Rift gradually quiets down, with the streets bathed in a soft twilight glow. Each member of the group carries with them a sense of anticipation and determination as they part ways, preparing for the meeting with the river witch.

In their homes, they gather their thoughts and finalize their plans, ensuring they have everything they need to help the river witch and seek the answers they seek. Excitement fills the air, mingling with a touch of nervousness, as they envision the possibilities that lie ahead. They exchange messages and phone calls, discussing strategies and sharing their hopes for the encounter.

As the night deepens, the residents of Foul Rift find solace in the comfort of their homes. The gentle hum of cicadas drifts through the open windows, lulling them into a peaceful slumber. Dreams of mysteries and revelations dance in their minds, fueling their eagerness for the coming day.

In the morning, the small town of Foul Rift slowly awakens to a new day, one filled with purpose and determination. The group gathers outside of Rambo's, their hearts filled with anticipation. They bring with them the offerings of food and drinks.

Embraced by the gentle warmth of the morning sun, the town of Foul Rift stirs to life. The vibrant hues of dawn paint the sky as the six friends gather their supplies and mount their bicycles, ready to embark on their mission. Their journey takes them across the town, navigating the quiet streets and relishing in the tranquility of the early morning.

Pedaling with purpose, they make their way towards the edge of town, where the old out-buildings behind the bio-science labs await their arrival. These abandoned structures, remnants of a bygone era, hold the secrets and stories of the past. The land, once belonging to the esteemed William Penn and later purchased by a wealthy industrialist to be used as a tile factory, were later entrusted to the state; they now stand as a testament to history and an open invitation to exploration.

The friends navigate the winding path that leads to the hidden gems of the property, passing through thickets of trees and catching glimpses of wildlife along the way. As they approach the old out-buildings, a sense of anticipation hangs in the air. The weathered structures stand as silent witnesses to the passage of time, their weathered facades hinting at the stories they hold within their walls. The group dismounts their bicycles and secures them against nearby trees, their excitement growing with each step closer to their destination.

Standing outside, the row of out-buildings, the kids find themselves captivated by the eerie atmosphere that surrounds them. The buildings, each constructed with brick and stone, create a hauntingly beautiful scene. Two of them display a surprising level of preservation, while the third succumbs to the weight of time with its collapsed roof.

As the morning sun casts long shadows across the worn facades, a sense of foreboding fills the air. The buildings, with their darkened windows and silent interiors, exude a haunting presence that sends shivers down the spines of the young adventurers. It's as if they hold untold secrets and stories within their walls, waiting to be discovered by those brave enough to venture inside.

The comparison to the buildings that housed the three little pigs does not escape Cassidy's observation. The stark contrast between the sturdy structures and the dilapidated one evokes a sense of caution and uncertainty. Like the fable, the kids can't help but wonder what lies within these enigmatic buildings.

Despite the creeping fear that tugs at their hearts, the allure of the unknown beckons the children forward. They exchange nervous glances, their curiosity outweighing their trepidation. With a shared understanding, they steel themselves for the mysteries that wait within the dimly lit interiors.

Taking a collective deep breath, they approach the entrance of the first intact building, their steps accompanied by the crunch of gravel beneath their feet. The creak of a rusty hinge echoes through the air as they push open the heavy door, revealing an empty space waiting to be explored. They brace themselves, prepared to face whatever secrets and surprises these ancient structures hold.

In the face of uncertainty, the six friends draw strength from each other, their bond growing stronger with every step they take into the unknown. As they cross the threshold, their hearts pounding with a mixture of fear and excitement, they venture deeper into the darkness. The friends are enveloped in an atmosphere of faded grandeur. Sunlight filters through cracks in the walls, casting ethereal rays that illuminate the dust particles dancing in the air. The creaking floors and echoes of their footsteps serve as a reminder of the history that lies dormant within these forgotten walls.

With cautious curiosity, they explore the rooms, their eyes scanning the remnants of the past. Each corner holds the potential for discovery, and the friends feel a connection to the stories that unfolded within these forgotten walls.

As they venture deeper into the heart of the first building, their anticipation reaches its peak. The river witch's dwelling awaits, tucked away somewhere in one of the buildings. It stands as a sanctuary for the enigmatic woman, who has found solace amidst the forgotten buildings.

The friends approach a closed door, their hearts filled with a mixture of apprehension and compassion. They carry their supplies, symbols of their goodwill and determination, ready to extend a helping hand to someone who has been cast aside by society. In their collective presence, they bring the warmth of friendship and a glimmer of hope to the river witch's secluded world.

In this moment, as they stand before a blackened door, the six friends embody the essence of adventure, resilience, and the power of human connection. Their journey has led them to this point, where mysteries intertwine with history and compassion intertwines with curiosity. They take a deep breath, their spirits alight with anticipation, and with a shared resolve, they knock on the door, ready to embrace the unknown that awaits within.

Ryan takes a step forward and lightly taps on the metallic door, calling out, "Hello, we've brought some food and other things for you." They pause for a moment, waiting in anticipation. Ryan glances back at their companions, shrugging his shoulders in uncertainty. Feeling a sense of persistence, he taps on the door once more, but there is no response.

Hayley, sensing the growing tension, bravely steps forward and firmly grasps the doorknob. With a steady hand, she slowly turns it and cautiously pushes the door open, creating a small gap to peek inside. Their hearts beat rapidly in their chests, their nerves intensifying as they await what lies beyond the threshold.

With determination, Hayley persists in pushing the door open wider, allowing the group of six to peer inside. The sight that greets them is an aging storage room, enveloped in an air of neglect. In the far corner, a small mattress lies, its surface marred by dirt and unsightly stains. A couple of steel shelves stand empty, devoid of any contents.

Across from the mattress, cracked plastic storage containers occupy the opposing corner, revealing the passage of time. Although there are no windows, faint beams of light manage to seep through minuscule cracks in the brick walls and roof, casting an ethereal glow upon the room. The collective tension within the group remains palpable as they take in the scene before them.

As the six individuals step into the room, their gazes fixate on the somber surroundings. Andy breaks the silence, his voice tinged with empathy, "This must be where she sleeps." The weight of the situation hangs heavy upon each of them, as they absorb the sight before them. A sense of melancholy grips their hearts, each person grappling with their own emotions.

Questions swirl within their minds, an unspoken chorus of concerns. They ponder the unfortunate circumstances that led this woman to seek solace within the confines of an abandoned building nestled deep within the woods. Their thoughts wander, contemplating the absence of her family and the reasons why they have seemingly allowed her to dwell in this desolate place. The room becomes a symbol of the mysteries and hardships this woman has endured, and the six individuals are left grappling with a mix of sympathy, curiosity, and a desire to understand her story.

Charlotte's voice breaks the pensive silence, her tone filled with curiosity and concern. "I wonder where she is," she muses aloud, her eyes scanning the room for any clues.

Bo, contemplating the possibilities, offers a suggestion. "Perhaps she saw us approaching and decided to leave," he speculates, recognizing the uncertainty of the situation. Ryan, ever the pragmatist, interjects with another possibility. "Or maybe she wasn't here at all," he suggests, acknowledging that their assumptions may not align with reality.

The group falls into contemplative silence once more, each grappling with the myriad of possibilities surrounding the absence of the woman they sought. Their minds swirl with unanswered questions, leaving them to ponder the enigmatic circumstances further. The room, once filled with a sense of hope to find her, now carries a lingering air of uncertainty.

Bo breaks the silence with a question that hangs heavy in the air, "So now what?" His words resonate with a mix of uncertainty and anticipation, as the group contemplates their next course of action. Yet, before any response can be given, an unexpected occurrence startles them all.

In a sudden and dramatic fashion, the door they had entered through slams shut with a resounding thud. The sound of a lock engaging echoes through the room, freezing everyone in their tracks. The six individuals turn swiftly, their eyes widening in shock as they collectively stare at the now securely sealed door.

Reacting swiftly, Hayley instinctively dashes towards the door, her heart pounding with a mix of fear and determination. She reaches for the doorknob, desperately attempting to twist it open. But her efforts are in vain, for the door remains steadfastly locked, refusing to yield to her touch.

A sense of alarm and unease fills the room, their minds grappling with the sudden turn of events. The realization of being trapped inside this enigmatic space takes hold, leaving the group with an unsettling blend of trepidation and a pressing need to uncover the truth that awaits them.

Driven by a mixture of fear and urgency, Hayley starts forcefully banging on the door, her voice intermingling with the sharp sound of her fists striking the unyielding surface. "Let us out!" she shouts, her voice filled with desperation. Andrew and Ryan swiftly join her, their combined voices resonating through the room as they implore the unseen individuals on the other side to release them from their confining predicament.

Their pleas reverberate through the air, echoing into the unknown, but there is no response, only an eerie silence. Yet, amidst the silence, a faint but distinct sound reaches their ears—a murmur, a rustle, evidence that there is indeed a person on the other side of the door. It fuels their determination, knowing that they have been heard, but the absence of any verbal reply deepens the mystery and raises more questions.

Undeterred, they continue shouting, their words punctuated by frustration and growing anxiety. The room seems to vibrate with their collective urgency, their voices carrying a plea for freedom and answers. But still, there is no answer, no reassurance from the other side. The enigmatic presence on the other end of the door remains silent, leaving the group to grapple with the unsettling realization that they are not alone and that their fate lies in the hands of the river witch.

As panic envelops the group, their collective efforts of banging and shouting through the door prove futile, leaving them increasingly trapped and desperate. Realizing the need for a different approach, Ryan takes charge, urging his companions to stay calm amidst the chaos. With a determined tone, he asserts that they must find an alternative way out of their confining predicament.

Ryan instructs everyone to search their surroundings diligently, hoping to discover a hidden exit or any sign of weakness that could be exploited. Bo promptly directs his attention to the door, examining it closely for any potential vulnerabilities. Meanwhile, Hayley and Cass turn their focus to the plastic bins, meticulously sifting through their contents in search of any clues or useful items.

Charlotte, torn between her reluctance to touch the dirt-streaked and stained mattress, steels herself and cautiously investigates the area around it, considering the possibility of uncovering something significant beneath its surface. Simultaneously, Ryan scans the room, assessing the shelves and surroundings, hoping to identify any overlooked possibilities or hidden pathways.

The room becomes a flurry of activity as each individual methodically explores their designated areas, driven by the shared goal of escaping their confinement. The urgency remains palpable, but amidst the chaos, a glimmer of hope emerges—the possibility of finding a solution and reclaiming their freedom.

Hayley's voice carries a hint of disappointment as she announces her findings, "There's nothing in here but a few shirts and blankets!" Charlotte echoes her sentiment, expressing her reluctance to touch the soiled mattress, inviting others to investigate it instead.

Meanwhile, Ryan's attention remains fixed on the steel shelves, his mind working through various possibilities of how they could be utilized. Andy, filled with a mix of frustration and desperation, steps closer to the door. He takes a deep breath, attempting to compose himself, before addressing the mysterious lady on the other side.

In a pleading tone, Andy's voice resonates through the door, his words laced with a genuine appeal, "Please, ma'am, we mean no harm. We're trapped in here and just want to find a way out. Can you please find it in your heart to let us go?" His voice carries a blend of sincerity and vulnerability, hoping that the lady will hear their plea and show them mercy.

Moved by Andy's plea, Hayley steps closer to the door, her voice intertwining with his as she adds her own earnest appeal. She emphasizes that they have brought food, water, and clothing, assuring the person behind the door that their intention is to help. Hayley implores the unseen figure to open the door so they can offer their assistance.

Suddenly, a voice breaks the silence, but the words uttered are unintelligible and garbled. "Reg Nad Reth Erb Reg Nad," it echoes, a jumble of nonsensical syllables. The peculiar language spoken confirms the unsettling truth— the river witch, the enigmatic figure they had heard whispers about, is the one who has locked them inside.

A shiver of apprehension ripples through the group as they exchange bewildered glances, realizing the true identity of their captor. The witch's actions raise more questions, leaving them to wonder why they have been trapped and what her intentions may be. Faced with this enigma, they must find a way to navigate the mystery that surrounds them.

Hayley's voice carries a mixture of urgency and desperation as she pleads once again, "Please, Miss, let us out!" Her words hang in the air, filled with a desperate hope for mercy. Meanwhile, Ryan experiences a sudden revelation, an epiphany that stirs within him.

Silently, Ryan retrieves his cell phone from his pocket, realizing that he holds a crucial piece of the puzzle within its digital confines. Accessing his photos, he scrolls through the images he took during the search party in the woods. His gaze lingers on the photographs of the carved logs, captivated by the engraved markings. As he examines them closely, a realization dawns upon him. He reads the engraving backward, and its meaning becomes clear - it spells "danger."

The revelation shakes Ryan to his core. The carvings were not the innocent markers he initially believed them to be. They were the handiwork of the river witch herself. But why? Questions flood Ryan's mind, diverting his attention from the immediate need to escape the locked room. He contemplates the meaning behind the witch's actions - why she yelled at the Snakehead River Derby, why she grabbed Bo at the boat launch. Is she truly insane, or is there a deeper purpose behind her seemingly erratic behavior? Could it be that she is attempting to protect them from something?

As the group continues their efforts to escape, Ryan's newfound understanding adds a layer of complexity to their situation. Uncovering the river witch's motives becomes not only a quest for freedom but also a pursuit of understanding, an exploration into the enigmatic nature of the witch and her intentions.

Ryan's voice cuts through the stillness, resolute and filled with a mixture of determination and curiosity. "Are you trying to protect us from something?" he calls out, hoping to elicit a response from the enigmatic river witch on the other side of the door. However, silence continues to reign, leaving his question hanging in the air unanswered.

Undeterred by the absence of a reply, Ryan's determination remains unwavering. He knows that escaping from this locked room is paramount, and he won't be swayed from his mission. His mind races, contemplating alternative strategies and possibilities to find an exit.

With a renewed focus, Ryan turns to his companions, sharing his determination. "We need to keep searching for another way out," he asserts, his voice resolute. The group's shared resolve strengthens as they rally behind Ryan's leadership, their determination to escape unscathed fueling their actions.

Amidst the uncertainty, the enigma of the river witch, and the unanswered questions, they press forward, united in their pursuit of freedom. The room becomes a scene of relentless exploration and resourcefulness as they continue their quest to find an escape route, refusing to be confined by the witch's locked door.

Andy's gaze shifts upward, scanning the roof intently as his eyes widen with a newfound hope. "Look up there!

The edge of the roof is rotting. You can see the light seeping through from the outside," he exclaims, excitement lacing his voice. The possibility of a potential escape route sparks a surge of determination within the group.

Embracing Andy's idea, Ryan swiftly springs into action, relying on his quick thinking. He positions the steel shelves beneath the compromised area of the ceiling that Andy had identified. With calculated movements, he arranges the mattress behind the shelves, providing a cushioned landing should he encounter any mishaps during his ascent.

However, realizing that his height is a hindrance to reaching the opening, Ryan yields his position to Andy, recognizing that his friend's taller stature may prove more advantageous. With a seamless swap, Andy takes Ryan's place, poised and ready to make his attempt.

With a focused determination, Andy begins punching and pushing at the weakened edge of the roof. Each strike carries a growing impact, causing the opening to widen gradually. Rays of light stream into the room, illuminating their path to freedom with each forceful blow. A renewed sense of anticipation fills the air as they witness tangible progress in their quest to break free.

As the opening in the ceiling becomes just large enough for a small person to pass through, Ryan recognizes that Bo, being the smallest of the group, is the most suitable candidate for the task. He carefully explains to Bo that he must climb out and make his way back inside the room they originally entered, in order to open the locked door.

Bo, aware of the importance of his role, begins climbing up the steel shelves, guided by Ryan's instructions. Despite his best efforts, he struggles to reach the opening. Ryan swiftly adapts his plan, instructing Bo to keep his hands against the wall to steady himself and maintain his balance. Adjusting their positions, Ryan instructs Andy to hold one end of the shelf, while Cassidy takes hold of the middle section.

With their combined efforts, Hayley, and Charlotte stand close to Bo, ready to assist in case he loses his footing. As the three lift the shelf off the ground, Bo is propelled closer to the opening. Ryan's voice resonates with urgency and encouragement, "Bo, jump and grab the opening! Pull yourself through!"

Bo summons his courage and propels himself upward reaching out for the opening with determination. The group holds their breath, their collective focus solely on Bo's successful escape. They stand ready to catch him if needed, their unwavering support fueling his resolve. Bo grabs the edge of the concrete blocks and hoists himself up using his feet and legs as leverage. With every ounce of strength, Bo pulls and advances himself though the opening enduring pokes and scratches from the decaying lumber. With a resounding thud, Bo's feet land on the soft earth, he looks up at the blue sky; he is free.

As Bo's footsteps carry him towards the building where he initially entered, a torrent of thoughts swirls through his mind. The possibility of encountering the river witch within the room fills him with apprehension. What would he do if she were there? How would he handle such a confrontation? These questions taunt his thoughts, adding an extra layer of tension to his actions.

Taking caution, Bo moves stealthily, seeking to approach the doors without revealing his presence. He cautiously peeks through the door, his eyes scanning the room beyond. To his relief, there is no sign of the river witch. It appears she has vanished, leaving no trace behind. A surge of anger courses through Bo's veins, fueled by the realization that she had seemingly abandoned them to their fate.

In the midst of his frustration, Bo's determination strengthens. He refuses to let the river witch's actions crush their spirits. Instead, he harnesses his anger as motivation, knowing that their escape relies on his ability to navigate the situation effectively.

Bo approaches the blackened door that had sealed shut behind them, cautiously examining the area for any signs of the river witch. To his surprise and a stroke of luck, he spots the key that she had used to lock them in, still lodged within the door. Relief washes over him as he realizes that the means of their escape lies within his grasp.

With a steadying breath, Bo reaches out, gripping the key firmly. He turns it in the lock, feeling the mechanism shift, and the door swings open before him. The sight that greets his eyes fills him with joy and a sense of triumph. The smiles on his friends' faces mirror his own feelings of liberation.

Hayley rushes forward, enveloping Bo in a warm, heartfelt hug, expressing her pride and gratitude for his bravery. The group rejoices in their newfound freedom, their shared ordeal now a testament to their resilience and unity.

In that moment, the weight of the locked room and the river witch's actions dissolve, replaced by the triumph of overcoming adversity. Together, they stand as a testament to the strength that lies within friendship, determination, and the unwavering spirit to reclaim their freedom.

As the six friends collect themselves, a sense of determination fills the air. They exchange knowing glances, silently affirming their shared understanding that it's time to leave the haunting building behind. Retracing their steps, they navigate their way out, stepping back into the open air that surrounds them.

Gratefulness washes over the group as they breathe in the fresh, untainted atmosphere, savoring the freedom they now embrace. They scan their surroundings, searching for any sign of the river witch's presence. The peacefulness that envelops the area brings them a moment of respite, but the nagging thought of the witch lingers in their minds.

Suddenly, Charlotte's sharp eyes catch sight of movement in one of the other outbuildings. She focuses her gaze, her heart skipping a beat as she locks eyes with the river witch peering out from a window. In an instant, the witch retreats, concealing herself behind the protective wall. Filled with a mix of astonishment and urgency, Charlotte calls out to her friends, "I saw her... over there... in the window!"

Ryan, sensing the need to leave the lingering presence of the witch behind, asserts, "Let's get out of here, like now."

Hayley's resolute voice cuts through the air as she objects to the notion of turning back. Her determination radiates from her as she declares, "No. We didn't come all this way to turn back now. She is more afraid of us than we are of her. Let's go talk to her."

Her words hang in the air, met with skepticism and concern from the rest of the group. They exchange uncertain glances, torn between caution and curiosity. Reluctantly, the others acknowledge Hayley's conviction, deciding to trust in her judgment and follow her lead.

With cautious steps, they join Hayley as she heads towards the second outbuilding, the air thick with anticipation. Each footfall carries a mix of trepidation and a determination to seek understanding. They approach the building, their hearts beating in unison as they brace themselves for the unknown encounter with the river witch.

Hayley approaches the door of the second building, her hand reaching out to gently knock on it. "Hello, I am coming in. We are not here to hurt you," she announces, her voice filled with reassurance. Slowly, she turns the doorknob and steps inside, her friends following closely behind.

Andy, concerned for their safety, volunteers to stay outside, keeping a watchful eye in case of any unforeseen circumstances. Hayley pushes the door open, revealing a dimly lit and dingy room, reminiscent of the one they had encountered in the first building. In the corner, they see the river witch, her expression reflecting fear and uncertainty.

Approaching the river witch with caution, Hayley introduces herself, her voice gentle yet firm. "Hello, my name is Hayley. We have come here to help," she says, extending a hand in a gesture of goodwill. She reassures the witch that they mean no harm and explains their genuine intentions to assist her.

The room holds an atmosphere of tension and apprehension, the air thick with unspoken questions. As Hayley reaches out, hoping to bridge the gap between them, the true test of empathy and understanding unfolds.

Ryan, recognizing the river witch's apprehension, carefully retrieves food and water from his bag. Holding them up, he locks eyes with her, his voice filled with sincerity. "This is for you," he says, extending a gesture of kindness. He places the provisions gently on the floor, near her feet.

His words hang in the air, as the river witch continues to gaze at the offerings, her emotions veiled behind a shroud of uncertainty. Ryan takes a step back, allowing her space to process the gesture and understand their intentions. Sensing that there is more they can offer, he continues, "We also brought you some clean clothes and other necessities."

The room remains silent, the weight of the moment palpable. Ryan's actions and words are an attempt to bridge the gap of understanding and extend compassion to someone who has been shrouded in mystery. As they await the river witch's response, hope lingers in the air, mingled with a sense of trepidation, as they wait to see if their offer will be accepted.

Hayley's voice carries a gentle tone as she poses a question to the river witch, seeking understanding and clarity. "Why did you lock us in the room and leave us? We could have died in there," she expresses, her concern evident in her words.

The river witch's gaze meets Hayley's, and the room fills with an expectant silence. The weight of their shared experience hangs in the air, the consequences of her actions still echoing within their hearts. Hayley's inquiry carries the hopes of uncovering the reasoning behind the river witch's choices, yearning for an explanation that could shed light on their encounter.

As time seems to stretch, they wait, their eyes fixed upon the river witch, awaiting her response. The room remains cloaked in uncertainty, the opportunity for understanding and connection hanging in the balance.

As the river witch extends her hands towards Hayley, her voice repeating the word that resembles "face," a poignant expression lingers on her face. Hayley, caught in a moment of confusion, echoes the word in a questioning manner, attempting to grasp its meaning. "Face? What do you mean by 'face'?" she asks, her voice tinged with bewilderment.

In that moment, Bo, ever perceptive, interjects, reminding them that the river witch's speech is reversed. He carefully begins sounding out the word "face" backward, his realization dawning upon him. "Safe," he blurts out, his voice filled with revelation. The word "safe" resonates within the room, unveiling the true intention behind the river witch's message.

A glimmer of understanding flickers across the faces of the friends. The river witch, with her limited ability to communicate, had been trying to convey a message of safety all along. The tear that rolls down her cheek serves as a testament to the genuine concern she holds for their well-being.

"You wanted to keep us safe?" Hayley's question hangs in the air, seeking confirmation from the river witch that her intention had indeed been to keep them safe. The river witch nods in response, affirming Hayley's understanding. Sensing the group's curiosity, Cassidy asks a probing question, "From what? What did you want to keep us safe from?"

The river witch's gaze shifts to Cassidy, a flicker of fear in her eyes. With a burst of emotion, she blurts out a word that sounds like "Eev Rahh" before tears stream down her face. Frustrated by her inability to fully communicate, she resorts to using her finger to draw an oval on the ground, with four lines extending from it.

Ryan's mind races to decode her message, drawing connections between her fragmented words. "Eev Rahh backwards is RV," he explains. The river witch confirms his interpretation with a nod. Curiosity lingers in the air as Cassidy speaks up, pondering the significance of RV. "Is that an RV, as in a recreational vehicle?" she asks, her voice filled with curiosity. Charlotte chimes in, connecting the dots, "I think she's drawing a motorhome."

The river witch's attention turns to the food nearby, the tantalizing aroma irresistible to her senses. She moves toward it, her actions speaking louder than words. It is a sub sandwich that Ryan had gotten from Rambos, the taste of which proves too enticing to resist.

The group observes the river witch's response, contemplating the newfound pieces of information they have gathered. The significance of the motorhome and the river witch's connection to it remains a mystery, but with each revelation, they inch closer to understanding her intentions and the depths of her fears.

As the river witch enjoys her sandwich, the six friends engage in a flurry of discussion, trying to unravel the mystery of the RV and its connection to the two individuals who had disappeared. Theories are shared, conjectures are made, yet none of the pieces seem to fit together seamlessly.

Amidst the puzzlement, Ryan retrieves his phone and takes a seat next to the river witch, his curiosity piqued. Introducing himself, he establishes a sense of familiarity and trust. "My name is Ryan," he says, his voice gentle. With a sense of anticipation, he poses his question, displaying the photo of the log with the carved word "Reg Nad" on his phone.

Ryan seeks confirmation, his gaze fixed on the river witch, waiting for her response. The river witch looks at the photo, her eyes filled with recognition. She nods in agreement, her voice repeating the words "Reg Nad... Face." Ryan echoes her words, connecting the dots. "So, danger... safe," he says, the realization washing over him. The river witch nods, affirming his understanding.

In this moment of clarity, a shared understanding begins to take shape. The carvings on the logs were indeed a warning, a way for the river witch to communicate the presence of danger while also ensuring their safety. A sense of gratitude and respect fills the air as they start to comprehend the river witch's actions and the lengths she went to protect them.

As Ryan continues to flip through the photos on his phone, a particular image catches his eye. It is a picture taken by Andy, depicting him standing proudly alongside Ambrose, both holding up a snakehead fish at the derby. Andy had forwarded it to everyone that day. The river witch's eyes lock onto the photo, her gaze fixated on the captured moment. In a burst of emotion, she points vehemently at the photo of the fish, repeating the words "Rets Nom... Rets Nom..."

Ryan's mind races to decipher the meaning behind her fervent outburst. His understanding sharpens as he connects the river witch's words to the image before him. "Rets Nom," he repeats softly, realizing that it translates to "monster." Suddenly, the river witch's behavior takes a drastic turn.

She springs to her feet, consumed by an uncontrollable rage. Her screams and shouts fill the room, her emotions spiraling out of control. The six friends, taken aback by this sudden change, attempt to calm her down, offering reassurances and gestures of understanding. However, their efforts only seem to intensify her distress.

Hayley's voice breaks through the chaos, her words tinged with concern. "I think we should go, guys," she suggests, her empathy guiding her decision. "She's upset, and our presence seems to be making the situation worse. Let's give her the peace she needs."

With a shared understanding, the group reluctantly acknowledges the wisdom in Hayley's words. They retreat slowly, casting one last glance at the distraught river witch. As they leave the building, a mix of emotions fills their hearts, recognizing the complexities of the river witch's existence and their own limitations in providing the solace she seeks.

As Ryan recounts the river witch's reaction to the photo of the snakehead fish, the group is left grappling with a new set of questions. Cass voices her confusion, expressing doubts about the connection between the fish and the disappearances. "That doesn't make sense," she remarks. "What about the RV? She drew an RV. None of this adds up."

Hayley interjects, attempting to piece together the fragments of information they have gathered thus far. She recaps the known facts, bringing a sense of order to their chaotic thoughts. "Here's what we know," she begins, her voice steady. "Two people are missing, and we witnessed a fawn being pulled under the water as if something had grabbed it. In the vicinity of these incidents, we have a homeless woman with a mental illness carving 'danger' on logs, and there's also the existence of a pirate treasure rumored to be in Foul Rift."

The group falls into a moment of contemplation, the weight of these interconnected events becoming increasingly apparent. The river witch's emotional response to the snakehead fish and her labeling it as a "monster" raises unsettling possibilities. Yet, the mysteries surrounding the RV, the disappearances, and the river witch's actions remain elusive, leaving them grappling for understanding.

As the six friends continue on their journey homeward, their path takes them past the entrance to the woods where the mechanic had last been seen. They notice the area still cordoned off with police tape, a lingering reminder of the unresolved mystery. To their surprise, they witness the local Foul Rift police escorting Greg, Sean, Rick, Sanj, and Erin out of the woods. The tension between the police and the group is palpable, evident in the officers' stern expressions.

Intrigued by the unfolding scene, the six friends inch closer, attempting to eavesdrop on the conversation between the police and the group. However, the distance proves too great, and they struggle to make out the details of the exchange, save for one officer's admonishment that they were not supposed to be in that area. They catch a snippet of dialogue, the police mentioning that they would bring them to their homes. Without further explanation, the kids are escorted into the back of two patrol cars, which swiftly drive away.

Bo's voice breaks the silence, offering a plausible explanation. "I guess they got caught trespassing," he suggests, his curiosity piqued. Hayley's mind, too, begins to wander, her thoughts swirling with possibilities and unanswered questions.

As the group resumes their journey, the encounter with Greg, Sean, Rick, Sanj, and Erin leaves them contemplating the reasons behind their presence in the restricted area. The incident adds another layer of intrigue to the ever-expanding web of mysteries that surround Foul Rift.

Chapter 10:

Beep-Beep

As the sun climbed higher in the sky, Foul Rift found itself enveloped in the embrace of a sweltering summer morning. The air was thick with humidity, clinging to every surface and causing a layer of perspiration to form on the brows of its residents. The streets shimmered with heat waves, as if mirroring the scorching intensity of the day. The trees stood tall and motionless, their leaves offering only limited respite from the relentless sun. The town seemed to pulsate with the palpable heat, creating a hazy, almost dreamlike atmosphere. The locals sought shelter in the shade, seeking solace from the unforgiving rays. Foul Rift was a town caught in the grip of summer's fiery grasp, where every breath carried the weight of the humid air, and the promise of relief seemed but a distant mirage.

While Foul Rift languished in the oppressive heat, the teens sought refuge within the cool sanctuary of their homes. With the air conditioning humming softly, they lounged on comfortable couches, enjoying the respite from the sweltering outdoors. The hum of electric fans provided a soothing soundtrack, circulating the chilled air and alleviating the stifling atmosphere. Ice-cold beverages perspired on coffee tables, their condensation forming tiny droplets that glistened in the artificial light. The teens reclined, finding solace in their favorite books, movies, or video games, as the outside world melted away in the face of their indoor retreat. They relished the luxury of cool temperatures, savoring the relief it brought to their bodies and minds. In the comfort of their air-conditioned havens, time seemed to slow down, allowing them to unwind and recharge amidst the scorching summer heat outside. Foul Rift may have been held captive by the sweltering sun, but within the cool embrace of their homes, the teens found their own oasis of comfort and relaxation.

Hayley sunk into the plush cushions of the couch, seeking refuge from the blistering heat that lay just beyond the walls of her air-conditioned sanctuary. The cool air gently brushed against her skin, providing a much-needed respite from the oppressive humidity outside. With her phone in hand, she scrolled through short video clips of frogs wearing hats, seeking a distraction from the sweltering summer day.

Suddenly, a familiar ping reverberated through the room, drawing Hayley's attention. She glanced at her phone, her curiosity piqued by the incoming message. It was Ryan, texting everyone in the group chat. Intrigued, she tapped on the notification and the conversation unfolded before her eyes.

Ryan: Hey guys, meet me at the Field of Dreams playground. It's important.

Hayley: What's up? Why are we meeting there?

Ryan: Can't say right now. Just trust me, it's important. Meet me there ASAP.

Cassidy: Ryan, come on! Give us a hint. Why all the secrecy?

Ryan: I promise I'll explain everything once you're there. Just come, please.

Charlotte: This is so mysterious. I hope everything's okay. We'll be there soon.

Bo: Yeah, Ryan, we're all a bit worried. Can you at least give us a clue?

Ryan: Sorry for being cryptic. I'll explain everything once we're together. It's something we need to see.

Hayley: Okay, Ryan. We trust you. We're on our way.

Cassidy: Yeah, we're heading there now. Just hope it's not something scary.

Andy: Count me in. See you all soon.

Ryan: Thanks, everyone. See you at the playground. It'll all make sense soon.

The cool air enveloped Hayley as she sat in the tranquil oasis of her living room, her mind abuzz with anticipation. The contrast between the scorching world outside and the comforting ambiance of her air-conditioned haven intensified her curiosity. She was ready for whatever awaited her at the Field of Dreams playground, where secrets and revelations often found their stage.

With a flicker of excitement in her eyes, Hayley swiftly typed her response in the group chat, eagerly confirming her presence. The promise of a new adventure beckoned, and she couldn't resist the allure of the unknown. In this cool cocoon of her air-conditioned haven, Hayley eagerly awaited the rendezvous that would soon unfold, her heart beating with anticipation.

Hayley, Bo, Andy, Cassidy, and Charlotte sat together on the wooden train, their bodies sticky with sweat from the relentless humidity that hung in the air. The heat seemed to wrap around them like a suffocating blanket, leaving them yearning for a cool respite. Their parched throats begged for a drink, and they eagerly searched their surroundings for any sign of relief.

Bo, seeking shelter from the scorching sun, ventured into the wooden globe with hopes of finding a momentary reprieve from the oppressive heat. However, his optimism quickly faded as he discovered that the enclosed space only amplified the stifling humidity. Beads of perspiration formed on his forehead, and he emerged from the globe, frustration etched on his face.

Sitting under the shade of the wooden train, the group's patience waned with each passing minute. The discomfort caused by the humidity seemed to amplify their thirst and weariness. Bo, exasperated by the conditions and the delay, voiced his dissatisfaction. He threatened to abandon the gathering and retreat to the comforts of home if Ryan did not appear within the next five minutes.

The minutes ticked by slowly, the humidity clinging to their skin, amplifying their discomfort. The anticipation of Ryan's arrival hung in the air, mingling with the stifling heat. Each passing second seemed to test their resolve, but the camaraderie and shared anticipation kept them rooted to their spots.

As the group sat on the wooden train, their patience tested by the unforgiving humidity, they hoped for the arrival of their friend. The minutes ticked away, and with each passing moment, the need for refreshment and relief grew stronger. Willing Ryan to appear, they yearned for the promise of companionship and the prospect of an adventure that would transport them from the sweltering heat to a realm of excitement and discovery.

The group of kids sat patiently against the wooden train, growing more restless by the minute as they awaited Ryan's arrival. The air hung heavy with anticipation, and the sweltering heat made their agitation more palpable. Beads of sweat trickled down their foreheads, mirroring their rising impatience.

Just as the tension reached its peak, a sudden noise pierced through the stillness. The distant sound of a car horn beeping twice echoed in the air, catching their attention. They turned their heads in unison to see a rusty Toyota Highlander pulling up beside them. The window rolled down, revealing Ryan's familiar face with a mischievous grin.

"Who wants to go for a ride?" Ryan called out, his voice carrying over the stifling air. The question hung in the atmosphere, momentarily suspending their restlessness. Excitement ignited within them, momentarily eclipsing their discomfort. In that fleeting moment, the promise of an adventure beckoned, luring them with the allure of escaping the heat and embarking on a journey.

Their expressions transformed from restlessness to eagerness as they scrambled to their feet, a renewed energy coursing through their veins. The thought of being whisked away in the rusty Highlander provided a welcome reprieve from the stagnant heat. They eagerly made their way towards the car, their anticipation evident in every step.

As they piled into the vehicle, their sweat-drenched bodies seeking refuge from the unforgiving humidity, they couldn't help but feel a sense of liberation. The air conditioning provided a refreshing blast, washing over them like a cool breeze. The car roared to life, ready to carry them away from the stifling stillness and into the unknown. With hopeful hearts and wide smiles, they embarked on their impromptu adventure, leaving the sweltering heat behind, if only for a little while.

Ryan smiled proudly as he adjusted the rearview mirror and shifted the car into drive. The engine purred to life, ready for their impromptu journey through the familiar streets of Foul Rift. Cass's suggestion to cruise through town resonated with everyone, as they were eager to soak in the sights and sounds of their beloved community.

As they drove along the tree-lined streets, Bo couldn't help but marvel at the Highlander's interior, admiring the spaciousness and comfort it provided. Hayley, Cass, and Char chatted animatedly in the middle row, their laughter and voices filling the car with a youthful energy. Andy sat in the back, observing the world passing by through the window, lost in his own thoughts.

Congratulatory remarks filled the air as the friends praised Ryan for passing his driver's test, celebrating this milestone in his life. They marveled at the Highlander's origin, learning that it had been a thoughtful gift from Ryan's parents, acquired at a bargain price from his uncle. The sentimental value of the car made their journey even more special, adding a layer of shared memories and familial connections to their adventure.

As they meandered through the streets of Foul Rift, their eyes captured familiar landmarks and cherished memories embedded in the town's fabric. They passed Rambo's where they shared countless meals and the library where they sought refuge in the pages of books. Each corner held a story, each street a snapshot of their shared history.

With the windows rolled up, the cool air from the AC brushed against their faces, carrying with it the scent of summer and the sounds of their town. The hum of conversations, the occasional honk of a passing car, and the laughter of children playing outside enveloped them in a comforting familiarity.

As they continued their leisurely drive, Ryan and his friends shared laughter, stories, and dreams for the future. In that moment, as they cruised through the heart of Foul Rift, the Highlander became more than just a car; it became a vessel for their shared experiences and the bond that connected them.

Together, they embraced the simple joy of being in each other's company, embarking on an adventure that held no particular destination. In the comfort of the Highlander, their laughter intertwined with the rhythm of the road, forming a soundtrack of friendship and the promise of endless possibilities ahead.

As Ryan drives the Highlander through town, laughter and excitement fill the air. The friends celebrate his new license and the freedom of the open road. Suddenly, Andy's sharp eyes spot a familiar red Jeep Wrangler parked outside the museum.

Andy: Hey, guys! Look, it's Greg's Jeep!

Hayley's eyes widen with realization, and she quickly connects the dots.

Hayley: Wait a minute... They know about the treasure! It all makes sense now.

Bo: What do you mean?

Hayley: Think about it. We saw them being escorted out of the woods, and now they're at the museum. They have class with Odrap before us. He must have told them about the treasure and Ambrose at the museum.

The group falls silent, contemplating Hayley's theory. Ryan, intrigued by the possibility, steers the car around the block, finding a spot to park at a distance from the museum.

Ryan: Let's wait here and see if they come out.

The friends anxiously peer out the windows, their gazes fixed on the museum's entrance, anticipation building with every passing moment.

Andy: There they are! It's Greg, Sean, Rick, Sanj, and Erin.

Hayley: I knew it! They're definitely up to something.

Cassidy: You're right Hayley. It makes sense. They are after the same thing we are after.

Hayley leans closer to the window, her eyes never leaving the group.

Hayley: We need to find out. If they're after the treasure, we can't let them get to it before us.

The friends exchange determined looks, a shared resolve passing between them. Ryan grips the steering wheel, ready to take action.

Ryan: Buckle up, everyone. We're going to follow them.

Hayley: Don't follow too closely. We don't want them to see us.

With a nod from the group, Ryan shifts the Highlander into gear, seamlessly merging into the flow of traffic. Their pursuit of answers and the hidden treasure begins as they tail Greg's Red Jeep, embarking on a chase that will test their courage, wit, and friendship.

As the engine hums and the road stretches out ahead, their minds race with possibilities and the unknown that lies within the museum's walls. Their summer adventure takes an unexpected turn, transforming into a thrilling quest to outmaneuver their rivals and unearth the secrets of Captain Kidd's treasure.

With each passing mile, their determination grows stronger, and the stakes rise higher. Bound together by a shared mission, the friends navigate the twists and turns of fate, ready to confront challenges, unravel mysteries, and claim the legendary treasure that awaits them.

The rusty Highlander continues to trail the red Jeep at a cautious distance, their mission to uncover the truth becoming more intense with every passing moment. As they reach the edge of the woods, where they had previously witnessed the group being escorted by the police, the red Jeep slows down and eventually comes to a stop. An air of anticipation fills the Highlander.

Hayley, with conviction in her voice, confirms their suspicions.

Hayley:(whispers) See? They're definitely searching for the treasure.

The red Jeep begins to move again, prompting the Highlander to follow closely behind. They travel north on Mununka Chunk Road, passing by the bio-science building. Sensing the need to maintain a low profile, everyone in the Highlander, except for Ryan, instinctively ducks their heads as the red Jeep U-turns and passes by them. Hayley's determination pushes them forward.

Hayley: We have to keep following them. We need to find out what they're up to and what they know.

Ryan hesitates for a moment, aware of the risk involved in being discovered.

Ryan: We should be cautious. They might notice us tailing them.

Hayley, undeterred, insists on the importance of unraveling the mystery.

Hayley: I don't care if they know. We need to know what they're doing and if they're going after the treasure.

With a firm resolve, Ryan makes a U-turn, skillfully maintaining a safe distance from the red Jeep. Their pursuit takes them through the familiar streets of town, across Water Street, and into Pennsylvania, where they continue following Riverton Road northward.

As the miles roll by, Hayley's conviction only grows stronger. She is convinced that the group's relentless search is directly tied to Captain Kidd's hidden treasure. The friends brace themselves for whatever lies ahead, determined to outwit their rivals and uncover the secrets that await them.

With each passing mile their bond grows stronger. They are united in their quest, their shared purpose propelling them forward. The chase continues, fueling their determination to protect the treasure's legacy.

As the sun beats down and the road stretches out before them, the friends remain steadfast, ready to confront whatever obstacles come their way. Their pursuit of the truth and the treasure becomes more than just an adventure—it becomes a testament to their friendship and unwavering spirit.

The red jeep abruptly veers down Shady Lane, catching Hayley's attention and fueling her determination to uncover the truth. She urges Ryan to stay on their tail, not willing to let the opportunity slip away.

Hayley: Ryan, keep following them! They're onto something, and we can't lose sight of them now.

Ryan's grip tightens on the steering wheel as he accelerates, skillfully navigating the twists and turns of Shady Lane. The friends brace themselves, holding their breaths with anticipation. The red Jeep comes to a stop at the end of the lane, its brake lights casting a crimson glow.

Ryan, concerned about being detected, hesitates for a moment, contemplating their next move.

Ryan: They've reached a dead end. What should we do now, Hayley?

Hayley, undeterred by the obstacle, leans forward, her eyes fixed on the scene ahead.

Hayley: We can't afford to lose them now. Pull over here and watch them. There might be something important they're about to reveal.

The Highlander slows to a stop, concealed from view but close enough for the friends to keep a watchful eye on their targets. The tension inside the vehicle is palpable as they wait in silence, their gazes focused on the red Jeep.

Hayley's voice breaks the silence, her determination evident.

Hayley: We've come too far to turn back now. Stay alert, everyone. We need to find out what they're up to without being noticed.

With bated breath, the friends peer through the windows, straining to catch every subtle movement. Greg emerges from the driver's side of his red Jeep, scanning the surroundings with caution. The friends instinctively huddle lower, their hearts pounding with anticipation.

Hayley's voice, barely above a whisper, conveys their shared objective.
Hayley: Keep low and observe their every move. We can't let them get ahead of us.

As the tension builds, the friends watch Greg beckoning to the others in the red Jeep, their conversation out of earshot. Hayley's mind races, contemplating their next course of action, eager to gather more information without jeopardizing their mission.

Hayley: We need to get closer, but we can't risk being seen.

United in their pursuit, the friends remain hidden, their gaze fixed on the unfolding scene before them. The mystery of Captain Kidd's treasure and the secrets surrounding Foul Rift hang in the air, igniting their determination to unravel the enigma that has captured their imaginations.

With each passing moment, the atmosphere crackles with anticipation. The friends stand ready, poised to seize their chance to decipher the secrets that lie just beyond their reach. The pursuit of truth intertwines their fates, drawing them deeper into the intriguing web of Foul Rift's hidden past.

Hayley's determination reaches its peak as she senses a pivotal moment unraveling before her. Ignoring the cautionary words of her friends, she decides to take matters into her own hands. With a determined expression on her face, she stealthily exits the Highlander and instructs the others to remain in the safety of the vehicle.

Whispering her intentions to the group, Hayley begins to stealthily approach the scene alone, her curiosity overriding any fears that may have lingered within her. Moving through the dense undergrowth, she navigates her way closer along the riverbank, careful not to create a disturbance that will notify the others of her approach.

Hidden amidst the foliage, Hayley observes Greg's actions. His gaze is fixed across the river, his hand pointing towards something of interest. Although the distance muffles their voices, Hayley's intuition leads her to believe that their objectives align with her own. The pieces of the puzzle fall into place, connecting the dots from Mr. Odrap's lessons to the unexpected encounter with Greg and his companions.

A surge of determination pulses through Hayley's veins as she contemplates their next course of action. The urge to uncover the truth intensifies, and she believes that Ambrose holds vital information that could shed light on the others' motives. A plan begins to form in her mind, prompting her to retrace their steps and seek answers from the enigmatic museum curator.

As she turns to head back to the highlander, her footing betrays her, causing a loose rock to tumble down the embankment and splash into the water below. The sound catches the attention of Greg, Sean, Rick, Sanj, and Erin. Curiosity piqued, they all rushed to investigate the source of the splash and what they thought might be a voice.

Hayley knows she must act quickly to avoid being seen, so she swiftly lies down on the muddy bank, hidden below the sightline of the five. She holds her breath, fear coursing through her veins as they scan the area above her. Their footsteps echo, just mere feet from where she lies concealed. Hayley's heart pounds in her chest as she hopes they won't spot her.

Greg breaks the tense silence, suggesting it might have been a groundhog or some other small animal that caused the noise. The others agree, and they continue to search the area for any sign of disturbance. Satisfied that there's nothing to be found, they start to make their way back to Greg's Jeep.

As soon as they are out of sight, Hayley seizes the opportunity to act. With a sense of purpose, Hayley retraces her path through the woods, her body wet and muddy and her heart pounding with anticipation. The mystery surrounding Captain Kidd's treasure and the entanglement of her friends and classmates become even more enthralling. Hayley is determined to uncover the secrets that lie dormant within Foul Rift, convinced that the truth will eventually reveal itself.

As she ventures back towards the Highlander, her thoughts race with possibilities, ready to share her discoveries and strategize with her friends. The quest for answers has taken an unexpected turn, pushing them further down the path of adventure and intrigue.

Hayley's urgency fills the air as she leaps back into the Highlander, urgently instructing Ryan to turn around and head back to the museum. Panic sets in as they realize the red jeep, seemingly one step ahead, is already heading towards them. The narrow escape route is now blocked, as Ryan steps on the gas pedal and pulls out onto the road as the two vehicles narrowly avoid a collision. Greg's furious honking reverberates through the air, a clear signal of their close encounter.

In a desperate attempt to avoid detection, the group instinctively ducks down, hoping to blend into the vehicle's interior and avoid catching the attention of the Jeep's passengers. The Highlander swerves and pushes forward. Fear and anticipation grip their hearts as Bo, Hayley, Cassidy, Charlotte, and Andy turn back and look behind them, praying that their identity remains unnoticed.

As the red jeep speeds away, Hayley and her friends breathe a collective sigh of relief. Yet, the encounter leaves them shaken and uncertain of their next move. They exchange concerned glances, contemplating the implications of this unexpected confrontation. The mysteries surrounding Captain Kidd's treasure and the actions of their peers continue to deepen, enveloping them in an ever-expanding web of intrigue.

Ryan shifts the Highlander into gear once more, their destination altered by this unexpected turn of events. Determination fuels their resolve as they decide to proceed with caution. The museum, where Ambrose awaits, becomes an even more crucial waypoint on their journey.

They yearn for answers, longing to unlock the secrets that have remained hidden within the depths of Foul Rift.

The rusty Highlander cuts through the humid air as it embarks on a new path, the weight of their shared mission etched into their minds. The road ahead is uncertain and fraught with danger, but the bond between Hayley and her friends remains unyielding. Together, they face the unknown, ready to confront the challenges that lie ahead and unmask the truth concealed within.

The six friends pull-up to the entrance of the museum, the air thick with anticipation. As they step inside, the familiar scent of aging artifacts and the soft hum of air conditioning wash over them. Their eyes quickly locate Mr. Ambrose, diligently tending to one of the display cases, a faint smile playing upon his lips.
"Hey there, what a pleasant surprise!" Mr. Ambrose exclaims, his voice filled with genuine delight. "It's been quite the busy time here with all the treasure hunters. Seems like Captain Kidd has sparked quite the frenzy."

Hayley's heart skips a beat as she exchanges a knowing glance with her friends. Her suspicions are confirmed, and a sense of vindication fills her being. In a hushed tone, she whispers to the group, "I knew it. They're after the treasure, just like us."

A mixture of excitement and trepidation fills the air as they approach Mr. Ambrose, ready to confront the enigma that surrounds the town's obsession with Captain Kidd's legacy.

Hayley, intrigued by Mr. Ambrose's statement, leans in slightly and asks, "Mr. Ambrose, who are these other teens that have been visiting you? Are they also searching for Captain Kidd's treasure?"

Mr. Ambrose chuckles softly and nods. "Yes, indeed. There have been quite a few curious young minds who have made their way here seeking information about Captain Kidd and his legendary treasure. It seems that our history teacher, Mr. Odrap, is that his name? He has been sharing the tale with his classes, igniting a spark of interest in the students."

The realization dawns on Hayley, her mind connecting the dots.

Mr. Ambrose states with a gleam in his eyes. "It's been quite a fascinating time for the museum. I should write a thank-you note to Mr. Odrap for sharing the story and bringing so many young enthusiasts to learn about our town's rich history."

Hayley's thoughts race, contemplating the significance of this newfound knowledge. The realization that their quest for the treasure is not theirs alone fills her with a mixture of anticipation and a hint of competition. It's a race against time and other determined seekers.

As the group exchanges glances, they understand that their journey has taken a new turn. The hunt for Captain Kidd's treasure has become a shared endeavor, with mysteries to unravel, clues to decipher, and rivalries to contend with.

Hayley asks Mr. Ambrose eagerly, "Did these other kids find anything? Did they tell you anything?"

Mr. Ambrose pauses for a moment, thinking. "Well, they didn't explicitly mention finding anything significant. From what they told me, it seems they explored the small caves in the cliffs at the edge of the eddy, but unfortunately, they didn't come across any substantial clues or treasures."

Hayley's excitement deflates slightly. "So, they were hoping for more ideas, just like us?"

Mr. Ambrose nods sympathetically. "Yes, it seems they were hoping to uncover some hidden secrets or hints that could lead them closer to Captain Kidd's treasure. But, much like our own search, they faced challenges and came up empty-handed. It's a reminder that the treasure hunt is not an easy endeavor."

Bo chimes in, "We won't give up! We'll keep exploring, and search for any leads that may have been overlooked." Mr. Ambrose smiles warmly at their determination. "That's the spirit! Remember, sometimes the greatest discoveries come to those who persevere and approach things from a different angle. Don't lose hope."

Hayley nods, feeling a renewed sense of determination. "Thank you, Mr. Ambrose. We appreciate your guidance and encouragement. We'll keep digging deeper. Do you have any other suggestions for us?"

Mr. Ambrose gathers the kids around and reminds them of the intriguing story they discussed before. "Remember, I told you about the fate of those four men connected to Captain Kidd's treasure? They were arrested and later executed in Philadelphia. Now, here's something to consider: if they had a hand in hiding the treasure, wouldn't they have made a map to ensure its retrieval? Kidd intended to lead his wife to Foul Rift, but he never revealed the exact location. That's where the mystery lies."

His words hang in the air as the kids contemplate the significance of his insights. Hayley's eyes light up with a newfound realization. "You're right, Mr. Ambrose. There must be a lost map, a key to unlocking the secrets of Kidd's treasure. If we want to uncover the truth, we need to think like the pirates and investigate further."

Mr. Ambrose nods approvingly. "Indeed, follow your instincts. Perhaps the Independence Seaport Museum in Philadelphia can shed more light on the matter. There's an exhibit there called 'Patriots and Pirates.' It might hold clues that will guide you on your journey. But remember, treasure hunting can be a dangerous pursuit. Proceed with caution and keep each other safe."

Mr. Ambrose's words were like a flint to fire, a glimmer of hope within the group. Hayley's eyes widen with excitement as she connects the dots. "A lost map... that could be the missing piece we've been searching for! If there's a connection between Kidd's men and the hiding of the treasure, the Independence Seaport Museum might hold valuable information."

Bo adds, "And the 'Patriots and Pirates' exhibit sounds like a good place to start our search. We might find clues or artifacts that shed light on the hidden map and the secrets of Captain Kidd."

The group's enthusiasm grows as they imagine the possibility of discovering a long-lost map that leads them to the elusive treasure. With newfound determination, they quickly make their way back to the highlander.

Excitement fills the air as the group settles back into their seats with their hearts set on the upcoming road trip. The engine roars to life, ready to carry them on their adventure. Andy's voice breaks the silence, "So, road trip tomorrow?" His words are met with unanimous agreement from the others, their enthusiasm palpable.

Cassidy adds with a grin, "Definitely! It's about time we unravel the secrets of Captain Kidd's treasure." The anticipation builds as Bo chimes in, "I just map-quested it, guys. It's only 81 miles away from us. Less than 2 hours to get there." Ryan nods in approval, saying, "Perfect. Let's plan for tomorrow then. But first, let's swing by Rambo's and grab some drinks. I'm really thirsty; it's ridiculously hot."

With their minds filled with visions of hidden maps, treasure chests, and thrilling discoveries, the highlander sets off towards Rambo's. Their road trip awaits, promising an unforgettable journey into the world of pirates, legends, and the elusive treasure of Captain Kidd.

Chapter 11: Patriots and Pirates

With excitement coursing through their veins, Ryan enthusiastically beeps the horn of the rusty highlander multiple times as they drive past Hotdog Johnny's. In response, Bo, Hayley, Andy, Cass, and Char erupt into joyful celebrations, exclaiming "Whooo Hooo! We are doing it!" Their voices mingle in exhilaration, their anticipation of the adventure ahead palpable.

As the car barrels down the road, Ryan reaches over and turns on the radio, filling the vehicle with the sounds of "Sweet Home Alabama." The iconic melody resonates through the speakers, and without missing a beat, Ryan joins in, singing.

"Big Wheels keep on turning...
Carry me home to see my kin."

Andy jumps in to the singing "Singin' songs about the Southland
I miss Alabamy once again, and I think it's a sin, I said."

Cassidy jumps in "Well, I heard Mr. Young sing about her
Well, I heard ol' Neil put her down
Well, I hope Neil Young will remember
A Southern man don't need him around, anyhow."

Everyone jumps in "Sweet home, Alabama
Where the skies are so blue

Sweet home, Alabama
Lord, I'm comin' home to you."

Ryan beeps the horn several more times as the teens drive down route 46, singing and swaying, leaving Foul Rift behind them in the rear view mirror.

As the car continues down Route 46, the conversation takes a turn toward dreams and aspirations. Bo initiates the discussion, pondering what they would do if they became millionaires. "What's the first thing everyone would buy?" he asks, sparking the imagination of his friends. I would buy a new drone."

Ryan, glancing at Bo from the driver's seat, chuckles and replies, "That's the first thing you'd buy? Well, I'm going to treat myself to a brand-new Mercedes." Charlotte eagerly adds, "I'd love to buy my parents a new house. Ours is on its last leg. That's the first thing on my list." Andy jumps in, sharing his excitement about getting his driver's license. "I think I'd buy myself a car too, maybe a bigger Jeep than Greg's."

Cassidy, considering her options, envisions a future that extends beyond material possessions. "If Charlotte is using her share to buy us a new house, I'd use my money for college and maybe buy a bookstore," she declares. Hayley listens intently, contemplating her own priorities. "You know; I feel like I have everything I need. I'd make sure my parents are comfortable and able to retire, and then I'd use the money for college, just like Cass," she concludes, nodding in agreement.

The car buzzes with anticipation and dreams as each friend envisions the possibilities that a fortune could bring.

Though their aspirations differ, a shared sense of gratitude and consideration for their loved ones shines through. As the highlander cruises along Route 31, the warm sun casts its radiant glow through the car windows, creating a sense of adventure and possibility. Bo, ever inquisitive, raises another question, sparking a lighthearted conversation among the group. "What if there are booby traps? Do you think the pirates left traps around the treasure?" he ponders.

Hayley, unable to contain her laughter, playfully responds, "You watch too many movies, Bo. We're searching for Captain Kidd's hidden treasure, not One-Eyed Willy's Rich Stuff." The group joins in the laughter, their spirits lifted by the playful banter. With each passing mile, their bond strengthens, fostering a sense of camaraderie and shared joy.

The idea of booby traps may have momentarily crossed their minds, but in this moment, the treasure hunt is imbued with a sense of adventure, reminiscent of the tales that captivated their imaginations as children. The laughter serves as a reminder that, despite the challenges and uncertainties that lie ahead, they are united in their quest and the shared thrill of the journey.

With the echoes of their laughter resonating in the car, the group continues their trek, eagerly anticipating what lies ahead on their path to uncovering Captain Kidd's hidden treasure.

As the rusty highlander pulls into the Independence Seaport Museum Parking Lot, after a nearly two-hour drive from Foul Rift, Ryan announces their arrival with a simple statement, "We are here." The group takes a moment to survey their surroundings, the city bustling with life and stories waiting to unfold.

Hayley, her gaze fixed on the urban landscape, softly utters the words "Patriots and Pirates." The phrase lingers in the air, encapsulating the essence of their quest. It serves as a reminder of the rich history embedded within the city's streets, where the echoes of both revolutionary heroes and notorious buccaneers can still be heard.

The juxtaposition of "Patriots and Pirates" evokes a sense of adventure and intrigue. The group's hearts quicken with anticipation, their imaginations brimming with the allure of hidden treasure and the echoes of the past. Philadelphia, a city steeped in history, is now their playground.

With a mix of excitement and determination, they step out of the car, ready to embark on their next chapter.

As the group enters the Patriots and Pirates exhibit at the Independence Seaport Museum, they are immediately transported into a world of rich history and captivating artifacts. The exhibit is carefully curated, with dim lighting casting an air of mystery and intrigue.

The first display showcases an array of authentic artifacts from the Golden Age of Piracy. A collection of weathered cutlasses, flintlock pistols, and intricately designed pirate flags adorn the walls. The group marvels at the sight of a preserved pirate hat, its brim worn and tattered from years of sea voyages.

Adjacent to the weapons display, an information panel provides a detailed account of notable pirates from history, including the infamous Captain Kidd. The panel features vivid descriptions of their exploits and the challenges faced by those who sought to suppress their activities.

Further into the exhibit, the room opens up to reveal a life-sized replica of a pirate ship, complete with meticulously crafted details. The ship's deck showcases the daily life of pirates, with replicas of cannons, navigational instruments, and a mock treasure chest filled with sparkling gemstones and gold doubloons.

The walls are adorned with framed maps and illustrations. Nearby, carefully preserved manuscripts and letters offer glimpses into the lives and exploits of notable pirates and Revolutionary War figures.

The exhibit unfolds within a spacious hall, filled with carefully curated displays and engaging multimedia presentations. Glass cases line the walls, showcasing a fascinating array of artifacts from the golden age of piracy and the Revolutionary War era.
A central focal point of the exhibit is a meticulously crafted diorama depicting a dramatic battle scene between a pirate ship and a colonial vessel. The intricately detailed models capture the intensity of the conflict, while accompanying audio recordings and visual effects further transport visitors into the heart of the action.

Interactive stations invite visitors of all ages to explore the maritime world. Children can dress up in replica pirate costumes, complete with tricorn hats and eye patches, while they embark on a virtual treasure hunt. At another station, visitors can test their navigation skills by using a replica navigational compass to chart a course across treacherous waters.

As visitors make their way through the exhibit, they are transported back in time, gaining a deeper understanding of the intertwined histories of piracy and patriotism. The Patriots and Pirates exhibit captures the imagination, inviting visitors to explore the rich tapestry of maritime history through a blend of artifacts, information, books, pictures, models, and interactive experiences.

The six teens stroll through the Patriots and Pirates exhibit, their eyes scanning the displays and their minds eager for new discoveries. They move from one exhibit to another, carefully examining artifacts, reading informative panels, and flipping through pages of books. However, despite their excitement and diligent exploration, they find themselves disappointed that the exhibits do not reveal any new information about Captain Kidd.

They pause in front of a display showcasing maps and navigational tools used during the Revolutionary War era. The intricately drawn maps depict the coastlines and trade routes of the time, but none of them hint at the whereabouts of Captain Kidd's hidden treasure. The teens exchange glances, a hint of frustration mingling with determination in their eyes.

Moving on, they approach a section dedicated to pirate legends and folklore. Here, vivid illustrations and gripping tales depict the notorious pirates of history, their exploits and treacherous lives. However, none of the stories shed light on the specific whereabouts of Captain Kidd's elusive treasure.

As they continue their exploration, they come across a display featuring replicas of Captain Kidd's personal belongings. A replica compass, a weathered journal, and even a worn leather satchel offers glimpses into the life of the infamous pirate. However, these items offer no clues to the hidden treasure's location.

With each passing exhibit, the disappointment of not finding any new leads grows, but the teens remain determined.

The six teens, disheartened by their fruitless search within the Patriots and Pirates exhibit, find solace in the museum cafeteria. They gather around a table, their plates filled with sandwiches and snacks, but their minds preoccupied with their unresolved quest.

As they eat, their conversation is tinged with frustration. Hayley leans forward and sighs, her voice laced with disappointment. "I thought for sure we would find something in there, some clue or hidden message." The others nod in agreement, their eyes reflecting the shared sense of letdown.

Bo pushes his half-eaten sandwich aside and leans back in his chair. "I mean, what are the odds of finding the exact location of Captain Kidd's treasure in a museum exhibit? It's like looking for a needle in a haystack."

Cassidy, her salad forgotten momentarily, chimes in. "I guess we were hoping for a breakthrough, something to spark our next move. But it seems like we're back at square one."

Charlotte takes a sip of her drink, her face reflecting a mix of determination and frustration. "We can't give up now.

We've come so far. We just need to think outside the box and approach this from a different angle."

Andy, his appetite still intact, eats his chips as he ponders the situation. "Maybe there's another lead we haven't explored yet. Something we missed or overlooked. We need to reassess what we know and find a new starting point."

Ryan, typically the voice of reason, adds, "Let's not forget that we have the advantage of local knowledge. We know Foul Rift better than anyone else. Maybe there's a hidden clue or a forgotten tale that could guide us in the right direction."

As the group continues their lunch, their conversation shifts from frustration to determination. They discuss various possibilities, brainstorming new ideas and potential leads. Their disappointment slowly transforms into renewed enthusiasm, their collective resilience shining through.

Though they may not have found the answers they sought within the museum walls, their hunger for the truth remains unyielding.

Andy, holding everyone's trash, walks over to the garbage bins and tosses it in, sighing in frustration. Just as he does, a young woman who does tours for the museum approaches him with a friendly smile. She asks if he's been enjoying his visit so far.

Andy, slightly taken aback, hesitantly replies, "Uh, yeah, it's been alright." The woman picks up on his lackluster response and offers a cheerful suggestion. "If you haven't already, make sure to check out the museum's 'ship model shack.' It's a hidden gem where you can see incredible model ships being built by members of the oldest ship modeling society in America."

Andy's interest piques, and he asks, "Are there any pirate ships in there? Like, Captain Kidd's ship?"

The young woman nods enthusiastically. "Absolutely! We have a model of the Quedagh Merchant, Captain Kidd's famous ship. And guess what? The model maker is quite the expert on Captain Kidd himself. He might be there today!"

Andy's eyes widen with newfound purpose, and he thanks the woman eagerly before rejoining his friends. As he walks back, he shares the exciting news, and they all agree to head straight for the "ship model shack" within the museum.

The group walks briskly through the museum, their anticipation growing with each step. They enter a small door labeled "Ship Model Shack," and inside, they find themselves surrounded by a workshop atmosphere. The air is filled with the scent of sawdust, and the room hums with the sounds of conversation and the delicate clinking of tools.

Workbenches line the space, adorned with various model ships in different stages of construction. The members of the ship modeling society are engrossed in their craft, meticulously bringing these miniature vessels to life.

Andy's eyes scan the room, searching for the model of the Quedagh Merchant. And there it is, placed on a dedicated pedestal, a stunning display of craftsmanship and detail. Standing beside the model is an older gentleman, his skilled hands delicately shaping a tiny piece of wood.

Approaching the expert model maker, Andy musters his courage and strikes up a conversation. "Excuse me, sir. Are you the maker of the Quedagh Merchant? My friends and I are really interested in Captain Kidd and his treasure."

The model maker, his eyes glimmering with enthusiasm, pauses his work and turns to Andy. "Ah, Captain Kidd and his treasure. A captivating tale indeed," he replies, his voice carrying a wealth of knowledge. "I've spent years studying Kidd's adventures."

Hayley takes a step forward, introducing herself and the rest of the group. "Hi, I'm Hayley, and we've been researching Captain Kidd and his treasure. We heard that four of Kidd's men were captured and hanged in Philadelphia. Do you happen to know anything about that?"

The man adjusts his bifocals, his eyes narrowing with intrigue. He takes a moment to study the group before responding to Hayley's question. "You kids looking for Kidd's treasure?"

Hayley nods eagerly. "Yes, we've been researching Captain Kidd and his treasure for a while now. We heard about the captured men, and we were curious if you had any additional information."

The man's eyes glimmer with a mix of wisdom and curiosity. He gestures for the group to gather closer and begins to speak in a low, measured tone. "Ah, the tale of the captured men. It is true that four of Kidd's crew were indeed captured and ultimately met their fate in Philadelphia. It was a dark chapter in Kidd's story."

He continues, sharing the historical accounts and providing additional context to the events surrounding the capture and execution of the four men. The group listens intently, absorbing every detail and trying to piece together the significance of this information in relation to their treasure hunt.

As the man concludes his narrative, he looks at the eager faces of the six teens. "You see, my young treasure seekers, the story of Captain Kidd is a complex one.

Hayley musters the courage to ask another question that lingers in their minds. "Do you have any insights or clues that could lead us closer to Kidd's treasure? Anything that might help us in our search?"

The man smiles warmly, a glimmer of mischief in his eyes. "Ah, my dear young adventurers, treasure hunting is a path paved with mystery and unexpected twists. And as fate should have it, you stumbled across the right person. It just so happens that we have a relic here that might be a clue to Kidd's missing treasure. Let me finish what I am working on and I can take you behind the scenes and show it to you."

Bo takes a step forward, his eyes filled with curiosity. "Sir," he asks, "can you tell us what you're working on? We noticed you're making a plaque for another model. What is it?"

The old man stops his work and looks up, a gentle smile forming on his weathered face. He adjusts his bifocals and gazes at Bo with a mixture of warmth and pride. "Ah, I am crafting a replica of a ship called the Orca. It holds a remarkable story that unfolded off the coast of New England in 1974."

The other kids gather around, their curiosity piqued by the mention of an intriguing tale. They eagerly await the old man's words, their imaginations running wild.

The old man continues, his voice filled with enthusiasm. "The Orca was a fishing vessel that encountered a great white shark, a fearsome predator of the seas.

Bo's eyes widened with fascination. "That's incredible!

"Indeed", said the old man. "My uncle was the captain of that ship. Unfortunately, a 'porker' got the best of him and the Orca. I am making this model ship in his honor."

As the old man shares his knowledge and passion for the Orca, the kids listen intently, their minds filled with visions of the vast ocean and the thrilling encounters that unfold within its depths.

As the afternoon sun gently bathes the quaint model ship shop in warm hues, the six friends exchange knowing glances and decide to let the skilled craftsman complete his work. With a collective nod, they step outside into the bustling hallway, where wooden benches offer a perfect spot to relax. As they settle down, a sense of anticipation lingers in the air, and the conversation naturally gravitates towards the intricately crafted ships they had just admired.

Their voices blend harmoniously, discussing the exquisite details and craftsmanship of each model. Enthusiasm bubbles within them as they share anecdotes and observations about the vessels, each one showcasing a unique tale of maritime history. The rhythmic clink of mugs and the occasional laughter form a melodious symphony, accentuating the camaraderie shared by the friends.

As they wait patiently for the craftsman to complete his day's work, time seems to slow down in the tranquil ambiance. The world around them hums with life, people passing by, and distant snippets of conversation. Yet, their focus remains on the intricately carved ships, marveling at the skill and passion poured into every piece.

The old man carefully cleans up his workspace, stowing away his tools in their designated chests. As he finishes, he steps outside and waves the kids back into the model ship shop. The six eagerly gather around him, anticipation written across their faces.

With a gleam in his eye, the old man begins to share a recent discovery that piqued his interest. "You see, my young friends," he starts, his voice filled with a mixture of excitement and intrigue, "I came across some intriguing information regarding four of Captain Kidd's men quite recently."

The kids lean in closer, their attention fully captivated by the old man's words.

"Well, my children, it may not be directly related to the treasure itself, but it sheds some light on the fate of those four men. You see, historical records suggest that after their capture, they were held in Philadelphia before facing a grim fate on the gallows."

The group listens intently, their minds racing with images of the past and the tantalizing pieces of history being shared with them. Bo, unable to contain his excitement, chimes in, "Do you know what happened to them after their capture? Did they leave any clues behind?"

The old man nods, his voice infused with an intriguing blend of mystery and history. "Legend has it that following their capture, these men were confined in a place of eerie significance known as Gallows Hall. Picture this, my young adventurers—a vast chamber where hangings were solemnly carried out, its air heavy with the weight of judgment and fate. The legend is that there was no space in any of the cells at the prison, so the 4 men were locked inside the very room that they would be executed in, faced to stare at the device of their demise.

About nine months ago, an incredible discovery unfolded as a team of skilled archaeologists unearthed a hidden treasure—an ancient beam that once formed a chilling part of the Gallows Hall's structure. This particular beam, believed to be one of the very beams where the noose of justice was once suspended, held a powerful secret within its weathered grains. With great care, the beam was carefully extracted from its resting place, a sealed room nestled within the historic grounds of Fort Mifflin, also known as Mud Island.

 The significance of this finding became apparent as the beam was transported to the museum, where it would undergo meticulous cleaning and preservation to ensure its lasting legacy. Upon closer examination, experts made a remarkable discovery—a delicate engraving etched onto the surface of the beam. The carving had remained concealed for centuries, a hidden testament to the actions and emotions of those condemned to meet their fate upon the gallows. It is believed that one of Captain Kidd's men, imprisoned within the confines of the Gallows Hall, seized a moment of respite and defiance. With a clandestine tool, perhaps a piece of loose stone, he carefully etched a message upon the beam. As time marched on, the gallows were dismantled, their purpose fulfilled. Yet, the beam, unknowingly carrying the weight of history, found its way to Fort Mifflin during the construction of the 1770s. Embedded within the very foundations of the fort, it stood as a silent witness to the trials and tribulations of bygone eras."

As the words leave his lips, the kids find themselves transported to another time, imagining the grim conditions faced by Kidd's men within the confines of the ominous Gallows Hall. The old man's storytelling prowess leaves an indelible impression, fueling their desire to uncover more secrets and untangle the threads of history.

Hayley: Can we see the beam?

Old Man: Absolutely! It's currently in our storage room. It is being prepared to be displayed in our Patriots and Pirates exhibit, which I am assuming you have visited already.

Bo: That would be amazing! I'm really curious to see it up close.

Andy: What's engraved on the beam? Is there anything significant about it?

Old Man: Ah, the engravings! They're quite intriguing. Let me explain as we head to the exhibit.

Cassidy: Do you think it could be a clue to Captain Kidd's treasure?

Ryan: Yeah, could this beam hold secrets that lead us closer to the treasure?

Old Man: It's certainly a possibility. Legends and stories surrounding Captain Kidd's treasure have always fascinated treasure hunters and historians. The engravings on the beam remain a puzzle yet to be fully deciphered, but I have a feeling that once this beam goes public, we will have treasure hunters from around the country visiting us searching for Kidd's gold.

They enter the storage room. their eyes immediately drawn to the table that the beam is resting on.

Hayley: Wow, look at it!

Old Man: Yes, take a closer look. Just don't touch it. It's preserved well, but parts are rotten and we don't want to risk damage to it. You can see the engraving and mark of the noose on the top. The pirate must have climbed to the top which is why it went unnoticed until it ended up on Mud Island.

Bo: How do you know that one of Kidd's men did the engraving?"

Old Man: Ah, my young adventurer, that is a good question. We are not 100% sure, but I'll show you why we think it may be." The old man gestures to the kids to the end of the beam. "Look closely right here, it's a little hard to make out, but you'll see the word, 'Sarah K'. That is the name of Kidd's wife, Sarah Kidd."

The kids' excitement grew as they closely examined the engravings on the beam. Their eyes widened with astonishment when they spotted the name "Sarah K" elegantly carved into the wood. They immediately realized the significance of this discovery—it could potentially be a hidden message, a note addressed to Captain Kidd's wife. Their hearts raced with anticipation, fueled by the possibility that this clue could lead them one step closer to unraveling the mysteries of the treasure and the legendary captain himself. They knew that Sarah K held a key to the secrets that lay dormant, waiting to be unveiled.

Andy: So, they could potentially be linked to Captain Kidd's treasure?

Old Man: Indeed, my inquisitive friend. Although we believe here at the museum that it was an attempt by Kidd's loyal followers to send a message to Kidd's beloved wife Sarah to help free her husband.

Ryan, Hayley, and Andy carefully examine the remaining portions of the beam, their brows furrowed in concentration. They find it difficult to decipher the faint carvings and markings. The old man nods understandingly and explains that advanced techniques such as X-rays and computer analysis were used to enhance the visibility of the engravings. He directs their attention to a particular area, where a wavy line leads to a carved notch, followed by what resembles a horseshoe. The meaning of this remains uncertain. However, on the other end of the beam, a clear message emerges: "Look up marque." The kids ponder the significance of these words, but the old man states that the team speculates that it may have been a message to Captain Kidd's wife, urging her to invoke the authority of his privateering letter of marque in an attempt to challenge the court's judgment. Nevertheless, the old man emphasizes that certainty remains elusive, leaving room for further exploration and interpretation.

Cassidy: So you don't believe that this has something to do with the treasure?

The old man looked down at Cassidy through his bifocals. "Well you never know, but we don't believe it does, but that's not going to stop the treasure hunters. As I mentioned, this is going to bring everyone here and have them searching.

Bo: Is it okay if we take some pictures?

Old man: Unfortunately, I cannot let you do that until this becomes part of the exhibit, but you're welcome to write down any notes and make a sketch. I have some paper here.

The six kids gather around the beam, their eyes focused intently on the engravings. With pencils and paper in hand, they carefully sketch the beam, making sure to capture every detail of the carvings. They lean in closer, observing the intricacies of the markings and jotting down their observations. Ryan suggests that each of them take their time to complete their sketches and notes, ensuring they don't miss any important elements. They all diligently follow his suggestion, quietly engrossed in their task, determined to capture the essence of the beam's enigmatic message.

Bo asks the old man about the theory that the numbers that Kidd gave his wife. He asked if they could be coordinates. The old man nods, acknowledging the popular belief among treasure hunters. "Yes, it is believed that they are coordinates to Deer Isle, a small area in Maine. Many have searched high and low on Deer Isle, hoping to uncover Kidd's treasure. But alas, nothing significant has been discovered so far," he responds, his voice tinged with a hint of disappointment.

Bo hesitates for a moment, contemplating whether to share the information about Ambrose and the poem he found in Kidd's treasure chest. However, he decides against it, realizing that it might be best to keep that piece of information to themselves for now. Instead, Bo focuses on the topic of Deer Isle. He asks the old man to tell him more about it.

The kids express their gratitude to the old man for his knowledge and the special tour of the gallows beam. They feel fortunate to have witnessed such a recent and significant discovery. As the conversation continues, the old man's eyes light up when he learns that they are from Foul Rift, referring to them as "river-kids." He shares his knowledge of a restaurant in Milford on the Delaware once called Ship Inn, now known as Descendants. The old man mentions that he had provided the restaurant with some of his model ships, which are on display there. He suggests that the kids visit the restaurant, as it holds a rich pirate history and may offer further insights. The kids listen attentively, excited by the prospect of exploring more pirate tales and enjoying a good meal at the same time. They thank the old man once again for his valuable information and bid him farewell, eager to continue their treasure-hunting journey.

The kids, tired but satisfied with their adventure, climb back into the highlander and begin their journey home.

Cassidy: Hey, guys, what do you think about stopping at Descendants in Milford? It's the restaurant the old man mentioned, and he said they have model ships and pirate history.

Hayley: Sounds like a plan! We can make it a whole day trip, and I'm starving right now.

Andy: I'm down for some good food and pirate stories. Let's do it!

Bo: Yeah, why not? It'll be a nice way to end our adventure.

Ryan: Agreed. Let's go grab some burgers and fries.

The group arrives at Descendants in Milford and enters the restaurant, greeted by the savory aroma of grilled burgers and the lively chatter of customers. They find a table and settle in.

Hayley: This place has such a cool atmosphere.

Cassidy: And check out those model ships! Just like the ones the old man made.

Charlotte: I'm excited to eat, I am starving.

Waiter: Welcome, folks! What can I get you today?

Bo: I'll take a cheeseburger, fries, and a Dr. Pepper.

The others follow Bo's lead and order similar meals.

Waiter: Coming right up! Enjoy your meal, and let me know if you need anything else.

As they wait for their food, the kids soak in the ambiance of the restaurant, taking in the pirate memorabilia on the walls and sharing their own excitement about the day's discoveries.

Ryan: This has been an incredible adventure. From the museum to the old man's workshop, and now here.

Hayley: Absolutely! We've come a long way, and it's been worth it. And who knows, maybe we'll find more clues or stories here.

Cassidy: It's been an epic journey, guys.

The kids laugh, talk, and indulge in their delicious burgers and fries, immersing themselves in the pirate-themed atmosphere and savoring every bite.

Hayley: So, guys, what did you think about the museum and our time in Philadelphia? And, more specifically, what do you think about the gallows beam?

Andy: It was fascinating to see all the history and artifacts related to Captain Kidd. And that beam... it gave me chills knowing that it was used for hangings.

Bo: Yeah, standing in front of that beam made everything feel more real. It's like we were face to face with the actual events of the past.

Cassidy: I couldn't help but imagine what those pirates went through. Knowing that they were connected to Kidd's treasure, it adds another layer of mystery and intrigue.

Charlotte: It's hard to believe that we were standing in front of the very beam where they were hanged. Those pirates probably knew something important about the treasure, and it's still out there waiting to be found.

Ryan: Exactly. It makes me wonder if the answers we're looking for are hidden somewhere in those old stories and legends.

Hayley: That's what I'm thinking too. I feel like we are so close. I don't think that I realized that most people don't know about the connection to Foul Rift. The general public thinks that the numbers connect to Deer Isle in Maine.

Andy: Yes, but people do know that there's a connection to the Delaware. They know about Kidd's' men traveling the river. They have searched the entire coast.

Cassidy: It wouldn't be hidden in plain sight though. What if that beam is not the message that the museum thinks it is?

Andy: You're right, Cass. It's unlikely that the treasure would be hidden in plain sight. We need to think beyond what's obvious.

Hayley: Exactly! (Hayley shows her notes to the group) Look at this line, the notch, and the horseshoe. It made me think of the river, the eddy, and the cave. What if these symbols are pointing us to something specific? And the message "Look Up Marque"... What if it's telling us to look up inside the cave near the eddy?

Bo: That's an interesting theory, Hayley. Actually, that makes a lot of sense. Maybe the carving is not about the letter of marque, but to look for a mark inside of the cave? Maybe people have always looked down or dug, but maybe the hidden treasure is actually up, hidden in the cave's ceiling.

Charlotte: That's actually smart. I would never think of looking up. My instincts would have me looking down, looking for someplace to dig.

Ryan: I agree. We have to consider all possibilities and think outside the box. This could be the breakthrough we've been waiting for.

The group's excitement builds as they discuss Hayley's theory. They realize that there may be more to the gallows beam and its carvings than meets the eye. The waiter returns to the table and asks if he can get them anything. Bo, excited about the group's epiphany about the beam, asks the waiter what he knows about pirates.

The waiter raises an eyebrow at Bo's question about pirates, clearly caught off guard. Ryan chuckles at the waiter's reaction. He then turns to the rest of the group, a determined look on his face.

Ryan: Well, now that we have a good idea of where to look, I think it's time to plan our expedition to the caves at the eddy. We need to gather supplies and make sure we're fully prepared.

Hayley: Agreed. We should take some time to gather all the necessary equipment and research the cave's location and any potential dangers we may encounter.

Andy: And we shouldn't forget about the river levels and weather conditions. We need to choose the right time to explore the cave safely.

Charlotte: How are we getting to it? The woods are still closed off. We also can't forget that two people are missing. We need to think about that.
Andy: Char's right. We can access through the river AND if we do find something, it will be easier to move it by boat than carrying it.

Bo: That's a really good point. We are going to need a boat then. This sounds like a plan, guys!

As the group leaves Descendants, their minds are filled with excitement and anticipation. Although they didn't uncover any new information about Captain Kidd's treasure during their time at the restaurant, they feel a renewed sense of purpose and determination. Their time together at Descendants was not only a chance to fill their stomachs and enjoy each other's company, but it also served as a bonding experience, strengthening their friendship and unity. As they drive off in the rusty highlander, heading back to their hometown of Foul Rift, they are filled with hope and the belief that their upcoming expedition will lead them one step closer to unraveling the mysteries of the treasure.

As the sun dipped below the horizon, casting a warm orange glow over Foul Rift, the six friends found themselves lost in a world of imagination and possibilities. Each of them lay in their beds, their minds consumed with thoughts of treasure and the adventures that lay ahead. In the stillness of the night, they contemplated the clues they had uncovered, the stories they had heard, and the paths they were yet to explore. Excitement coursed through their veins as they envisioned the untold riches and the thrill of unraveling the mysteries that awaited them. With hearts filled with anticipation, they drifted off to sleep, dreaming of the next chapter in their quest for Captain Kidd's treasure.

Chapter 12:
S. N. A. P.

On July 2nd, the town of Foul Rift basked in the warmth of a beautiful summer day. The sun shone brightly in a cloudless sky, casting its golden rays upon the picturesque town. The air was heavy with humidity, creating a balmy atmosphere that wrapped the streets in a gentle embrace. The excitement for the upcoming 4th of July celebration filled the air, as the townspeople eagerly prepared for the grand parade that Foul Rift was known for.

Throughout the town, preparations were in full swing. Dedicated individuals ensured that every detail was taken care of to create a festive atmosphere. Park maintenance crews diligently mowed the lush green grass, transforming the parks into welcoming spaces for families and friends to gather. Flagpoles proudly displayed the stars and stripes, as vibrant flags fluttered in the gentle breeze, evoking a sense of patriotism and unity.

The spirit of celebration extended to the houses as well. Colorful decorations adorned the facades, with streamers, banners, and balloons creating a lively scene that reflected the joy and anticipation in the hearts of the residents. From porch railings to windowsills, the town wore a festive dress, beckoning visitors and locals alike to join in the festivities.

As the day progressed, the sound of laughter and cheerful conversations echoed through the streets. The aroma of delicious food filled the air, as families gathered in backyards and parks for picnics and barbecues, savoring the flavors of summer. Children ran about with excitement, clutching small flags and eagerly awaiting the parade that would soon fill the streets with color and music.

In the midst of the preparations, there was a palpable sense of unity and community. Neighbors exchanged friendly greetings, lending a helping hand where needed. The anticipation of coming together to celebrate the nation's independence created a shared bond that transcended individual differences, fostering a spirit of togetherness and pride.

The people of Foul Rift reveled in the sense of anticipation and camaraderie. With hearts brimming with excitement, they eagerly awaited the dawn of the 4th of July, when the grand parade would march through the streets, filling their lives with joy, laughter, and a deep sense of patriotism.

With hearts filled with anticipation and a renewed sense of purpose, the six friends embarked on a mission to share their newfound insights with Mr. Ambrose. They made their way to the museum, where they had first delved into the fascinating world of Captain Kidd's treasure.

Entering the familiar halls, they sought out Mr. Ambrose, their trusted guide in this captivating journey. As they approached him, excitement radiated from their faces, eager to disclose the discoveries they had made during their recent adventure to Philadelphia.

Mr. Ambrose greeted them with a warm smile, sensing their enthusiasm. The group gathered around him, their voices brimming with excitement as they recounted their visit to Philadelphia and the intriguing details they had learned about the gallows' beam and the possible location of Captain Kidd's treasure.

Their words spilled forth, painting a vivid picture of their theory, the beam's engravings, and their interpretation of the symbols. Mr. Ambrose listened intently, his eyes gleaming with curiosity and appreciation for the dedication and determination of these young treasure seekers.

As the group finished sharing their story, a moment of silence hung in the air, anticipation mingling with the museum's hallowed atmosphere. Mr. Ambrose, always the knowledgeable guide, pondered their words, contemplating the significance of their findings.

With a gentle smile, he commended their perseverance and resourcefulness, acknowledging the validity of their observations. He assured them that their discoveries had added a new layer of intrigue to the tale of Captain Kidd's treasure, igniting fresh possibilities and avenues for exploration.

Encouraging their curiosity, Mr. Ambrose offered his support and guidance, emphasizing the importance of thorough research and meticulous investigation. He reminded them of the significance of teamwork, reminding them that their combined efforts had brought them this far.

Hayley's eyes sparkled with determination as she spoke up, her voice filled with conviction. "We are going after it,

Mr. Ambrose. We are going to cut you in on whatever we find. Without your guidance and the knowledge, you shared with us, we wouldn't have even known where to begin or about the significance of those numbers leading to Foul Rift."

Mr. Ambrose's eyes twinkled with a mix of pride and concern. He chuckled softly and replied, "Oh, you kids are something else. But in my old age, I've found my true gold right here in the peaceful town of Foul Rift. I don't need any more riches. However, I do appreciate your kind offer. I do want you all to be careful. I also suggest you go for it on the 4th. The town will be busy that day. You don't want any interference."

Hayley nodded, understanding the sentiment behind Mr. Ambrose's words. "We will be careful, Mr. Ambrose. We'll follow your advice and go on the morning of the 4th when everyone is busy with the parade and park activities. We'll find a way to explore the back of the eddy, perhaps even using a boat to bypass the park rangers guarding the woods entrance."

The rest of the group nodded in agreement, their expressions reflecting a mixture of determination and excitement. Ryan chimed in, "We'll make sure to be cautious, Mr. Ambrose. Thank you for your guidance and for believing in us."

Mr. Ambrose smiled warmly, appreciating their genuine concern. "You're welcome, my young adventurers. Just remember to stay safe and take care of each other. You have the spirit of true explorers within you. Now go, and may fortune favor your quest. AND remember to come back here and show me what you find. We can dedicate a section of the museum to your discoveries."

With a renewed sense of purpose, the group bid their farewells to Mr. Ambrose, feeling a deep sense of gratitude for his wisdom and support. As they left the museum, their hearts brimmed with anticipation and determination, eager to uncover the secrets hidden within Foul Rift.

Throughout the town, the preparations for the upcoming 4th of July parade continued. The streets were adorned with flags and decorations, the air filled with an atmosphere of excitement and anticipation. Amidst the bustling energy, the six friends felt a sense of connection to their community, knowing that their quest was intertwined with the history and spirit of Foul Rift.

As they walked through the lively streets, their minds buzzed with plans and preparations. Hayley tells the others, "We need to prepare. We need supplies."

Andy nodded, adding, "We need to pack wisely, knife, rope, first aid-kit…"

Ryan: We need a boat.

Cass chimed in, her eyes shining with enthusiasm. "Make sure your phones are charged and we need waterproof bags for them."

Ryan glanced at the group, a spark of determination in his eyes. "Let's all go home and start getting ready. I'll see if I can get us a canoe or some kayaks. Let's text tonight and take inventory and then make a solid plan."

The group nodded in agreement, their minds set on the upcoming adventure. They were filled with a renewed sense of purpose, eager to explore and uncover the secrets hidden within their town. As they continued their journey, their hearts brimmed with optimism, knowing that their unity and unwavering determination would guide them toward the treasure that lay just beyond their grasp.

As the day drew to a close, the sun painted the sky with hues of orange and gold, casting a warm glow over Foul Rift. The night whispered promises of excitement and possibility, as the six friends prepared themselves for the remarkable journey that awaited them on the morning of the 4th. The town's anticipation for the upcoming parade merged with their own eagerness, creating an air of enchantment that filled every corner of Foul Rift.
On the early morning of July 4, in a dark bedroom, a pair of heavy leather work boots walked across the dark-stained hardwood floor and stood near their stereo, his fingers carefully placing a CD inside. With a gentle press, activated the play button, and the soft melody of "Stand by Me" by Skylar Grey filled the room.

"Stand by me, oh, stand by me," Skylar Grey's voice sang, carrying a sense of longing and determination that resonated with the unknown person. The lyrics wrapped around him like a comforting embrace, providing a sense of strength for the journey that lay ahead.

In sync with the music, the person turned their attention to a small duffel bag, carefully placing essential items inside. Binoculars, a large hunting knife, and a coil of sturdy rope spoke to his preparedness and resourcefulness. A generous bottle of water, some candies for sustenance, and a lucky rabbit's foot hinted at a touch of superstition intertwined with their practicality. A sweatshirt, perhaps a shield against the unknown or a reminder of comfort in uncertain times, completed the selection of items.

Leaving the bedroom, the person stepped outside, his eyes adjusting to the soft light of the morning. A gentle breeze pressed against his face, carrying the scent of adventure and anticipation. With purposeful strides, he approached a waiting canoe, its aluminum frame sturdy and inviting. Placing the duffel bag inside the canoe, he secured it carefully, ensuring everything was in place for the upcoming journey.

As the person focused on their preparations, another figure emerged from the driveway donning heavy boots and jeans. Together, they silently communicated, a shared understanding passing between them. With practiced coordination, they positioned themselves on opposite ends of the canoe, their strength evident as they effortlessly lifted it above their heads.

In perfect synchronization, they maneuvered the canoe onto the roof of a vibrant red jeep, its doors and roof removed, signifying freedom and adaptability. The juxtaposition of the robust vehicle and the delicate vessel atop it captured the essence of their upcoming expedition — a harmonious blend of resilience and the ability to navigate both land and water.

As the final notes of "Stand by Me" lingered in the air, Greg and Rick stood side by side, a silent acknowledgement passing between them. With a nod, they began their journey, the red Jeep rolling forward, carrying them towards Sean's house and the unknown with a steadfast resolve and a hint of curiosity.

Meanwhile, on the other side of Foul Rift, Ryan, with a mischievous grin, parked his highlander in front of Bo and Hayley's house. The familiar rumble of the engine ceased, signaling the arrival of their friends. As the door swung open, Andy eagerly jumped out of the passenger seat, his eyes gleaming with anticipation. Soon after, Cass and Char arrived, effortlessly maneuvering their bicycles to a halt beside the parked vehicle.

With a playful gleam in his eyes, Ryan swung open the back of the highlander, revealing an assortment of deflated river tubes. Their vibrant colors lay dormant, waiting to be filled with air and carried along the currents of adventure. It was a humble offering, but it held the promise of joy and laughter on their forthcoming expedition.

"Behold!" Ryan announced with a flourish. "The best I could do, my friends." His voice held a hint of excitement as he gestured toward the deflated tubes, a testament to their shared eagerness for what lay ahead.

Bo's eyebrows arched in surprise, while Hayley's face lit up with a mix of gratitude and excitement. The sight of the river tubes sparked images of sunlit days and laughter-filled escapades, floating along the gentle waters of their beloved river. It was a simple but thoughtful gesture from Ryan, a symbol of their friendship and shared enthusiasm for the journey they were about to embark on.

Cass and Char exchanged a knowing look as they unzipped their backpack, unveiling their carefully crafted creation. Nestled within the bag was a vividly colored flag, meticulously stitched and adorned with a patchwork design. The fabric unfurled, revealing a captivating symbol that represented their shared values and aspirations.

Cass grasped the flag with pride, holding it high for all to see. Its dimensions, two feet by three feet, emphasized its significance, commanding attention and respect. The patchwork design showcased a remarkable fusion of elements, each carrying its own symbolic weight.

With a gleam in their eyes, Charlotte began to explain the profound meaning behind the flag's composition. They spoke with a sense of purpose, emphasizing the importance of preparedness, empowerment, and inspiration in their quest for treasure and noble endeavors.

As the flag fluttered in the breeze, the crossed wrenches beneath the luminous lightbulb caught the sunlight, symbolizing preparedness. Cass's voice rang out, underscoring the notion that a well-equipped mind, armed with knowledge and mental tools, was the foundation of preparedness in the face of any challenge.

Charlotte picked up the thread, drawing attention to the vibrant lightbulb symbol with a map of the earth inside. They spoke of inspiration, the spark that ignites creativity and fuels the pursuit of dreams. The lightbulb stood as a beacon, a reminder that within each of them burned a wellspring of ideas and solutions, ready to illuminate their path.

The conversation shifted, as Cassidy's voice intertwined with Charlotte's, describing the eye patch that lent the flag a captivating skull and crossbones appearance. Empowerment was their message, inspired by the indomitable spirit of pirates who commanded their own destinies. Cassidy's words resonated with conviction, urging their friends to embrace their own sense of empowerment, to fearlessly chase their dreams and conquer their goals.

But their intentions reached beyond their own ambitions. Cassidy's voice softened, conveying a deeper purpose. They spoke of the noblemen, of striving for nobility through acts of kindness, integrity, and unwavering principles. The flag became a symbol of their collective journey, a visual reminder of their commitment to embody nobility and make a positive impact on the world.

As the flag fluttered proudly in the breeze, its patchwork design capturing the essence of preparedness, inspiration, empowerment, and nobility, the group felt a renewed sense of purpose. It served as a reminder of their shared values, a beacon of unity that would guide them through the trials and triumphs that lay ahead.

Hayley: Wow, Cass and Char, this flag is incredible! I love it!

Andy: Yeah, it's so creative. I can't believe you guys made this. It's awesome!

Cassidy: Thanks, guys! We put a lot of thought into it, and we're glad you appreciate it.

Charlotte: Absolutely! The flag represents our purpose.

Ryan: This is fantastic! It's a symbol of our shared journey and reminds us of what we're striving for.
Hayley: I think it's going to be our lucky charm. With this flag, we'll face any challenge.

Bo: Hey, guys, hold on a second! I've got an idea to make it even better. I'll be right back!

[Bo rushes off to the garage and returns with several zip ties and a sturdy stick from his yard.]

Bo: Check this out, everyone! I've got some zip ties and a perfect stick to attach our flag to!

Cassidy: That's brilliant, Bo! Let's secure it to the stick, so we can display it.

[Bo skillfully attaches the flag to the stick using the zip ties, ensuring it's securely fastened.]

Bo: And voila! Look at this magnificent flag on its mighty staff!

[Bo holds up the flag on the stick, its vibrant colors fluttering in the breeze.]

Andy: That looks incredible, Bo! It's like our own personal banner of adventure.

Hayley: I love it, Bo! It's a symbol of our determination. We're ready to conquer any challenge!

Ryan: This is perfect. It's truly remarkable.

Charlotte: It's amazing how a simple flag can hold so much meaning. It was so much fun to make.

Cassidy: I couldn't be happier with how it turned out. I feel like we are ready for today.

[The group stands together, marveling at their flag, appreciating the craftsmanship, and feeling a renewed sense of purpose and unity.]

Hayley: We'll have to figure out a way to attach it to the tubes.

Andy: Absolutely! I really love the whole thing…it's awesome!!!

[They share a moment of excitement and camaraderie, their spirits soaring as the flag dances in the wind. Their treasure hunt awaits, guided by the flag and fueled by their unwavering friendship.]

Andy pulls out two waterproof bags. He brought a small one to store all of their cell phones and a larger one to store supplies that they didn't want to get wet. He tells the group that they are going to do an inventory check and when he calls the item, place it in the bag.

Andy: Alright, let's do an inventory, guys. First Aid Kit?

Hayley: Check. (drops it in the bag)

Andy: Flashlights?

Hayley: Check. (drops 3 headlamps in the bag)

Andy: Small military shovel?

Andy: (answers himself) Check. (places the foldable shovel in the bag)

Andy: Hatchet?

Ryan: Check. (places the hatchet in the bag)

Andy: Rope?

Ryan: Check. (places a thin bound rope in the bag)

Ryan: (Oversteps Andy) Flares?

Ryan:(Answers Himself) Check. (drops 3 in the bag) You never know, we may need these.

Bo: Drone. (places the his foldable drone and remote carefully in the bag)

Hayley: I wouldn't bring that. That was a gift. You don't want to break it.

Bo: Just like Ryan said, you never know. We may need to send it into the cave.

Andy: Granola Bars, snacks, and sandwiches?

Hayley: Check. (drops a bunch of granola bars and sandwiches that she made in the bag)

Andy: Does everyone have a pocket knife?

Ryan: Yeah, I've got one.

Bo: Me too.
Hayley: Good!

Andy: Great. Keep those on you. Are there any other things that you think we need?

Bo: Duct Tape (Bo runs to the garage and returns with a role of gray duct tape and drops it in the bag)

Andy: Good thinking.

Ryan: I think that's it. Oh, I also have an inflatable cooler we can use to hold the bags of equipment.

Andy: Perfect. Let's pack up and head out.

Cassidy: Wait, what about water? We should bring plenty of water bottles with us.

Hayley: Good point. I have a few reusable water bottles that we can fill up before we leave.

Andy: Speaking of hydration, does anyone have sunscreen?

Charlotte: I've got us covered. I brought sunscreen.

Hayley: Alright, everyone. This is it. We've planned, we're prepared, and now it's time to find Captain Kidd's treasure.

The group raises their hands in a show of unity and determination, ready to face the challenges that lie ahead.They load up the rusty highlander eager to take off.

Bo: Alright, guys, let's drink to the Noblemen and Captain Kidd!

(Bo pulls out a bunch of soda cans and passes them around to everyone.)

Hayley: Cheers to the legends and the adventure ahead!

(They raise their soda cans and clink them together before taking a sip.)

Andy: Here's to the thrill of the unknown.

Ryan: May our journey be filled with excitement and discovery.

Charlotte: Cheers to the treasure that awaits us.

Bo: Cheers to lifelong friendships.

(They all take a sip from their cans, relishing in the moment and the anticipation of what lies ahead.)

Bo: Alright, everyone. It's time to make our mark on history!

(Bo collects the empty cans and throws them away in a can next to the garage while everyone gets inside the Highlander)

As the six friends drive through the lively streets of Foul Rift, they are greeted by an atmosphere brimming with anticipation and patriotic cheer. The town is adorned in vibrant shades of red, white, and blue, with American flags proudly waving in the warm breeze. Families and neighbors gather on the sidewalks, setting up their lawn chairs to secure the perfect viewing spot for the upcoming parade. The enticing aroma of grilled hotdogs fills the air, tempting their taste buds and reminding them of the festive feast to come.

Young children run around with sparklers in hand, their faces lit up with joy as they create mesmerizing trails of light. Colorful patriotic pinwheels spin and twirl in the hands of excited little ones, adding a touch of whimsy to the joyful atmosphere. Floats are being meticulously arranged, adorned with vibrant decorations, ready to showcase the town's creativity and pride. The sounds of laughter and conversations fill the air as people eagerly prepare for the grand celebration.

In the park, a lively band tunes their instruments, their melodies echoing through the town, setting the festive ambiance. Smiling faces, filled with excitement and unity, can be seen everywhere. Despite the sweltering heat and humidity, spirits remain high as the community comes together to celebrate their shared history and values.

As the six friends drive through the heart of Foul Rift, they feel the energy and excitement of the town pulsating around them. They exchange glances filled with anticipation, knowing that while they may miss the spectacle of the parade, their own adventure awaits, beckoning them with the promise of mystery and treasure. With determined smiles on their faces, they continue their journey, fueled by the spirit of the day and the collective enthusiasm of their community.

As the familiar tune of "Country Roads" fills the cabin of the rusty Highlander, the six friends embark on a contemplative drive up Manunka Chunk Road. The rhythmic melody weaves its way into their thoughts, each lost in their own reflections and the weight of the impending adventure. The road stretches ahead, leading them closer to their destination—the river's access point on Route 46, just north of Dildine Island.

An air of excitement mixes with a hint of apprehension as they approach the small parking area by the side of the road. However, their enthusiasm quickly gives way to a sense of unease as their eyes land upon an empty red jeep. The doors and top have been removed, a clear indication that it belongs to Greg. The realization strikes them like a bolt of lightning—Greg and his group are already ahead of them on the same quest.

A wave of panic washes over the six friends as they grapple with the implications of this unexpected encounter. Thoughts race through their minds, fueled by a mix of determination and a nagging fear of being left behind. The urgency to catch up and stay one step ahead intensifies, urging them to act swiftly and decisively.

In the face of this unforeseen setback, the six friends take a moment to gather their thoughts, seeking solace in the camaraderie they have forged. They draw upon their shared determination and resolve, knowing that they must remain focused and adaptable to navigate the challenges that lie ahead. With hearts pounding and minds racing, they brace themselves for the next phase of their journey, determined to overcome any obstacles that stand in their way.

In a flurry of activity, the six friends spring into action as they jump out of the Highlander. Ryan takes charge, quickly instructing Andy to retrieve the tubes from the back. With a swift motion, Andy opens the hatchback and lays the deflated tubes on the ground. Meanwhile, Ryan seizes the electric pump, determined to fill the tubes as efficiently as possible.

Hayley and Bo take out the waterproof bags and begin collecting the necessary items. Hayley checks if everyone has their phones and swiftly gathers them, sealing them securely in the small airtight bag. She then places the bag next to the floating cooler, ensuring its protection from water.

As Ryan diligently fills the tubes one by one, the anticipation in the air is palpable. The six friends watch eagerly, their eyes fixed on the growing inflated tubes. The excitement mounts with each passing moment, their impatience growing as they anxiously await the completion of the task at hand.

Amidst their preparations, a young couple strolls by, coming down from the above mountain on a hike, offering a warm greeting. Hayley seizes the opportunity to engage them, inquiring if they happened to notice when the red Jeep arrived. The couple nods, confirming that they did see the group of kids with a canoe. Hayley further probes, asking if they noticed whether the group all got into one canoe. The couple recalls that it appeared that way, confirming Hayley's suspicion.

Seeking further information, Hayley queries how long ago the group arrived. The couple pauses for a moment, reflecting on the time, and responds that it was approximately an hour or perhaps a little longer before the arrival of the six friends. Panic begins to grip the group as they realize the implications of this revelation. Time is of the essence, and the urgency to catch up with their rivals heightens.

A sense of determination and urgency permeates the air as the six friends exchange glances, understanding the gravity of the situation. They know they must act swiftly and decisively to close the gap and continue their pursuit. With a renewed sense of purpose, they redouble their efforts, their minds focused on the task ahead as they strive to overcome the unexpected challenges that lie in their path.

As Ryan continues to inflate the remaining tubes, Cassidy seizes the roll of duct tape from the bag and steps forward to take charge of their flag. With swift fingers, Cass carefully affixes the flag to the inflatable cooler/tube, ensuring that it stands tall and proud. The vibrant colors of the flag catch the sunlight, fluttering in the breeze as a symbol of their unity and determination.

The sight of the flag standing tall amidst the chaotic scene brings a renewed sense of purpose to the group. It serves as a reminder of their shared goals and the bond that holds them together as they embark on this adventure. The flag becomes a beacon of hope and a symbol of their unwavering commitment to their quest.

As the last tube is filled, Ryan turns off the electric pump and stands up, surveying their preparations. The six friends stand in a tight circle, their eyes locking on one another, a silent understanding passing between them. The time has come to set off on their journey, to follow in the wake of the group that preceded them, and to pursue the elusive Captain Kidd's treasure.

With hearts racing and determination fueling their every step, they gather their belongings, securing them in the tubes and floating cooler. Each member of the group takes a moment to check their gear, ensuring they have everything they need for the challenges that lie ahead. Their excitement blends with a tinge of nervous anticipation, creating a potent mix of emotions as they prepare to launch into the river.

As they stand by the water's edge, the reflection of the sun dances on the rippling surface of the river. The balmy summer air envelopes them, heightening the sense of adventure that pulses through their veins. With the red Jeep left behind in the parking area, their eyes are fixed on the vast expanse of water stretching before them, ready to embrace the unknown and chase after the dreams that lie on the horizon.

In unison, the group steps into the water, the coolness enveloping their feet, signaling the beginning of their grand expedition. With tubes floating beside them and the flag standing tall, they push off from the riverbank, their hearts brimming with hope and anticipation. As they set sail, their determined expressions catch the attention of the young couple who had shared valuable information with them moments before.

The young couple watches from the riverbank, their faces lit up with curiosity and encouragement. They wave goodbye, their smiles carrying the warmth of well wishes. The six friends return the gesture, their eyes filled with gratitude for the unexpected kindness they encountered on their journey.

With each passing stroke, the group glides further into the heart of the Foul Rift, propelled by a mixture of determination, camaraderie, and the gentle current beneath them. The rhythmic sound of water lapping against their tubes echoes in their ears, merging with the distant sounds of festivities and laughter from the shore.

Unaware of the trials and triumphs that lie ahead, they navigate through the twists and turns of the river, their minds filled with anticipation for the hidden treasures that await them. The sun's golden rays dance upon the water's surface, casting an ethereal glow on their path, as if nature itself is guiding them towards their destiny.

As they venture deeper into the Foul Rift, the young couple's presence lingers in their thoughts, a reminder of the connection formed through shared stories and serendipitous encounters. Their encouragement fuels the group's resolve, amplifying their determination to unravel the mysteries that lie within the cave's dark recesses.

With the wind caressing their faces and the river embracing their journey, they press on, united by a shared purpose and the unwavering belief that they are on the brink of uncovering a treasure that has remained elusive for centuries. The young couple's wave lingers in their memories, symbolizing the support and encouragement that will guide them through the challenges and trials they may face.

Meanwhile, farther down the river, Greg paddles fiercely at the back of the canoe, his muscles straining against the force of the rapids, Rick calls out to the group, his voice filled with determination. "Keep it straight, guys! We're almost there!" Sean grits his teeth, his paddle slicing through the churning water. "Hold on tight, everyone. We've got this!" Sanj, focused on the task at hand, adds, "Just a little bit more."

Erin, in the middle of the canoe, feels the adrenaline coursing through her veins. "We can do this! Keep pushing!" The five friends paddle with synchronized effort, navigating the treacherous rapids, their eyes fixed on the tributary up ahead.

As they reach the entrance of the tributary, Rick's voice rises above the rushing water. "This way! Paddle towards the opening!" The group maneuvers the canoe into the narrow waterway, its path obscured by overgrowth and tangled vegetation.

Amidst their intense paddling, Sanj manages to catch his breath and speaks up. "This place gives me the creeps. It feels eerie." Rick nods in agreement. "Yeah, it's definitely unsettling. But we have to push forward. The treasure could be waiting for us there."

Sanj scans the surroundings, his eyes darting from the overgrown banks to the murky water below. "Be careful, everyone." Erin glances at the foreboding scenery and shivers. "It's like something out of a horror movie."

The tributary gradually opens up into an eddy, and the atmosphere takes on an ominous tone. The water becomes still and stagnant, reflecting the twisted forms of dead trees scattered throughout. Thick mud clings to the edges, creating an almost swamp-like appearance. At the far end of the eddy, imposing cliffs rise, leading up to a towering mountain, casting long shadows over the water below.

The five friends exchange concerned glances, a mixture of excitement and trepidation in their eyes. Greg breaks the silence. "This is it, guys. We've reached the eddy. Let's stay focused and keep our eyes peeled."

With hearts pounding and anticipation hanging in the air, the group steels themselves for what lies ahead. In unison, they take a deep breath, ready to dive into the depths of the unknown and uncover the truth that has eluded countless seekers before them.

As the canoe glides steadily through the eerie eddy, the excitement in the air is palpable. The five friends can't contain their elation, their voices blending together in a symphony of laughter and animated conversation. Greg, a wide grin on his face, shouts over the water's surface, "Man, when we find that treasure, I am going to buy a new and bigger Jeep and get the heck out of Foul Rift!"

Sanj, his eyes gleaming with anticipation, joins in, "You know what? I've always dreamed of owning a Bronco. That's exactly what I'm getting, top of the line!" Erin, her voice filled with enthusiasm, adds, "I'm going for a sleek and rugged Hummer! It'll be perfect for meeting cowboys and off-road adventures!"

Sean, caught up in the moment, exclaims, "Since the theme is cars, I'll be buying a Mercedes. I'm treating myself to the ultimate luxury ride!" Rick, grinning from ear to ear, chimes in, "Guys, you know what I'm thinking? A fully restored Z28. Classic and powerful!"

The group erupts in laughter, their words blending with the sounds of the water. Greg playfully teases Rick, dubbing his choice as "Rick-Diculous," prompting another round of laughter.

As they paddle through the eddy, their dreams and aspirations fill the air. They talk animatedly about their future purchases, sharing ideas and envisioning the possibilities that the treasure will bring. In this moment, their spirits are buoyant, their hearts filled with anticipation, as they continue their journey towards the cliff, guided by hope and the promise of adventure. Meanwhile, up the river, as the six friends float lazily down the calm stretch of the Delaware, their once vibrant pirate flag hangs low, mirroring their feelings of despair. The still air amplifies the silence that envelops them, broken only by the occasional sound of their tubes dragging on the shallow river bottom or bouncing off rocks. Each of them is lost in their own thoughts, grappling with the realization that Greg, Sanj, Sean, Rick, and Erin may have reached the treasure before them.

Andy, breaking the silence, looks ahead and notes, "Don't worry, guys. The river will pick up its pace a little further down. We'll catch up." His voice carries a flicker of determination, trying to inspire hope in his friends. Yet, the weight of disappointment lingers in the air, making it difficult to fully embrace his words.

Hayley, her voice tinged with a hint of disbelief, speaks up, "I can't believe they got ahead of us. We worked so hard, put in so much effort..." Her words trail off, a mixture of frustration and resignation evident in her tone.

Bo, his brows furrowed, breaks the silence with a sigh. "We can't dwell on what we can't change. We have to keep going. Who knows, maybe they missed something, and we'll find the treasure right under their noses."

Ryan, always the optimist, adds, "That's right. We've come this far, and we can't give up now. Let's stay focused and keep going. We're still in the game."

Cassidy and Charlotte exchange a glance, their determination mirrored in their eyes. They understand the challenges they face, but their resolve remains unyielding. Cass speaks up, her voice filled with determination, "We've faced obstacles before, and we've overcome them. This won't be any different. Let's stay strong, keep paddling, and trust that our efforts will be rewarded."

With renewed determination, the six friends push aside their despair and embrace the notion that their adventure is far from over. They continue floating down the river, the water gradually picking up its pace, as they remain committed to the belief that there might still be surprises and opportunities awaiting them along the way.

Back at the eddy, as an eerie silence hangs in the air, the five friends paddle slowly, their thoughts consumed by the anticipation of the treasure. A sense of unease lingers, as if the very atmosphere is cloaked in mystery. Suddenly, their progress is halted, and an unsettling feeling washes over them.

The canoe scrapes against an obstacle beneath the water's surface, causing it to pivot and jolt. Greg's frustration boils over, and he takes his oar, striking it against what he assumes is the riverbed. The others follow suit, a chorus of rhythmic thuds echoing through the eddy.

Sensing the urgency, Sean calls out a plan, urging everyone to push off with their oars. Determined, they dig their oars into the water, summoning every ounce of strength to dislodge the canoe. With a collective grunt, they push together, their combined efforts slowly inching the canoe forward.

Greg, noticing the shallow water, hatches a plan in an attempt to free the canoe. Stepping out onto the uncertain ground, the water barely covering his boots, he braces himself against the back of the canoe. "Hold on!" he calls out, preparing to exert all his strength to dislodge the obstacle. But as he pushes off with all his might, a startling realization dawns upon him—the ground beneath him gives way, abruptly tipping the canoe and throwing everyone into the water.

In an instant, the once-sturdy vessel capsizes, spilling its occupants and their precious supplies into the murky depths of the eddy. The air is filled with splashes and gasps as they resurface, their shocked expressions mirrored in the ripples of the water. Their hopes and dreams momentarily submerged, they find themselves in a disheartening predicament, their supplies scattered and at the mercy of the eddy's murky water.

"What the heck?!" The five friends can feel the ground beneath the water shifting, unsettling them with an eerie sensation. Suddenly, in a jolt, they are propelled upwards, disoriented by the unexpected force. Confusion and panic grip them as the ground beneath them swiftly descends back below the surface, now in motion. Erin's screams pierce the air, heightening their fear and desperation.

Reacting instinctively, Greg and Sean swim towards a nearby tree partially submerged in the water, seeking refuge and a vantage point to assess the situation. Meanwhile, Erin, Sanj, and Rick forge ahead towards the shore, their strokes fueled by fear and adrenaline. Rick, slightly ahead of the others, glances back, his eyes widening in terror.

As the water churns and splashes with a tumultuous energy, the true cause of their distress reveals itself. Emerging from the depths, an immense two-ton turtle emerges, its formidable size casting a foreboding shadow over the unfolding tragedy. Greg and Sean watch in horror from the safety of the tree as the colossal alligator snapping turtle fixates its attention on Rick, Sanj, and Erin. Rick, determined to reach the safety of the shore, continues his desperate swim, never letting the haunting image of the pursuing creature fade from his sight. With calculated movements, the colossal turtle advances, its slow and deliberate approach intensifying the terror. Sanj and Erin struggle against the murky depths, their efforts impeded by the treacherous, muddy bottom.

In one swift lunge, the beast springs forward, crushing Sanj under its massive plastron and capturing Erin in its formidable beak. The water becomes a scene of chaos and tragedy as Sanj is pulled beneath the turtle's armored shell, his struggles silenced in a watery grave, while Erin becomes the unfortunate prey of the ferocious creature's hunger.

Greg and Sean, gripped by the horror unfolding before their eyes, shout desperately at Rick, urging him to run for his life. Rick's heart pounds in his chest as he summons every ounce of strength to propel himself towards the sanctuary of the eddy's shore, his mind haunted by the horrifying fate that befell his companions.

Rick, waist-deep in the water and closer to the shore, watches in horror as the giant alligator snapping turtle crushes Erin's bones and tears her flesh apart. Greg and Sean, sickened and terrified, debate whether to stay on the trees or flee in the opposite direction. In a sudden shift of instinct, the turtle fixates on Rick, abandoning its current meal and pushing through the water. Its prehistoric spiked shell breaks the surface, and its menacing beak emerges. Greg and Sean urgently scream at Rick to run, warning him of the approaching danger. Rick glances back, the shore within reach, his confidence initially intact. As he trudges through knee-deep mud, his shoe gets stuck, leaving him barefoot and slowing his progress. The sinking realization sets in that he won't make it in time. Determined, Rick turns to face the approaching reptile, gripping his pocketknife tightly. Greg and Sean watch in horror, yelling desperately from their perch. Rick readies himself to fight, prepared to defend his life. In a swift, ferocious strike, the turtle lunges forward, biting off Rick's entire arm. A scream of agony fills the air as blood gushes from his wound. Despite the devastating injury, Rick refuses to go down without a fight. Gripping the knife in his remaining hand, he swings with all his might. However, the turtle's immense strength overwhelms him, crushing his body and silencing his screams. Greg and Sean, paralyzed with shock, bear witness as the two-ton turtle drags Rick's lifeless body back into the depths of the eddy, resuming its macabre feast beneath the murky surface.

Greg and Sean, perched in the dead tree, sit in shock, their bodies soaked and covered in mud. The reality of the horrific events that just unfolded weighs heavily upon them. They glance around the eerie scene in silence, searching for answers amidst the devastation. Below them, the remnants of their supplies rest at the bottom of the eddy, inaccessible and useless. The overturned canoe, now fully submerged, sinks deeper into the murky depths, disappearing from sight. As they sit in their isolated sanctuary, bubbles suddenly rise to the surface, capturing their attention. Slowly emerging from the dark waters is a hand, adorned with a distinctive Tag Heuer watch on its wrist. They realize that the detached forearm belongs to their once friend, Sanj. It hovers momentarily, releasing trapped gasses, before descending back into the depths of the eddy. The sight is chilling, a grim reminder of the lives lost and the dangerous nature of their surroundings. Greg and Sean realize that they are stranded, trapped in their refuge atop the dead tree, with no means of escape. Fear and despair grip their hearts, leaving them paralyzed with the harsh reality of their situation.

Back up the river, as the six friends float down the river, their spirits dampened by the knowledge that the other group is ahead of them, a sense of disappointment and regret hangs heavy in the air. The once lively conversation has faded, replaced by a somber silence that envelops them all. Each individual grapples with their own thoughts and emotions, lost in their own solace.

Suddenly, a sharp crash breaks the tranquility, startling Ryan as a rock comes hurtling towards him, narrowly missing his tube. The others turn their heads in alarm, only to witness another rock landing perilously close to Hayley. Confusion turns to concern as they realize the source of the disturbance.

They look towards the riverbank and there, with a fierce and angry expression, stands the river witch. Her eyes burn with an intense fury as she hurls rocks in their direction, her power evident in the forceful throws. The friends exchange worried glances, unsure of how to handle this unexpected encounter. Fear and tension fill the air as the river witch continues her assault, each rock a reminder of her wrath and their vulnerability in this precarious situation.

As the rocks continue to rain down upon them, the six friends raise their voices in a desperate attempt to reason with the river witch.

Hayley: Please, stop! Why are you throwing rocks at us?

Bo: We mean no harm! We just want to pass through peacefully!
Cassidy: Please stop? We don't want any trouble!

But their pleas fall on deaf ears as the river witch persists, her shouts becoming more frenzied and incomprehensible.

River Witch: Ret Snom, Reg Nad, Reg Nad, Reth Erb!"

The friends strain to decipher her words, their hearts pounding with both fear and curiosity. The urgency of the situation pushes them to take action.

Ryan: Quick, everyone! Catch the current north of Mack Island! We need to get away from her!

With renewed determination, they paddle with all their strength, propelling themselves towards the swift current that will carry them away from the reach of the river witch. Their bodies lean forward, ready to dodge any incoming rocks, their eyes fixed on the turbulent waters ahead.

As they successfully navigate the current and emerge past Mack Island, a sense of relief washes over them. They look around, searching for any sign of the river witch, but she is nowhere to be seen.

Hayley: Did anyone catch what she was saying?

Andy: I couldn't make out a word, it sounded like French.

Charlotte: Whatever it was, she was clearly not pleased with our presence.

Cassidy: I think I got a couple of the words. I think she said breather or breath and danger.
Bo: I have no clue what she means by that. Should we keep going?

Hayley: We have to.

As the six friends float lazily on the river, their minds still buzzing from the encounter with the river witch, Bo addresses the group.

Bo: (thoughtfully) Hey, guys, I've been thinking about something since this morning when we were discussing the flag. Remember what Cass said about striving for nobility through acts of kindness and unwavering principles?

Hayley: (nodding) Yeah, it was a good idea. It really stuck out with all of us.

Bo: Well, I've got an idea. Let's condense that into an acronym that represents the tenets of the Noblemen. How about S.N.A.P?

Ryan: What does S.N.A.P. stand for?

Bo: It stands for Striving for Nobility through Acts and Principles.

Cassidy: (surprised) Wait, you turned my words into an acronym? That's brilliant, Bo!

Bo: Thanks, Cass. It was your thought that sparked this idea. I just put it together.

Andy: I love it! S.N.A.P.

Charlotte: And it's catchy too. S.N.A.P. will stick in people's minds.

Hayley: So, let's embrace S.N.A.P. as a reminder to uphold our principles and engage in acts of kindness and nobility.

The group repeats the acronym, S.N.A.P., with enthusiasm, their voices carrying across the tranquil river.

Bo: We can use S.N.A.P. to help get our message out there making a difference and continue to build out what it means to be a Nobleman.

The others cheer and express their agreement, feeling a renewed sense of purpose and unity. S.N.A.P. becomes their symbolic guide as they continue floating down the river, ready to face whatever challenges lie ahead, striving for nobility through their actions and unwavering principles.

Meanwhile, back at the eddy, Greg and Sean sit motionless on a dead, half-submerged tree, their hearts heavy with grief and shock. The weight of what transpired weighs heavily on their minds, and silence hangs in the air. After a long, agonizing pause, Greg finally breaks the silence.

Greg: (voice trembling) We have to do something, Sean. We can't just stay here. Nobody knows we're stranded here. We need to find a way off and get help.

Sean's gaze is distant, his eyes reflecting the pain of their recent losses. He takes a deep breath before responding, his voice filled with sadness and resignation.

Sean: (softly) Greg, I understand that you want to do something, but you have to understand... They're gone. Rick, Sanj, and Erin... they didn't make it. They're... they're dead."

Greg's face pales as the reality of their friends' fate sinks in. He looks down, unable to comprehend the enormity of the situation.

Greg: (whispering) They were just here with us... and now... they're not.

Sean places a comforting hand on Greg's shoulder, his own emotions evident in his voice.

Sean: (solemnly) I know, Greg. But we can't dwell on what we can't change. Right now, our priority should be getting ourselves to safety and finding help.

Greg raises his head, his eyes filled with determination mixed with grief.

Greg: (firmly) You're right. We can't let their deaths be in vain.

Sean nods, a glimmer of hope emerging in his eyes.

Sean: Let's focus on finding a way off this tree.

Together, Greg and Sean begin to assess their surroundings, searching for a viable solution to their predicament. With their fallen friends in their thoughts, they begin the daunting task of planning their escape from the eddy, hoping to find help and ensure that their friends' lives were not lost in vain.

Hayley's voice echoes through the air, filled with a mix of excitement and unease, as she calls out the sighting of the tributary opening. The six friends swiftly use their hands to paddle their tubes, pushing themselves towards the entrance. Ryan, determined and cautious, keeps a firm grip on the inflatable cooler, ensuring their precious cargo remains secure.

As they float towards the tributary, Bo's voice cuts through the anticipation, a hint of concern lacing his words.

Bo: Keep your eyes open, everyone. Stay vigilant for any signs of the river witch.

The group's excitement is tinged with a sense of urgency and uneasiness. Though their spirits are lifted, a lingering worry tugs at their thoughts. They are torn between their eagerness to continue their adventure and the fear that their nemeses, Greg, Sean, Rick, Sanj, and Erin, may have reached the cave before them, claiming Captain Kidd's gold as their own.

Hayley, her eyes scanning the river ahead, wrestles with conflicting emotions. On one hand, she eagerly anticipates the sight of the five, imagining them paddling past with a canoe filled with treasure and then on the other hand, she pictures her and friends thwarting the 5's efforts and finding the treasure before them.

The mixture of excitement, anticipation, and worry fills the air as the six friends navigate through the entrance of the tributary. They remain vigilant, both hopeful and apprehensive about what lies ahead, their hearts yearning for discovery, but also bracing for the possibility that their rivals may have already claimed the legendary treasure.

"Sean, look!" Greg excitedly taps Sean on the shoulder, his eyes fixed on distant figures approaching from the far end of the eddy. As the movement draws closer, hope blooms within them, replacing the lingering sadness. A surge of joy fills their hearts, and they can't contain their excitement any longer. They raise their voices, calling out with all their might, desperate to catch the attention of those floating towards them.

Greg: Hey! Hey, over here! Look!

Sean joins in, their voices carrying across the water, carrying the weight of anticipation and relief.

Sean: We're here! We're here!

The air is charged with a mix of hope and uncertainty, the sound of their voices echoing through the eddy. Greg and Sean eagerly wave their arms, their gestures a beacon of hope and rescue amidst the vastness of the river.

Bo's voice breaks through the tension, drawing the attention of the group to the distant sound of yelling. Hayley's heart sinks as her mind races, immediately jumping to the conclusion that it must be the five friends celebrating their discovery of the treasure. A surge of panic and anger washes over her, mingling with the deep sense of loss and betrayal.

Hayley: Oh no, it's them. They found it... they found the gold.

The others quickly scan the eddy, searching for the source of the noise. Andy's sharp eyes catch a glimpse of movement amidst the downed trees at the center of the eddy. Excitement fills his voice as he points out the figures perched on the dead tree.

Andy: Look! Over there, on that dead tree. There are people!"

Curiosity replaces Hayley's initial feelings of panic and anger. The six friends find themselves torn between conflicting emotions - the desire to know what has happened and a sense of trepidation about the unknown.

Their eyes remain fixed on the distant figures, hoping for answers.

The determined group paddles closer to the figures on the dead tree, their voices growing louder with each stroke. As they draw near, Ryan's keen eyesight allows him to recognize the familiar faces of Greg and Sean.

Ryan: It's Greg and Sean! They're up there!

Bo, perplexed by the sight, poses a question to the group.

Bo: But why are they in the tree? What's going on?

Hayley, piecing together the puzzle, offers a plausible explanation.

Hayley: I think they're keeping lookout for the others. They're here to alert them that we're coming and delay us from getting to the cave. It's a trick.

The group's attention turns towards the absence of a canoe, their eyes scanning the shoreline and the expanse of the eddy. Their confusion deepens as they fail to spot any sign of a canoe.

Ryan, still scanning the surroundings, raises his voice with a tinge of concern.

Ryan: Where is their canoe? I don't see it anywhere.

The six friends exchange puzzled glances, their minds racing with questions. The sight of Greg and Sean perched in the tree, the missing canoe, and the overall mystery of the situation fill them with a mix of curiosity and anticipation.

Greg's voice echoes through the air, filled with urgency and fear as he calls out to Ryan. He desperately tries to convey the danger they faced.

Greg: Ryan, listen! There's a giant snapping turtle...it's massive! Turn back, get help! Our friends...they didn't make it! They are dead! Please, go back!

Sean's voice joins Greg's, their pleas intertwining as they implore the group to reconsider their course of action.

Sean: Listen to us! It's too dangerous! We lost our friends…they are dead. The thing is massive.! Turn back and get help!

The six friends exchange alarmed glances, their expressions mirroring the gravity of the situation. The words of Greg and Sean hang heavily in the air, revealing the treacherous encounter that claimed the lives of their friends. Fear and uncertainty grip their hearts as they grapple with the decision before them.

Hayley's voice carries a mixture of frustration and determination as she addresses the group, voicing her suspicion about Greg and Sean's warnings.

Hayley: They're lying! They're just trying to scare us. The others must have ditched the canoe and made it to the cave. Let's ignore them and keep going.

The rest of the group nods in agreement, their trust in Greg and Sean waning. They paddle by, confident in their belief that the others are in the cave.

Hayley: We know what they're up to! Rick, Sanj, and Erin are in that cave, and we're going to find them. Don't let their lies fool you!

With renewed determination, the six friends continue paddling, their focus firmly set on reaching the cave and uncovering the truth about Greg and Sean's missing companions.

Ryan's voice carries determination and a sense of responsibility as he addresses the group, making a decision to approach Greg and Sean alone.

Ryan: You guys keep going. I'm going to talk to them.

He reaches into the cooler and pulls out the large waterproof bag, containing essential supplies, and hands it to Bo.

Ryan: Here, take this. It has the flashlights, rope, shovel, and hatchet. Take it to the cave. I'll be right behind you guys.

The others nod in agreement, understanding Ryan's intentions. Hayley, Bo, and the rest of the group continue paddling towards the cave while Ryan separates from them, making his way closer to the tree where Greg and Sean are perched.
Ryan's heart pounds in his chest as he approaches them, ready to confront their warnings and unravel the truth

behind their claims. He maintains a steady focus, determined to understand the situation.

Ryan maintains a skeptical expression as Greg and Sean continue to plead for help, insisting on the presence of a giant snapping turtle. He crosses his arms, unconvinced by their words.

Ryan: Let me guess, you're going to film my reaction like you did at school and put it on the Internet.

Greg's desperation is evident as he tries to convey the seriousness of the situation.

Greg: Ryan, I'm sorry, but I am not kidding. There is a giant snapping turtle in the eddy. It's enormous. Please go get help.

Ryan chuckles, thinking it's another one of their pranks. But as he looks up, ready to join the others at the coast, Greg's voice interrupts him.

Greg: Ryan, don't move!

Ryan stops in his tracks, curiosity piqued by the urgency in Greg's voice. He scans the water's surface, trying to spot what Greg sees.

Ryan: You are so full of it. (In an act of defiance, Ryan begins kicking his feet and slapping his hands against the water. I'm not stupid, Greg. I know what you're trying to do. Look, if you guys want, I'll grab two tubes once the others get out and bring them to you so you can get off that tree.

The others, 20 feet away from the coast, turn their attention back towards Ryan and Greg, their expressions filled with concern.

Greg and Sean's pleas for Ryan to climb onto the tree intensify as they witness the chilling sight of the giant turtle's silhouette gliding beneath him. Fear grips their hearts as they desperately try to warn Ryan of the impending danger. But before Ryan can react, a terrifying scene unfolds.

Suddenly, the massive head of the snapping turtle emerges from the depths, its jaws wide open, ready to claim its prey. Greg and Sean's cries of alarm fill the air, their voices drowned by the sound of rushing water. In a swift and horrifying motion, the enormous beak clamps onto Ryan's backside, gripping him tightly. With an unstoppable force, the turtle pulls Ryan down into the murky depths, creating a flurry of splashing and churning mud that obscures any view of the tragic encounter.

Ripples spread across the water's surface, resonating with a haunting echo. The once serene river is now filled with an eerie stillness, broken only by the faint echoes of the struggle that took place just moments ago. The remaining friends only feet away from the coast are frozen in shock and disbelief, their expressions a mix of terror and sorrow as they comprehend the loss of their companion to the merciless jaws of the river's fearsome inhabitant.

Bo, Hayley, Cassidy, Charlotte, and Andy stand frozen in disbelief, their hearts heavy with grief and shock. The reality of their friend's sudden and tragic demise sinks in, leaving them overwhelmed with fear and despair. The weight of the situation bears down upon them, rendering them momentarily paralyzed and unable to comprehend the magnitude of what has just occurred.

Time seems to stand still as their minds race, searching for a way to cope with the unimaginable loss. Their thoughts are filled with a mix of emotions—anger, sadness, and a profound sense of helplessness. They struggle to find a path forward, unsure of what actions to take next.

Greg, snaps his head away from the scene and locks his eyes on Hayley. He yells at the group to move. "Paddle!!! Get to the shore!"

With Greg and Sean's urgent pleas echoing in their ears, Hayley snaps out of her frozen state, her eyes meeting Greg's with a mix of fear and determination. She realizes the gravity of the situation and knows they must act swiftly to ensure their safety. Without hesitation, she commands the group to paddle with all their might, their arms working in a frenzy against the current.

The five friends propel themselves forward, their tubes skimming across the water's surface with desperate determination. The coast, mere feet away, offers a small stretch of sandy beach nestled against the sheer cliff wall. It is their only refuge in this perilous moment, their final chance to find sanctuary from the unknown terrors lurking in the depths of the river.

Their hearts pound in their chests as they draw closer to the coast, their muscles burning with exertion. With each stroke of their hands, the cave carved into the cliff's base looms larger and more inviting. It is a beacon of hope amidst the chaos, a sanctuary that promises respite from the horrors that haunt the eddy.

As the five friends paddle frantically towards the safety of the cave, a sudden ripple disturbs the water behind them. The snapping turtle, its instincts triggered by the movement, senses prey in its domain. With a surge of power, its massive body rises from the depths, its spiked shell breaking through the surface with a thunderous force.

The towering presence of the snapping turtle commands the scene, its ancient form creating a chilling spectacle. The top of its shell, adorned with sharp spikes, emerges like a prehistoric creature from the primordial depths, sending shivers down the spines of the terrified friends.

Its beady eyes fixate on the moving targets before it – Hayley, Bo, Cass, Char, and Andy – as they paddle with every ounce of strength they can muster. The turtle, driven by primal instinct, begins to close the distance between them, its massive jaws opening wide, revealing its razor-sharp beak.

The friends' hearts race with fear as they glimpse the snapping turtle's relentless pursuit. Panic intensifies their efforts, their paddles slicing through the water with frantic desperation. But the turtle's power and speed outmatch their frantic strokes, and it inches closer with every passing moment.

The friends can feel the snapping turtle's presence looming over them, its cold, predatory gaze fixated on their vulnerable forms. The sound of its powerful movements fills the air, a terrifying reminder of the imminent danger they face. They can almost taste the terror, a bitter taste of despair and helplessness.

Their minds swirl with thoughts of survival as the snapping turtle's monstrous form draws nearer. The cave's mouth beckons them, a glimmer of hope in the face of impending doom. With a final surge of adrenaline, they push their limits, propelling themselves forward with sheer determination.

Gasping for breath, they scramble out of their tubes, their bodies trembling with a mixture of exhaustion and fear. The entrance to the cave stands before them, a dark opening that beckons them with an air of mystery and trepidation. It is a threshold they must cross, a doorway to potential salvation.

As the five friends scramble into the safety of the cave's mouth, relief washes over them, their hearts pounding in their chests. But their momentary respite is shattered when they hear a thunderous crash behind them. They turn in horror to witness the snapping turtle, driven by relentless determination, lunging towards them with all its might.

Charlotte, the last of the group to enter the cave, feels a rush of adrenaline as she senses the turtle's presence closing in. She pushes herself to the limit, her limbs pumping with every ounce of strength, desperately trying to reach the safety of the cave's shelter. But time seems to slow down as she hears the terrifying sounds of the turtle's clawed feet scraping against the rocky shore.

With a surge of primal power, the snapping turtle lunges forward, its massive body pressing against the cave's entrance. Its spiked shell scrapes against the rocky walls, the sheer force of its momentum vibrating the ground. Charlotte can see the grotesque visage of the turtle's head and snapping jaws coming perilously close to her, its sharp beak glinting in the dim light.

In a heart-stopping moment, the snapping turtle's maw snaps shut just inches from Charlotte, the rush of air from its fierce bite sending a chill down her spine. The opening of the cave barely provides enough space to contain the beast's fury, as its relentless attempts to squeeze its colossal form into the confined space prove futile.

Driven by primal instinct, the snapping turtle extends its head further, its eyes fixated on its prey. Its muscular limbs scrabble against the sandy, rocky shore, leaving deep furrows in its wake. The scene is a terrifying tableau of the creature's overwhelming power and the group's narrow escape.

As the snapping turtle's claws scrabble in vain against the unforgiving rocks, the friends watch in a mixture of awe and dread. They can almost feel the beast's frustration, its primal rage seeping through the cave's entrance. The sound of its enraged growls echoes through the narrow passage, a haunting reminder of the danger that lurks just outside.

Charlotte, shaken but unharmed, breathes a sigh of relief as she gazes upon the immense creature, its head poised just beyond her reach. She takes a moment to collect herself, her heart pounding in her chest, thankful for the narrow margin that spared her from the snapping turtle's deadly jaws.

The snapping turtle's futile attempts continue for a brief moment before it settles at the cave's entrance blocking the 5 friends from escaping.

Hayley leads the way, stepping into the cool darkness of the cave. The others follow, their resolve unwavering, as they venture deeper into the unknown, their hearts pulsating with a mix of apprehension and fear.

Andy, in an attempt to console Hayley and Cassidy, places a comforting hand on their shoulders. "It's going to be okay," he says, his voice filled with a mixture of concern and determination. "We're in this together, and we'll find a way out."

The five friends huddle together in the safety of the cave, their bodies trembling from the adrenaline coursing through their veins. Their hearts race, pounding against their chests, matching the rapid pace of their thoughts. Silence hangs heavy in the air as they try to process the magnitude of the situation.

Charlotte, her voice filled with fear and uncertainty, breaks the silence. "What do we do now?" she asks, her voice quivering. Her question hangs in the air, unanswered, as the group grapples with their own overwhelming emotions.

Hayley, her mind racing for a solution, suddenly remembers the possibility of using their phones. With a glimmer of hope in her eyes, she rummages through the big waterproof bag that Ryan had given to Bo. She spills its contents onto the ground, searching desperately for the phones they need to reach out for help.

As the items scatter around them, Bo's voice quivers as he breaks the news to Hayley. "The phones... they were in the smaller waterproof bag that we left in the cooler with

Ryan. They are out in the eddy," he says, his words heavy with disappointment. A sinking feeling washes over the group as they realize their means of communication are floating out of their reach.

Hayley's tears start to flow uncontrollably, her hope shattered by this realization. Cassidy, feeling the weight of the situation, joins her in silent tears. The cave echoes with their shared sorrow and frustration, mingling with the sounds of dripping water and their own trembling breaths.

Andy, the pillar of strength amidst the emotional turmoil, steps forward to console his friends. He wraps his arms around Hayley and Cassidy, offering a gentle embrace. "We'll figure something out," he says, his voice filled with determination. "We won't give up. We'll find a way to get through this together."

His words provide a glimmer of comfort in the midst of despair. In that moment of vulnerability and solidarity, the five friends find solace in their togetherness.

Bo strains his eyes, trying to spot the cooler in the distance, bobbing in the eddy beyond the reach of the turtle. He feels a pang of disappointment, realizing their only means of communication is drifting further away. Bo raises his voice, projecting it towards Greg and Sean.

"Our phones are in the cooler, but it's out of our reach," he calls out, his voice tinged with frustration. "We need to come up with a plan. Are there any other ways we can get help?"

Greg and Sean exchange worried glances, their faces reflecting the weight of the situation. Sean shouts back, his voice laced with concern. "Our phones were in the canoe when it tipped over. We need to come up with a plan."

Bo nods in agreement, his determination fueling his words. "You're right. We need to focus on getting to shore first."

The communication between the two groups, though strained by distance and the looming presence of the turtle, provides a sense of reassurance. Even in the face of adversity, their voices bridge the gap, strengthening their resolve to find a way out of their predicament.

Inside the cave, Hayley, Cassidy, Charlotte, and Andy listen intently to the exchange, their hopes lifted by the knowledge that Greg and Sean are still with them, fighting their own battles. The reassurance of the others' presence brings a renewed determination to overcome the challenges that lay ahead.

Together, the two groups share a moment of solidarity, their voices carrying across the divide, echoing in the darkness of the cave and the vastness of the river.

Andy takes inventory out loud, carefully listing the items they have at their disposal. "Alright, let's see what we have here. We've got three headlamps, three flares, a survival shovel, hatchet, rope, snacks, sandwiches, and a first aid kit. Oh, and Bo's drone!"

Hayley's eyes light up with a glimmer of hope. "Bo's drone could be a game-changer for us. We can use it to scout the area or send a distress signal."

Cassidy nods in agreement. "It's definitely worth a shot. Bo, how good are you at flying that thing?"

Bo: I am pretty good.

Bo's eyes light up with a spark of ingenuity. "Wait, I've got an idea," he exclaims. The others turn their attention to him, eager to hear his suggestion. "We have my drone here, right?" Bo continues. "What if we attach something heavy, like that hatchet or shovel, to a rope and tie the other end to the drone? I can fly it over to the cooler, land the hatchet on top, and then use the drone to drag the cooler back to Greg and Sean."

The group exchanges glances, considering Bo's plan. Hayley nods approvingly. "That could work," she says. "It's worth a shot, and it's our best chance of getting those phones."

Andy chimes in, "We'll need to make sure the attachment is secure and the drone can handle the weight. But if we can pull it off, it might just save us."

Cassidy adds, "It's a risky maneuver, but I believe in Bo's piloting skills. Let's give it a try and hope for the best."

The group agrees, hopeful that this creative solution might be their ticket to reaching the phones and calling for help.

The five friends jump into action, fueled by a renewed sense of hope and determination. Bo takes out his drone, ensuring it is fully charged and ready for the mission ahead. Meanwhile, Andy grabs the hatchet, assessing its weight and sturdiness. "I think the hatchet will work better as the weight," he suggests, securing it to the rope with precise knots and reinforcing it with duct tape.

With the makeshift attachment complete, Andy carefully ties it to the bottom of the drone. "Alright, Bo, it's all set," Andy says, his voice filled with a mix of excitement and anticipation. "You'll have to fly the drone over the turtle, then gently land the hatchet on top of the cooler. Make sure it's securely positioned. Once it's squared on top, fly the drone over to Greg and Sean, dragging the cooler, so they can reach it."

Charlotte, her eyes shining with admiration, interjects, "This is a brilliant idea, guys. I'm confident that this will work."

The others nod in agreement, their focus laser-sharp as they prepare for the critical moment. They know that the success of this plan rests on Bo's steady hands and precise maneuvering. With a deep breath and a determined look, Bo takes hold of the controller, ready to navigate the drone over the daunting presence of the giant turtle and deliver the cooler to their stranded peers.

The scene unfolds with Andy standing at a safe distance from the immense turtle, his voice projecting loudly across the eddy. "Greg! Sean!" he calls out urgently, catching their attention on the dead tree. "Listen up! We've got a plan!"

Both Greg and Sean turn their heads towards Andy, their faces showing a mixture of surprise and curiosity. "What is it?" Greg shouts back, his voice tinged with hope.

"We've got Bo's drone here," Andy continues, motioning towards Bo who is holding the drone near the cave's entrance. "We're going to attach a rope to it with a hatchet tied at the other end. Bo will fly the drone over to the cooler, land the hatchet on top of it, and then bring it back to you guys. Our phones are inside."

Sean's eyes widen in realization, a glimmer of hope shining through. "You're going to use the drone to bring us the cooler and the phones?" he asks, almost incredulous.

"Exactly!" Andy confirms a sense of determination in his voice. "Once you have the cooler, you can use our phones to call for help."

Greg smiles, nodding in approval. "That's a good plan!" he exclaims.

With the plan settled, Bo takes the drone in hand, preparing it for its crucial task. The other four keep their eyes on the drone as it hovers above the turtle, ready to make contact with the inflatable cooler.

"Be careful, Bo," Hayley calls out with a mixture of concern and encouragement.

"I've got this," Bo responds with a reassuring smile. He takes a deep breath, steadying himself, and begins the drone's flight towards the cooler, keeping a careful eye on the hatchet hanging below it.

As the drone hovers over the cooler, Bo expertly guides the hatchet to land on top of it, creating the necessary friction to move it. The five friends watch with bated breath as the drone pulls the cooler across the water's surface towards Greg and Sean.

With a sense of relief and gratitude, Greg and Sean watch as the cooler gets pulled closer to them. "You guys rock!" Sean calls out, his voice filled with emotion.

The others smile, their hearts lifting with the success of their plan. They know that the journey isn't over yet, but for now, they have a renewed sense of hope.

As Bo expertly maneuvers the drone the others watch in awe as the cooler is gradually pulled across the eddy towards Greg and Sean. Excitement fills the air as they see the plan coming together. Bo's focus is laser-sharp as he concentrates on guiding the drone through the obstacle course of trees and rocks.

"Looking good, Bo!" Andy calls out, trying to encourage his friend.

"Yeah, you've got this!" Hayley adds with a nod of approval.

Bo nods back, determined to succeed. He carefully navigates the drone, inching it closer to the boys. Everyone is holding their breath, anxiously anticipating the moment when the cooler will reach its destination.

But just as the cooler is about to reach Greg and Sean, disaster strikes. A cord that had been attached to the side of the cooler gets snagged on a submerged branch of a dead tree. The drone tugs at it, but the hatchet, serving as the weight to create friction, slides off the top and plummets into the water. The drone's propellers thrash the water wildly, causing the hatchet to get entangled with another branch underneath.

"No, no, no!" Bo exclaims, desperately trying to fly the drone off the branch.

The rope tightens around the tree branch, and the drone becomes hopelessly stuck. Panic surges through the group as they realize their lifeline to Greg and Sean is now compromised.

"We need that cooler!" Cass cries out, her heart sinking.

Bo's hands tremble as he frantically tries to free the drone, but the hatchet remains lodged beneath the water. The weight of the situation weighs heavily on everyone's shoulders.

"We can't give up!" Hayley urges, her eyes locking with Bo's.

Andy scans the area, looking for any potential solution.

Bo takes a deep breath, determination returning to his eyes. "I'll try again," he says, refocusing on the drone.

Bo takes the controls once more, his fingers steady as he tries to fly the drone, "Come on, come on," Bo mutters, willing the plan to work, but it is hopeless. The drone is stuck and the hatchet is submerged.

The group huddles together, seeking comfort and solace in each other's presence. Cass sits on the cold wet ground folding her arms over her knees, "The parade will end soon, the barbeque will begin. Our parents will be looking for us. They'll try to call us and then they will call each other. They will come look for us. Someone will come look for us."

"You're right," Hayley says, her voice shaky. "Our parents will realize we're missing, and they'll come looking for us. We just need to sit tight until help arrives." Hayley thinks about Ryan's parents. They are going to be devastated. She is devastated.

Bo nods in agreement. "We just need to stay strong and stay together. We'll get through this."

But Charlotte can't help but voice her concerns. "What if the turtle doesn't leave? What if nobody comes? They don't know where we are."

"We'll find a way to deal with it," Andy asserts, trying to sound confident even as his mind races with worry.

"We need a plan," Hayley says, taking charge. "Let's take stock of what we have and figure out our next move."

They gather around the bag of supplies, taking inventory of what remains. The headlamps, flares, rope, food and water and other items are still there, giving them a sense of security.

"We need to conserve our food," Andy says, looking at the limited supplies. "We don't know how long we'll be in here."

Inside the cave, the atmosphere is tense, with the five friends anxiously awaiting rescue. Hayley keeps glancing towards the entrance, her heart racing every time the turtle makes a move.

"We can't stay here forever," Charlotte says, her voice trembling. "We need to find another way out."

Andy nods. "She's right. We can't rely on someone finding us. We have to take action."

Cassidy looks around the cave, searching for any hidden passages. "Maybe there's another way out, like a secret tunnel or something."

Bo sits against the cave's wall, rubbing his eyes. "I wish we had more options. The drone idea was our best shot."

"We still have the flares," Hayley says, her voice hopeful. "If we hear or see someone nearby, we can signal them with the flares."

Greg and Sean, still perched on the dead tree, continue to debate their next move. "We should make a run for it," Sean says. "The turtle is just sitting there; we can see it." Greg considers the idea and says, "NO! You saw it go after the others. It attacks anything that moves. I don't want to take that risk yet."

As the discussions continue inside the cave and on the tree, time passes slowly. The kids try to stay as calm as possible, attempting to keep their fears at bay. They take turns keeping watch near the entrance, alert for any signs of help.

After what seems like hours, the massive turtle stirs again, its colossal form shifting and attempting to push itself into the cave once more. The five friends inside the cave hold their breath, fearing the worst. But then, a glimmer of hope arrives in an unexpected sound.

Cass's keen ears pick up on something over the turtle's movements. "Do you hear that?" she whispers to the others, her voice barely audible in the confined space. "I hear something."

The others strain to listen, and then they hear it too—a distant rumbling. The unmistakable sound of an engine. The five friends stand up, their hearts pounding in anticipation, as the noise grows louder, echoing through the cave.

"It's a boat," Bo exclaims, disbelief and hope mixing in his voice. "A jon boat is coming!"

Their eyes widen with astonishment as the sound gets closer and closer. The driver of the boat cuts the engine and lets the boat drift towards the cliffs.

The turtle seems to sense the incoming disturbance, and its movements intensify. Panic threatens to take over the kids again, but they fight it, knowing that help is finally on its way.

Cassidy notices the sudden silence, and her heart leaps with anticipation. She whispers to the others, "They turned off the engine! They must have spotted us!"

Filled with relief, the five friends start yelling and waving their arms frantically. Greg and Sean, still on their perch, join in, waving even more vigorously to catch the attention of the approaching boat.

The rescuers on the boat notice the kids' frantic gestures and hear their calls for help.

One of the rescuers calls out to Greg and Sean on the tree, asking if they are okay.

"It's huge and aggressive! Be careful," Greg warns, pointing at the turtle trying to convey the seriousness of the situation.

The jon boat creeps closer as the driver spots the drone and the floating cooler. Their eyes widened in surprise and confusion, not expecting to see a drone in the middle of the eddy. They cautiously approach the scene, unsure of what they might find.

As the boat gets closer, the kids inside the cave wave their arms frantically, trying to catch the driver's attention. "Help! We're trapped in here!" Hayley shouts, her voice desperate and urgent. "There's a giant turtle blocking the entrance, and it's already attacked some of our friends!"

Hayley's heart leaps with relief when she realizes that men on the jon boat are Mr. Ambrose and Mr. Odrap, two familiar faces, coming to their rescue. "Mr. Ambrose! Mr. Odrap!" she calls out again, her voice filled with gratitude. "Oh my God!!! Thank goodness you're here!"

Mr. Odrap smiles warmly at the kids.

"We're so glad you came," Bo chimes in, his voice shaky with emotion. "There's a giant snapping turtle blocking the entrance to the cave, and we've been stuck here for what feels like forever."

Mr. Ambrose nods, understanding the seriousness of the situation. "We'll call the police right away," he assures them. "You all did a great job staying calm and taking care of each other while waiting for help."

As the boat gets closer Mr. Odrap reaches over and pulls the cooler on board, followed by carefully detaching the drone from the tangled rope. The hatchet unfortunately slips from the rope and sinks to the bottom of the eddy. Mr. Odrap leaves the drone on the branch where he found it. He opens the cooler to find the water proof bag filled with kids' phones. He reaches into the bag and pulls out the phones one by one, turning them on and going through them. Hayley's voice trembles as she urgently calls out, "Please, Mr. Odrap, call the police. We need help. We want to go home."

Meanwhile, Mr. Ambrose carefully stands up from his seat on the boat and looks at the group of kids, seemingly unfazed by their distress. Ignoring their plea for help, he calls out from the deck of his craft with a curious smile, "So, did you find the treasure?"

Chapter 13: Pirates and Noblemen

Hayley, feeling a mix of frustration and desperation, responds, "No, there's no treasure! We aren't looking for any treasure. We just want to go home. Please, Mr. Ambrose, call the police."

Odrap glances over at Ambrose in anticipation. Ambrose nods at Odrap and he dumps the kids' phones over the boat into the eddy. The kids stand there in shock and disbelief. Their expressions shift from anxiety to confusion and then to anger. Greg and Sean are the first to react, their voices raised with frustration and concern.

"Why did you do that? What is your problem?" Greg shouts, his face flushed with anger.

"Yeah, we needed those phones to call for help!" Sean adds, his voice filled with frustration.

Hayley steps forward, trying to maintain her composure. "Mr. Odrap, we don't understand. We needed those phones to call for help. Why would you do that?"

Mr. Odrap looks at the kids with a solemn expression. "I'm sorry, but I had to do it," he says calmly.

Greg, frustrated by the lack of help and the focus on the treasure, starts to climb down the tree with a look of anger on his face. He's about to jump into the water, intending to take over the boat, when Ambrose's warning stops him dead in his tracks.

"I wouldn't do that if I were you," Ambrose says, his gaze never wavering from Greg.

Fear seizes the group as they realize the danger they are in. Ambrose has a gun, and they are trapped in the cave with no means of escape. The situation has gone from bad to worse, and the kids know they must tread carefully if they want to survive this ordeal.

As Hayley's scream echoes through the cave, the other kids stand frozen in panic. The gravity of the situation sinks in as Mr. Ambrose aims the revolver at Greg, his gaze unwavering. Fear courses through their veins, and they realize they are at the mercy of these men.

"What are you doing? We want to go home! What do you want?" Hayley cries out, desperation in her voice. Her heart races as she tries to reason with the men, hoping to find a way out of this nightmare.

Ambrose's cold eyes lock onto Hayley's, the revolver still pointed at Greg. He smirks, clearly enjoying the power he holds over them. "We want the treasure. You get us the treasure, and you get to go home," he replies in a chillingly calm tone.

Hayley's mind races, trying to understand the situation. "There is no treasure, the cave is empty!" she yells back, hoping to convince them that their quest is futile.

Ambrose's smirk widens, and he chuckles darkly. "No, dear, you figured it out, remember? 'Look Up Marque.' Kidd's treasure is in there, and you're going to get it," he taunts, reveling in the knowledge that he has the upper hand.

The kids exchange terrified glances, realizing they are trapped in a deadly game of wits with these dangerous men. The hope of rescue vanishes, and they must now face the grim reality that they are in grave danger.

Hayley takes a deep breath, trying to steady her nerves. She knows they have no choice but to comply if they want to survive this ordeal. In a shaky voice, she asks, "What do you want us to do?"

Ambrose's smile widens, his eyes gleaming with malice. "You're going to find the treasure. And if you try anything foolish, well, let's just say it won't end well for any of you," he says ominously, making it clear that he means business. The kids swallow their fear and nod, realizing they have no other option but to play along for now.

The kids huddle together at the back of the cave, their faces reflecting a mix of fear and determination. Hayley speaks up, her voice trembling but resolute, "They are not going to let us out. Let's try and find the treasure."

Bo recalls the clue they discovered back in Philadelphia, "Look up Marque - Everyone look up for clues..." He reiterates the message, hoping it will lead them to the answers they desperately need.

With their headlamps illuminating the cave's dark corners, the five friends begin their search, scanning every inch of the walls and ceiling for any sign of a clue. They move carefully, their hearts pounding with anticipation.

After what feels like an eternity, Bo's light falls upon a small carving in the rock at the back corner of the cave. He calls out, "Guys, look! There's something here!" The others rush over, their excitement building as they see the marking.

"It's an X! X marks the spot!" Bo exclaims, his eyes widening with realization. But Cassidy quickly corrects him, "No, that's not an X. It's two swords crossed. Look, those are the handles, and those are the blades."

Cassidy's observation brings a surge of excitement among the group. "That's Captain Kidd's flag. That's his marque! Oh my god, that's it!" she exclaims, her voice filled with awe and excitement.

They all shine their lights on the rock, revealing the intricate carving of the crossed swords - Captain Kidd's iconic flag. The evidence is right in front of them, confirming that they are on the right track.

Their fear and desperation begin to fade away, replaced by determination and hope. They know they have to find the treasure to get out of this dangerous situation.

"We can do this," Hayley says, her voice filled with newfound confidence. "It's our only way to get out of here and put an end to this nightmare."

Ambrose and Odrap sit on the boat, keeping a watchful eye on Greg and Sean as they wait for the rest of the group to return. Ambrose's grip on the gun has eased slightly, but he still holds it, ready to use if needed.

Greg can't help but feel a mix of fear and anger towards Ambrose. He decides to push his luck, hoping to get some answers or even a reaction from the mysterious man. "Why don't you shoot that thing in the head and then go get the treasure yourself?" Greg asks, a hint of defiance in his voice.

Ambrose glances at Greg with a bemused smile. "Dear boy, do you know how thick that shell is?" he replies, his voice calm and collected. "Even the turtle's skull, you would need a military assault rifle to penetrate that skull. Besides, don't you think I've tried already?"

Greg's eyes widened in surprise at the revelation. Ambrose lifts up his pant leg, revealing his prosthetic limb. "Where do you think I got this from?" he adds, tapping the metal leg for emphasis.

Greg is taken aback, suddenly realizing the dangers and challenges Ambrose and Odrap have faced in their pursuit of the treasure.

Ambrose continues, "You see, boy, the snapping turtle is a formidable creature. One doesn't simply conquer it with brute force. It has guarded the treasure for a long time, and it will continue to do so. Every pirate treasure has its curse and right now that curse is hunting you."

Greg's eyes narrow, a mixture of anger and betrayal welling up inside him. "So you used us? All of us?" he accuses, his voice tinged with frustration. "You wanted us to do your dirty work. AND YOU, YOU, Mr. Odrap, trustworthy teacher, you tell the story of Captain Kidd and his treasure to your students. You get them interested. You get them asking questions. Then you send them to Ambrose at the museum who entices them even more. You fill them in on what they need to know, encouraging them to pursue what you were unable to get yourself. Then, once they find the treasure, you take it from them."

Ambrose smirks, his smile seemingly unaffected by Greg's outburst. "That's exactly right, dear boy," he admits with a hint of amusement. "You are smart; I'll give you that."

Mr. Odrap chuckles softly, a glint of pride in his eyes. "Greg, I never thought you would catch on so quickly, too bad you never used your ability to deduce in class" he says, almost admiringly. "You and your friends were the perfect candidates for this plan. Brave, curious, and eager for adventure."

Sean with a feeling of sadness, "You were the nicest guy. You seemed like you cared about our wellbeing. You didn't care at all."

Ambrose leans back in the boat, looking satisfied. "Ah, that was just a way to keep you motivated," he explains, his tone dismissive. "But in the end, the treasure is all that matters. With it, we'll have the means to change our lives and start over."

Greg's anger flares up again. "You're willing to put our lives at risk just for some treasure?" he retorts, his voice trembling with emotion.

Ambrose raises an eyebrow. "Isn't that what pirates have always done?" he responds casually. "Risked everything for the promise of unimaginable riches?"

As the realization sinks in, Greg and Sean feel a mix of anger, fear, and disappointment. They are pawns in a dangerous game, caught between the pursuit of treasure and the looming threat of a giant snapping turtle.

Mr. Odrap glances at his colleague, concern evident in his eyes. "Ambrose, maybe we should reconsider," he suggests, a hint of doubt creeping into his voice.

But Ambrose shakes his head, his resolve unwavering. "No, we're so close," he insists, his gaze fixed on the cave entrance. "We stick to the plan. The treasure is within our grasp."

The boat drifts slowly, Ambrose and Odrap immersed in their plans, while Greg and Sean struggle with the weight of the truth. In the distance, the snapping turtle remains a silent guardian, its presence a constant reminder of the danger that surrounds them.

Greg's eyes narrow, his frustration mounting. "Why did you need all of us? Wasn't one group enough?" he asks, his voice tinged with anger. "Why would you risk all of our lives?"

Ambrose looks at Greg, a glint of amusement in his eyes. "Maybe you're not as smart as I thought," he taunts. "I hate to break this to you, but you were the decoys, or one might say, the bait."

"The bait?" Greg repeats, incredulous. "For what?"

Ambrose smirks. "Do you know how hard it was to coordinate two groups of kids to embark on a national holiday, one leaving slightly before the other?" he explains. "That took a lot of planning and a bit of luck, I may say."

Greg's face contorts with realization. "You chose the 4th because everyone, including cops and emergency personnel, would be busy with the parade and festivities," he deduces.

Ambrose nods, confirming Greg's suspicions. "That's right," he says. "The whole town would be too busy celebrating to notice a few missing kids."

Greg continues, the pieces of the puzzle falling into place. "And if you needed to use your gun, people would think the shots were just fireworks," he adds, a mix of anger and disbelief in his voice.

Ambrose and Odrap chuckle, pleased with their cunning plan. "You catch on quick, boy," Ambrose says, his tone condescending. "But don't think for a second that this treasure isn't worth the risk."

Sean glares at them, unable to contain his anger any longer. "You're willing to put innocent kids' lives at risk for your own selfish gain?" he demands, his voice shaking with rage.

Ambrose and Odrap exchange a knowing look before Ambrose speaks again. "In the grand scheme of things, a few kids are a small price to pay for the chance to change our lives forever," he says callously.

Greg and Sean are left stunned, realizing they were merely pawns in a dangerous game. Their anger and fear mix with the overwhelming sense of betrayal.

Inside the cave, the kids gather around underneath the stone with Captain Kidd's mark, the excitement growing in their eyes as Andy retrieves the collapsible military shovel from the bag. "Bo, here," Andy says, handing the shovel to Bo. "Climb on my shoulders, and let's see if we can loosen that stone."

Bo nods, taking the shovel and quickly unfolding it to its full length. He positions himself on Andy's shoulders, carefully balancing as he brings the shovel up to chisel around the stone with the crossed swords. "Be careful, Bo," Hayley warns, worriedly looking up at them.

"I got this," Bo says with determination, carefully chipping away at the rock with the shovel. As he works, small pieces of stone begin to fall, narrowly missing Charlotte's head. Charlote catches one of the pieces and examines it. "Wow, this is heavy," she remarks, passing it to Cassidy.

Bo continues to chip around the rock with precision, and the others eagerly watch the cavity being revealed. "There's an opening up here," Bo announces, his voice filled with excitement.

"Maybe we can get out through it," Cassidy suggests, hope filling her voice.

Bo, with his curiosity piqued, responds to Cassidy, "I don't think it's very deep. Andy, can you push me higher? I cannot see inside."

Andy nods, understanding the situation. "Sure thing," he says, calling Cassidy over. "Push on Bo's right foot while I push on his left. Let's lift him higher."

Cassidy positions herself behind Bo and pushes upward on his right foot, while Andy boosts him from the left. Bo gains a better view inside the cavity. "Guys! There is a chest in here," Bo exclaims, his eyes widening with excitement.

Hayley, still skeptical, replies, "Bo, stop lying. There's no way."

"I'm not lying, I promise!" Bo insists, his voice filled with determination. "I'm going to pull it out."

With a deep breath, Bo braces himself against the cave wall and uses all his strength to wiggle the ornate chest out of the cavity. He pulls with one hand while keeping his balance with the other.

The chest emerges from the cavity, and the kids gasp at its sight. It's an ornate chest made from hammered steel and wood, in surprisingly good condition despite its time in the cave. It's heavy, and Bo struggles to keep it steady.

The weight becomes too much, and the chest slips from Bo's grasp, falling to the ground with a loud thud. It opens upon impact, and a breathtaking sight unfolds before their eyes. Hundreds of gold coins and sparkling gems spill out, forming a magnificent display of wealth on the cave floor.

Hayley's disbelief turns into awe as she realizes the truth. "Bo... you weren't lying," she says, her voice filled with wonder.

Bo grins triumphantly, proud of his discovery. "Told you," he replies, taking in the breathtaking sight before him.

Andy kneels down and picks up one of the gold coins, his eyes wide with astonishment. "This is incredible," he says in amazement.

The kids gather around the treasure, their excitement palpable. "We did it," Cass exclaims, a mixture of joy and disbelief in her voice.

As they inspect the treasure, they feel a sense of accomplishment and vindication. Their risky adventure and determination led them to a real pirate's treasure. They can't believe their luck and the magnitude of their discovery.

Hayley grins at Bo, her eyes shining with gratitude. "You're a genius, Bo," she says.

Bo chuckles humbly. "Just a little bit of luck and a lot of curiosity," he replies.

They spend a moment savoring the sight of the treasure before them, knowing that their lives have changed forever.

As the kids marvel at the gleaming gold and sparkling jewels, their faces are a mix of wonder and excitement. For a brief moment, they forget about the danger surrounding them and are captivated by the historical significance of the treasure.

Hayley sets down the gold coins gently and picks up the engraved rock, running her fingers over the intricate design of the crossed swords. "Think about it, guys," she says, her voice filled with awe. "This treasure has been hidden away for over 300 years. The last time anyone saw this was during the time of Captain Kidd himself. It's like we're touching history."

Bo nods, understanding the gravity of the moment. "You're right, Hayley. This is something truly extraordinary," he agrees, his eyes still fixed on the engravings.

Cassidy chimes in, "It's hard to believe that we're holding something so ancient and valuable in our hands."

But soon, Hayley's sensible nature kicks in, and she realizes the perilous situation they are in. "As amazing as this treasure is, we can't forget that we're still trapped here," she says, her tone serious. "We need to figure out a way to get out of this cave and away from those monsters."

The others nod, bringing their attention back to the immediate challenge at hand. They carefully place the gold and jewels back into the ornate chest, taking one last longing look before closing it.

"We can't let that treasure blind us from the danger we're facing," Cassidy adds, determination in her voice.

Andy agrees, "We need a plan. We can't just stay here and hope that they'll go away."

Bo suggests, "Maybe we can use the treasure to negotiate with them. Ask them to share it."

Hayley considers Bo's idea, but then shakes her head. "I don't know if we can trust them. They already betrayed us once," she says, remembering how Ambrose and Odrap dumped their phones into the eddy. "Let's not forget that they pulled a gun on us. I don't think they are planning on us leaving here alive."

"Besides," Charlotte adds, "there's no guarantee they'll let us go even if they say they will.

The group falls silent, contemplating their next move. They know that time is of the essence, and they can't afford to make any more mistakes.

"We need to find another way out of this cave," Hayley says finally, her voice firm.

Inside the cave, the kids freeze as they hear the scratching and movement outside. Hayley clutches the flashlight tightly, her heart pounding in her chest. "Guys, be quiet," she whispers urgently. "The turtle is moving."

They all huddle together, their eyes fixed on the cave entrance. The sound of the turtle moving rocks and sand outside sends shivers down their spines. They know they must remain still and silent to avoid attracting its attention.

Outside the cave, Ambrose, Odrap, Greg, and Sean watch the massive turtle's clumsy movements. The creature's dark silhouette against the water is both eerie and intimidating. The boys can see the concern in Ambrose's eyes as he grips his gun tightly.

Greg leans towards Sean and whispers, "That turtle is no joke. It's like a living tank."

Sean nods in agreement, his heart racing with anxiety.

As the turtle continues to move rocks and debris, the ground beneath the kids' feet slightly trembles. The turtle's movements are powerful and unnerving.

The kids inside the cave freeze as they hear the sound of movement outside. The ground beneath them trembles slightly, and their hearts race with fear.

They listen intently, the scratching and dragging sounds growing louder, and then suddenly, the massive turtle begins to turn. Its enormous body pivots, kicking up dirt, rocks, and sand as it propels itself towards the water.

Bo grabs Cass's arm, and they huddle closer together, their eyes locked on the cave entrance. "Oh my goodness," Cassidy gasps, "it's enormous!"

The turtle's scaled legs scrape against the rocks, and its powerful claws dig into the ground as it pulls itself under the water. Its spiked shell reflects the dim light from the cave, and its eyes glint with an ancient, primal wisdom.

Fear grips the kids as they watch the creature's movements. Andy whispers, "It's going back to the water. Maybe we're safe."

But Hayley isn't convinced. "Don't let your guard down," she cautions. "That thing is dangerous."

Greg and Sean, still outside, watch the turtle with awe and trepidation.

As the turtle continues its movements, the ground finally stops vibrating. It drags its massive body into the water, and with one last splash, it disappears beneath the surface.

The kids inside the cave release the breaths they didn't realize they were holding. Bo wipes sweat from his forehead. "That was intense," he says, his voice shaking.

Andy nods, "Tell me about it. Let's hope it's gone for good."

Hayley looks at the group with determination. "We can't wait around. We need to find a way out of here. Let's keep thinking."

The kids huddle closer together, their eyes wide with fear and uncertainty. Cassidy speaks up, her voice trembling slightly, "Maybe we should wait it out. We have food and water. Maybe they'll just leave."

Hayley shakes her head, "No, we can't just sit here and hope they'll give up. We need to come up with a plan."

Andy adds, "And what about Greg and Sean? We can't leave them out there with those guys. They're dangerous."

Cassidy nods in agreement, "You're right. We can't abandon them."

Outside, Odrap's voice echoes into the cave again, "Come out, we won't hurt you. The turtle is gone. We just want to talk."

Hayley looks at the others, her face determined. "We can't trust them. They lied to us from the beginning. They used us to find the treasure, and now they won't hesitate to get rid of us."

Bo chimes in, "I think that one of us should make a run for it and go get help."

Hayley: It's too dangerous, Bo. Nobody will make it. The coast on the banks is all mud. You would get stuck.

Ambrose's voice echoed through the cave, commanding the kids to come out. "If you don't come out in 3 minutes, I am going to shoot one of them!" His words sent a shiver down their spines, and panic spread among the group.

Hayley grabbed Andy's arm, trying to hold him back, "We can't go out there. He'll shoot us!"

Andy hesitated, torn between the fear for his friends and the dread of what would happen if they didn't comply. Bo, feeling the weight of the situation, whispered to Andy, "We have to go. We can't risk it."

Reluctantly, Andy nodded, and the two of them stepped out of the cave, hands raised in surrender. Ambrose's sinister grin widened as he aimed his gun at them, and the other kids followed behind, fear and uncertainty etched on their faces.

"Now, the treasure," Ambrose demanded. "Did you find it?"

Andy nervously answers Ambrose, "Yes, we found it, but how do we know you'll let us go if we give it to you?"

Ambrose pulls back the hammer on the revolver and points it straight at Bo's head. "Get it! Now!" he demands, his voice tense and threatening.

Andy turns to get the chest, but Ambrose interrupts, "Not you, her," he points at Charlotte. "Bring it out here."

Charlotte takes a deep breath, her heart pounding in her chest, and steps forward to face Ambrose. With determination in her eyes, she turns and walks into the dark cave alone, leaving the others standing at gunpoint outside.

As she ventures into the cave, Andy tries to reason with Ambrose, desperate to buy more time. "How do we know you won't shoot us as soon as you get the gold?" he asks, his voice shaking slightly.

Ambrose's grin widens as he relishes the fear he's instilled in the group. "Do what we tell you, and nobody has to get hurt," he responds coldly. "We'll leave you here to figure out a way to get out, and by then, we'll be on a plane heading out of the country with the treasure."

Inside the cave, Charlotte locates the ornate chest, marveling at its craftsmanship and the shimmering treasure inside. She starts to drag it, but stops to admire the stone with Kidd's Insignia. She picks it up and stares at it. She thinks to herself that this might make a good weapon.

Outside, the others anxiously await Charlotte's return, their thoughts filled with concern and dread. Charlotte struggles to bring the heavy chest to the mouth of the cave where everyone has been anxiously waiting. She presents the chest to Ambrose, her small frame trembles with the effort as she drags it forward. Ambrose, impatient and menacing, comments, "What took you so long? Open it! Show it to me."

Char takes a deep breath and unlatches the chest, lifting the lid with the hinges facing Ambrose. She reaches inside and grabs a handful of glittering gold coins, holding them up to the light before letting them cascade back into the chest. With a tone of defiance, she yells, "Here!" and tosses a coin towards Ambrose. It misses its mark and lands on the boat.

Ambrose picks up the coin, studying it carefully. His face shows a mix of excitement and greed. "Finally... Kidd's treasure," he whispers, unable to hide his elation. He raises his voice, demanding, "Bring it to me!"

Hayley, unable to keep quiet, shouts back, "No, you come and get it!"

Ambrose's eyes darken with fury, and he points the gun back at Bo. "You two, swim it out to us!" he commands, his voice threatening.

Hayley's fear for her friend and her little brother takes over, and she yells, "That thing will come back, we'll all be dead!"

Ambrose cocks the hammer again, the sound ringing through the air, and puts his finger on the trigger, aiming the gun at Bo's head. "I am not going to ask a second time," he growls.

Bo looks at Hayley and the others, seeing the fear in their eyes. He knows he has no choice but to comply, no matter how risky it might be. Slowly, he steps forward, making his way to the water's edge with Andy close behind him, clutching the chest with trembling hands.

The kids watch in horror as Bo and Andy start wading into the murky water, the weight of the chest slowing their movements. The snapping turtle's presence lingers in the back of their minds, but they have no other option if they want to protect each other.

Bo and Andy exchange nervous glances as they wade through the dark and murky water, carrying the heavy chest towards Ambrose. Hayley's voice echoes in their minds, urging them to move slowly and cautiously to avoid attracting the attention of the snapping turtle lurking beneath the surface.

The water rises steadily, and Bo feels it creeping up to his neck, sending shivers of fear down his spine. He holds the chest with all his strength, trying to keep it steady and prevent any coins from spilling out. His heart pounds in his chest, each beat reverberating in his ears as he struggles to focus on the task at hand.

Andy, just as terrified, clutches the chest tightly on his end, his eyes darting around, searching for any sign of movement in the water. He knows the snapping turtle could be anywhere, waiting for the opportunity to strike.

Ambrose's cold voice cuts through the tension, warning them not to make a mistake. Bo's head barely remains above the water's surface as he inches forward, each step feeling like a step closer to danger. He can feel the weight of the chest pulling him down, making every movement more difficult.

Both Bo and Andy are acutely aware of the danger they are in. One wrong move, one misplaced step, and the snapping turtle could be upon them. They feel the weight of responsibility for their friends and their own lives. The chest feels heavier with the burden of Ambrose's threats.

As Bo and Andy reach the boat, Ambrose and Odrap reach out to grab the chest from them. Ambrose's greedy eyes lock onto the treasure, but he hesitates, knowing the danger that lies beneath the water's surface. They try to keep their composure as Ambrose and Odrap take the treasure from them, but inside, their hearts race with anxiety.

"Good," Ambrose sneers, satisfied with the loot he now possesses. "Now get back to your friends and don't try anything foolish."

As Bo and Andy begin to slowly make their way back to the cave, Ambrose picks up an oar from the boat and starts smacking it on the water, creating loud splashes. The sound reverberates across the eddy, echoing like a call to the lurking snapping turtle. Hayley, Cassidy, and Charlotte are filled with a mix of anger, fear, and despair as they watch Ambrose's cruel behavior. With each echoing smack of the oars on the water, the kids' fear rises.

"You murderer! You have the gold, leave us be!" they scream at Ambrose, hoping to reason with him, but he only responds with uncontrollable laughter. He seems to be enjoying the power he holds over them, knowing that he possesses both the treasure and the threat of the deadly turtle.

As Hayley scans the water's surface, her heart sinks as she spots a large, dark shape rising above the water about 100 feet away. The carapace of the snapping turtle emerges, revealing the creature's enormous size. It's as if the turtle has sensed the commotion and is now heading directly towards the source of the splashing - Ambrose's oar.

The reality of the situation hits the kids like a tidal wave. Panic sets in as they realize they are at the mercy of both the snapping turtle and Ambrose's sadistic intentions.

Bo and Andy quickly turn around and see the turtle approaching. Fear shoots through their bodies, knowing the danger that lies ahead. They rush back pushing through the water to Hayley, Cassidy, and Charlotte, their faces pale with dread.
Hayley's mind races, trying to come up with a plan to escape this deadly situation. The snapping turtle moves steadily closer, propelled by curiosity and a potential source of food. The kids stand there, frozen with fear, unable to see a way out.

As Bo and Andy struggle against the water, their arms burning with exhaustion, the snapping turtle continues its relentless pursuit, drawing ever closer to them. Ambrose's cruel laughter echoes in the air, fueling their desperation and fear. Greg and Sean watch helplessly from their perch on the tree, their hearts pounding with anxiety for the others.

But just as all hope seems lost, a mysterious figure emerges from the shadows and enters the eddy, splashing and making a commotion. It's the river witch. She chants in her backwards language, her words foreign and haunting. "Reth Erb, Reth Erb, Ret Snom." She charges towards the boat.

The river witch moves closer to Ambrose and Odrap's boat, luring the attention of the snapping turtle away from Bo and Andy. Her presence intrigues the turtle, causing it to shift its focus towards her.

Ambrose, taken aback by the sudden appearance of the river witch, stares at her in disbelief. He tries to regain his composure but finds himself transfixed by the strange and unexpected turn of events.

Meanwhile, Bo seizes the opportunity to act. Instead of continuing towards the cave, he decides to make a bold move. With the river witch successfully distracting Ambrose and the turtle, Bo changes direction and heads for the coast. He knows that the turtle's instincts will lead it towards the source of commotion—the river witch—and away from him.

With the extra time and space, Bo and Andy push themselves harder, battling against the water's current to reach the safety of the coast. Each stroke feels like an eternity, their muscles screaming in protest, but their determination to escape keeps them going.

As the river witch continues her mesmerizing chant, the snapping turtle remains fixated on her, drawn by her splashing. The distraction proves to be enough for Bo and Andy to gain some distance from the creature, allowing Andy to reach the cave and Bo to get to the shore on the far side of the eddy.

Breathing heavily, Bo steps heavily onto the muddy coast. He is exhausted, but a sense of relief washes over him knowing he is almost out of the turtle's reach. Soon he will be able to run for help. Step by step he fights the deep sucking mud.

Back at the boat, the river witch's splashing and moving towards the boat has captured Ambrose's attention, but it has also made him uneasy.

The river witch, pushes the water and miraculously makes her way towards the jon boat. Ambrose, surprised by her sudden appearance, instructs Odrap to help her up onto the boat.

"Help her up, Odrap," Ambrose commands, his eyes fixed on the mysterious woman. Odrap hesitates for a moment but obeys, extending his hand to assist her.

As the river witch reaches for Odrap's arms, her presence seems to cast an eerie aura over the boat. The turtle, now just a few feet away, makes its way to its next meal.

Greg and Sean watch in bewilderment from their perch on the tree, unsure of what to make of the river witch's intervention. The kids in the cave cautiously peek out, trying to make sense of the situation.

Bo, still struggling to make his way through the mud on the far shore, glances back at the boat to see the commotion.

As Odrap begins to pull her up, the massive turtle lurks just a few feet away, its hulking form gliding silently through the murky water. Ambrose's attention shifts momentarily as he spots Bo struggling on the far shore, trying to fight the thick and unforgiving mud.

Bo's heart pounds in his chest as he tries desperately to free himself from the mud's grasp. He turns back towards the boat, sensing the danger, just in time to see Ambrose raise his revolver and take aim at him. Fear grips Bo's entire being, but he pushes on, fighting the mud with all his strength.

With a calculated precision, Ambrose lines up Bo's body in his sights, his finger tightening on the trigger. In an instant, a loud bang reverberates through the air, and time seems to slow down. Greg and Sean flinch at the sound, while the rest of the kids scream in shock.

Bo's body falls face down into the mud, unmoving. The world around Hayley blurs as she witnesses the horrifying scene in slow motion. She drops to her knees, her heart breaking into pieces. "NOOO!! That's my brother!" she cries out in anguish, her voice trembling with grief and despair.

Amidst the chaos and cries of anguish, Odrap struggles to lift the river witch into the boat, but she surprises him with a sudden shift in weight. She swiftly grabs onto Odrap's arms, using her strength to pull him overboard. He splashes into the water with a startled yelp, catching Ambrose's attention.

As Odrap falls into the water, the massive turtle, ever watchful, senses the movement and starts to make its way towards the boat. Its large, spiked shell scrapes along the side, creating a shiver of fear. Just as Odrap is dragged under, the boat is pushed away by the turtle's massive form, and the creature submerges once more, leaving a trail of ripples in its wake.

Amidst the confusion, the river witch is knocked backward by the force, but she manages to keep her grip on the boat's edge. Ambrose calls out to her, "Polly, give me your hand!" With a determined effort, he pulls her back up into the boat, his dark eyes narrowing as he looks at the terrified group of kids.

Greg and Sean sit in paralyzed fear, their hearts racing as they witness the horrifying events unfolding before them. Hayley, her eyes filled with tears, cries in hysterics, her hands trembling as she looks over at her brother's lifeless body lying face down in the unforgiving mud.

The river witch, now on the boat, sits quietly, her expression inscrutable. The weight of loss and terror presses heavily upon them, as they grapple with the reality of what has just occurred.

The once sought-after treasure now lies forgotten, overshadowed by the tragedy that has unfolded. The kids, their spirits shattered, can only watch helplessly as Ambrose gets to his feet on the drifting boat. They are left with the painful realization that their lives will never be the same, forever marked by the darkness they have encountered in the depths of the river.

Hayley's anguish boils over as she stands up, her face contorted with rage and sorrow. She screams at Ambrose, "You killed my brother, you son of a..." But she stops herself abruptly, her eyes darting to Bo's lifeless body in the mud.

With tears streaming down her face, she glares at Ambrose, her voice shaking with emotion. "You killed him! You have the gold! Leave! Get out of here!" Her words fall on deaf ears as Ambrose only smiles back at her, unmoved by her pain.

"Sorry, darling, but you might be right," Ambrose retorts casually as he starts the engine of the boat, preparing to leave with the river witch. The engine roars to life, its sound echoing eerily in the air. Polly, next to Ambrose, begins to drag the chest towards the edge of the boat, determination etched on her face.

With trembling hands, she pulls the chest closer to the edge with the intention of dumping it. But before she can toss it overboard, Ambrose halts the boat's movement. He limps forward pushing Polly with his cane.

"Polly, my dear sister, don't do that."

His hands grasp the edge of the chest, and he pulls on it, wrestling it away from his sister, Polly. In the struggle, the chest opens, and its contents spill all over the deck of the jon boat.

As the chest spills its contents, Ambrose's eyes widen in disbelief and rage. A bunch of ordinary rocks mingled with a few gold coins, littered the deck of the boat. He picks up one of the rocks, tracing the etching of two crossed swords with his thumb. The realization of Charlotte's deception hits him like a thunderbolt, and his face contorts with rage. He glares up at the coast, where Charlotte stands, seemingly unshaken by the peril she had just put herself in.

Fury overtakes Ambrose as he glares at Charlotte, a sly smile dancing on her lips. She nods subtly to the right, indicating that the real treasure is hidden in the cave. The knowledge that he had been outsmarted by a young girl ignites an anger within him like never before.

Andy and Cassidy, standing nearby, catch on to Charlotte's cunning plan. Their faces light up with astonishment and admiration. Charlotte, undaunted by the danger she had put herself in, bounces her eyebrows at them playfully, her smile full of mischief.

The situation has taken an unexpected turn, and Ambrose is consumed by his anger and the humiliation of being outwitted by a child. He lets out a bellow of rage, causing the kids on the shore to shiver in fear.

Ambrose stares down at the mess before him, his anger growing with every second. The pile of rocks and a few gold coins lay before him, mocking his greed. He clenches his fists, feeling frustration and humiliation creeping in.

Polly watches the scene unfold with concern in her eyes, realizing that her brother has been tricked by the clever young girl. She opens her mouth to say something, but Ambrose's focus remains on the spilled treasure before him.

Ambrose raises his gun and takes aim at Hayley, Cassidy, Andy, and Charlotte. Panic fills their eyes as they brace for the worst. But in the frenzy of the moment, Ambrose's aim is off, and the shot misses its mark. The bullet whizzes past their heads, causing them to duck for cover inside the cave.

Seeing this opening, Sean gathers his courage and decides to take action. Fueled by adrenaline and the desire to end this chaos, he leaps into the water, forgetting about the lurking danger of the snapping turtle. With his pocket knife firmly in hand, he makes his way towards the boat, determined to confront Ambrose.

Ambrose, still preoccupied with the chaos around him, doesn't notice Sean at first. As Sean gets closer, he uses the boat for cover, hoping to take Ambrose by surprise. His heart pounds in his chest as he prepares to make his move.

With a swift and decisive motion, Sean lunges out of the water and attempts to swipe Ambrose's leg with his knife. But as he does so, he hears a metallic sound and his momentum plunges the knife into the top of the plastic gas tank causing fuel to spit out onto the deck of the jon boat. Confused and shocked, he falls back down below the edge of the boat in the water. Ambrose turns and looks down at him.

"Too late, boy. The turtle already got that one," Ambrose taunts, pointing at his prosthctic leg. His sinister grin sends shivers down Sean's spine.

Ambrose raises his pistol at Sean, takes aim and says out loud, "go join your friend". Ambrose fires a shot into Sean's shoulder. Just as he is about to take another shot, as if on cue, the turtle swims below grabbing Sean's legs and dragging him down into the murky depths of the Eddy.

Ambrose turns his attention on the kids in the cave and starts firing the remaining bullets inside.

Panic and fear grip the kids inside the cave, as they hear Ambrose's shots echoing through the narrow passage. The reverberating gunshots intensify their sense of impending danger. Hayley peeks out from the mouth of the cave and sees Ambrose, now out of bullets and loading more in. He places the gun down on the jon boat before starting the engine.

"He's coming! He's going to shoot us if we stay in here," Hayley exclaims, her voice trembling with fear. "We need to do something. We can't just wait for him to come to us."

Cass chimes in, "She's right. We can't let him get any closer."

Andy, filled with determination, adds, "We have to stop him before he reaches the cave."

Meanwhile, on the jon boat, Ambrose steers the boat towards the mouth of the cave with an eerie grin on his face. He believes he has the upper hand and that the kids are trapped. Polly, the river witch, picks up the revolver and stares at her brother, switching her eyes back and forth between him and the gun.

With the gun in her hands, Polly takes a deep breath, her heart pounding in her chest. She knows the stakes are high, but she's determined to protect the children. As the boat draws closer, she gathers her courage and positions herself to confront Ambrose.

Back inside the cave, Hayley glances at the others and says, "On my count, we rush out and overtake him. If we all work together, we can disarm him."

Charlotte, who had been quietly observing, nods in agreement. "We can do this; we won't let him hurt any more people."

As the boat approaches, the kids brace themselves, their hearts racing. They know it's now or never. They count down silently, synchronizing their movements, and as Hayley signals with a determined nod, they rush out of the cave, shouting and screaming to distract Ambrose.

Surprised by the sudden commotion, Ambrose turns his attention away from the boat's controls, and that's when Polly seizes the opportunity. With a fierce determination, she raises the gun and points it at Ambrose.

Ambrose freezes, shocked by the turn of events. The tables have turned, and he now finds himself at the mercy of his younger sister with a gun. He glares at Polly, his anger and frustration boiling within him.

The kids charge towards the boat, their hearts pounding with adrenaline. They're determined to overpower Ambrose and stop him from hurting anyone else. As they splash through the water, their attention is fixated on the boat, unaware that the snapping turtle is stealthily approaching, its enormous back rising out of the water.

Cassidy senses something is off and glances around, and that's when she spots the turtle getting dangerously close. "Watch out! The turtle!" she shouts, her voice echoing in the air.

The kids turn their attention to the massive creature just as it lunges forward, its jaws snapping close to their feet. Fear seizes them, and they scramble to climb onto the front of the boat. As they haul themselves up, Polly aims the gun at her brother, yelling, "Pots! Pots!" Cassidy knows instantly that she's saying "stop."

But Ambrose, fueled by desperation, throws the boat into reverse, forcing the boat to lodge itself in the tree that Greg is in. The boat jerks backward, pushing up against the tree and lifting the motor out of the water. In the commotion, Polly becomes distracted, giving Ambrose the opportunity to snatch the gun from her grasp.

He points the gun at Hayley, Andy, Cass, and Charlotte, who are trapped at the front of the boat. "Back off!" he snarls, his face contorted with rage. The kids stand still, fear in their eyes, but they refuse to back down.

The snapping turtle continues its relentless pursuit, inching closer to the boat and using its claws to climb up the front to reach his next meal. The back of the jon boat lifts higher against the tree from the turtle's weight. Greg, still watching from the tree, feels a surge of adrenaline. He knows he needs to do something to help.

Ambrose aims the gun at Hayley's head who was advancing forward. He tells her "Go join your brother and squeezes the trigger. Hayley flinches, but nothing comes out. The gun doesn't fire. Ambrose squeezes the trigger again and again, but no shots. He immediately looks at his sister, Polly in shock. Polly opens her hand revealing the bullets that she took out of the gun. She drops them in the eddy. Ambrose is outraged. At that moment, the turtle climbs onto the boat using its legs to push itself up.

As Ambrose's anger intensifies, he clenches his fist in frustration. "You little traitor!" he growls at Polly, his plans foiled by her quick thinking.

Meanwhile, the snapping turtle clambers onto the boat, its massive body causing the vessel to tilt slightly more. Its cold, unblinking eyes fixate on Charlotte.

Ambrose, now facing the wrath of both the kids and the powerful creature before him, feels his control slipping away. He glances at the empty gun, then at the defiant faces of the children who have outsmarted him at every turn.

In a desperate move, he lunges for Hayley, hoping to overpower her and push her into the mouth of the turtle. But before he can reach her, the snapping turtle lunges, pulling its massive body higher on the boat, its massive jaws snapping and almost biting Charlotte.

In a heart-stopping moment, a bone-chilling scream pierces the air as Greg leaps off the tree branch, propelled by an unstoppable surge of courage. With fearless determination, he hurls himself at Ambrose, catching the treacherous man off guard. Their bodies collide, and Ambrose loses his footing, he tumbles awkwardly down the slanted jon boat. Hayley, Andy, Cassidy, and Charlotte instinctively dodge Ambrose's falling form, narrowly avoiding the potential danger. But as fate would have it, Ambrose's metallic leg becomes ensnared on a menacing spike protruding from the turtle's carapace.

With a mixture of shock and horror, the once mighty treasure hunter now finds himself trapped and helpless on the turtle's back. His prosthetic leg, a twisted reminder of past misdeeds, has turned against him. Ambrose's desperate cries for his sister's aid reverberate across the eddy, only adding to the turmoil.

Polly, watching from the boat, hesitates for a moment, torn between her loyalty to her brother and her newfound mission to protect the children.

In that poignant moment, Polly makes a life-altering decision. She steps back, distancing herself from the clutches of her brother's twisted fate. She can't help but think of the countless lives he's ruined in search of the treasure. It's time to break free from the shackles of her family's dark legacy.

As Polly moves away, Ambrose's desperation intensifies, but there is no saving grace for him. In a harrowing twist of events, the relentless snapping turtle remains undeterred, completely unfazed by Ambrose's entangled plight on its back. With a determined persistence, the massive creature continues its advance, scaling the jon boat with a haunting determination.

Ambrose's struggles on the turtle's back are futile, his flailing body held captive by the very leg that once symbolized his arrogance and cruelty. The kids and Polly, cornered at the back of the boat, have no escape route. Fear and panic fill the air as they find themselves at the mercy of the beast.
In this moment of desperation, Andy's quick thinking takes center stage. He detects the pungent scent of gasoline lingering in the air, a remnant of Sean's attempt to stop Ambrose. Without hesitation, Andy seizes the opportunity to use it as a last line of defense.

With a swift motion, he rips the plastic tank from the tubing, embracing this risky gambit to stave off the impending danger. He opens the tank and lunges towards the turtle, dousing its scaly form and the boat itself with fuel, hoping to deter the creature from its relentless pursuit.

However, the turtle, driven by a primal instinct, strikes back with terrifying force. In a moment of pure terror, it lunges at Andy, clamping its powerful jaws around his arm. Despite Andy's brave attempt, he finds himself ensnared by the formidable predator. In a chilling twist of fate, he falls beneath the protection of the turtle's plastron, crushed by the sheer force of its weight.

The scene erupts in chaos as the girls scream in anguish, their hearts heavy with the weight of another friend lost to the relentless snapping turtle. Emotions of fear, sorrow, and anger mingle together, enveloping the group in a shroud of profound grief.

The turtle, seemingly unaffected by the gasoline, continues its inexorable ascent. Its intentions remain a mystery, and the kids and Polly are left to confront this enigma with hearts heavy and courage waning.

As they stand on the precipice of a perilous situation, the indomitable spirit of the remaining friends stirs. Driven by grief and determination, they resolve to stand strong together, to face their imminent demise.
In the midst of darkness and uncertainty, they find solace in each other, finding strength in their unity. Armed with Andy's sacrifice and the memory of their fallen friends, they prepare to confront the beast with every ounce of courage they possess, knowing that in the face of

adversity, they are bound together by an unbreakable bond of friendship and love.

Amidst the dire situation, the kids find themselves trapped on the precarious boat, surrounded by the murky waters, and facing the relentless snapping turtle inching closer. Grief, fear, and sadness grip their hearts, and hope seems distant and unattainable.

But then, a faint sound emerges, growing louder and more distinct with each passing second. Hayley's eyes dart upwards, and to her astonishment, she spots her little brother's drone soaring through the air, carrying two lit flares taped to its legs like a beacon of hope. The sight is almost surreal, and the kids cannot believe what they are witnessing.

Hayley scans the shore for the pilot. In a breathtaking twist of fate, Hayley's despair transforms into sheer joy and disbelief as she realizes the truth. Her little brother, Bo, is alive and well, guiding the drone towards them, a glimmer of hope amidst the darkness that surrounds them.

As the drone hovers above, Bo's voice comes across through the built-in speaker, "Get ready to jump", a smile lighting up his eyes as he pilots the device with skill and precision. His presence alone breathes life into their desperate situation, igniting a flame of hope within their hearts.

With tears streaming down her face, Hayley calls out in triumph, "He's not dead! Bo is alive!" The words spread like wildfire, and the kids are overcome with a mix of disbelief and pure elation. The impossible has become a reality, and their long-lost friend and ally has returned to them in their moment of need.

With newfound hope surging through their veins, the kids find the strength to face the menacing turtle and the dangerous waters. They stand together, unified by a bond that transcends time and trials, ready to confront whatever challenges come their way.

The moment is tense as the drone approaches, and the kids wait for the perfect opportunity. Hayley's voice is steady but filled with determination as she commands, "Not yet, let him climb higher." The turtle continues its relentless ascent, drawing closer to them with each passing second. Ambrose's futile struggles against the turtle's back are now overshadowed by the impending danger.

The drone approaches the critical point, and at Hayley's signal, they make their move. With adrenaline coursing through their veins, they leap from the jon boat, their eyes fixed on the fiery fate that awaits them if they hesitate for even a second. Polly, showing a remarkable courage that rivals her brother's, leaps alongside them.

In a breathtaking display of timing and precision, Bo expertly pilots the drone, guiding it straight toward the open maw of the approaching turtle. A triumphant cheer resounds through the air as Bo's voice booms through the drone's speaker, a mixture of joy and exhilaration in his tone, "Woooo-Hoooo!!! Open up and say ahh!!" He smashes the drone and flares directly into the turtle's mouth, sacrificing his creation to save his friends.
In an instant, chaos erupts as flames consume the turtle, the boat, and Ambrose. The kids, now in the water, swim

vigorously towards the cave where Bo stands, anxiously waiting for them.

They reach the safety of the cave just as the inferno behind them intensifies. Hayley, Greg, Cassidy, Charlotte, and Polly huddle together, gasping for breath and trembling from the adrenaline rush. Their eyes meet Bo's, and in that moment, they know that they have overcome insurmountable odds.

The crackling of the flames outside serves as a testament to the courage and unity that brought them through the darkest of trials. They share a moment of relief and gratitude, understanding that their bond is unbreakable, forged through shared experiences, and their collective strength.

As the flames continue to rage outside, the kids find solace in knowing that they have emerged victorious, not only against the turtle but against the darkness that Ambrose had brought upon them.

Chapter 14:
Foul Rift

In Foul Rift, a day of pure splendor embraces the town as the radiant sun graces the sky with its warm, golden rays. The air carries a gentle warmth, inviting everyone to step outside and relish the beauty of the day. Soft, billowy clouds float gracefully overhead, casting playful shadows on the vibrant landscape below. A gentle breeze sweeps through the streets, causing leaves to rustle and creating a perfect harmony with the cheerful chirping of birds and the delightful fluttering of butterflies. Squirrels dart and play, adding their liveliness to the joyful scene. The picturesque houses stand proudly, adorned with colorful flowers and manicured lawns, a testament to the care and love of the community. Everyone is beaming with happiness as they go about their day, their hearts lifted by the sheer magnificence of the surroundings. In Foul Rift, this day is a true celebration of life, where beauty, happiness, and contentment blend harmoniously, creating a sense of bliss that permeates every corner of the town.

Amidst the quaint streets of Foul Rift, an old, rusty red Jeep with its top down, doors off, and a lucky rabbit's foot hanging from its mirror, is parked outside the charming Rambo's Deli. A distinguished gentleman, dressed in jeans and a sport coat, steps out of the deli carrying a neatly wrapped pork roll egg and cheese sandwich in his hand.

He climbs inside the Jeep, placing the sandwich on the seat beside him, and starts the engine. As the car hums to life, he turns on the radio, and the soulful melody of "Stand by Me" fills the air. Lost in the song's soothing rhythm, he takes a moment to reflect on the memories it evokes.

Driving slowly through town, he passes the enchanting Field of Dreams playground, a place that holds cherished memories for many. He continues on, passing the inviting entrance to Wind Chime Woods and the familiar trail leading to the mystical eddy. As he drives on, he glimpses the bustling old mechanic's station, where familiar faces wave at the passing Jeep.

He arrives at his destination, the Foul Rift High School. The parking lot is calm and serene, and he parks the Jeep gracefully. Stepping out, he walks towards the entrance, and before him stands a beautiful marquis adorned with an engraved board that proudly declares, "Home of the Noblemen," a testament to the town's rich history.

He enters the empty hallway, the echoes of footsteps from bustling days now replaced by tranquility. Navigating the corridors with familiarity, he reaches Room 33, the place where countless students have sought knowledge and wisdom throughout the years. With a key in hand, he gently unlocks the door, revealing a space filled with memories and stories of a lifetime, a place where learning and growth have thrived, and where countless lives have been shaped.

The gentleman steps inside, feeling a sense of nostalgia and reverence, surrounded by the echoes of laughter, discussions, and dreams that have echoed within its walls. As he gazes upon the empty classroom, he can't help but smile, knowing that within these hallowed halls, the legacy of Foul Rift's Noblemen continues to live on.

The man sits at his desk, enjoying his sandwich while browsing an article about the upcoming 4th of July festivities on his computer. Time seems to fly by, and before he knows it, the familiar school bell rings, signaling the start of the class. The students file into the room, greeting him with a warm, "Good morning, Mr. Pardo."

Returning their smiles, Mr. Pardo reciprocates the greeting, "Good morning, everyone." With their attention now on him, he continues, "As promised, today, on the last day of school, I'll share with you the thrilling tale of the notorious pirate, Captain Kidd and the discovery of a part of his treasure right here in the caves at Foul Rift."

The students lean in, their curiosity piqued, as their teacher weaves a captivating narrative filled with adventure, mystery, and daring escapades from a bygone era. They listen with rapt attention, hanging onto every word, as if transported to another time and place.

As the story reaches its exciting conclusion, Mr. Pardo finishes with a flourish, leaving the students eagerly wanting to know more. "So, does anyone have any questions?" he asks.

Hands shoot up in the air as the students eagerly ask about the treasure, the pirate's exploits, and the history of Foul Rift. One hand waves frantically from the middle of the room. "Yes, Autumn. What is your question?" Mr. Pardo calls on the girl, who asks with intrigue, "So the little boy faked his death? He wasn't shot?"

Mr. Pardo smiles warmly, pleased with the engagement of his students. "That's correct," he confirms. "He was incredibly resourceful. After hearing the first shot, which fortunately missed him, he took advantage of his predicament. Realizing that the old man would likely continue firing until he hit his target, the boy acted swiftly. He laid flat in the mud pretending he was dead, patiently waiting for the right moment to make a move."

As he continues the tale, the room becomes hushed, captivated by the unfolding story. "With steely nerves, he slowly pulled himself out of the mud and skillfully made his way back to the cave, where he piloted his drone off of the tree branch where it was perched, back to him. Then, using duct tape, he attached the flares on its legs. He did this just in the nick of time to save his friends from the clutches of the treacherous turtle."

The students listen with awe and admiration, their curiosity piqued by the thrilling tale. Autumn's hand fires back up, eager to learn more. "What happened to the river witch?" she inquires with genuine interest. "Was she really the sister of the museum manager?"

Mr. Pardo smiles, appreciating her enthusiasm for the story. "Polly is still around," he replies, "living with a caretaker who looks after her. Occasionally, the caretaker brings her to the banks of the river so she can sit and enjoy the view. And yes, she was the sister of the curator. He loved her, but he was abusive to her so she left and lived out in the woods. She tried to warn the friends except they misunderstood her. They tried to translate her words and they thought she was saying 'breather' and 'RV', but what she was trying to say was 'brother Harvey'.

Suddenly, another student raises his hand and chimes in, recalling a sighting of the river witch. "I think I've seen her. She's in a wheelchair, right?" And before Mr. Pardo could answer, he blurts out a statement. "My father told me this story too. He told me it's how the school club and mascot 'Noblemen' came to be."

Mr. Pardo nods in agreement. "Your father is correct. The club started the year after the treasure was found. It was the little boy's idea. When I became a teacher here, I took the club over. I have been running it for 15 years and it was my idea to make "The Noblemen" our mascot and S.N.A.P. our motto. The Andy Zzobi Library and Ryan Shawl Theater were named after the two boys in the story."

Autumn raises her hand again, but can't contain her curiosity, calling out, "What about the treasure? Did they find all of it? Are they rich?"

Mr. Pardo glances up at the clock, realizing the bell is about to ring, signaling the end of the class. "I'm sorry, Autumn," he apologizes, "but our time is up. If you want to learn more about the treasure and Captain Kidd, I highly recommend visiting the Foul Rift Museum. There's a dedicated section there that delves into this fascinating story. Go speak to the curator; she'll be more than happy to tell you all about it. She's quite the expert."

As the bell rings, the students gather their belongings, still buzzing with excitement and curiosity. Mr. Pardo bids them farewell, "Have a great summer, everyone! I hope to see you around town. Don't forget to explore and go on your own adventures." The students disperse, carrying with them a newfound sense of wonder and a desire to seek out their own thrilling tales in the world beyond the classroom.

Several weeks later, on July 3rd in Foul Rift, a gentle summer rain falls outside, accompanied by occasional bursts of thunder. Undeterred by the weather, Autumn and her little brother, Cole, step into the Foul Rift Museum, causing an old-fashioned bell attached to the door to chime merrily. Excitement and curiosity fill their faces as they enter a place they have never been before.

Inside, the museum is peacefully empty, allowing Autumn and her brother to freely explore. They wander around, their footsteps echoing softly on the wooden floor. Autumn finds herself drawn to a section of the room labeled "Pirates and Noblemen." As she glances at the framed photos on the wall, her imagination begins to run wild.

One photo catches her attention - a group of six teenagers who seem to be in high school. They are all smiling, standing inside a charming restaurant. Above them, the word "Descendants" is displayed on the wall, capturing her curiosity. Her gaze shifts to another photo, showing the same six teens holding up inner tubes, their faces glowing with happiness.

As Autumn examines the photos, she notices what resembles a pirate flag draped across the wall. It is a lightbulb donning an eye patch and two crossed wrenches beneath it. Next to it are old newspaper articles, each revealing intriguing stories. One headline reads, "Teens Find Part of 300-Year-Old Missing Treasure," sparking her imagination further. Another article's headline reads, "Infamous Treasure Hunter Sisters, Open Pirate-Themed

Book Store in Maryland," adding another layer of intrigue to the tale. The young girl's eyes widen as she reads another, "Mystery of Missing Mechanic and Detective Solved."

Surrounded by the history and mysteries of the past, Autumn finds herself immersed in the captivating stories of the people in the photographs and the articles. With each new piece of information, her fascination with the past grows stronger.

As she scans the room, Autumn can't help but feel a sense of wonder at the connections between the photos and articles, as if they all hold clues to an incredible story waiting to be unraveled. The museum becomes a treasure trove of history, and Autumn eagerly delves deeper into its secrets, eager to uncover the truth behind the fascinating stories before her.

Behind her, a person appears and walks softly over to her. She greets the children. "Hello, children. My name is Hayley," she says with a warm smile. Autumn turns around swiftly and looks up at the older woman. "Hi. My teacher sent me here. He said that you know all about the story of Foul Rift and Captain Kidd's treasure."

Hayley smiles softly and says, "That I do. What would you like to know?" Autumn's face lights up with excitement, and she says, "Everything."

Hayley proceeds to tell Autumn and her little brother Cole all about what happened in Foul Rift many years ago. Just as she is about to finish, a man pushes the door open, ringing the antique bell hanging above. Hayley looks up and smiles at the person with warmth and gratitude.

She then walks over to Autumn and gently places a hand on her shoulder. "I hope you enjoyed the story," she says warmly. "History has a way of unfolding secrets to those who seek them."

Autumn nods eagerly, still mesmerized by the captivating tale she just heard. "It was amazing," she exclaims. "Thank you for sharing it with us."

Hayley's smile broadens. "You're very welcome," she says. "I'm glad you found it intriguing. Foul Rift holds so much history, and it's wonderful to see young minds like yours eager to learn about it."

Autumn and Cole express their heartfelt thanks to Hayley for sharing the incredible stories with them. "Thank you so much for telling us all of that," Autumn says with genuine gratitude.

Hayley smiles warmly at the children. "You're welcome, my dear. It was my pleasure to share these stories with you," she replies.

As they prepare to leave, Autumn walks past the man who is now standing by a display case, seemingly lost in thought. She pauses for a moment before turning back to Hayley. "Do you think there's more treasure out there, waiting to be discovered?" she asks with a hopeful glimmer in her eyes.

Hayley's smile widens as she gazes at Autumn. She then subtly glances at the man who has entered and is now smiling back at her. "Oh, I know that there is," she says with a hint of mystery. "You just have to be willing to look for it."

Autumn smiles back, feeling inspired and intrigued. With a final wave to Hayley, she turns and walks out of the museum, her little brother Cole following closely behind.

As they step outside, they are greeted by the fresh scent of rain-washed air and the warmth of the sun breaking through the clouds. The world around them feels filled with endless possibilities and hidden treasures waiting to be discovered.

Meanwhile, the man approaches Hayley with a knowing smile. "Hello, sis," he says with affection in his voice.

Hayley looks at him with a mixture of surprise and joy. "Hi, Bo" she replies, embracing her brother. "Are you ready for tomorrow?"

Bo nods, "I am."

Hayley disappears behind the wall that Ambrose disappeared behind so many years ago. She returns carrying a familiar inflatable cooler. "It's still good after all of these years, if you can believe it."

The siblings share a moment of understanding, their bond strengthened by their shared love for history and the enchanting tales of Foul Rift.

The next day, as the Foul Rift 4th of July festivities come to an end, the town starts to settle into a tranquil evening. Bo and Hayley find solace in the gentle shallows of the Delaware River. The sun, painting the sky in hues of orange and pink, begins its descent, casting a warm glow over the landscape.

Walking side by side, they cherish the quiet reflective moments they have shared on this day for many years. Between them, an inflatable cooler holds a precious reminder of their extraordinary adventure— a stone etched with two crossed swords and six gleaming gold coins, an emblem embodying the unity of the six friends who once embarked on their unforgettable journey down the Delaware.

As they stroll through the water, the setting sun turns the river into a canvas of shimmering light. The ripples on the water's surface catch the last rays of the sun, creating a dance of glimmering reflections. The river seems to come alive, as if whispering the secrets of centuries past.

Bo and Hayley, immersed in the moment, feel the weight of their shared history and the bond forged by their adventures. The silence between them is comfortable, filled with unspoken memories that connect them on a profound level.

They continue walking, their silhouettes elongated by the descending sun, moving in harmony with the river's flow. The air is filled with a sense of peace and contentment as they bask in the beauty of the fading day.

As the sun finally sets below the horizon, the town embraces the stillness of the night. Bo and Hayley find themselves in the gentle darkness, grateful for the memories they have created and the treasure they carry in their hearts.

And as they head back home, they know that they will return to this spot next year, on the 4th of July, to continue their tradition and relive the tales of their daring adventure—forever united by the shimmering memories of Foul Rift.

Addendum

Many of the places in the story are real or they were inspired by real places. Scan the QR to view a slide show of different places that inspired the locations in the story.

Unveil your thoughts! By scanning the QR code, you can share a video message that encapsulates your impressions of the story or simply drop a friendly "hello" to let me know you've journeyed through the pages. Your words will bring the story to life in a whole new dimension. Your feedback matters, and this QR code is your gateway to express it.

Return to Foul Rift

Made in United States
North Haven, CT
29 August 2023

40895369R00212